THE END OF A WILD RIDE

Zigzagging down the slope, he was picking up speed, being pulled down the mountain by an invisible force. The brake pads screeched as he made a fist with one hand, then the other, gripping the handlebars and brake levers with a sudden urgency. Ground sped past beneath him as he leaned to follow the trail. He bounced over a mound of rocks and grass and lost his balance.

Suddenly Ray was airborne, arms outstretched, legs spread wide, Superman performing a goofy, low altitude flyby. Unlike the man of steel, Ray couldn't maintain his body position in flight. He landed with a thud and rolled gracelessly into a thicket of berry bushes. He cursed aloud as he crawled out on shaky legs. Fatigue? Fright? Hunger? Probably a combination of the three. Maybe a shot of carbs would help. Digging an energy bar from his fanny pack, he devoured it in three bites. He was about to tear open another when he noticed something . . .

It was lying at the foot of an enormous stump, surrounded by pines, camouflaged by shadows. Ray squinted, trying to make out details. It almost looked like . . . No. Couldn't be a body. Maybe he had hit his head harder than he thought. Still . . . What if it was?

Ray decided to investigate . . .

Other Inupiat Eskimo Mysteries by
Christopher Lane
from Avon Twilight

ELEMENTS OF A KILL
SEASON OF DEATH

CHRISTOPHER LANE

A SHROUD OF MIDNIGHT SUN

AN INUPIAT ESKIMO MYSTERY

AVON
TWILIGHT

This is a work of fiction. Names, characters, places, and incidents either
are the product of the author's imagination or are used fictitiously. Any
resemblance to actual events, locales, organizations, or persons, living or
dead, is entirely coincidental and beyond the intent of either the author or
the publisher.

AVON BOOKS, INC.
1350 Avenue of the Americas
New York, New York 10019

Copyright © 2000 by Christopher Lane
Inside cover author photo by Melodie Lane
Published by arrangement with the author
Library of Congress Catalog Card Number: 99-94992
ISBN: 0-380-79873-5
www.avonbooks.com/twilight

First Avon Twilight Printing: January 2000

AVON TWILIGHT TRADEMARK REG. U.S. PAT. OFF. AND IN OTHER COUN-
TRIES, MARCA REGISTRADA, HECHO EN U.S.A.

Printed in the U.S.A.

WCD 10 9 8 7 6 5 4 3 2 1

➤➤ AUTHOR'S NOTE ◄◄

NORTH TO ALASKA . . . again. I'd like to express my appreciation for those who made the journey possible, as well as issue a broad disclaimer regarding the fiction herein.

First, *quyanaqpak* to my wife for the role she played in the development of the manuscript and for her patient support through the process. I'd also like to thank my editor, Lyssa Keusch, for helping to sculpt the manuscript with her provocative ideas and constant encouragement. The staff at Avon Books did a wonderful job in turning out a very handsome book. My agent, Karen Solem of Writers House, deserves a hardy "tanku" for her diligent efforts on my behalf. Lastly, I'd like to thank the noble Inupiat people—the Real People. It is their perseverance and courage in the face of a rapidly changing cultural climate that make this book possible.

While the setting of the story is real, the characters themselves, the events, and many of the locales are imaginary, created solely for the purposes of this story. Any and all mistakes in the information conveyed about Alaska or the Native people are my own.

I hope that you enjoy reading the book as much as I enjoyed writing it. As was the case with the previous Ray Attla mysteries, *A Shroud of Midnight Sun* proved to be an *aarigaa* experience.

Christopher A. Lane

Christopher A. Lane
1999

➤➤ PRELUDE ◀◀

THE DEAL CLOSED on Friday evening at 6:27, pens assaulting documents with swift, taut precision. There was a sober pause, fourteen eyes studying the contract that had been on the table, in one form or another, for almost seventy-two hours. An unvoiced question hung in the air: Was this a marriage made in heaven or in hell?

The spell was broken when the first chair slid back. Others followed. Stiff bodies rose. Faces contorted, smiling, yawning, sighing in resignation and relief. Handshakes were exchanged, files gathered, briefcases repacked and snapped shut.

At 6:31 the door opened and a young lady swept into the room, a gleaming silver platter balanced gracefully at shoulder level. The platter bore an attractive arrangement of thin-stemmed glasses, flowers, and two perspiring bottles of Dom Perignon. Before she could set it on the table, the bottles were snatched away, the corks released. Bubbly froth spilled to the carpet. The glasses were filled generously, recklessly, droplets of champagne splashing to the table like golden tears. Someone called out a toast. "To the deal!"

Thirty seconds later, a phone buzzed. A cellular. Heads bobbed, checking breast pockets and satchels. When he determined that it was *his* cellular, he excused himself and stepped to the corner of the conference room. He had to take this call. This was *the call.*

Swallowing hard, he flipped the device open. "Hello?"

The noise level was escalating, the other six men venting the stress of three long, difficult days of tooth-and-nail negotiations. Snippets of Japanese and English merged into an indistinguishable din.

He cupped a hand around the phone, straining to hear. "Hello?"

Someone noticed his plight and called for silence.

Suddenly the room was quiet. Uncomfortably quiet. Robbed of conversation, the men stood watching him, as if he were about to perform a feat of magic. He waved them off, frowning to assure them that the hush was unnecessary.

It was at that moment, before the others had resumed their celebratory mood, that the message was delivered.

He nodded, silently indicating that he understood, as if the speaker could discern this via the telephone line. A tap of his thumb extinguished the phone. He calmly folded it shut, stuffed it into a jacket pocket, and followed the others as they trailed out of the room.

A motion for drinks was made. This was seconded by animal calls and hoots. It was decided that they would meet in thirty minutes in the bar to launch an offensive against the hotel's supply of liquor.

He stood with them at the elevator, chuckled absently as one of the Japanese told an off-color joke. When the doors opened and they filed on, he made his apologies, begging off for the night by complaining of indigestion and fatigue. The others pleaded with him, reminding him that there was a nursing conference taking place in the hotel. This was met by a chorus of wolf whistles. The party would be wild, he was assured.

Resisting their efforts, he wished them well and went to his room. There he removed his tie, changed out of his suit, into a pair of Dockers, a polo shirt, a thin jacket. He sat at the table by the bed and wrote his wife a letter on hotel stationery. It was short, less than a page, and he left it open on the desk. After withdrawing a small manila envelope from his briefcase, he folded it, slid it in a jacket pocket, donned a pair of Rockports.

He checked his watch: almost seven. He would have to hurry. Jogging down the back stairs, he hit the roll bar and exited into a glare of light. The sun was balanced on the crest of a mountain to the west, as low as it would sink in its trek along the horizon.

The parking lot was nearly full, the majority of the vehicles bearing stickers from Avis, Hertz, and Budget. He picked out his white Ford from among the rows of white rental cars, got in, and started the engine. The tires squealed as he raced out of the lot.

The clock on the dash read 6:57. His watch gave the time at 6:53. He hoped his watch was right. Stepping on the gas, he urged the Ford south, toward the resort.

Two minutes later he skidded to a halt in an unpaved parking area and leapt out of the car. He left the keys in the ignition and locked the doors. Sprinting past the lodge and up the trail, he was relieved to find the lift still operating: chairs floating up the slope before disappearing into a thick, overgrown carpet of berry bushes and stunted evergreens.

As he approached the lift house, the attendant, a scruffy-looking kid in his early twenties with the burnt bronze complexion of a surfer, shook his head at him, muttering something about having just missed it, that the lift had closed at seven.

A twenty-dollar bill brought a change of mind. The kid waved him to the loading area.

Panting from the effort, he stood on the thick white line, awaiting the next chair. It hit him in the back of the knees, scooped him up, and accelerated skyward.

The kid called after him, reminding him to catch a ride down by 7:30 sharp.

He nodded, intent upon ignoring the directive. Ushered up the mountain on the high-speed quad, he was struck by the majesty of it all: the lush greenery, the snowy blue peak looming above ... Behind him the curling inlets of Turnagain Arm had been transformed into pools of liquid copper by the ever-present sun. It was a dizzying sight.

No wonder people who visited Alaska came back exhilarated, blathering about the grandeur and majesty. This truly was a Great Land, as the tourist material boasted.

Watching the treetops glide past under him, he judged the distance to the ground: a good fifty to sixty feet in spots. A fall here would be fatal. He gripped the armrest.

If a person could choose the setting for his own death, he thought morbidly, this would be a worthy one. Right here, halfway up the face of Mount Alyeska.

 **ONE**

ALL HAIL THE power of Jesus' name, let angels prostrate fall ...

Ray mouthed the words without issuing so much as a hiss.

Bring forth the royal diadem and crown him Lord of all.

As a boy, he had begrudgingly chanted the traditional songs at festivals. It was either that or listen to endless lectures from Grandfather about the value of the old ways. He had given up all forms of singing as a rebellious youth and had seldom so much as yodeled in the shower or hummed along with the car radio since.

Let every kindred, every tribe on this terrestrial ball . . .

The hymn seemed endless. He glanced at Margaret in desperation, but she was the picture of contentment: smiling, lifting her voice, eyes sparkling. Ray imagined that his own face was the yang to Margaret's yin: frowning, brow sagging, pinched expression.

Sitting between him and Margaret, Keera was beaming, excited about the service without understanding why. Her eyes were locked onto her mother, her lips mimicking every syllable, as she exuberantly mutilated the song. She had an impressive vocabulary for a four-year-old. But *diadem* and *terrestrial* weren't part of it.

Ray checked his watch: 7:22. Only twenty-two minutes had elapsed since the start of the service? Impossible.

According to the flyer he had been handed on the way in, there were still several items left: the offering, the sermon, the closing hymn, the benediction.

What a way to spend a Friday night. And this was supposed to be a vacation. For him at least. Why had he agreed to this? At the moment, with the organ blaring, he couldn't remember. If it had been up to him, they would have gotten off the plane, rented the car, and hopped right on the Seward Highway.

Ray sighed in relief when the song mercifully found an end. The organ finished with a flourish, the last note echoing through the building. On cue, a pair of men carrying what appeared to be bread baskets strode up the center aisle. The minister, a Tlingit in his mid-forties, popped up from his chair next to the podium.

Dark heads in the row ahead of Ray bobbed forward as the minister launched into a marathon prayer, giving thanks for everything under the sun. As the man droned on, Ray surveyed the congregation of the First Native Church of Anchorage. Most of the attendees were Native. Many appeared to be blue-collar. A few, especially the couple up front encased in oil-stained down jackets, could well have been homeless, residents of a local mission or shelter.

When the minister finally summed up his remarks, Ray consulted the schedule to see what else stood between him and freedom. Keera flinched and hit him with an elbow.

"Are you okay, honey?" he whispered.

Her lips moved, but the answer was swallowed by the organ. It erupted into a lavish intro that allowed a large female choir member to plod to the right side of the podium. When the organ paused, she sucked in enough breath to inflate a small raft, then let it out in an ear-splitting note. Ray bent his face to Keera's. "Are you okay?"

She was slightly pale, her eyes wide. "That man's in trouble."

Ray nearly burst out laughing. "That man is a woman," he told her. And we're the one's who are in trouble, he thought.

"He's in trouble."

Ray nodded. "Uh-huh." He checked his watch again. "But it'll be over soon."

One of the bread baskets came down the pew and he handed it to Margaret. The song ended with a noise that must have driven every dog within ten miles mad.

"Wasn't that wonderful?" the minister remarked.

Ray could think of a number of things to call it, but wonderful was not among them. He mentally scratched off the offering. The sermon was next.

The minister ran through a few announcements, something not accounted for on the menu of events. As Ray fidgeted in his seat, trying in vain to find a comfortable position on the wooden pew, he wondered how these people could survive such extreme boredom and come back next week for more. His watch read 7:39. Twenty-one minutes. That was saying this thing was an hour and the preacher didn't run over with his sermon. Ideally, in under half an hour, give or take an unexpected delay, they would be rolling south toward Girdwood. The trip would only take about fifty minutes. They could easily be in the condo, unpacked, and relaxing by 9:30.

In the morning, the first session of Margaret's law seminar started at ten. A friend in Barrow had assured Ray that the lifts opened at seven. Which meant that he and his Trek mountain bike could be at the top of Alyeska by 7:30. If he rode hard, he could probably do the mountain three times before having to be back to watch—

Keera pulled on his sleeve. "Daddy, Raven's after him."

"What?"

"Raven's gonna get him."

"Get who, honey?"

"The man that's in trouble."

He put his arm around her and whispered, "It's okay. Raven won't get him here in church." Even as he said this, Ray realized how ludicrous the statement was. *Raven . . . church . . . ?* The words and the images they elicited belonged to wholly separate worlds. The former was part of their Native heritage, a history rich in lore and myth. The latter represented the introduction—some would say the "intrusion"—of white society. And Ray, like every other contemporary Eskimo, was caught in the middle, struggling to make sense out of the confusing, identity-blurring marriage of the two.

Grandfather had raised him to honor the People and their ways. He had taught him about the tuungak, the ruling spirits, and the system of taboos that had to be upheld in order to appease them. He had shown him how to hunt, fish, live from the land, respect nature in all its varied and marvelous forms. Ray had been obedient until his teen years when he left his village and his mentor to attend high school in Barrow. It was then that he had come face to face with American culture: television, fast food, name-brand clothing, basketball. . . . The effect was dramatic. By the time he graduated and went to Anchorage to do his undergraduate study in criminal justice, he had decided that Grandfather, his kind, and his belief system, were an endangered species, a primitive people best suited to a more primitive age.

If the Inupiat hoped to survive this upheaval and continue to exist at the dawning of the twenty-first century, Ray realized, they had to be willing to adapt. That meant balancing their unique heritage with and against the powerful, constant, nearly ubiquitous influences of modernity and change. White culture had forever altered life above the Arctic Circle. This was a fact that couldn't be denied or ignored. Only embraced.

Glancing up at the stage, Ray saw the minister turn and energetically mount the raised podium. In the process, he either tripped on the step or caught his robe with a shoe. Whichever, he disappeared behind the podium for an instant before bouncing back up, an embarrassed smile on his face.

"They call me Grace," he said. This elicited polite laughter from the audience.

"He fell down," Keera said. "He's hurt."

"No, honey," Ray whispered. "He's fine."

Her lower lip began to tremble. "He's not getting up."

Ray blinked at her. "What?" He glanced at the minister.

"He fell and he won't get up. Raven got him!"

"Honey, this will be over in just a little while. But you have to be quiet, okay?"

"But he fell, Daddy! Raven got him!" she screeched.

Heads turned and the minister lost a beat in his reading.

"He's okay, honey." He directed her attention to the podium. "See?"

"No. Not him. The other man."

"What other man?"

A woman in the row ahead "shhhed" them.

"The man on the mountain."

"Let's talk about it later," he whispered.

"But Daddy . . . Raven got him!"

Margaret gave them both the evil eye.

"He's dead, Daddy!"

"Ray . . . !" Margaret warned, as if Keera's behavior were his fault.

"Raven got him . . . !" Keera whined, on the verge of tears.

Ray scooped her up in his arms. He had no idea what she was blathering about, but recognized that she was about to lose it.

"Daddy!" This outburst qualified as a major disruption. The entire congregation was looking at them now, demanding silence with their glares.

Hurrying down the aisle, he felt his cheeks blushing. Keera didn't usually throw fits. Not in public anyway. Why now? Why here of all places? As soon as they got to the entryway they would have a little father-daughter discussion.

As he pushed through the exit, the irritation began to subside as he realized that he would miss out on the rest of the sermon, the closing hymn, *and* the benediction. Aw, shucks.

TWO

TO THE RIGHT, Cook Inlet was a sea of burnished bronze, water ablaze as the sun dipped like a honey ladle toward the Alaska Range, yet refused to set. To the left, Potter's Marsh was a living advertisement for Mutual of Omaha's *Wild Kingdom:* rushes darting through the low brush, two loons circling overhead. And was that a moose off beyond the parking area? It was difficult to tell at sixty-eight mph.

"You better slow down," Margaret warned as they streaked past the marsh and entered the first series of twists that skirted Turnagain Arm. "You're way over the limit."

Ray obediently tapped the brake. Margaret seldom gave him a hard time about his driving. But then, she was seldom five months pregnant. He glanced into the back and saw that Keera was slumped over in her car seat like a lifeless doll, neck drooping to one side, asleep.

"What happened? What did you say to her?" Margaret wanted to know.

"Nothing. We were just sitting there and she lost it."

They raced past a series of waterfalls dropping from the rugged stone cliffs that lined the highway. "Remember how pretty these are in the winter when they freeze up?"

"What was the fit about?" Margaret asked, without glancing at the waterfalls.

"I'm not sure. She started babbling about the preacher after he tripped going up to give his sermon. She was all concerned that he was hurt. You heard her."

"That doesn't make any sense."

"I think she was just overexcited about the trip, tired from the plane ride."

Across the water, beyond the swirling tide pools, the Kenai Mountains were a glowing watercolor: green slopes rising to blue peaks streaked with thin rivers of snow.

"Did you bring the chips?" she asked, digging into her overnight bag. "I had a sack of Fritos out on the cabinet. Did you pack it?"

Ray tried to recall whether Fritos had made the cut. They had been preparing for the trip for a full week. But the actual packing had been accomplished a slim hour before leaving for the airport. Ray had gotten off duty and hurried home to find Margaret just pulling up with Keera. What followed was a frantic, chaotic attempt to stuff everything, unceremoniously and indiscriminately, into suitcases.

Ray was nearly certain they had forgotten something. Probably several somethings.

"I don't see them," she grumbled. "No Fritos, but at least we've got your mountain bike, and your helmet, and your riding packs, and your pump . . ."

Ray swallowed hard. This was moving in the wrong direction. The remark about the bike went deeper than Margaret's inability to locate a snack, he realized. She enjoyed biking as much as he did and was bummed out about not being able to go. That Ray got to do the mountain and its network of trails while she had to attend a seminar, avoid overeating, and down eight glasses of water a day didn't exactly thrill her.

"Here they are," she said, pulling the sack out. "Good thing for you."

Ray relaxed.

She handed him a chip. "You missed meeting the minister. He was nice."

The all-season radials hummed on the asphalt as they snaked around another of the countless jogs in the road.

A bore tide was gathering strength in the arm, a long row of water standing up in an abbreviated wave that would rush toward Portage. The inlet was shallow, muddy, with a forty-foot tidal range, the second greatest in North America. Not a place for boating or swimming. Every so often someone got stranded out there. Most of them drowned.

"He said there's a church down here."

Ray's heart sunk. "Down where?"

"In Girdwood. It meets on Sundays."

His mind raced, looking for an excuse not to attend. "You have the seminar."

"The early session on Sunday is tax law. I could skip it."

In the back, Keera tried to reposition herself in the constrictive seat. She muttered something about falling, then peeped, ". . . in trouble . . ."

They were rolling by Bird Creek when Margaret leaned across and kissed him. "I love you." Her lips found his again and pressed with a sudden passion. The rental car drifted over the center line and a horn from an oncoming pickup warned Ray to move back to the right.

"I don't know why you put up with me," Margaret said with a sigh.

Ray tried to think of a response but couldn't. The pendulum was swinging again, the grouchiness dissipating, transitioning to a mushy, warm medium. She would probably be weeping uncontrollably in a matter of minutes.

"I think maybe she was talking about one of Grandfather's old stories," he said in an effort to distract her.

"Who?"

"Keera."

"You mean when she threw the fit?"

"Yeah. She kept saying 'he fell,' and 'Raven.' Then she started getting all upset because he was dead."

"Dead?!" Margaret's face twisted and she removed her hand from Ray's shoulder.

"I'll bet Grandfather told her a tale about Raven and it scared the bejeebers out of her. They used to scare me something awful. Some of those fables are creepy. The imagery is right out of a nightmare: shadows and mischievous animals, trickery, revenge, death . . ."

They passed a sign: GIRDWOOD 12.

"I'll talk to Grandfather when we get back. Tell him to lay off the stories."

"I could see her having bad dreams about that," Margaret observed. "But she was awake. Why do you suppose she was suddenly afraid of—?"

"There's no telling. It's impossible to follow a four-year-old's train of thought. That's saying a four-year-old actually has a train of thought." He shook his head. "Falling . . . Getting hurt . . . Dying . . . All of that from an old wives' tale about a bird."

"Huh-uh!"

They jerked their heads around and saw Keera sitting upright, eyes wide, straining against the straps. "It was real. I saw it. The man fell. He fell at the way down!"

"Okay, honey," Ray tried in a consoling voice. "We believe you."

"No, you don't!"

"Keera . . ." Margaret reached to stroke her face with the back of a hand. "Honey, you're tired. Try to go back to sleep. We'll be there soon."

"I'm not tired!" On the heels of this screeching denial, she began rubbing her eyes. "He fell," she contended with a little less volume. "And he didn't get up 'cause he was so hurt." She sniffed, sighed, yawned, and within a few seconds was asleep.

"Well, she's been a low-maintenance kid," Margaret

observed. "Skipped the terrible twos altogether. Maybe she's planning to make up for it now."

"One can only hope."

Margaret tossed two more Fritos into her mouth before blurting, "Ray!!"

The tone was so panicked and shrill that he instinctively jerked the steering wheel to the right, away from opposing traffic. The result was a fishtailing skid along the shoulder that brought them perilously close to the edge of the precipice.

When Ray had steered back onto the road, Margaret grumbled, "I told you to slow down," then took his hand and slipped it under her shirt.

Ray cut his eyes at her. "What are you doing?"

"Be still." After a long pause, she shouted, "There! Did you feel that?!"

"Feel what?"

"He moved!"

Ray waited as a half-dozen vehicles whizzed by, headlights playing in the shadows of the cliff. *He* was not moving. If *he* was, in fact, a *he*. The doctor thought so. But then, doctors made mistakes. And it would be just like this kid to pull a switcheroo.

Keera had come easily, seemingly of her own accord. All he and Margaret had done was discuss having a child and voilà! Enter Keera. This little one on the other hand . . . Talk about a labor of love! They had planned, tried, endured a miscarriage, worried over charts and graphs, studied temperatures and cycles, experimented with all manner of methodology. Ray had even changed his style of underwear. Which combination of factors had finally worked, they would probably never know.

"There!" Margaret said excitedly.

"I don't feel anything," he said, moving to withdraw his arm.

"Wait!" This was an order, not a request. She stuffed in more Fritos.

Ray drove on, one hand on the wheel, the other

stretched against his wife's protruding belly. Pregnant or not, Margaret was beautiful, he thought. In fact, she seemed especially attractive when "with child." The proverbial inner glow. Maybe the weekend wouldn't be a total loss. Maybe after they put Keera to bed . . . He was about to comment on Margaret's loveliness when she blurted, "There he goes again! Did you feel him?"

"No."

"He's about to do it again. Hang on."

Ray did. For a mile. Two miles. They were in view of the gas station that signaled the turn off to Girdwood when *he* finally decided to humor old Dad. "Wow!"

"He's a strong one," she remarked.

"Or maybe *she's* a strong one."

"The doctor knows what to look for."

"I know what to look for too."

"He said he was ninety-five percent sure."

"But not one hundred percent."

"We need to discuss names." She sniffed. "What about . . . Alfred?"

"Alfred??"

"What? That's my father's name. You're the one who's always talking about tradition. It's traditional to name the first son after the maternal grandfather."

"I know but . . . It seems cruel to do that to a kid. *Alfred* . . . He'd either learn to be really tough or he'd grow up with lots of bruises."

"Okay then, let me hear your suggestions."

Somehow Margaret's intonation made the request seem ever so slightly insincere. Ray groaned. Going to church . . . having Keera throw a screaming fit . . . arguing with his pregnant wife about baby names . . . Were they having fun yet?

As they approached the turnoff, Ray flicked on the blinker, braked for a bus, and exited the highway. He smiled and gestured at the mountain: manmade fingers of grass and brush running down through a forest of sun-bleached pines and their long, deep shadows. Tall metal towers dotted the runs, wooden houses marking the midway and top.

"Well?" she prodded.

"Uh . . . I don't know. Something like . . ." His mind was a blank. He could hardly think of any names, much less good ones. Grandfather's was Charles. That was rather boring. So was Raymond. Lewis? No! Billy Bob? Ha!

A green metal road sign told them that they had entered Girdwood. A quarter mile later they were greeted by a more elaborate billboard that depicted a pair of skiers shushing down a slope of deep powder. Bold letters exhorted: SKI ALYESKA!

"How about Alyeska, 'the great land'?"

It was a joke, and for the seven minutes it took them to reach the condo, he regretted it.

 THREE

RAY CARRIED HIS bike into the breezeway with slow, deliberate steps. Leaning it against a concrete wall, he carefully swung the door closed behind him. Success! He had managed to get up, dress, collect his gear, and escape without waking Margaret or Keera.

Glancing at his watch, he felt the adrenaline start to flow: 6:20. He had promised to be back by 8:30. That gave him over two hours to ride, climb, rock-hop . . .

Gathering his long black hair into a ponytail, he fastened an elastic band in place and pulled on his helmet. With the strap snapped tightly against his chin, he re-positioned his fanny pack and mounted up. His mind ran down the checklist: pump, extra tubes, tire wrench, water bottles, energy bars, sunglasses, mosquito repellent, gloves with fingers, gloves without fingers . . . He was wearing thigh-length biking shorts, but had dressed heavy on top: tank, long-sleeved T-shirt, squall jacket. All systems go.

As he rolled along the breezeway and rattled down the trio of concrete steps into the parking lot, he realized that the jacket probably wasn't necessary. It was mild, almost muggy. The sun was up, as always at this time of year, balanced on the peak of Mount Alyeska like a basketball caught on the rim.

Since the lift didn't open until seven, he had a choice: explore the network of dirt roads surrounding the lodge, or stop by the Bake Shop for a cup of coffee and one of their sensational sweet rolls. The latter was tempting. But he needed to warm up and stretch, he told himself. Besides, he could take Keera down for a sticky bun later.

Pooling his resolve, he set off at an enthusiastic pace, pedaling past the support buildings and through the main parking area. It wasn't until he had gone a half mile down the hill and was coasting around a gravel turn that he caught his first glimpse of the arm. It was an iridescent puddle of caramel this morning, the cold, silty water gleaming as if it were in the process of engulfing and extinguishing a bonfire.

He streaked down to the bridge before squeezing the brakes. The trip back to the lifts would be uphill with a vengeance. Time to turn around. As he was about to perform a 180, an ancient, rust-weary pickup rattled out from a dirt artery and stopped just a few feet from him. He found himself staring into the wrinkled face of an old man in a soiled cowboy hat. The man glared at him as though he had never seen anyone on a bicycle.

Ray nodded at the man and offered a friendly smile.

He got a frown in return. The truck lurched forward and headed for Girdwood, showering Ray with gravel.

Bike riders in general were looked down on by motorists, Ray thought as he took hold of the bar ends and stood to pump. They got in the way, moved too slowly, were something of a nuisance. The same could be said for Natives. According to the naluaqmiut, Eskimos got in the way in terms of progress, especially when it came to oil exploration. They worked too slowly and were something of a cultural nuisance.

So an Inupiat on a bike, Ray conceded, legs burning, was a double negative.

He was about to pull over and catch his breath when he realized that the lifts were already running. It was another half mile to the slope. A half mile with a grade of probably 25 percent. There was nothing more severe than a 15 percent grade within a hundred miles of Barrow. It wasn't a prime training ground.

Standing again, he ordered his thighs and lungs to ignore the pain and keep going. He was on the verge of collapse, amazed that he was in such sorry shape, despite getting on the bike three times a week back home, when the road leveled out and fed into a trail that ran downhill to the chair lift.

Braking along the bumpy trail, he decided that two hours was far more time than he needed to exhaust himself. Twenty minutes would probably do it. The good news was that from here on out, the body punishing uphills would be conquered by a high-speed quad. All he had to do was get off at the top, point his bike toward Turnagain Arm, and hold on.

The chair operator was facing the mountain, head raised toward the sun. In shorts and a crumpled Gor-tex parka, he looked like he had just stumbled out of the bush.

"How's it going?" Ray said, hoping not to startle him. If the guy heard the greeting, he did a convincing job of not letting on. Ray wheeled up next to him. It was a kid of maybe eighteen with a sunburned face.

"You open?"

The kid's head swiveled and he observed Ray with a blank face.

Ray pointed to a clock in the window of the lift house. "7:02."

The head turned slowly, regarded the clock, turned back. "Yep."

"So can I go up?"

"Got a ticket?"

Ray shook his head. "Where do I get one?"

"Ticket window opens at nine." He motioned with a gloved hand.

"But I thought the lift . . ."

". . . opens at seven. Gotta buy your ticket the day before if you want first run."

"But I have to be back by nine."

The kid sniffed. "Bummer."

"Can't I just pay you?"

This drew a yawn. "I don't sell tickets. The office is real particular about that."

Ray could see his morning ride evaporating. "How about if I give you the money and then you give it to the ticket office when it opens up?"

Frowning, he said, "Then I gotta go all the way up there. Takes time and energy."

Ray produced a pair of ten-dollar bills. "What's a ticket, twelve?"

"Yeah."

He handed him the money. "Maybe the extra will make up for the inconvenience."

For the first time, the kid evidenced a hint of interest. "Okay," he grunted.

Together they loaded his bike on the back of a chair and the kid positioned Ray to catch the next one. "Have a good one."

"I'll try to," Ray replied as he was scooped up.

The chair accelerated, conducting him above the treetops, toward the ball of yellow fire enthroned on the summit. Streams percolated beneath him, coursing unseen through the dense undergrowth. Barren dirt maintenance roads violated the terrain at odd intervals.

Surging by the midway house, he looked back and was rewarded with an expansive view of Turnagain Arm: the highway, the inlet, the coast of the Kenai Peninsula . . . The tide was shifting again, the water steely gray.

As the chair made another rise, the lodge disappeared. Ray could still see the Bake Shop. Its chimney was billowing smoke. He imagined the crew of talented cooks working like maniacal ants to satisfy the glut of morning customers: pulling sourdough loaves from ovens, flipping flapjacks, cutting apart those enormous cinnamon rolls . . . Maybe after this run he would stop by for a quick refueling.

Above him, the peak glistened with the regal majesty of a reigning monarch. Anointed in brilliant sunlight, the blue ice of the rugged cornice seemed as impenetrable as the wall of a mighty fortress.

Mountain biking down this monster of a mountain would be a thrill, he thought: 2,500 vertical feet. The fact that there was no one else up here—he hadn't seen another soul since getting on the lift—made him a little nervous. He glanced up and down the drooping wires, following the towers with his eyes: empty chairs. He was alone. What if something happened? What if he lost control, went off the trail and hit a tree? Would anyone find him? Did they sweep the slopes daily, like the ski patrol did in winter?

The upper house and lodge came into view five minutes later. The latter was fashioned after the ski chalets of the German Alps: A-frame, cedar construction, wide deck. The upper house was manned by a young lady in her early twenties. She had the same leathery, tanned face as her counterpart at the bottom. She had the Trek waiting for Ray when he arrived.

"There you go. Have a good one."

Ray gave his bike a cursory inspection. It was a delicate piece of machinery and the ride up could have jostled something. Of course, the ride down would do more than just jostle it. Satisfied that the Trek was trailworthy he said, "I was wondering about your safety rules."

"Ride on trails only. Don't ride in mud. If possible don't leave tracks," she clicked off from rote. "Observe the carry in—carry out rule. No littering. Downhill rider has the right of way. Watch your speed. No jumping. Ride under control at all times."

"Sure. But actually, I was interested in . . . you know . . . rescue policies."

"Rescue?" Her face contorted. "You planning to crash?"

"I was just wondering, you know . . . what if something happened and . . ."

"We sweep at noon, four, and after the lifts close at seven. There are phones on the mountain at every house." Frowning, she added, "Ride under control. Take your time getting down. Stay on the trails. You won't have any problems."

"Thanks." He wheeled down the ramp and onto the mountainside. After snapping his helmet strap, he slung a leg over the bike and stood gazing down the slope. After a deep breath, he stuffed his feet quickly into the stirrups. And he was off. Rolling, picking up speed, being pulled down the mountain by an invisible force. A strong force.

The brake pads screeched like wounded birds as he made a fist with one hand, then the other, gripping the handlebars and brake levers with a sudden urgency. Ground sped past beneath him, Turnagain Arm reaching up at him. When he bottomed out at the base of the first terraced step, he was breathing hard, sweating, without having turned the pedals.

Zigzagging down the next section, a black-diamond run called Widowmaker, he spotted a single track that led into the trees under the chair lift. It was relatively flat, less aggressive than the run, more like a nature trail than a racing chute. Leaning to follow it, he bounced over a mound of rocks and grass that probably accounted for a killer mogul in winter and lost his balance. His back tire left the ground, his rear end leapt up from the seat, and he flailed his right arm like a cowboy fighting to stay on a bucking bronco. His left hand reacted, seemingly of its own accord, by squeezing the front brake.

The Trek skid to a halt like a horse confronting deep water and Ray was airborne: arms outstretched, legs spread wide, Superman performing a goofy, low-altitude flyby. Superman with a fanny pack. Unlike the Man of Steel, Ray couldn't maintain his body position in flight. He sailed forward, executing a half layout before landing with a thud and rolling gracelessly into a thicket of berry bushes. Since he was covered almost entirely in Gor-tex, nylon, and fiberglass, the thorns had little to attack. They did, however, find his face.

Sprawled on his back, gasping for air, he silently swore at the calamity and at the sheer stupidity that had made it possible. Hitting the front brake was the cardinal sin of mountain biking. Only an idiot would stop the front tire on a downhill ride. He was lucky he hadn't broken his neck. Remarkably, *nothing* seemed to be broken or even dented. Aside from a stinging cheek, he had survived intact. He touched his face. Blood.

He cursed out loud and began clamoring out of the brush on all fours. Talk about a close call . . . Talk about scary . . . *Ride under control,* the girl had warned.

He found his bike leaning innocently against the hill, as if he had merely stepped off for a moment to appreciate a nearby patch of fireweed. Traitor, he thought, picking it up. The frame was unscathed. As for the tires . . . Still inflated. He gave the pedal a twist, watched the back rim spin in perfect circles, tried the front. Nothing bent.

He led his fickle, tubular steel mount to the edge of the treeline to inspect the trail. After the brief but memorable aerial maneuver, he wasn't about to take off into the forest without knowing what was there. The thirty paces left his legs shaky. Fatigue? Fright? Hunger? Probably a combination of the three, he decided. He would take it easy the rest of the way down, riding within his means and ability. *Not* using his front brake. And . . .

He dug an energy bar from his fanny pack. Maybe a shot of carbs would help. He devoured the bar in three bites. His stomach signaled its appreciation, and he was about to tear open another when he noticed something: an object twenty yards down the hill. It was lying at the foot of an enormous stump, surrounded by pines, camouflaged by their elongated shadows. A fallen branch? If so, it was a big one, maybe six feet in length, a foot or two thick. An animal? It seemed lumpy enough. But it wasn't moving. Something that big wouldn't be sleeping in the open like that. Would it?

Ray squinted, trying to make out details. From where he was standing, the contours almost made it look . . . No. Couldn't be. That was ridiculous. Maybe he had hit his head harder than he thought. The wreck had knocked the sense out of him.

Still . . . What if it was?

He decided to investigate.

⟫⟫ FOUR ⟪⟪

DESCENDING THROUGH THE underbrush, bike in tow, Ray lost sight of the body. *The body*... He chided himself for jumping to conclusions. In his line of work, the word body implied a person, specifically someone who was no longer living. Until he verified it, the object was nothing more than a dark lump in the woods. A log. An abandoned ski patrol stretcher. A broken-down snow machine. A combination of natural shapes and shadows.

A pair of squirrels skittered into the brush ahead of Ray. He could hear a stream, gurgling and trickling through the thicket. Looking straight up he saw the chair lift.

A body... It was laughable. Here? In this serene, alpine paradise? Ridiculous. The entire valley seemed magical, immune from issues of mortality and health.

If it did turn out to be a person, there would be a simple explanation. A backpacker zonked out for the night. A biker taking a break. A staff member catching a few Z's.

It couldn't be a body, he stipulated silently. The lift operator had said that the mountain was swept three times a day. The patrols would notice someone lying in a shallow grave. Wouldn't they?

He was mentally debating the issue, wondering how

thorough a "sweep" really was, when he came upon it. Or rather, *him*. A man. Dressed in khaki slacks and a blue jacket. Lying facedown, arms spread wide, legs together.

Ray studied the scene with the stunned amazement of a sleepwalker rudely awakened from a convincing dream. Or maybe this was a dream. A nightmare. Maybe in falling from the bike he had smacked his head and was now unconscious.

The blood and bruises on the man's neck seemed real enough. So did the way the first two fingers on the left hand were bent backward, folded skyward.

As he gawked at the body, Ray vacantly released his bike. It bumped against a stump, then a root before collapsing. He ignored this. Kneeling, he gently examined the man's right hand. It was cold, stiffened into an unnatural, clawlike position. He felt for a pulse. Nope. No heartbeat. No evidence of life. It realy was a body.

Rising, he scowled at the man, as if he had died on purpose, just to make Ray's life more difficult. His eyes raked the area for a bike, a tent, a pack . . . anything that might tell him what the guy was doing there. Nothing. As he slowly circled the body, he realized that the area was clean. No tire marks. No footprints. The moist ground was smooth, the brush wild. There wasn't so much as a broken limb or a depression in the grass.

Ray sighed at this and bent to examine the man's shoes. They were Rockports, the soles dry, bearing a fine layer of dust. Dust? How could someone end up on a mountainside, a slope riddled with tiny brooks, and covered with wet tussock grass and boggy trails, without filling the soles of his shoes with mud?

He glanced up as a chair hummed overhead. *Directly* overhead. Of course. The guy had fallen from the chair. Ray estimated that the cable was a good sixty feet above him, the chair it carried almost that high. A drop of even thirty feet could kill you.

Ray gingerly felt the man's neck. Broken. Watching another chair glide over in route to the lower lift house,

he envisioned the event: the man nodding off, maybe
he'd been drinking, slipping from his seat, falling forward, losing control in the air, impacting in a clumsy,
tilted layout, head meeting the ground slightly before the
rest of his body. Wham! The neck would have snapped.
The back too. Not to mention the damage such a fall
would do to the organs. The man didn't linger, Ray decided.

Using two hands, he lifted the head. It was a gory
mess: cheekbones flattened, nose sunken into the skull,
the chin imploded. Thin crusts of dried blood snaked
from the ears to the chin. The skin around the eyes was
blue-gray, the eyes themselves open but expressionless.
It was more a death mask than a face. The jaw hung
open, as if the man had something left to say but
couldn't quite verbalize it. Two incisors were missing,
along with pieces of four others. Ray stared at the exposed gums, then glanced at the ground beneath the
head. There was a miniature crater where the forehead
had impacted, a protrusion of buried granite where the
rest of the face had touched down.

What a way to go, Ray thought as he respectfully laid
the man's head back down. On vacation and you fall off
the chair. Do a face plant into a rock.

Ray guessed that the man was around forty. Upper-
middle class: good haircut, brand-name clothing . . . A
professional. Probably had a family.

He fished into the man's pockets for ID. There was a
bottle of Binaca in the jacket. The inside pocket held a
trail map and a small manila envelope. The envelope
was folded in half and held something heavier than mere
paper. There were no marks on the outside, no address
or name. Replacing it, he found a passport: Richard M.
Gleary of San Francisco. No international stamps. The
booklet was clean and new. Ray tucked it back into the
jacket and fished an eelskin wallet out of the hip pocket
of the Dockers. A driver's license confirmed the man's
identity and home, offering a street address. Wedged be-

hind an assortment of credit cards Ray discovered pictures: a woman in her early twenties, smiling from beneath a broad-brimmed sun hat; the same woman in glasses, cradling an infant; a naked toddler messily consuming a cupcake; the woman sitting with the toddler, a new baby in the child's arms. Gleary's wife and kids. Tragic.

The other pockets were empty. No house keys. No car keys. No condo or hotel room keys. Odd. But then Gleary was from out of town. He was probably there on vacation. Except where was his family? Okay, maybe he had come to Alaska on business, attended a meeting or a seminar in Anchorage. The meeting was over on Friday. He came up to Alyeska to relax and take in the natural beauty. Rode the bus. No. Not an executive. He rented a car and checked into the hotel at the base. Left his keys at the desk.

Ray studied the photo on the license. Richard Gleary had been a handsome guy.

He replaced the ID and put the wallet back where he had found it. As he did, his mind continued to analyze the scene, addressing the questions it posed, methodically proposing, discarding, and embracing various answers. When had Gleary fallen off the lift? This morning? No. Not from the looks of the body. Yesterday? The patrol hadn't spotted him on their sweep. Why? Because there was no way to realistically "sweep" an entire mountain? Because they seldom if ever found anyone lost or in need of first aid? Because they were a bunch of college kids in a hurry to get down the mountain and knock off a few cold ones? Because it was easy to overlook a body lying in the woods?

A better question: Why hadn't Gleary been missed by his business partners or traveling companions? Had he come up alone? Up the lift by himself? Or had he been part of a tour group? Doubtful. He wasn't tour group material. At least, Ray didn't think so.

All of this conjecture was moot, of course, since Ray

would not be working the case. The North Slope was the largest incorporated borough in Alaska, weighing in at a stunning 89,000 square miles, roughly the size of Minnesota. But it ended just above the Arctic Circle. His jurisdiction expired somewhere in the upper Brooks Range. Alyeska belonged to what? The municipality of Anchorage? Was Girdwood a first- or second-class city? He wasn't sure. But he was sure about Gleary. The incident was a no-brainer. Gleary had slipped from a chair lift and fallen sixty-some feet. End of story.

Ray had worked a few cases like this back in Barrow. A hunter freezing to death, a drunk succumbing to hypothermia, accidents involving firearms. Explanations were usually self-evident, though not always as glaringly plain as this.

Retrieving his bike, he wondered if the poor guy would have lain there all summer, even through the ski season, if he hadn't stumbled onto him. Apparently the body blended so well with the landscape that it was virtually invisible from the chair. Either that or those riding the lift simply hadn't bothered to notice. Why look straight down when you could sit back and gaze at a vision of Eden?

Eventually someone would have come looking, Ray decided. Gleary's colleagues, his family . . . someone would have missed him and traced him to this mountain.

A chair floated over, rattling as the cable led it past a tower. Ray squinted at the white numbers stenciled near the top of the tower: 42. That would serve as his reference point. Richard Gleary's corpse was lying in the shadow of tower forty-two.

He gave the motionless form a sympathetic shake of his head before leading his Trek to more rideable terrain. The first order of business was to locate a lift house. According to the girl at the top, each house had a phone. He would call in his discovery and either hike back up or catch the lift at midway to assist in the recovery process.

Mounting up, Ray was struck by the dramatic shift in his mood. The morning was still incomparable, the scenery overwhelmingly beautiful, yet he found himself distracted, unable to fully appreciate it any longer. He was no longer a man on holiday. He was a law enforcement officer with a job to perform. A distasteful job. A job involving death.

To the Inupiat Eskimo, death was a transition. Good hunters went to an intermediate place of plenty to await reincarnation, sometimes as animals: caribou, foxes, whales . . . Lazy men were resigned to the Land of the Crestfallen, a humiliating netherworld. But the dead themselves, the bodies, were feared and avoided at all costs.

As for finding a corpse . . . Grandfather would call that a bad omen, a portent of coming evil. Of course, Grandfather saw signs everywhere, attributing nearly everything from the weather to the success of a hunt to the activity of the fickle, malevolent tuungak.

Ray had stopped worrying about appeasing the spirits and observing all the old ways as a teen. He was no longer concerned about whether the tuungak found him worthy of blessing or deserving of curses. Any of those traditional Inupiat beliefs would have made his vocation impossible. You couldn't be a policeman without encountering the dead. Still, he found it draining. Sobering.

He tried to shake free of these gloomy, morbid thoughts as he bumped down the trail. *Find a lift house,* he reminded himself. *Report Gleary. Go back to enjoying the thrill of recklessly bombing a 4,000-foot mountain on a fat-tire bike.*

The trail ran parallel to the ski run for a quarter mile. Ray slowed as the steep single-track made an abrupt turn and traversed the slope. The entire world seemed visible from here. Everything except the midway house. Eventually the trail would lead him to a phone. Either that or wind into the Chugach National Forest and dump him out at Whittier.

Fifteen minutes later he reached a fork. The more heavily traveled track continued on, bisecting another run. The other, a subtle, curving line of matted grass, fell away to the left, wrapping through an array of hay bales, moguls in winter, before entering the trees. Which way?

Frustrated, Ray looked to his watch for an answer, then caught himself. What was the big hurry? Gleary wasn't going anywhere. Still, there was something propelling Ray, demanding that he share the news with someone. A cloud of mosquitoes materialized and he fled by, pedaling into the hay bales.

The trees presented a challenge. Or, more accurately, the narrow path that jinked in and out of them. It was wide enough for a single tire, deep enough to swallow that tire and cause the pedals to drag the ground on either side. Once in the track, there was no escape. The grade abruptly became severe and his speed increased despite a steady, insistent application of the brakes.

By the time he reached the clearing, he was totally out of control: Mr. Toad piloting a Trek. He was in the process of abandoning the bike, loosing his feet from the stirrups with the intent of leaping to safety, when the midway house presented itself: a square wooden building slightly larger than an outhouse sitting directly in his path.

He squeezed the brakes and braced for impact. The pads shrieked and the bike slid sideways, skidding gracelessly to a halt a slim yard from the house.

A head poked out of the glassless window and a fresh-faced teenager blinked at him. "Dude . . . that was gnarly."

"Thanks," Ray managed between gasps.

"I thought you were gonna bite it—big time."

"Me too," he admitted, still puffing. "I need to use your phone."

The head retracted and in a moment the door popped open. "Be my guest."

Ray leaned his bike against the house and stepped inside. It was cramped and reeked of wet wool and dope. A rotary phone sat on a wooden ledge, next to an open box of Fruit Loops and an assortment of rolling papers bearing leftover shreds of marijuana.

As Ray dialed 0, the attendant opened a small cooler on the floor. "Care to join me in a Dew this morning?" He snapped the top of a wet can of pop and offered it to Ray. "Doin' the Dew—it's like, part of my religion, man."

And dope must be part of it too, Ray thought but decided not to add. "No thanks." The kid couldn't have been much older than sixteen or seventeen. His hair was long, scraggly, unwashed, his eyes pinpricks. He was as high as a kite. What a combination, Ray thought, sugar cereal, caffeinated pop, and hash. At eight in the morning. The breakfast of champions.

When someone answered the line, Ray said, "Uh . . . Yeah. I . . . uh . . . spotted someone . . . a man . . . lying in the trees, under tower forty-two."

"Was he hurt?" the kid asked. He gobbled a handful of Froot Loops and washed them down with a messy gulp of pop.

"No, he wasn't hurt," he said, answering the same question for the person on the phone. "He was dead."

The kid was in mid-swallow when Ray made the disclosure. He responded by first choking on, then spewing Mountain Dew and flecks of cereal across the inside of the hut.

▶► FIVE ◄◄

"I'M POSITIVE," RAY told the phone, ignoring the kid who was wiping down his shirt. "Yes, I'll hold."

The kid's face pinched into a pained expression. "Dead?!" He cursed before asking, "Dude! What happened?!"

"Broken neck . . ." The receiver clicked and a man calling himself Hans Heiberg came on the line. With a thickly accented voice, but little enthusiasm, he asked how he could be of service. "I'd like to report a body on the mountain." He waited as the man voiced the obvious questions. "A dead body. Under tower fourty-two . . . No . . . Yes. I'm sure he was dead . . . Because I checked for signs of life . . . Well, for starters, I'm a police officer."

The kid dropped his pop can and began passionately invoking God's eternal damnation. "You're a *pig!?*"

Before Ray could answer or object to the term, the kid went into a panic, frantically brushing the rolling paper and marijuana remnants into an open backpack.

Ray shook his head, listening as Hans described his plan to come up and take a look at the body himself. To be sure it actually existed and that it was really dead.

"The bike and the tail had me fooled, dude," the kid whined. "And the Native American routine. I thought you were an Eskimo. I thought you were cool."

"I'll wait for you at the top," Ray told the phone. After hanging up, he glared at the kid. "I *am* an Eskimo. And I *am* cool. So cool I think I'll bust your butt right here and now for possession." He let this hang in the air and watched the kid squirm. "Unless you make me two promises."

"Anything, dude. Name it. Anything."

"First, never again compare a policeman to a farm animal."

"Oh . . . like, wow, dude. I'm sorry," he stammered. "I didn't mean . . ."

"Second, promise me you'll lose the dope."

The kid bit his lip.

"I assume your boss, Mr. Heiberg, frowns on employees getting high on duty."

This drew a glum nod.

"You could be arrested, go to jail, *and* lose your job in the same day."

The kid sighed heavily, ready to concede defeat.

"And since it's bad for you anyway . . . Let's make a deal. You kick the habit and I look the other way, this one time."

"But like, dude . . . It's a nonaddictive chemical substance. I don't have a habit."

"Mr. Heiberg will be up here in fifteen minutes. I can read you your rights and tell him about your 'nonaddictive chemical substance' problem or . . ."

"Okay . . . Okay . . . I won't smoke on the job. Be boring as heck without it though."

"An occupational hazard."

"I'm still gonna toke on my own time," he proposed rebelliously.

"Fine. Smoke your brains out. Just don't let me catch you." Ray stared until the kid swallowed hard. "Mind helping me with my bike?"

The boy hurried to the task, clearly anxious to be rid of the "pig." He hoisted the Trek onto a chair and invited Ray to take the next one. As he rode the lift, Ray glanced back periodically and found the kid watching through the house window, waiting for him to top the rise. Probably waiting to roll a doobie and light up.

Drugs . . . Squinting into a fierce sun, Ray focused his loathing on mind-active chemicals of all shapes and forms. He had witnessed their ability to derail even the most promising of lives. Especially among the Inupiat. Especially alcohol. But the frightening thing was that drugs and booze weren't particular. They could destroy people from any ethnic background, culture, religion, age group, class . . . Maybe Grandfather was right. Maybe they weren't inanimate substances, but evil spiritual entities capable of entrancing, taking captive, and ultimately conquering mankind.

These distressing thoughts were still haunting Ray when he reached the top. The same girl was there, holding his Trek for him.

"Back again?" She asked this in a bright tone, with clear, innocent eyes and a winning smile. Dope-free, Ray was certain. Her face fell when Ray hopped off the chair and she noticed his cheek. "What happened?!"

"Did a header." He was blushing, the rush of blood causing the scratches to burn.

She winced at the mental image. "Hit the front brake?"

He nodded apologetically. "Stupid . . ."

"No. I've been riding for four years. All summer every summer, on the rescue patrol for two seasons." She rolled her eyes melodramatically. "I still hit the front brake every once in a while. And usually regret it." Rolling up a sleeve, she displayed a thin scar. "Thorn bush." She tapped a raised, round mark on her neck. "Low branch. I'd show you where I pegged a pine, but I'd have to take off my shirt."

Ray nearly choked. The girl was about twenty-one, disgustingly tan, in remarkable shape. He had to fight to avoid visualizing the souvenir from her encounter with the tree.

She slipped into the lifthouse and returned seconds later with a first aid kit.

"It's nothing," Ray protested.

"A little disinfectant and a Band Aid. You'll be ready to rock and roll." Once the wound was clean and the bandage was in place, he thanked her and walked his bike down the ramp.

"If you can hold on about ten minutes, I'll ride down with you," the girl called.

"Actually I'm waiting for someone."

"Oh . . ." Her disappointment was evident, though Ray couldn't imagine the source. She was ten-plus years his junior.

"You da von who sawed da body?" a voice boomed in clipped English.

Ray looked up to see a man arriving on the lift. He was short, silver-headed, and frail, thin upper body swallowed by an oversized Alyeska parka. Nikes dangled from bronze sticks that protruded from a pair of miniature biking shorts.

"Mr. Heiberg?" Ray asked, watching with concern as the man stepped from the lift and hobbled stiffly down the ramp.

"Coal me Hans," he ordered in an accented baritone that seemed impossible for a man of his slight, broken stature.

"I'm Ray Attla." He grimaced as Hans attempted to crush his hand. As Ray stared down into the sun-darkened face, he found a pair of youthful blue eyes. Hans was either a forty-year-old who had led a hard life or a seventy-year-old in terrific shape.

"Vat a beeg von you are," Hans remarked. "Gotta be da beegest Eskimo I seen."

"Inupiat," he specified, nodding.

Hans refused to release his hand, apparently expecting an explanation for Ray's size. Granted, six-two was large for a Native. Ray towered over his friends back in

Barrow by a good four to six inches. He towered over Hans by eight.

"I ate all my Wheaties."

Hans laughed heartily at this. "You deedn't say you vas Native on da phone."

Ray shrugged. "It didn't seem relevant."

"Jest dat I vould have trusted you more. Day tried da cope routine before."

"*Cope?*"

"Police officer," he corrected. "Dees kids, day call from da houses and pretend to be copes. Report all sorts of vierd stuff: beegfoot, U-eff-Os . . . I thought maybe you vas da kids, pulling my leg again."

Ray nodded, pretending to understand.

"Now vere's dees body of yours?"

Pointing, Ray said, "Down in the trees under tower forty-two. I guess we could walk down there . . ." He wondered how long it would take Hans to walk that far. Half a day?

"Valk?" He chortled. "Vee ride." The girl wheeled a bike down: oversized chrome frame, shocks on both forks. Ray had seen one in a magazine going for $2,000.

"Now Hans," the girl said, smiling mischievously, "you take it nice and slow. Don't go off and leave this guy in the dust. Okay?"

Hans winked at the girl. "But I like to ride fast. Speed is my only vice."

The girl winked back, then whispered to Ray, "Be careful. Hans is a wild man."

Ray was trying to decide whether she was serious when the little man threw a leg over his bike and pushed off. He was rocketing down the hill before his feet were even in the stirrups. Ray had to hustle to keep him in sight.

Hans's strategy for riding a mountain turned out to be painfully simple: point the front tire toward the base and hold on. The guy was a lunatic, Ray soon discovered.

Ten heart-pounding minutes later, wheezing like an

asthma sufferer, Ray was relieved to see Hans dart into the bramble under the lift. When Ray reached the brush, he dismounted and walked in to find Hans waiting.

"Vers dis body of yours?"

"Down there," Ray told him, nodding toward the tower. As they hiked down, he said, "You're quite a rider. Fearless."

"Riding is just a hoe-by. You should see me ski."

"You're head of the ski school?" he said, referring to the logo on Hans's jacket.

"Yah. And I supervise da summer activities. Like mountain biking."

And body recovery, Ray thought as they reached Gleary. He was just as Ray had left him: irreparably without life. Still in the position of a man crucified. Except one arm was slightly bent. Ray decided that he must have done that when checking for ID.

Hans crouched and tried to find a pulse. A minute passed before he gave up.

"Name's Richard Gleary," Ray informed. "From San Francisco."

"Any idea vat happened to eem?" Even as he inquired about this, Hans tilted his head at the chair sailing overhead. "Maybe ee vell off da lift?"

"That's my guess."

"Dat vould kill ya, sure enough." He pondered the chair. "But how come? I vork here tvelve years. Only had a coo-ple people fall off da lift. Day all fall off in winter and all right up by da houses. Couple a broken legs. Nobody died."

"Maybe he just lost his balance and slipped off."

"Da chairs, day angle back, to keep you from doing dat."

"Fell asleep?"

Hans cocked his head, challenging this. "More den likely drunk."

They stared at the body. Ray asked, "How are we going to get him down?"

"Oh . . . You don't have to vorry bout dat. I got help coming."

On cue a voice called out of the wilderness: "Hans?!"

"Over hee-er," he responded.

Thirty seconds passed before the same voice cried, "Where?"

"By da pole."

Branches rustled twenty yards uphill and a man staggered into view pulling a ski patrol sled, this one equipped with wheels instead of ski pontoons. The man was taller than Hans, shorter than Ray, with tufts of carrot-colored hair sticking out at odd angles from beneath a Burton Snowboards cap. Another ski bum, Ray thought at first glance. But as the man approached, panting at the effort of leading the heavy sled, he changed his mind. The guy was a Native. Or . . . part Native? It was an unnerving mix: red hair, broad nose, full cheeks, almond-shaped *blue* eyes . . . Intensely blue eyes.

The man dropped the sled and wiped his brow on the sleeve of his polar fleece jacket. Blinking at the body, he puffed, "What happened?"

"Fell off the lift," Ray submitted.

The piercing blue eyes gave him the once over.

"Ray Attla. I found him."

"Glen Redfern," the man responded. As he shook Ray's hand his face adopted a look of curiosity. "Inupiat?"

Ray nodded. "Tareumiut."

"Biggest one I ever seen. I'm Yupik."

Ray's eyebrows rose. Glen was the first redheaded, blue-eyed Yupik he had encountered.

"*Part* Yupik," Glen specified. " 'Bout half. Give or take." Turning his attention to the body, he knelt to examine the head. "Nasty." He retrieved a 35mm camera from the sled. "Guess I should take a few snaps."

"What for?" Ray asked. "Insurance?"

"That," Glen said, "and for the State Police."

"Glen is da sheriff of Girdvood," Hans explained.

"The title's honorary," Glen stipulated. "It's a volunteer position. No pay. I'm also the designated chaplain and the rector of Girdwood Chapel."

The hair on the back of Ray's neck stood up. *Rector?* "Sounds like a lot of hats."

Glen clicked off shots from a variety of angles. "It would be. But I don't do much sheriff work. The State Police handle any real crimes. Every so often I have to get after a reckless snowboarder or lean on some twelve-year-old shoplifter. That's about it." He paused, trading the SLR for a video camera. "I do even less chaplaincy work. Folks don't come to Alyeska for spiritual advice or crisis counseling. They're here to ski, bike, play, party ... Emphasis on the last." He panned the body before switching off the camera. "Maybe that's what happened to this poor guy."

"Dat's my guess," Hans agreed. "Too much brew."

Stuffing the video camera back into its bag, Glen fished a walkie-talkie out of his jacket. "Base, this is *Sheriff* Redfern," he told the device. "We've got a body at ..." He paused and checked the tower. "At fourty-two. I'm about to load up and head down."

The reply took the form of a blast of static.

"Yeah," he said, depressing the button with a thumb. "Go ahead and give the State Police a jingle. Tell them we've got a package for them."

"He's got ID," Ray told him.

Glen frowned at this. "I'll let the real cops deal with all that." Glancing at his watch, he sighed, "I've got Mass in forty minutes." With that he bent to gather the body. Ray and Hans helped him hoist it into the sled.

"Mass?" Ray asked. "So you're Catholic?"

"Temporarily." He laughed. "I'm filling in until they get a replacement for Father Michael."

Ray was about to ask about this when he caught a glimpse of Hans's watch. He examined his own and swore: 8:23. He was due back at the condo in seven minutes.

"I gotta go. Nice meeting you, Father . . . or Reverend . . . or . . ."

"*Glen.* Same here, Ray. See you around."

Not if I see you first, Ray thought as he mounted his Trek. "If you need me, I'm at the Highland Condos until Monday."

"I doubt if there will be anything," Glen said. "Pretty cut and dried."

"I tell you," Hans shouted as Ray started pedaling. "I tink da best vay down is—"

"Yeah. I know, Hans," Ray called back as he reached the trail. "*Straight* down."

SIX

"RAYMOND ATTLA!"

It was amazing, Ray thought, how a name, even one's own, could be made to sound like an indictment. "I got here as fast as I could." He hustled his bike through the kitchen and leaned it against the couch, pulling off his helmet and gloves.

"I said eight-thirty, not eight-fifty," Margaret reminded.

"Sorry."

"Hi, Daddy!" Keera hugged his leg as though he had been gone for weeks.

"I can't believe you sometimes," Margaret muttered. He considered telling her about the body, but decided against it. In her present mood, a volatile state accentuated by hormones, no excuse short of his own death would suffice. "I'm sorry. I really am."

She brushed by en route to the door, then turned on her heels and marched back. Ray braced himself for a parting tongue-lashing. Instead Margaret opened her mouth and froze. "What happened?!" A hand gently brushed his bandaged cheek. "Did you crash?"

He shrugged. "It's nothing."

Without warning, she took his head in her hands and kissed him with a wild, reckless passion. Releasing him, she whispered, "Sorry for being such a witch."

Ray could think of no safe response to this statement. Denying it would require her to build an argument for her witchhood. Agreeing would be insane. "I love you."

Her eyes sparkled at this and a smile beamed up at him. "Me too." She gave him a final squeeze before whispering, "Maybe tonight we can . . . *you know.*"

Ray swallowed hard. "Sounds good to me."

She winked at him, then bent to peck Keera on the cheek. In the next instant, her demeanor changed radically as she adopted a professional air. Heading for the door, briefcase in hand, she said, "See you at five."

"What about lunch?" Ray asked, feeling like an abandoned housewife.

"There's a practicum." She paused in the open doorway. "Keera's had juice and a banana. She wants to watch Bugs Bunny. She needs a bath."

"And I wanna cinner-men roll, Daddy. Please? Can I have a cinner-men roll?"

"We didn't bring any, but I mentioned the Bake Shop." She waved, the look on her face implying that Ray was going to have his hands full. "Have fun, you two."

"We will, Mommy!" Keera shouted. When the door was shut, she began chanting, "Bugs Bunny, cinner-men roll, Bugs Bunny, cinner-men roll . . ."

"How about a bath first?"

This elicited a yelp—a hound dog in severe pain.

"Come on. We'll be quick. Get the icky stuff out of the way so we can have fun." He waited for her pouty frown to fade. "When does Bugs come on?" He stepped to the TV and found a guide. "Here we go. Bugs is on . . . in six minutes! We'd better hurry."

Keera dashed to the bathroom, ripping her clothing off as though it were on fire.

In four short minutes, his daughter had washed her hair, given her skin a cursory once-over with a bar of soap, and was wrapped in a towel. She continued to stutter her mantra through chattering teeth: "B-B-Bugs B-B-Bunny, c-c-cinner-m-men r-rolls . . ."

After helping her get dressed, Ray set her up in front of the TV and flicked it on in time to catch Bugs and his pal Daffy doing the song and dance opening.

"I'll be in the shower," he told her. She was transfixed by the cartoon images, oblivious to Ray, her surroundings, life in general. Grandfather was right, he thought as he disrobed and turned on the water. Television was an anjatkut: powerful, magical, able to hypnotize and influence.

He exited the shower five minutes later, toweled off, and drew his wet hair into a ponytail. Sliding on a pair of Levi's and a Nike sweatshirt, he looked at himself in the mirror. Despite the modern trappings, he caught a glimpse of Grandfather: the same dark, brooding eyes, same prominent cheekbones, the full mouth. The resemblance went beyond physical traits. He had inherited something of Grandfather's spirit: the critical gaze, the suspicious attitude toward all things new and different. No, Ray didn't religiously observe the old ways. But he had his own set of rules, gods, and taboos.

These rather disturbing thoughts were still with him when he returned to the living area and found Keera entranced by a commercial for Malibu Barbie.

"That's what I want, Daddy. I want Barbie for my berf-day."

"Is that right? What's so great about Barbie?"

"She's neat, Daddy. She really is."

Ray blinked at the screen, trying to decide why a Caucasian doll with long peroxide hair, tan skin, and an exaggerated hour-glass figure would appeal to a short, dark Eskimo child who would grow up to be a short, dark Eskimo woman. Indoctrination, he decided. Keera had already been impressed that slender, large-chested, and blond were the ideal.

He shook off the observation. This was supposed to be a vacation, not a gloomy condemnation of modern values. He fixed a bowl of cereal and slumped onto the couch next to Keera. After several slapstick shorts featuring Bugs, Tweety and the Road Runner, the closing credits began to roll and Keera sprang from her seat to switch off the TV. "Cinner-men rolls! Can we get a cinner-men roll now, Daddy? Please?"

"Maybe we should wait until after lunch," he suggested.

"Awww . . . ! I want a cinner-men roll now! Pleeeeeeeeezzzzz!?"

"Okay. Put your shoes and socks on." Ray slipped on his own shoes and glanced at his watch. Straight up ten. Seven hours until his shift was over. He loved Keera and enjoyed caring for her. But usually Margaret was around to act as relief. Seven hours?

Keera raced back from the bedroom. "Is this the right one?" She plopped onto the floor and began to work her left foot into a sandal marked with an oversized R.

"Right shoe. Wrong foot." He switched them for her and watched as she grunted and yanked her way into them. "Grab a jacket."

"I don't wanna jacket." She balled her fists for emphasis. "I'm not taking one."

"Grab a jacket or no *cinner-men* roll."

"O-kay . . ." She stomped to the bedroom.

Ray pocketed his wallet and slung a Gor-tex shell over his arm. It was warm enough to warrant short sleeves, but if it clouded over and started to drizzle though . . . Better to be prepared for the worst, especially when venturing forth with a preschooler. The walk to the Bake Shop was maybe a quarter mile. There was a bike shop right next door to the condos. They probably rented child trailers. Ray considered getting one and riding to the Bake Shop. It would be easier, quicker . . . But he needed to pace himself, activity-wise, and Keera needed the exercise. With any luck the big Bake Shop outing would wear her down. By the time they returned, maybe she would be ready for a nap. After that, they could pack a little lunch, rent a trailer, and go for a biking picnic.

Ray calculated the time involved and was satisfied that, if all went according to plan, he could make it to five o'clock without losing his mind.

"I'm ready, Daddy." She was wearing a fire engine–red jacket over her purple sweats, river-runner sandals strapped to socks that glowed fluorescent green. Margaret would have sent her back to put on something less casual that actually matched.

Ray squinted at her. "You need a brightness knob." He led her outside into a glare of sunshine.

"Where's the cinner-men rolls?" Keera asked before he could even lock the door.

"We have to walk down to—"

"Walk! How far? Can you carry me?"

He took her hand and pulled her down the sidewalk. "Maybe on the way back."

She made a noise like a wounded shrew and Ray gazed longingly at the bike shop. It was open and he could see a row of trailers lined up in the window.

"Come on," he urged, determined to stick with his original itinerary. "It's not that far. And if we look, we might see some animals."

"Animals!" She leapt forward, yanking him along. "What kind of animals?"

"Rabbits . . . moose . . . birds . . . bears . . ."

"Bears?!"

"Maybe. But you have to be really quiet if you want to see them."

The ruse worked. For the next half hour they crept along, conversing in whispers, stalking whatever wildlife might be lurking around the next bend in the trail. The area proved to be void of big game: no bears or moose. But they saw several ground squirrels, startled a gray hare, and spotted a bald eagle lazily riding thermals over the valley.

"Maybe on the way back we'll see a bear," Keera said when they reached the parking area of the main lodge complex.

The lot was almost full now, the sidewalk along the row of shops thick with tourists. Asians with Nikons slung around their necks chattered happily as they poured off of one charter bus, Europeans in hats toting pregnant packages filing onto another.

Ray was eyeing the Bake Shop, wondering how bad the line would be, when a man hurried into their path.

"Peek-cher?" He was Asian; Korean, Ray guessed. Grinning like a lunatic, he jabbed a camera at them, then cut his eyes at a nearby woman. His wife?

"You want me to take your picture?" Ray asked, reaching for the camera.

The man took a step back. "Peek-cher?"

"You want *our* picture?" Ray asked.

The man stared, still grinning. "Re-ah Ez-kee-mo?"

Ray sighed and nodded. "Inupiat."

Turning to his fellow travelers, the man jabbered something, repeating the word Ez-kee-mo several times. In a matter of seconds, Ray and Keera were adrift in a sea of lenses.

"Where dogsled?" someone asked from behind a video camera.

"I left it back at my igloo," Ray deadpanned.

"Ee-gloo!" Shutters clicked. A woman moved in for a close-up of Keera.

"We see ee-gloo?"

"I was joking," Ray replied. The paparazzi circled, fingers focusing, eyes stuck to viewfinders, teeth gleaming behind telephotos the size of summer sausages. "Back off!" he warned, waving them away as if they were insects. This seemed to fan them to action.

Ray was about to use force, to put his fists to his chest and plow a path through the crowd like a football lineman, when someone shouted something.

There were gasps, wide-eyed stares, a flurry of final snapshots, and suddenly the frenzy was over. The group moved like a wind-driven cloud toward the Bake Shop.

Ray turned to see Sheriff Glen Redfern standing behind them, a Jimmy bar in his hand.

"What did you say to them?" Ray asked.

Glen repeated himself, though to Ray it sound like he was clearing his throat.

"I caught that. What's it mean?"

"It's Korean for cannibal."

"Cannibal . . . Gee, thanks."

SEVEN

"WHAT'S A CANNER-BULL?" Keera wanted to know.

Glen bent to her level. "And who is this beautiful little lady?"

"My name's Keera!" she answered enthusiastically.

"My, what a pretty name. How old are you, Keera?"

She shot a hand up, her thumb folded into her palm.

Glen's eyebrows rose into his forehead. "Four? I have a little girl who's four."

"Really?!" Keera squealed in delight, eyes wide, as if this just couldn't be possible.

"That's right. Her name is Ruby. She's named after my grandmother."

"Ruby's a pretty name too," Keera acknowledged in a dreamy voice.

Glen rubbed her head affectionately before rising. "Mind giving me a hand?"

"With what?" Ray sighed.

"Car over here." He held the bar up. "I don't know how to run one of these."

"What makes you think I do?"

"Hans says you're a cop."

"Yeah. A cop on vacation."

"It'll just take a second," Glen promised. "Besides, you know what they say about one good turn . . ."

Ray blinked at this, wondering if being called a cannibal in front of a throng of tourists constituted a "good turn."

Glen started toward a white Ford parked by itself on the edge of the lot, away from the shops, near the path to the lifts. Ray grudgingly followed.

"Daddy, I wanna cinner-men roll!" Keera whined, trailing after them.

"In a minute," Ray told her. "This won't take long."

"Hope you weren't planning on getting one at the Bake Shop," Glen whispered.

"Why's that?" Ray asked.

Glen glanced at his watch. "By this time, especially on a Saturday, they're long gone. They don't even have muffins past about nine."

Ray decided that he would find out for himself. "What happened to your Mass?"

This drew laughter. "It was a bust. No one showed. Well, one old guy did, but as soon as he saw me, he turned right around and went home. Something about a Protestant half-breed serving up Holy Eucharist. Doesn't exactly bring people in droves."

"I want a cinner-men roll, Daddy."

"I know, honey. Hang on a minute."

As they approached the car, Glen said, "I managed to get the other matter taken care of. Delivered the *package* to the State Police."

Ray nodded disinterestedly, then peered into the Ford. A set of keys dangled in the ignition. "What'd you do, lock your keys inside?"

Glen shook his head. "It's not my car."

"Whose is it?"

"No idea. It's a rental."

"Daddy . . ."

"Honey . . ." Ray put a finger to his lips. "Then why are we breaking into it?"

"To find out who it belongs to." He gestured to a nearby sign that warned motorists not to park in the lot overnight unless they wanted their vehicles towed away. "I try to give people the benefit of the doubt." Handing Ray the bar, he said, "I thought I'd check the rental agreement, make a few calls, give the guy a chance to move it before I call the truck."

"Daddy . . ."

Ray began to work the bar, feeding the chrome hook into the rubber window seal.

"Daddy . . . !"

"I know, Keera," he said, jabbing the tool farther inside.

"Daddy . . . !"

"Keera, we'll get you a cinnamon roll in a minute." He wiggled the bar.

"But Daddy . . . this is the man's car!"

The bar snagged the lock. Ray pulled. The bar slid off. "What man?"

"The man who fell," she told him in a voice that conveyed concern.

"I don't know what you're talking about, Keera. If you'll be quiet for just a second . . ." He hooked the lock, yanked, popped open the door.

"So that's how you do it," Glen observed. "You make it look easy."

"I've had lots of practice," Ray confessed. Unlocking cars was one of his more common responsibilities in Barrow. That and confiscating contraband liquor.

"Daddy!" Keera shouted in a shrill voice. "This is the man's car!"

"What man?" he asked again, actually listening this time.

"The man who fell," Keera answered. She was agitated, breathing hard.

"Oh . . ." Ray suddenly remembered the fit in church. "It's okay, honey."

"You told her about the body?" Glen asked in surprise.

"No. You think I'm crazy?" He glared at Glen. "We were at a service last night and the minister stumbled. She thought he fell and got all upset."

"No! Daddy, not *that* man. The other man. The man who fell. Up on the mountain. The one that Raven got."

Glen shot Ray a puzzled glance. "Raven?"

Ray dismissed it with a shake of his head. "Let's get that cinnamon roll, honey."

"Don't you want to know who the car belongs to?" Glen asked.

"Not particularly."

"What if it was rented by . . . you know . . ." Glen gave the slopes a sideways nod.

"What if it was?"

Glen crawled across the front seat and opened the glove box. He emerged with a fistful of papers and began rifling through them. "The cops checked the guy for ID," he told Ray. "His name was—"

"Richard Gleary," Ray interrupted. "I checked him too. I told you that."

Glen found the rental agreement and examined it carefully. "Rented in Anchorage last . . . Monday. By . . ." His lips pursed.

"Who?" Ray grumbled, failing to mask his irritation.

"Michael Cox . . ."

"Hmph . . . Come on, Keera."

". . . of Suntron International."

Ray sniffed at this. Gleary's employer. So Cox was a colleague. Maybe he had driven Gleary to Alyeska. Maybe Gleary had borrowed Cox's rental and driven himself. Who knew? Better yet, who cared? "See you around," Ray offered in parting.

"I appreciate the assist," Glen said. "Goodbye Keera."

"Bye-bye! Daddy, now can we get a cinner-men roll?!"

"Yes, honey." They turned and started across the lot. Even from a distance of a hundred yards Ray could tell that the bakery was crammed: people milling about the entrance, a line stretching from the door to the Sno-Bored Hut, two shops down.

"The bakery looks pretty full, honey."

"But I wanna cinner-men roll!" she demanded.

"I know," he said. "Don't worry. We may have a wait. But we'll get you that . . ." Ray's voiced trailed off as he saw the oversized chalkboard next to the entrance. Someone had scrawled the message: *Sorry. No more cinnamon rolls.* "They're out, honey."

"But Daddy! I wanna cinner-men roll!"

Ray took a deep breath, determined not to lose his cool. There was just something about a child's voice, especially your own child's voice, that made you want to scream and pull your hair out. That high-pitched whine, the sing-song intonation, the relentless repetition . . . Nature's way of ensuring that offspring weren't neglected.

"I wanna cinner-men roll!!" The volume was escalating.

Ray was about to try to reason with Keera, to explain

that the Bake Shop was out of rolls and that perhaps they could find a snack elsewhere, when an old, pumpkin-orange Jeep Wagoneer puttered up beside them.

"Told you." It was Glen and he was pointing at the sign, as if Ray hadn't seen it.

"Daddy! I wanna cinner-men roll!" Her fists balled, she stamped a foot.

Ray wanted to throw in the towel. Anything to avoid another fit.

"How about a sticky bun?" Glen asked in a calm tone.

The effect was magical. The energy that had been building in Keera evaporated. "What's a sticker bun?"

"Kind of like a cinnamon roll. Only I like them better." Glen winked at Ray. "My wife makes them every Saturday, for the reception we have after church on Sunday. But I usually nab a few samples early."

"What are they like?"

"Big." He exaggerated with hand gestures, implying that the buns were the size of a suitcase. "Sweet. Lots and lots of sugar. And sticky." He made a face and Keera laughed. "Takes a couple of days to lick the goo off your fingers."

Giggling, Keera looked to Ray. "Can we get a sticker bun? Can we, Daddy?"

"I don't know . . ." Ray's mind raced to find an excuse.

"We live right down the road." When Ray hesitated, Glen added, "It's the least I can do to return the favor."

"Really, it's not necessary. We're square."

"Daddy! Can we? I wanna sticker bun!"

Rolling his eyes, Ray grumbled his consent. "Okay."

Keera scurried to the passenger door like an overexcited rabbit and clamored inside. Ray followed at a trudge. As if finding a dead body *and* incurring Margaret's wrath by being tardy weren't bad enough, now they were going to the local preacher's house for refreshments, and, undoubtedly, some hard-sell prose-lytizing. Talk about a fun morning.

Glen goosed the Wagoneer and it made noises like a sick helicopter before dying. A minute later, he got it going again. After a backfire, they rumbled out of the parking lot.

"Needs a timing adjustment," he muttered.

What it needed, Ray decided, was serious carburetor work.

Glen snatched a mike from a shortwave unit seated under the dash and mumbled something into it. The response was a shower of static. As he continued to converse in hushed tones with the indistinguishable return, Ray noted that the Wagoneer was a true beater: no air conditioner, no knob controls on the heater, the speedometer needle stuck on zero, the exterior rusted out, the faux leather interior peeling badly. According to the odometer, the thing had over 300,000 miles on it. And the crackling exhaust made the number believable. Apparently being the sheriff, chaplain, rector and fill-in priest of a ski town didn't exactly pay big bucks.

"Well, could you check it out for me?" Glen was saying into the mike. He waited a beat. "Call me at home when you find out." He replaced the mike. "Geez . . ."

"Problem?"

Glen pulled the wheel to the right and the shocks groaned as they bounced down another gravel road, this one offering an assortment of ritzy ski chalets and vacation homes. Scattered among them were decrepit, overgrown cabins.

"The trials and tribulations of being a volunteer law enforcement officer," he answered philosophically. "Getting people to cooperate is like pulling teeth."

"I'm hungry for a sticker bun," Keera told them.

"Well, you're in luck," Glen said, aiming for an unpaved driveway. "We're here."

➤ EIGHT ◄

THE LOG HOME resembled an Alaskan postcard: A-frame of stripped pine, crooked steel chimney extending from a mossy roof, smoke curling up from the stack. The front yard was a sea of waist-high wildflowers. In the side yard, the carcass of a '57 Chevy pickup served as a planter, forget-me-nots sprouting from the dash.

As they were disembarking from the Jeep, a little girl pedaled up on a bicycle equipped with training wheels. She was about Keera's size, with a dark complexion and gleaming black hair. Dismounting gracelessly, she raced to hug Glen. "Daddy!"

The front door opened and a woman wearing an apron waved. She was a larger version of her daughter: olive skin, ebony hair pulled back into a bun.

"Brought some company home to sample your baking," Glen told her. Ushering them inside, he made the introductions. "Jean and Ruby, this is Ray and Keera."

Keera and Ruby examined each other cautiously.

"Nice to meet you," Ray said.

Jean shook his hand. "Come on in. Don't mind the mess."

The mess she was referring to was a carton of overturned Legos. The colorful blocks littered an oval rug that covered most of the living room floor. Otherwise, the home was in order: a precise row of framed photographs on the hearth, newspapers and magazines collected neatly in a pine caddy, a wooden rocker with an attractive Native blanket draped over an arm. An upright piano was pushed against one wall. The accoutrements were well-kept, attractive, decidedly Alaskan. Not exactly what Ray had been expecting. Especially after riding in Glen's clunky Jeep.

"I smell donuts, Daddy," Keera whispered.

"No donuts," Jean said with a frown. "Just sticky buns and chocolate chip scones." She laughed as Keera's eyes bulged. "The scones will be done in about ten minutes." Turning to Ruby, she suggested, "Why don't you show Keera your dolls?"

Ruby inched forward. "Wanna see my dolls?" she asked in a somber tone.

After glancing at Ray, Keera nodded and the two girls departed down the hall.

"What brings you to Girdwood, Ray?" Jean asked.

"Vacation," he answered.

She led them into the kitchen. It was cramped, cluttered with baking tins and mixing bowls, overly warm. As Jean donned a hot mitt, Ray pulled off his jacket.

"Where are you from?"

"Want some coffee?" Glen asked before he could answer.

"Sure. Thanks." To Jean he said, "Barrow."

Jean glared at the contents of the oven before shutting the door. She fiddled with the controls and discarded the mitt. "Barrow? Wow. You're a long way from home."

"My wife's attending a legal conference."

"Ray's a policeman," Glen informed. He handed Ray a mug and poured another.

"Is that right?"

"Yes, ma'am." Ray tried the coffee. It was wonderful: rich, full-bodied.

The phone rang and Glen answered it. "Yeah? So what did you find out?"

"How old's your little one?" Jean asked. She was using a wooden spoon to stir a bowl containing a porridgelike substance.

"Four."

"So's Ruby." She scooped flour into the concoction. "Say, you don't happen to know Ruth Odfish, do you?"

"I don't think so." Barrow was small. But even so, Ray wasn't personally acquainted with all the residents.

"She teaches up there. Third grade, I think."

Glen hung up. "That was the manager of the Prince. They had a Michael Cox registered there."

"So?"

"So that was his rental car that was left in the main lot overnight."

"I remember." Ray presented his mug for a refill. "So?"

"He was there for a business deal. His colleagues are checking out this morning. Cox missed their breakfast meeting."

"Hmph . . ."

"They don't know where he is. He hasn't been seen since yesterday evening." When Ray didn't say anything, Glen prodded, "Don't you think that's a little suspicious? We find the guy's car, with the keys locked inside. And he turns up missing."

"*Missing* is a little strong."

"What would you call it?"

"Busy . . . Tardy . . . Off doing his own thing . . . AWOL . . ."

Glen squinted, his nose wrinkling.

"Maybe he went hiking."

"All night?"

"It's light enough. Today's the longest day of the year."

"He's an executive. A VP," Glen retorted.

"VPs don't hike?" Ray took a sip of his coffee.

"Being gone all night doesn't sound good," Glen asserted.

"He could have stayed the night with a friend," Ray suggested. "A lady friend."

"Doubtful," Jean inserted. "At least, not a prostitute, if that's what you mean. He would have to go to Anchorage for that."

"Who says he didn't?"

"His car was in the lot," Glen reminded. "I spotted it around . . . eight."

"Okay," Ray said, giving in. "You win. Cox was kidnapped by Iranian terrorists and is now being held, blindfolded, in a basement in Tehran. It's a job for the CIA."

"Anybody ever tell you you're a smart aleck," Glen observed clinically.

"I try." Ray set his cup down, ready to leave.

"They're heading for Anchorage in an hour," Glen told him.

"Who?"

"Cox's associates. If we head straight over there, we can catch them."

"Why would *we* want to do that?" Ray wondered.

"To ask some questions. We could get a description of Cox. Compare it with—"

"Oh . . . I get it." Ray frowned at the hypothesis. "You're trying to say that it was Michael Cox that fell off the lift."

"Right."

Ray shook his head. "We both saw his ID. His name was Richard Gleary."

This put a damper on Glen's enthusiasm. "Yeah . . ." He gulped the last of his second cup, grabbed the carafe, and poured a third with brisk motions. Blowing at the steam, he stared vacantly at the floor. "I still think we should check into it."

Ray started to object to Glen's misuse of the word we, but decided to let it slide. He concentrated on his own mug. It bore a colorful Emma Flatbush print of two Eskimo women folding blankets. The silence stretched.

"Daddy!" Keera shrieked.

Ray flinched and instinctively rushed down the hall. The tone of Keera's voice implied that she was in trouble, possibly hurt. It was the same sort of cry she emitted when she fell and skinned her leg or woke up in the middle of the night, reeling from a bad dream.

He hurried past a bathroom, a study, toward the bedrooms. "Keera?"

"Daddy!!"

The panicked plea came from the other direction.

"In here, Ray," Glen called.

Ray did an about-face and ran to the living room. There he found Keera and Ruby, dolls in arms, standing next to the couch. Neither one of them was bleeding or visibly injured.

"What is it, honey?" he asked, slightly out of breath.

"Look at this, Daddy!" Eyes wide, she pointed at a large knife on display in the bookcase. It had an elaborately carved handle and a broad blade bearing several crudely painted images.

"It's a Yupik story knife," Glen informed. He lifted it out of its holder and bent to show it to the girls. "Do you know what a story knife is, Keera?"

Ray had heard of them, but was certain Keera hadn't, since they were unique to the southwest and south-central Native tradition.

"Back in the old days," Glen explained, "people used to tell stories with these. Especially grandmothers and grandfathers."

"They drew pictures in the mud," Ruby added, "before TV."

"That's right," Glen affirmed. "And see this?" He pointed to the images. "There's a story painted right on it."

"But Daddy doesn't know the story," Ruby complained.

"No," Glen admitted. "Something to do with a bird and a wolf and deer."

"Raven," Keera submitted. "That's Raven."

Glen examined it. "Could be, I guess. It's hard to tell." He turned to Ray. "It's not all that authentic. More of a souvenir."

"And that's not a wolf," Keera said. "It's a fox. She's trying to catch that caribou."

Glen eyed the knife again. "If you say so." He replaced it in the shelf. "But it's not a toy, is it, Ruby?"

"Huh-uh."

"And we don't touch it, do we?"

"No."

Keera inched up to it cautiously, as though it might bite. "That's the story of how Raven made the caribou fall. Just like he made the man fall."

"Oh, yeah?" Glen shot Ray a puzzled look.

Ray shrugged. "Her grandfather tells her all the old stories. You know, the ten-footed polar bear, the blind boy and the loon, the caribou man . . ."

"The fox and Raven aren't friends," Keera said, shaking her head at the knife. "But they both made the man fall."

"What story is that?" Glen wondered.

"One she's making up," Ray said in a low voice.

"Daddy! I'm not making it up! The man fell and he's dead. All 'cause of Raven." With that she and Ruby took the dolls and drifted down the hall.

Leading Ray back to the kitchen, Glen said, "If I didn't know any better, I'd say your daughter knew about the case."

"What case?" Jean asked as she extracted a tray of sticky buns from the oven and placed the sheet on a cooling rack.

Ray shrugged. "It's not really a case, per se. A man died up on the mountain. It was an accident. Another man locked his keys in his rental car and didn't feel like joining his coworkers for breakfast." He threw up his hands.

"But Keera seems to think Raven's involved," Glen said.

Ray couldn't tell if he was joking or not. "She just has an active imagination."

"Maybe she's got the gift," Jean suggested.

Ray bristled. "What gift?"

"What the angulcaq used to call 'seeing into the night.' "

"Angulcaq?"

"The old shamans," Glen said. "How else do you explain her ability to read the story knife and apply it to the case?"

Grandfather's face flashed through Ray's mind. On the day that Keera was born, the old man had blessed her with the name "spirit eyes," promising that she would grow to be a seer: someone who could look beyond the veil of this world, into the next, into the realm of the tuungak. But that was crazy. Wasn't it?

"It's not a case," Ray objected. "And she didn't 'read' the knife. She just looked at it."

"And interpreted the characters and the tale they tell."

Ray sagged at this. "I thought you were a minister."

"I am."

"Then how can you buy into that seer mumbo-jumbo?"

"It's not a matter of buying into it," Glen argued. "It's a matter of understanding and acknowledging that the supernatural exists. There are forces operating outside ourselves."

Ray braced himself. Here came the hard sell: an invitation to attend Glen's church and some in-your-face proselytizing.

Instead, Glen said, "I have a gut feeling that Keera's right."

"About what?"

"About this case. That the man didn't just fall. What if he was . . . pushed."

"Wait a minute," Ray said. "Are you trying to say—"

"You have to admit, it's a possibility."

"Almost anything is a possibility," Ray scoffed. "I suppose next you'll be telling me that Raven is behind the whole thing."

Glen's eyebrows rose. "He is known for being a trickster."

NINE

RAY'S EYES SHIFTED to the door. He mentally measured the distance, four long steps, and toyed with the idea of making a break for it. If Keera hadn't been playing somewhere in the back . . .

He had encountered anjatkuts, shamans with supposed prophetic powers, who boasted the ability to influence the powers of nature. He had even met a young girl who could discern the answers to perplexing questions via a voice that spoke to her out of thin air. Or so she claimed. But this . . . quasi-police work, amateur sleuthing, by interpreting story knives? Relying on four-year-olds to conduct an investigation? Deciding that a mythical bird was responsible for committing a crime? It was worse than nonsensical. It was insane.

Even Jean seemed stunned. "Uh . . . Did you say . . . ?"

Glen nodded. "Raven."

"Raven . . ." she repeated in a whisper.

"I'm using that term in the broadest sense, of course,"

Glen backpedaled. "Think about it. Raven stole the sun, he played pranks on other animals, he lied, he even killed. He's a powerful entity, troublesome, malevolent . . ."

"In lore," Ray pointed out. "In reality, there is no Raven."

"I don't know. Maybe the legend of Raven came about because there's a force like that at work," Glen suggested. "An evil presence. There's evil in all of us, you know."

Ray blinked at him. "What does that have to do with—?"

"All I'm saying is that we need to keep an open mind here."

"Open to what? Fairy tales?"

Jean began removing sticky buns from the baking sheet. "I think Glen's right. You have to follow whatever leads turn up."

"But we don't have any leads," Ray pointed out.

She produced dessert plates and served them both a steaming bun.

"Just for the sake of argument," Glen said, biting into his, "what if someone did push that guy off the lift?"

Ray took a bite of his roll. It was as good as it smelled: moist, sweet, with a chewy texture. "Playing 'what if' won't get us any closer to figuring out what really happened."

"Exactly," Glen said excitedly. "Which is why we need to go over and question those businessmen before they leave for Anchorage."

Ray chewed his bun, unable to see a way out of this circular, illogical line of reasoning. "But if he fell off, if it was an accident, like it seems to have been—"

"Raven pushed him!" a mouselike voice told them.

Ray glanced toward the hall and saw Keera and Ruby wearing floppy pink hats, their cheeks unnaturally red. They'd either been running or had gotten into Jean's makeup.

"Raven did it, Daddy!" Keera insisted from beneath the hat. " 'Member? 'Member I told you?"

"Yeah. I remember, Keera."

Jean offered the girls sticky buns. Ruby took two and Keera, cutting her eyes in Ray's direction, grinned and did likewise. The girls giggled and dashed madly down the hallway, as if they had stolen the buns from a side-walk vendor.

"See," Glen said with a satisfied look. "Even your own daughter thinks it was murder."

"Don't even start using that word," Ray warned.

"Why not? It could have been."

Ray shook his head. He started to explain the basics of how an investigation was conducted, how it revolved around meticulous, painstaking inquiries, interviews, re-search, forms, procedures . . . not wild guessing games over sticky buns and coffee. But he decided it would be a waste of breath. Glen and Jean seemed to be exhila-rated by the suggestion that an act of foul play might have taken place in their sleepy community. Ray had been a police officer long enough for the romance factor to wear off, if it had ever been there in the first place.

Jean presented the sheet of buns again.

"No thanks. They're wonderful. But—"

"Go ahead," she prodded. "I make dozens. We always have leftovers."

Ray took an especially fat bun: bronze dough gleam-ing with glaze. "Thanks."

Glen took one, munched, and asked casually, "So are you in or out?"

"Of what?"

"This case."

"What case? There is no case."

"No case?" Glen set his mug down and began using his hands to sculpt his argument. "A man falls off the lift. A sad accident. But nothing to call home about. Then we find a car left in the lot, and the owner—"

"Renter," Ray corrected, watching Glen's hands fly.

"The renter is missing."

"He skipped a breakfast meeting," Ray shot back.

"Whatever. He hasn't been heard from. And now this." He spread his arms expansively, as if the kitchen itself would turn the debate.

"This?"

"*This,*" he repeated. "We've all got a sense that there's more to it."

"Not all," Ray corrected.

"Even your daughter says—"

"Let's leave her out of this," Ray warned.

"Fine. All I'm saying is that someone needs to poke around a little, get a few answers to some of these questions. By default, that someone is me. And in all seriousness, Ray, I could use some help. You're a pro." He paused, blue eyes as pitifully sad as a puppy begging for table scraps. "I'm just a small-town chaplain who puts on a badge once in a blue moon to read reckless snowboarders the riot act. I'm more experienced with preaching sermons than with giving suspects the third degree."

"I'm on holiday," Ray groaned.

"It won't take long," Glen promised. "We'll just run over to the Prince, talk to Cox's business associates . . ." He shrugged as if interrogations were something every cop secretly hoped to incorporate into his vacation. "I'll write up the results. That'll be that."

Somehow Ray was certain that *wouldn't* be that. Things were seldom as cut-and-dried as Glen was trying to make them out to be. Even the simplest case could be a time-consuming burden.

"My wife is at that conference all day," Ray tried, "so I have to watch—"

"You can leave Keera here," Jean interrupted. "I'd be glad to take care of her. She and Ruby seem to be hitting it off anyway."

Good point, Ray thought, but didn't concede. Keera would probably appreciate the chance to play with some-

one her own age. He took a bite of bun, sipped his coffee, mind racing to find a viable excuse. Unable to come
up with one, he grumbled, "As long as it doesn't take
all day. Keera and I are going for a ride later."

"Great." Glen abandoned his mug and the remainder
of his bun. Digging keys out of his pocket, he started
for the door. "Let's get going."

Ray thanked Jean again and went to tell Keera goodbye. He found her in Ruby's bedroom. Still in their oversized hats, the girls had donned lacy dresses that dragged
the floor. They were hunched over a miniature table, in
the process of serving tea to a pair of button-eyed Rag-
gedy Ann dolls.

"Honey, I have an errand to run." When this failed to
draw a glance, he added, "How would you like to stay
here and play with Ruby?"

"Yea!" both girls chimed. The news sent them into a
flurry of hops and twirls.

TEN

THE PRINCE HOTEL was a monolithic island of modern
architecture adrift on an otherwise calm green sea of
thin-trunked evergreens and gentle alpine slopes. Its
twenty-two floors gleamed in the sunlight, mirrored
windows and golden crossbeams reminding the world
that it was the tallest structure on Turnagain Arm.

The parking lot was nearly full: plain-looking Ford

and Toyota rental cars scattered among sport utility vehicles, BMWs, Saabs, Volvos . . . Formerly owned by the Westin chain, the Prince had been purchased by a Japanese company, refurbished at a cost of nearly a billion dollars, and upgraded from four-star to five-star status. Ray had read about the transaction in the newspaper. He had also read that the new and improved Prince was now a hot spot, popular with businesspeople from Outside, wealthy tourists from the Lower Forty-eight and beautiful people in general.

Glen aimed for the covered drive-through where a pair of uniformed attendants waited next to a sign that promised valet parking. They stood up straighter when they saw the Jeep, slumping as Glen pulled into a reserved space twenty-five yards from the entrance.

"Here we are." He killed the motor, but the Wagoneer didn't want to stop. The engine gasped, dieseling as they climbed out. "Gotta get that timing checked."

"Yeah." Ray coughed, his nose stinging with the stench of burnt oil.

They reached the entrance before the Jeep gave up.

"You can't park it there, sir," one of the valets informed. He and his partner could have been brothers. Each was blond, about twenty, clean-cut, muscular.

Glen dug a wallet out of his pants pocket. Flipping it open he flashed it at them.

The two young men blinked, squinted. "You've got a license to drive," the one on the left observed. "Congratulations, sir. You still can't park there. It's reserved."

Fishing out another card, Glen said, "Girdwood Sheriff's Office."

"Girdwood's got a sheriff?" the shorter valet wondered.

"You're looking at him. Glen Redfern." He extended his hand.

The valets shook it warily.

"Watch out," Ray warned. "He's also a chaplain."

Ignoring this, Glen asked, "Is there a time limit on that slot?"

"Don't worry about it," the kid on the right said. "Take as long as you want."

"Thanks." As they were passing through the gauntlet of automatic glass doors, Glen said, "See. It pays to be clergy. You get the best parking spaces."

"Handicapped people get the best parking spaces," Ray shot back. "But that doesn't make me want to go out and lose a limb."

They entered a spacious, marble-tiled lobby, and a solicitous bellman in a forest-green jacket rolled his brass cart at them, ready to take their bags. He slowed when he realized that they had none, but seemed reluctant to give up. "May I be of service?"

"No," Ray grunted. "Listen," he said to Glen, "let me handle this."

"Fine." Glen sighed. "You're the pro."

"Gentlemen! How are we today?" The question was cheery, almost unnaturally so, issued from a woman confined to a freestanding oval station near the center of the lobby. Gold letters designated her as a concierge.

"*We* are fine," Ray returned. He pointed at an oak and brass counter that ran the length of the far wall. "Is that the check-in desk?"

She nodded enthusiastically. "If you would like to join us for brunch, our Turnagain Room will be open in another thirty minutes. I would be glad to reserve a—"

"No, thanks." Ray started for the desk, Glen and the bellman trailing after him.

"Reservations for dinner, perhaps," the woman called. "I can arrange tickets for the theater in Anchorage . . . a dinner show?"

Ray shook his head without looking back.

Three bright, college-aged faces, belonging to two women and a man, watched them from the desk, all smiling as though Ray and Glen were old friends returning home.

"Good morning," they chimed in unison, hurriedly converging on a single computer terminal. One of the women stepped to the keyboard, the man reached past her for the mouse, leaving the other woman without an input device.

"How can I help you, gentlemen?" the woman at the keyboard asked.

"Hi," Ray said, making an effort to return the smile. "We're from the Girdwood Sheriff's Office."

Glen produced his ID card and proudly presented it to them. The trio deflated visibly. One of the women and the man retreated, hurrying off as though they had important tasks to attend to. The hostess at the terminal repeated, "How may I help you?"

"We're looking for . . ." Ray paused, realizing that he didn't know who they were looking for. If Michael Cox was actually missing, he wouldn't be around to talk to. Who were Cox's colleagues? Ray had no idea. He glanced at Glen.

"Mr. Ehrlich," Glen said. "I talked to him earlier. But I don't have a room number."

She entered the name into the keyboard, sniffed, and smiled without displaying any teeth. A half minute passed before the terminal chirped. "Mr. Ehrlich . . . checked out."

Ray wanted to cheer. If Cox's buddies were already gone, the "investigation" was over before it could begin. No witnesses. No one to question. Chances were good that Cox had drifted back from wherever he had been and had departed with the gang. They were probably on their way to the airport in Anchorage at this very moment.

"What about Michael Cox?" Glen asked.

The woman attacked the keys. Another sniff. The terminal chirped. "Room 1734."

"He hasn't checked out?" Ray asked, the sense of relief fading.

"No, sir. Is there anything else?"

"Can we see his room?" Glen asked.

"See his room?" Her face contorted. "You'll have to speak with the manager."

Ray couldn't help hoping that the manager would turn down the request. He really wasn't in the mood to poke around, inquiring into the whereabouts of a man who probably wasn't missing. It was the policy of most law enforcement agencies to disregard missing person reports until the individual in question hadn't been heard from for forty-eight hours. The exceptions were children and people in dangerous locales: hunters, hikers, climbers . . .

Taking a deep breath, Ray vowed to adopt a better attitude. Even if this wasn't his idea of a good time, he was a police officer and had taken an oath to serve and protect. Whether Cox was really missing or not, Ray needed to give this his best effort.

"Could you ask the manager to meet us on the seventeenth floor?" Ray said. Maybe they would be denied entry and this little field trip would be over. If not, they would take a cursory look at Cox's room, guess at where he might be, and do the rest of the scavenger hunt via phone. A call to Cox's home office, a call to the rental agency . . . This affair could be over in an hour if Ray applied himself.

"I'll page her for you," the woman promised.

Ray started for the elevator and found the bellman still shadowing them. "We don't have any bags."

Undeterred, the man abandoned his cart, darted past them, and punched the elevator button. Looking for a tip, Ray decided. Apparently he hadn't heard who they were.

"We're from the sheriff's office," Ray told him.

Glen added, "I'm also a pastor."

The bellman's eyes grew wide, the concept of a law enforcement officer with a religious bent clearly having a chilling effect. The elevator arrived and Ray and Glen stepped on.

"Works every time," Glen said, obviously pleased with himself.

They stood watching the lighted display blink off the floors. When the elevator floated to a stop and the doors slid open, they got off and followed the doors down the hallway. Room 1734 was the last one on the southwest corner of the building.

Glen tried the knob. "Locked." He rapped on the door. Waited. Knocked again. "Mr. Cox?"

"Guess we'll have to wait for the manager." Ray stepped to the floor-to-ceiling window at the end of the hall. It offered a view of the mountain, the lodge, the inlet, the Kenai Peninsula . . . Cox's room had to have one of the best views in the hotel.

There was a metallic click. Ray turned around to find Glen swinging the door open.

"I thought you said it was locked?"

"It was." Glen grinned and waved an American Express card.

Ray checked the digital keypad next to the door and found a red dot blinking. "Where, exactly, did you get your law enforcement training?"

"At a special school in Anchorage. Why?"

"A school? What, six months?"

"Two weeks." Glen squinted at him. "What's the problem?"

"For starters, your little credit card trick constitutes illegal entry," Ray pointed out. "Second, you just set off the hotel security system." He tapped the blinking dot.

Before Glen could respond the door at the other end of the hallway flew open and two enormous shapes rushed toward them.

"Down!" a deep voice ordered. "On the floor! Hands in the air!"

Ray sighed, dropped to his knees, and raised his arms.

"I said down!"

As the shadows sprinted toward them, eclipsing the light from the far end window, Ray realized that the welcoming committee was made up of a short, stout Asian man and an Asian woman, an enormous Asian woman. And they were both bearing bulky firearms.

"Down!!" a hoarse voice demanded.

"Get down," Ray urged. But Glen seemed to be in a trance, paralyzed by the oncoming Amazon and her husky sidekick. The spell was broken when a beefy arm knocked him to the carpet. Ray was about explain who they were and ask the brute squad to take it easy when something hit him in the chest, propelling him backward.

Spread-eagle on the floor, he gazed up into the business end of a gun. It was so close that he had to cross his eyes to focus on the barrel. Beyond the weapon was a mammoth: pillarlike legs, tree-limb arms, broad shoulders, no neck to speak of, a tiny head with a butch haircut. Except for the mascara and breasts, this "lady" could have been a member of the Seattle Seahawks defensive line.

Cutting his eyes, he saw Glen on the floor next to him, face to the carpet, the thick, muscle-bound man astride him, poised to put a bullet into his brain.

When he caught his breath, Ray said, "We're from—" A knee crushed his torso.

"Shut up and don't move!"

⊶ ELEVEN ⊷

RAY STARED UP at the gun for what seemed like an eternity. He was contemplating another attempt at speech when the elevator chimed. Footsteps sprinted toward them.

"I got here as fast as I could," a harried, panting voice said. "What's going on?"

"We caught these two breaking into a room," the woman towering over Ray answered, eyes never wavering from her prey.

A face appeared: vibrant eyes, full lips, high cheekbones, and slender chin accentuated by carefully applied makeup and framed by long, jet-black hair. She too was Asian. Japanese, Ray guessed. With a mix of something. African American? The result was a dark, brooding beauty who, even from Ray's present point of view, was stunning.

"We're—" A forearm pressed against his windpipe. "*Police*," he hissed.

His guardian laughed, as though cutting off someone's air supply was a great game.

"Police?" the attractive woman asked.

Ray tried to nod, but this drew an increase in the pressure of restraint. Stars were encroaching on the outer edges of his vision.

"Did you check them for ID?"

The she-monster shook her head grumpily. The man riding Glen cursed. They obviously couldn't be bothered with such trivial matters.

"Check," the woman insisted.

They did. The forearm lifted from Ray's Adam's apple and he sucked in sorely needed oxygen. A pair of paws patted him down roughly. He was jerked to his side, spun to face the floor, spun to face the ceiling again, the knee returning to his sternum. He heard Glen cough as he was flopped onto his back.

"This one's from Barrow," Ray's guardian grunted. A second later, she stood upright and sighed. "He's a cop."

"So's this guy. Sheriff of Girdwood." The man gripped a handful of shirt and lifted Glen to a standing position. "Didn't know Girdwood had a sheriff."

"That's all well and good," the attractive woman said. "But there's still the matter of burglarizing one of our rooms."

As he scrambled to his feet, Ray realized that their accuser was tall, probably close to five-eight, with a striking figure that was punctuated by long, slender legs.

"We weren't burglarizing it," he argued, stretching.

The woman glanced at the open door. "Is this your room?"

"No."

"Do you have a key?"

"No. But—"

"Then you were burglarizing it."

"We needed to take a look inside," Glen said.

"I understand that. They told me at the desk that you wanted to see 1734. And I was about to come up and find out why. I don't make a habit of opening people's rooms without their consent. We strive to preserve the privacy of our guests."

"But this guy is missing."

"So I've been told. Mr. Ehrlich notified me. And if you would have simply waited for me and shown me the proper ID, I'm sure I would have allowed you to go in." She admonished them with a scowl. "That's all for now," she told the security guards.

The dynamic duo holstered their weapons and drifted back down the hall.

"We still need to look around." Ray smiled, hoping to gain her approval.

"You cops think you can just do whatever you want to. Don't you?"

Ray was about to answer the question, making at least a show of defending his profession, when she extended her hand.

"Amy Yasaka."

"Ray Attla. Sorry about this."

"It was my fault," Glen confessed. "I broke in. Glen Redfern."

"You're the sheriff?"

Glen nodded. "I know, I know . . . I should be more conscientious about the law."

A finger assailed him. "You're the chaplain. You run that little church down the road."

"Guilty as charged."

Yasaka was suddenly animated. "My sister visited that church."

"Is that right?" Glen considered this. "Was her name Jackie?"

"Yeah."

"Sure, I remember her. But I don't recall seeing you there."

Amy shrugged. "I'm not much on church."

"Me either," Ray threw in. "Now if we could check the room—"

"I was raised Buddhist."

Glen nodded knowingly. " 'Believe nothing, no matter where you read it, or who said it, unless it agrees with your own reason and your own common sense.' "

"I'm impressed." Yasaka blinked at him, long lashes fluttering.

"My mother was half-Korean. A staunch follower of Buddha."

"My father's Japanese. He lives in Tokyo and he's still upset that I'm not a practicing Zen Buddhist." She examined Glen thoughtfully. "What else are you? Aleut?"

"Yupik."

She nodded. "You look more Native than Korean."

Actually, given the color of his hair, Ray thought, Glen looked almost Irish. He eyed the open door and wondered if they would miss him if he went inside.

"Is this your cousin or something?" She gestured to Ray.

"Or something," Ray mumbled. "Could we . . . ?" He aimed a thumb at 1734.

"We're not related," Glen said.

Ray stepped into the room and glanced around. It was clean, the bed had been made, but bore the telltale signs of occupation: suitcase lying on a foldaway, a hanging bag and a pair of sport jackets hanging in the open closet, a three-ring binder and a copy of *Fortune* magazine on the table. The *Wall Street Journal* sat on the nightstand.

Ray stuck his head into the bathroom. There was a leather toiletry kit next to the sink, a toothbrush and the handle of a razor sticking out. A can of shaving cream, a bottle of aftershave, and a travel-sized container of Advil were lined up in front of the mirror.

In the hall, Glen was saying something about his "partner." Ray caught the words "Inupiat" and "big." Glen whispered something, then he and Ms. Yasaka laughed heartily.

The joke, Ray knew, was on him. Why had he agreed to this? Why had he let Glen talk him into rifling some businessman's room? Better yet, why was he in here attending to the chore while Glen, the ever-charming sheriff, was in the corridor making time with the hotel manager?

"Tell her about Jean," Ray called as he felt through one of the jackets. According to the label, it was an Armani, gray wool with salt and pepper flecks. The inside pocket contained a business card: WILLIAM SHERMAN, BUTTERFIELD ELECTRONICS. He replaced it and moved on to the other jacket, another Armani.

"Jean's my wife," Glen was saying in what sounded a lot like backpedaling.

"Your wife?" Ms. Yasaka said. She sounded disappointed.

Ray heard them enter the room behind him.

"Find anything?" Glen asked.

"Not yet." Ray unzipped the hanging bag and found a pinstripe suit. Also Armani. It looked as though it had been freshly cleaned and pressed. He zipped the bag shut and stood on tiptoes to scan the upper shelf. Empty.

"What are you looking for?" Yasaka asked.

"I'm not sure," Glen admitted. "I've never really done this sort of thing before."

There was a beeping noise and Ms. Yasaka bent to deactivate her pager. "If you'll excuse me for a moment . . ." She strode out of the room.

"Getting a little friendly with management, aren't we?" Ray said. He sniffed the air. Either Cox went heavy on the aftershave or Ms. Yasaka had left behind an invisible cloud of perfume. It was a sweet, intoxicating scent that made Ray slightly dizzy.

"Just making conversation," Glen said. "Besides, I'm married. And I'm a—"

"Chaplain. Yeah, I know. That's what makes this so humorous."

"What?" Glen asked defensively.

"The goo-goo eyes you're making at *Amy*."

"I was just being nice. In my line of work, you build bridges where you can."

Ray noticed a legal-sized envelope lying on the suitcase. He picked it up: sealed, no stamp, no address. Setting it down, he turned his attention to the binder on the table. According to the glossy cover, it was a prospectus on the Suntron Corporation. He fanned pages and watched graphs, charts, and shiny photos flash by. "Cox worked for Suntron, right?"

"Uh-huh."

Ray closed the binder and knelt to look under the bed, secretly hoping to find Michael Cox hiding there so that he could be on his merry way. "Was his home address on the rental car agreement?"

"Maybe," Glen said. "Actually . . . yeah. I think it was. But . . ."

"You don't remember what it was?"

"Well . . . um . . . let's see . . . uh . . ." After a pause, Glen conceded, "No."

The nightstand had two drawers and a shelf. He pulled open the first drawer: phone book, room service menu, complimentary postcard. "Maybe you should go check."

"You mean go all the way back to the lodge lot and—?"

"Just call the rental agency," Ray said. The second drawer turned out to be a fake. On the shelf he discovered a shopping guide to Girdwood and a Gideon Bible.

"What agency was it?" Glen wondered aloud.

Ray groaned.

"You don't have to do that." It was Ms. Yasaka. She was standing in the doorway with a man. Though he was taller than Glen and only moderately overweight, the guy looked dumpy next to Yasaka's shapely, statuesque form. "This is Mr. Ehrlich. Mr. Cox's associate."

The man nodded, frowning. He reached up and rubbed the gleaming, pink skin above his forehead, then combed greasy strands of hair across an expansive bald spot.

"I'm Ray Attla and this is Sheriff Redfern."

Ehrlich cleared his throat. "No sign of Mike?"

"Not yet, Mr. Ehrlich," Yasaka responded politely. "But I'm sure there's nothing to worry about. We're doing everything we can to locate him."

We? Ray thought.

"I appreciate that," Ehrlich said. He shot Yasaka a goofy smile then went to work, raking, rearranging, desperate to hide his bare scalp.

"Mr. Cox missed a breakfast meeting?" Ray asked.

"Yes."

"What about yesterday?"

"We had meetings all day."

"And he was there?"

"Yes."

"What time did you finish?"

Ehrlich examined the ceiling. "About . . . between six-thirty and seven."

"What about afterward?"

"We all went for drinks, here in the hotel. Sort of a celebration."

"What were you celebrating?" Ray wondered.

"A new contract. It'll mean a lot of business for us. For Suntron."

"Was Mr. Cox at the party?"

Ehrlich shook his head. "He went back to his room. Nobody's seen him since."

Ray sighed, still not sure where the mystery element was. So the guy skipped out on pancakes and sausage. So what? "Did you have any other meetings today?"

"Just breakfast. And it was more of a casual thing. The middle managers weren't invited. Just me and Mike and Bill. Bill Andrews. Our VP of R&D."

"Maybe Mr. Cox decided to do some sightseeing today."

"Without us?"

Ray shrugged. "Why not?"

Ehrlich rubbed his head instead of answering. "We had a two P.M. flight."

Glancing at his watch, Ray said, "It's only eleven."

"But check-out was an hour ago," Yasaka threw in.

"It takes almost an hour to get back to Anchorage," Glen pointed out helpfully.

"Bill already left," Ehrlich said.

"Maybe Cox went to see the glacier," Ray suggested, "and lost track of time."

"Without a car?" Glen said. "How'd he get there?"

"Bus," Ray responded. Nothing like getting ganged up on.

"No. Mike wasn't a bus kind of guy. He was first-class all the way."

Ray caught the past tense. "Was?"

▶ TWELVE ◀

"FRANKLY," EHRLICH SAID, "I'm a little worried that something may have happened to him."

"What makes you think that?"

Ehrlich sank to the bed as he considered Ray's question. "Just . . . I don't know . . . He was acting . . . kind of . . . funny."

"Funny?"

"Mike's head of marketing. His job is a prescription for a heart attack: sixty to seventy hours a week of sheer hell. He's always in a meeting. And when he's not, he's traveling to one." Ehrlich swore softly. "He's my boss. I'm familiar with his schedule. It's murder. Something crammed into every second of the day. He's the first into the office, the last to leave. Luckily he's got the personality for it. Stress is like a narcotic to him."

Ray waited, hoping there was a point to this.

"But lately . . . I don't know . . . he's been distracted. A little down. Like something's been bothering him. I asked him about it but . . ." Ehrlich shrugged. "He said it was nothing. And last night . . . Closing that deal was a big victory for us. But instead of celebrating, Mike just went back to his room."

"Maybe he didn't feel well," Ray suggested.

"No. I don't think that was it." Ehrlich bent forward and rested his chin in his hands. "Short of being flat on his back with the flu, Mike wouldn't miss an opportunity to party. He's a hard-core workaholic *and* a party animal."

"What does Mr. Cox look like?" Glen asked from out of the blue.

Ehrlich stuck out his lower lip. "A little taller than me. Thinner. A lot more hair."

The description fit approximately half the males on the planet, Ray thought. He mentally recalled the face of the man lying beneath tower forty-two. It was a mass of swollen, broken blood vessels. But the pictures on the license and passport. . . . A face materialized. No stats. He hadn't even bothered to look at the listed height, weight, or eye color. Good work. Here he was jumping on Glen for not knowing more about Cox, and Ray couldn't have IDed the corpse in a lineup. "Hair color?" Ray asked.

"Dishwater blond," Ehrlich answered.

A match. "Height and weight."

"About six foot, 185 or so . . . He works out at the gym."

The right size, Ray thought. "Mustache? Beard?"

"No. Clean shaven. Nice clothes. Stylish haircut. Mike's pretty *GQ*."

"Sounds a lot like our man," Glen observed.

Unfortunately, Glen was right. But then, the description was still vague. And the guy under the lift was named Gleary. Without something much more tangible. . . .

"What man?" Ehrlich wanted to know.

Ray dismissed the question with a shake of his head and a frown.

"Maybe we could get a photo from the State Police," Glen said.

"Of Mike?" Ehrlich's eyes grew wide with concern.

"Is he married?" Ray asked.

"Yeah."

"Maybe his wife could fax us a picture." Even as he said this, Ray decided that it was too aggressive. Cox had been "missing" for a matter of a few hours. There was no reason to alert his wife yet. Certainly no reason to terrify her by asking that a photograph be electronically sent. Even if they didn't tell her what they needed it for, she would panic.

Glen lifted the phone. "I'll contact the state patrol and then Mrs. Cox."

Ray took the receiver and hung it up. "We're not there yet."

"But if these two guys are one and the same . . ."

"What two guys?" Ehrlich wondered. "Did you already find Mike?"

"Maybe," Glen said.

Ehrlich sprang up from the bed. "What happened? Is he okay? Is he hurt?"

Ray wanted to strangle Glen. The first rule of investigation was controlling the flow of information. You didn't go around blurting out unconfirmed hypotheses or sharing every idea that entered your skull. You told people only as much as they needed to know. This not only helped you dredge through suspects, evidence, and witnesses, it allowed you to keep things simple. And most crimes were astoundingly simple.

Warning the sheriff with a glare, Ray said, "We don't know anything right now."

"But we found—" Glen started to say.

Ray silenced him with an outstretched hand. "We

don't know anything," he repeated. "All we have are a few leads."

"What sort of leads?"

Ray sighed and glanced around the room. "Is there any paper in here?"

Seated on the desk, feet in a chair, Ms. Yasaka was watching with amusement. Reaching between her legs, she pulled out a shallow drawer, withdrew a pad of hotel stationery, and tossed it onto the bed. "Need a pen?"

"No," Ray grunted. "A pencil." A second later a mechanical pencil flew at him.

"What are you doing?" Glen asked.

"Putting this whole matter to rest so that I can go back to my vacation." Ray sat down at the table and began sketching. Closing his eyes, he concentrated on the passport: cheekbones, eyebrows, cleft in the chin. . . . He tried to reproduce these shapes on the paper, erased several lines, shook his head, scribbled some more, erased again.

Two minutes later he gave the sketch a critical scowl. It looked like the passport photo. A little. Kind of. There was a resemblance. Maybe.

Glen hunched to peer over his shoulder. "Wow! You're good."

"No," Ray admitted. "I'm not. But in the absence of a better means of doing this . . ." He stood and flashed the drawing at Ehrlich. "Recognize this guy?"

After studying it for a moment, Ehrlich said, "Sharpen the chin. Make the eyes . . . smaller, the ears bigger."

Ray made the adjustments, littering the tabletop with bits of eraser. When he finished, the side of his hand was black. "Now?" He held it up for Ehrlich's approval.

Ehrlich swore at it. "That's Mike."

Turning it around, Ray studied the contours of the face. As much as he hated to admit it, Ehrlich's constructive criticism had been right on. The sketch was now remarkably close to the photo on the passport. The passport of Richard Gleary.

"You're sure? This is Michael Cox?"

"Yep."

"I told you so," Glen said, obviously pleased with himself.

Ray closed his eyes, willing the entire mess away.

"How did you know what he looks like?" Ehrlich asked.

"We found someone up on the mountain this morning," Ray confessed. "A man. He fell off the lift. And died."

"And it was . . ." Ehrlich grimaced at the sketch, swore, and slumped to the bed.

Ray paced the room, disgusted. That Gleary was Cox or vice versa made this complicated. Disorderly. A royal headache. And it meant more work.

Why would a corporate exec have false ID? Why would he go up a chair lift after begging off from a post-contract celebration? And the million-dollar question: Why did he fall off? The obvious answer to all but the perplexing double identity was depression. If, as Ehrlich had told them, Cox was "off his game," maybe he had gotten blasted, gone up the lift to be alone, lost his balance. . . . It made as much sense as anything else.

"Did Cox drink?" Ray asked.

"Not on the job. But in the evenings: cocktails, wine, nightcaps . . ."

"Did you see him drink last night, before he went to his room?"

"No. Well, we had champagne, but not enough to do any damage."

"What about drugs? Do you guys 'celebrate' with coke, crack, heroin . . . ?"

Ehrlich was horrified. "No! Of course not."

"Cox wasn't into that?"

"Maybe on his own personal time. But I never saw anything like that. Suntron doesn't tolerate illegal substance abuse."

"Good for Suntron."

There was a low cabinet between the bed and the

bathroom. Ray tried the doors. Locked. "Do you have a key?" he asked Yasaka.

She hopped down from her perch and tossed him a key ring. "The gold one."

Ray fit the gold key into the lock. It clicked and the doors creaked open to reveal a mini-bar: neat rows of tiny liquor bottles; a shelf of candy, chips, and assorted snacks; a mini-refrigerator. Ray checked the fridge. It held several bottles of beer and a bottle of champagne. The bar had either been restocked recently or Cox had abstained.

"Can you check with housekeeping to find out what condition this was in this morning?"

Yasaka reached for the phone. "I can do better than that." She punched a button. "It's all computerized. We keep a running tally of what our guests use and it shows up on their bill." Into the receiver, she said, "This is Amy. I need a bar count on 1734."

As she waited for the information, Ray drifted to the closet. He picked up the blank envelope and held it up to the light. It contained a letter. Handwritten. In black ink. The stationery had been double-folded, like a business letter.

Across the room, Yasaka huffed, "Not 1743. 1734."

Ray examined the suitcase: black leather with a Ralph Lauren logo. Beneath the foldaway stand was a smaller, matching bag. A carry-on. Together the luggage amounted to some major dollars. Ehrlich was right. Cox was a first-class kind of guy.

"The bar was full?" he heard Yasaka saying. "You're sure?"

Opening the larger suitcase, Ray stared down at a colorful selection of socks, boxer shorts, undershirts. Each item was neatly folded and arranged. He fingered a pair of chinos. On the right side was a heavy maroon sweatshirt with bronze letters: Harvard.

"Cox went to Harvard?" he asked without looking up.

"Harvard Business School," Ehrlich confirmed.

Next to the sweatshirt, a pair of white Nikes were

stacked heel to toe. Beneath the layer of clothing there was a trio of file folders and a book. Ray slid them out. The folders contained computer printouts and drafts of a contract. The book was a hardback edition of Martin Cruz Smith's latest thriller.

Replacing the material, Ray ran his hands along the inside edges of the suitcase. He discovered a packet of antacid tablets, a fountain pen, and a package of condoms.

Closing the suitcase, he knelt to retrieve the carry-on. It was heavier than he expected. He set it on the bed and began rummaging through the contents: a copy of *Money* magazine, a text on business management, notepads, a plastic case of pens and pencils, a leather cell phone satchel, pager, another packet of condoms. He spread the treasure out on the bed and was wondering why the bag still felt so bulky, when he saw the zipper. It ringed the bottom of the bag, creating a notebook-sized compartment.

"Mr. Cox hasn't used the mini-bar," Yasaka told him. "I could get a breakdown on the lunches and dinners he had in the hotel facilities."

"Don't bother. I was just wondering if he was sloshed last night. Or if maybe he pocketed a few bottles before he went out." He unzipped the compartment and found the source of the weight: an Apple Powerbook. Six eyes watched as he flipped it open and hit the power button. There was a chime, then a whir as the hard drive activated.

"What's that?" Glen asked.

"A laptop computer," Ray answered, watching as icons popped into the screen.

"No kidding . . . I meant in your hand. The envelope."

"I don't know. It's sealed." He handed it to Glen. "See what it is." The desktop blinked into existence: a rectangle half the size of the screen bearing a dozen miniature folders. Most of the folder titles contained the name of the corporation, a date, and the words spreadsheet or market report. Another prominent title was "NVSC."

Glen tore open the envelope.

"Ever hear of something called NVSC?" he asked Ehrlich.

"Sure. That's the project we signed the deal on last night."

"What do the letters stand for?"

"Nonvolatile Superchip," Ehrlich explained. "It's an advanced microchip that—"

"Oh, my God!" Glen muttered.

Ray looked up from the glowing screen. "What?"

"I think this is a suicide note."

THIRTEEN

RAY PLUCKED THE letter from Glen's outstretched hand. It was just four sentences:

Dear Diane,

I'm sorry for the way I've treated you. I don't expect or deserve your forgiveness. My only hope is that without me around, you can get on with your life. I wish you the very best.

Love,
Mike

"He jumped," Glen said in amazement. "He didn't fall. He jumped. On purpose."

Ray read the letter a second time, a third. Was it a suicide note or a Dear John letter? "How did Cox get along with his wife?"

Ehrlich didn't answer. He was breathing hard, bent over, face in his hands.

Yasaka's pager beeped. She glanced at it. "I'll be right back."

When she was gone, Ray repeated the question.

Ehrlich wiped at his eyes. They were red and swollen. "Not very well." He sniffed and cleared his throat. "They were separated. Diane was about to file for divorce."

"Was he unfaithful?" Ray asked, pretty sure he knew the answer.

"Oh, yeah. Every chance he got."

"What about Diane?"

Ehrlich glared at the floor. "She was lonely . . . hurt . . . confused . . ." He swallowed hard. "She needed someone to talk to. That's why . . ." His voice trailed off. "I didn't plan for it to happen. I really didn't. Mike was my friend."

Ray looked at Glen, hoping the chaplain would step in to field the confession. This was clearly clergy territory. He pantomimed, urging Glen to say something.

"Uh . . . so the two of you . . . uh . . . you . . ." Glen stammered. "You . . . uh . . . did it?"

Smooth, Ray thought. Real smooth.

The bald head nodded, then Ehrlich bawled, "I killed him! I killed Mike!"

"How do you figure that?" Ray asked.

"Mike wouldn't have taken his own life if I hadn't . . . if Diane and I hadn't . . ."

Ray struggled with the equation. If Cox was promiscuous, wasn't he ultimately responsible for his wife's dissatisfaction with their marriage? The letter admitted that much. Or at least intimated it. That Ehrlich had stepped into the fray was inconsequential.

"It's okay," Glen was saying in a soothing voice. "We all make mistakes."

The words had little impact on Ehrlich.

As Glen worked to comfort the broken junior executive, Ray's mind wandered. According to Ehrlich, Cox had been acting strangely. Why? Perhaps he had learned of his wife's plan to divorce him. And despite the fact that he regularly played around on her, maybe he still loved her. A highly competitive man like Cox might not have taken the news too well. He could have grown depressed . . . suicidal?

Leaping from the chair lift made more sense than slipping from it. The point of impact had been below one of the highest towers on the mountain. Ray envisioned Cox using the trip up to research the area and determine the best spot for the jump, then spending the short ride down summoning the courage to actually do it.

He glanced at the bed: laptop, cellular, folders, pens . . . Cox had left the hotel sometime yesterday evening. After the meeting. Close to seven. Yet his carry-on and suitcase had been packed and ready to go. Ready for a flight that didn't leave for some seventeen hours. It almost looked as if he had arranged his affairs. With his bags in order, he had driven his rental to the lodge and locked the keys inside. On purpose? Because he wasn't coming back? Then he had taken the lift just before it was scheduled to shut down, when there would be no one around to witness or interfere with his self-destructive course of action. This required planning. In Ray's experience, suicides were often thought out well in advance of their execution. The successful ones, at least.

The long string of conjectures flowed unimpeded right up until the moment Ray had discovered the body and the troubling identification. Who in the heck was Richard Gleary? And why, if you were determined to take your own life, would you carry a fake passport and a fake driver's license? Ray had heard of cases where a man lived two separate lives with separate families. Was that what Cox had been doing? Did he have another wife?

Ray suddenly recalled the pictures in the "Richard Gleary" wallet. A wife and two children. "Did Mike have any kids?" He turned his head and realized that Ehrlich was weeping openly, shaking, blubbering something about being "*so* sorry" for his affair with Cox's wife. Glen might not have been much of a sheriff, Ray thought as he watched them embrace, but he was proving to be one heck of a chaplain. Glen had only just met this man, and here he had the guy bawling his guts out, confessing his "sins."

"Excuse me," Ray said. "I hate to interrupt, but . . ." He waited for Ehrlich to regain a modicum of composure before asking, "Did Mike have kids?"

Ehrlich shook his head. "He didn't want any. Diane did, but Mike said that with his job and commitment to work, it wouldn't be fair."

Then who were the children in the wallet photos? Ray wondered.

The laptop chirped at them. Ray bent to examine it and found an icon near the top of the screen blinking. He wasn't sure whether it represented a stylized letter or a poorly illustrated face. When the thing beeped again, he asked, "What's wrong with it?"

"Mike's got e-mail," Ehrlich told him.

"E-mail?" Ray hunched over the Powerbook and moved his finger across the touchpad. "Don't you have to be hooked up to the Internet for that?"

Ehrlich nodded. He was recovering quickly, the penitent pilgrim reverting to the polished businessman. "Everybody in management at Suntron has a Powerbook and we're all on-line. The units are preloaded with DUs that log when we boot."

Ray squinted at him, wishing he had paid more attention to Margaret's PC and her insistent efforts to drag him into the computer age. DUs? Log? Boot? "Try that again."

"When we turn on our laptops, a desktop utility automatically hooks us into the Internet by way of a cellular modem. So we're on the Net all the time. That way we can send and receive flash e-mail whenever we need to."

Ray nodded, pretending to understand. "Can we get this message?"

Ehrlich looked at the screen, at the keyboard, at the screen again. "Not without a code." He pressed a button bearing an apple symbol, then hit several keys in rapid succession. An empty box appeared, a message above it requesting a user pass code.

"I don't suppose you know his pass code?" Ray asked.

"Sure." Ehrlich tapped in P-L-A-Y-E-R. "I told you we were friends. He knew my code, I knew his. It just made things easier." Using the touchpad, he moved the arrow to the blinking icon and double clicked on it. A document unfolded on the screen. It was laid out just like a regular business letter, complete with a company logo: Northwest Airlines. The text explained that since Cox had failed to make Flight 773 and had not canceled two days in advance, they would be forced to charge him a no-show fee that amounted to half the price of the ticket. The balance would be returned to him in the form of a cashier's check. The closing paragraph requested that he contact the Northwest billing office by phone, e-mail, or fax with any questions.

Ray checked his watch. "How can he be charged for missing a plane that hasn't left yet?"

"That's not ours," Ehrlich said. "We're on Alaska Airlines."

"Northwest doesn't go to San Francisco," Glen threw in.

Ehrlich typed something into the keyboard and a blue world map materialized. It was crisscrossed with red arching lines: air routes. "Flight 773 left at . . ." He entered more information and an oval superimposed itself onto the left side of the screen. ". . . One-fourteen this morning," he read. "Bound for . . . Tokyo."

"Tokyo? Another business trip?"

"If it was," Ehrlich said, fiddling with the mouse, "he didn't tell me anything about it." More clicking. "The reservations weren't made through our San Francisco office."

"So?"

"So our in-house travel agency handles all the booking for the company. Everything. You can't go to the can without getting it approved through them."

Ray tried to determine what that meant. Cox had booked passage to Tokyo for something other than business. Vacation? But instead of catching the red-eye, he had killed himself by vaulting from a chair lift. None of the above made sense.

Cox didn't sound like a vacation kind of guy. More like the a type-A workaholic. And since he was apparently having marital trouble . . .

"How many tickets did he have?"

Ehrlich tapped the keys. "Hmm . . . Says here the reservation was for two. A Mr. and Mrs. R. Gleary."

Ray felt a headache coming on. Traveling overseas under an assumed name. With a companion. Undoubtedly not his wife.

He dismissed the confusing array of information and returned his attention to the supposition that Cox had killed himself. Why would he do that? Suicide never seemed logical to the survivors. You had to experience severe depression in order to fully understand it. Ray hadn't. He did, however, have an appreciation for pain. If he ever decided to do himself in he would find a quick, simple means. Skydiving from a metal bench sixty feet in the air would not be his first choice. Surely there had to be a better way.

"What company did you make the deal with last night?" Glen asked.

"Fukutomi Research Technologies."

"We'll need to talk with representatives from Fukutomi," Glen announced in a tone that suggested expertise in this field. "And we'll to need to contact your co-workers."

"We'll need to notify the authorities," Ray corrected, "and let them handle this."

Ignoring him, Glen said, "I'm afraid you'll have to stick around for a few days."

"Not necessarily." Ray lifted the phone and dialed an outside line. "The state police can decide what to do. They may or may not need you to hang around that long."

"It's okay." Ehrlich sighed. "I have to . . ." He shook his head. "If that was Mike that . . . I guess I have to . . ." He shrugged.

"Identify him," Glen said.

Ehrlich nodded gloomily. "And I suppose I'll have to make arrangements to . . . to have his . . . his body flown home." Swallowing hard, he whispered, "And . . . tell Diane."

"This is Ray Attla, Barrow PD." Ray recited his badge number. "I'm following up on a body that was recovered from Mount Alyeska this morning. The ID said Richard Gleary. We believe he also went by the name of Michael Cox. . . . Yes, I'll hold."

"I should probably have a talk with Mr. Fukutomi," Ehrlich lamented. "If he reads about this in the paper . . ." He swore. "FRT's already skittish. It took us almost a year to convince them to hop into bed with us. This . . . It could spook them."

"I thought you signed the deal last night," Ray said.

"We did. But there's a remorse clause. Both sides

have forty-eight hours to back out. So we're not out of the dark until seven tomorrow evening."

"Yes, I'm still holding," Ray told the receiver. He asked Ehrlich, "What exactly is the agreement?"

Ehrlich hesitated like a man being ushered toward a dentist chair. "Suntron markets computer equipment: mainframes, business systems, communication hardware. . . . We don't manufacture anything. We just sell high-tech components for other companies. Mostly Japanese companies. That's where FRT comes in. They've developed a microchip—the NVSC—that's going to give Intel a run for their money. And we landed the contract to distribute it in the U.S."

"What was Cox's role in the project?" Ray asked, still on hold.

"It was his baby," Ehrlich said. "Don't ask me how, but he got wind of what Fukutomi was working on and started courting them. Pulled out all the stops."

"It obviously worked," Ray observed.

"If it sticks, Mike will make senior VP of marketing." Ehrlich paused, frowning mournfully. "*Would have* made senior VP."

Ray nodded and was about to ask what the deal meant to Ehrlich and whether he was next in line for Cox's old position, when someone finally picked up the line. "Yes . . . This morning . . . Mount Alyeska. No . . . On the run itself . . ." He sighed, "Yes, I'll hold.

"Hang up," Glen instructed. "We can handle this thing."

"Right . . ." Ray groaned. Glen's grasp of police work was tenuous. Investigating something as seemingly innocuous as a suicide was enough to keep a pair of full-time cops busy for days. Maybe longer in this case. There was the problem of Cox's double identity and the fact that he had been involved in an international business venture. Even with the note to his wife, the first objective would be to rule out foul play.

"Yes, I'm here," Ray assured the woman on the

phone. Thirty seconds later, he said, "You're kidding."
Unfortunately, she wasn't. "Did you check with Anchorage PD? . . . What about . . . ? There has to be some
sort of . . . No, I'm not accusing you, I'm just . . . Listen,
all I'm saying is that . . . Hello?" He glared at the phone.

"What's the matter?" Glen asked.

"They don't have any record of him."

"Of who?" Ehrlich asked.

"Of Michael Cox or Richard Gleary. Nothing. At the
state or the city level."

"That's impossible," Glen said. "Who'd you talk to?"

"State patrol office. They said they haven't had any
patrolmen up here all day."

"But I talked to them," Glen said.

Ray shrugged. "Apparently you talked to ghosts."

"What's all this mean?" Ehrlich wondered.

"It means your friend Mr. Cox is missing again. Missing *and* dead."

➤ FOURTEEN ◄

RAY DIALED AGAIN. "Are your people still here?" he
asked Ehrlich.

The bald head nodded. "Everybody but Anderson. He
left early. The rest of us are supposed to head out in . . ."
He glanced at his watch. "Ten minutes."

"Stall them." Ray gestured at Glen. "Go with him.
Ask about Cox: when he was last seen, what he was

wearing, how he was acting, that sort of thing. Don't tell them about the body. I'll be down in a minute."

As they were exiting the room, a female voice answered the line, "Barrow PD."

"Hey, Betty. This is Ray. How's life at the top of the world?"

"The party's on," she answered, laughing.

It was the longest day of the year, Ray remembered. Barrow celebrated the occasion with a blanket toss, midnight softball games, fun runs, dancing, special foods . . .

"What can I do for you?"

"I need you to run a couple of names." He gave her the information.

"I thought you were on vacation."

"I was. Listen, I need a hard-core search, Betty. Do you still have an in with the Feds in Seattle?"

"Yeah . . ." she answered suspiciously. "What's going on?"

"A body turned up down here. I'm trying to help the locals rule out a few worst-case scenarios." When she grunted at this, he told her, "Thanks. I'll check back in an hour." He hung up and was shutting down Cox's computer when Yasaka returned.

"Where is everyone?"

"Downstairs." Ray shut the suitcase, stowed the carry-on back in the closet, and put the letter back on the table. "Can you have your people guard this room?"

She nodded, then sighed dramatically when he held the door open for her.

"What? Should I let it slam on you?" When she didn't answer, he added, "I was raised to respect women."

"I'll just bet you were." She followed him to the elevator.

"I'm serious. Women play an important role in Eskimo culture." Ray punched the down button. "They clean game, cook, make clothing . . . Leaving the men to attend to—"

"Eating, sleeping, general laziness. Japanese culture isn't that different."

"The men hunt," Ray continued, undaunted. "Or at least they used to. For weeks, sometimes months at a time. Braving the elements to obtain sustenance for their families."

They stepped onto the elevator.

"Just a half century ago," Yasaka said, "the prevailing 'traditions' in Japan included killing baby girls at birth and enslaving women. In some places that still goes on. Women are considered second-class citizens, chattel, treated like work animals."

Ray shook his head. "But among the Inupiat women are honored by . . ." His voice trailed off as the elevator rose. He glanced at the button panel. "I pushed L."

"Must be the penthouse," Yasaka explained. "It overrides the panel."

"Penthouse?"

"The entire top floor is a suite that we keep reserved for our most elite clientele."

"Who's up there now?" Ray wondered. "Bill Gates?"

"At the moment it's occupied by Ronald Mancini," Yasaka replied.

"Ron the Don is staying here?"

Yasaka explained diplomatically, "We don't refer to our guests by nicknames."

"I saw him on TV, during his trial last year. Talk about a greasy little rat."

"We also avoid referring to our clients as 'greasy little rats.' "

The elevator slowed and the P button illuminated with a ping. When the doors slid open, Ray found it difficult to mask his surprise. Instead of a short, pudgy Italian male with a hard face and slicked back hair, the only person in view was a woman who looked remarkably like a high-priced call girl: dark, permed hair, heavy makeup, long lashes, full red lips, spike heels, tinted hose, skin-tight black dress that barely reached to her upper thighs and exposed an alarming amount of cleavage. As she energetically snapped a lump of gum, an invisible cloud of sickly sweet perfume drifted into the elevator.

"Good morning, Mrs. Mancini," Yasaka offered politely.

Mrs. Mancini twitched a smile that caused her cheeks to crack with wrinkles, then turned and bellowed with a hoarse Bronx accent, "Ronny!"

"I'm comin'," a raspy, smoker's voice answered from somewhere in the suite.

Mrs. Mancini tapped her way onto the elevator, teetering on the high heels. "Ronny!" she shrieked again. She batted her lashes at Ray. "He'll be right out."

Yasaka held the Open door button like an obedient servant girl. "Where are you off to today, Mrs. Mancini?" she asked brightly.

"Oh," Mrs. Mancini gushed, "we're going to see the glacier."

A man appeared in the hall. Fastening his jacket, he walked briskly toward the elevator, eyes darting about, taking in Ray, Yasaka, Mrs. Mancini. Without greeting them, he stationed himself just inside the elevator door. This wasn't Ron, Ray was certain. Aside from the fact that Mrs. Mancini didn't acknowledge him, he wasn't the right shape. This guy was fit, wiry, his movements swift and exact. A bodyguard. In fact . . . Ray studied the man's profile: gaunt cheeks, sharp nose, serious eyes, callous expression, jagged scar under his right ear. Not just any bodyguard. It was Hat Trick Benny, Mancini's main man. According to some, his hit man. Benny had reportedly earned his nickname by battling a trio of men with a hockey stick, sending all three to the hospital and maiming one for life. And yet, as far as Ray knew, the guy had never done time.

Benny's head swiveled and a pair of intense, brown eyes considered Ray.

"Hi," Ray said cheerfully. "How's it going?"

Without twitching a single facial muscle, Benny somehow managed to sneer. Though Ray had at least six inches on Benny, and a good fifty pounds, he felt small and defenseless. If Benny was even half as good at hand-to-hand combat as lore suggested, he could have Ray on the floor of the elevator, nose to the carpet in the blink of an eye.

"Ronny!!" Mrs. Mancini hollered.

Another man bounded down the hallway at a labored trot. He bordered on obesity, chest and waist a singular jiggling mass. His legs were short, thick stubs, his head too small for the rest of his body. The man's gleaming black hair had been combed straight back into an abbreviated ponytail.

"Sorry," he hissed. "Lobby, please."

Yasaka reached to comply but Benny beat her, thumbing the L button. The door slid shut and the elevator fell back toward the ground floor.

"Well . . ." Mrs. Mancini said with a smack of her gum. She grinned mischievously and turned a slow, tottering circle: a working girl displaying her wares. "Whattaya think?"

"Hubba-hubba," her husband growled. He drew her close, using her buttocks like a handle. After nipping her neck, he turned his attention to Benny. "Where we goin'?"

"To see a glacier," Benny replied in a monotone, barely moving his lips.

Mancini swore, wincing as though he had been slapped. "What for?"

"Now Ronny," Mrs. Mancini droned. "You said we could go sightseeing today."

"I know, baby, I know . . . but . . . a glacier? That ain't sightseeing. A strip club, a horse track . . . Now that's sightseeing." He nudged his bodyguard with an elbow. "All this natural beauty . . . Gets a little boring, you know?"

"Well . . . There ain't no horse tracks or strip joints,

so we're goin' to the glacier," Mrs. Mancini told them. "Both of youse just shut up and enjoy yourselves."

"Enjoy ourselves?" Mancini slumped. "We're gonna freeze our butts off."

Ray felt certain that Mrs. Mancini would.

"Maybe we should take jackets," Mrs. Mancini proposed.

"Jackets? All I brought was leather. It's summer. I figured it would be warm."

Ray almost interjected that it was, in fact, quite warm by local standards. By Barrow standards, it was a heat wave. Still, on Lake Portage, at the foot of the glacier, with wind blowing down over blue ice, it would be chilly. "You'll need coats."

All three heads jerked in his direction, eyes glaring.

"Our concierge can provide you with the appropriate attire," Yasaka assured them.

Mancini grunted at this. Still giving Ray the evil eye, he produced a cigar, bit off the end, and prepared to light up.

"You can't . . ." Ray started to say. His arm was in motion, about to point to the conspicuous no-smoking sign, when Yasaka grabbed his wrist and shook her head. "You can't go to the glacier without coats," he amended. "Even on a beautiful day like today."

"He should know," Benny grumbled.

"Yeah," Mancini chuckled, belching smoke. "If an Eskimo tells ya to put on a coat, ya better do it er else ya might frostbite some important body part."

Frowning, Yasaka apologized with her eyes. As a minority, she obviously identified with Ray's position. She had probably been the butt of a few jokes herself.

Ray was more offended by the cigar than anything else. The stench of Mancini's stogie combined with his wife's perfume was enough to knock a strong man to his knees.

"Say . . ." Mancini pivoted to face Ray. "You Indians got any gambling up here?"

Ray shook his head, biting his tongue to keep from saying something spiteful. For starters, he wasn't an Indian.

"Nothin'? No poker? No backroom joints?"

Another shake.

"Virgin territory," he snickered to Benny. "Maybe we should consider expandin' up here. Bet we could make some good money."

"Especially on the reservations. Right, Chief?"

These idiots didn't even know that there were no reservations in Alaska, that the Natives lived in villages and were organized into corporations that played a role in harvesting and distributing the natural resources.

Breathing through his nose, he felt Yasaka's hand brush his. He glanced at her and saw her roll her eyes: Blow it off. He forced a smile and nodded, silently vowing to personally visit pain and anguish on Ron the Don if he ever so much as set foot in a village.

The mob could have Anchorage if it wanted it. Even Fairbanks. But coming after the People would be a big mistake.

FIFTEEN

As THEY STEPPED off the smoky elevator, into the fresh, breathable air of the lobby, Ray left the members of the mafioso to Yasaka and headed for a cluster of men standing near the desk. They were all wearing overcoats, suitcases and bags at their feet. He could see Glen standing in the middle of the group, gesturing wildly, talking. Apparently the sheriff had yet to learn that the best way to gather information was to shut up and listen.

Ray arrived at Glen's side and flashed a badge at the men. "Officer Attla. Who was the last person to see Mr. Cox before his disappearance?"

"You mean his suicide," one of them said. This elicited a chorus of profanity.

A woman in a maroon hotel uniform strode up and addressed the group with a raised voice. "Suntron party, your shuttle to Anchorage International is waiting outside."

Heads bobbed and the men bent to pick up their baggage.

"If you'll hang on just a moment," Ray said, "I have a couple of questions."

"I think we pretty much covered everything," Glen assured him. "Thanks guys."

As the men hurried across the lobby and through the entrance, Ray rubbed his temples, which were now pounding with the authority of symphonic timpani drums. Sighing, he chided, "I specifically asked you not to tell them about the suicide."

Glen shrugged. "I wasn't going to. But one of them asked, point blank, if we had any idea what might have happened to Cox. I couldn't lie."

Ray exhaled his frustration. "Did you find out anything about Cox?"

Glen referred to a small notepad. "He left the meeting, turned down dinner and drinks, went to his room. Said he was tired. That was the last time anyone saw him."

"That's a big help." Ray watched as the glass elevator rose, carrying a load of guests toward the vaulted ceiling of the atrium. "Did you get names and numbers?"

"I figured Ehrlich could give us that." Before Ray could complain, he added, "But I took them down anyway." He displayed the pad. It contained a neat list in clear handwriting: names, job titles, addresses, telephone numbers, e-mail addresses.

Maybe there was hope for Glen after all. "Where's Ehrlich?"

"He went to check on the folks from Fukutomi. Listen, after we touch base with the Japanese, we might want to go up and speak to the lift operators who were on duty yesterday evening."

Ray nodded. "Good idea."

Ehrlich approached from the hall. "They're in a meeting."

"All we need is ten minutes," Ray said.

"It's a closed meeting," Ehrlich explained. "I couldn't even get in. They're sequestered until three this afternoon. Probably scrutinizing and rethinking our agreement." He cursed the idea and began anxiously combing limp strands of hair across his bare, pink scalp. "What should I tell Diane?"

"What do you mean?" Ray said.

"If the State Police lost Mike . . ." He swore again, energetically this time.

"I'm sure it's just a clerical error," Ray assured. "But you should probably hold off on making that call. At least until we can get a fix on who has the body."

"I need a drink," Ehrlich groaned. He examined his watch and apparently decided that even though it wasn't yet noon, cocktails were in order. "You guys wanna join me?"

"We have a few things to attend to," Ray said, purposely vague. "Stick around the hotel. We'll contact you."

"I'll be in the bar." He wandered off toward the sound of clinking glasses and silverware.

On the way out to the Jeep, Ray tried to think of an excuse that would extricate him from the investigation. It was growing more and more complicated, his vacation taking on the appearance of police work as usual.

As they climbed into the Wagoneer, Glen suggested,

"Lift operators?" Before Ray could answer, the sheriff was thumbing the radio. "Hans . . . Hans, you around?" The receiver crackled and he adjusted the knobs before repeating the call.

"Dis is Hans," a tinny, accented voice squawked. "Who's dis?"

"Hans, this is Glen. I'm with Officer Attla and we're headed for the lodge. We'd like to talk to the operators who were on duty last night at closing."

"Shoor." There was a pause, then, "Jason Simms . . . Ee vas on dee bottom house. Ee's off today."

"Got a Girdwood address on him?"

"Shoor." Paper rustled, causing the static to spike. "Lives down at da Voodlands. Number 2-3-3." More crinkling. "Deen dars Gary Bond . . . He vork dee mid-vay house. Still dere too. Prolly high as a kite . . . da hop-head."

"What about the upper house?" Glen asked. "Was Sheri up there last night?"

"Ya. But she gone today," Hans informed. "Gotta get ready for da Bird."

"Ah . . ." Glen said. "I forgot that was tonight. You up for it?"

"Ya betcha I am. Gonna vin too."

"I wouldn't doubt that. Thanks, Hans." Glenn replaced the microphone.

"What's the Bird?" Ray asked.

"The Solstice Mountain Race. At Bird Creek." They turned into the lodge parking area. "It's a running race they have every year on the longest day. Used to start around six. But now I think the gun goes off around nine or ten P.M. It's a real killer: three miles of mountain trail with an elevation gain of 3,500 feet. I ran it two years ago and nearly killed myself." He blew air at the race. "Some people thrive on that sort of thing. Not me."

Skidding into a slot, Glen twisted the key and extracted it from the ignition. The Jeep didn't seem to notice. It hiccupped and jiggled unevenly, as if it were still idling.

"Know anything about setting the timing?" Glen asked as they disembarked.

"It's not the timing," Ray said, trying not to inhale exhaust smoke. "It's the carburetor. The timing might be a little off, but your carb is on its deathbed."

"Maybe we can take a look at it later," Glen said.

Ray checked his watch. Later was now. The day was nearly half over. He wanted to go pick up Keera and do the picnic ride he had planned. Not ride the lift up the mountain again to talk to the dope-smoking Mountain Dew poster boy stationed at the midway house.

"Listen, I really need to—"

Glen waved him off. "I understand." Ushering Ray toward the lift, he dug a cellular phone out of his jacket, punching the buttons, and handed it to him.

By the time Ray brought it to his ear, Jean had already answered.

"Hi, Jean. This is Ray. Ray Attla."

"Hi. Where are you guys?"

"At the bottom of the ski runs. How's Keera doing?"

"Great," Jean gushed. "She and Ruby are having a wonderful time."

"Could I speak with Keera?"

"Sure. Hang on a sec." There was a clank as Jean set the phone down. Then Ray heard her calling the girls. The girls called back, shouting something about being busy. Several seconds and another shouted conversation later, Jean was back on the line. "They're right in the middle of a game. Can you call back in five minutes?"

"Never mind. It's not important. I was just—"

"Don't worry, Ray," Jean consoled. "She's fine. She and Ruby are like kindred spirits. In another hour, they'll be inseparable."

Which was exactly what Ray was dreading. So much for using Keera as an excuse to bag out on Glen. "Thanks for watching her for me."

"No problem, Ray. Keera's a wonderful little girl. She's no trouble whatsoever. You guys take your time. Finish your work. We'll be here."

Ray handed the phone back.

"Is Keera okay?"

"Yeah," he grunted.

Glen stuffed the phone into a pocket and fished out his wallet. When they reached the lift, he offered his badge for examination. "Official sheriff's business," he said.

The operator, a wispy girl in her late teens, nodded, eyes wide. "Mr. Heiberg called and said that you'd be coming." She positioned them to catch a chair, only too ready to please. "Enjoy your visit," she chimed from habit.

The chair scooped them up and accelerated out of the gully, seemingly anxious to reach the top. The air was warmer than on Ray's first ride, heavy with the sweet scent of fireweed. The sun was a quarter of the way up in the southern sky, impotent to rise higher, yet unwilling to relinquish its hold on the Arctic. It would continue to dispel even the suggestion of darkness for another three weeks.

Ray and Glen fell silent as they ascended the mountain face. Evergreens consumed the rolling foothills like a great army, their shadows pointing north. Above, a crystalline head gleamed at them: cornice, bowl, and descending rivulets white with snow and ice. A pair of mountain bikers bumped their way down a rutted path directly below the chair.

The midway house was in sight when Glen said, "Amazing, isn't it?"

"What's that?"

"Creation."

Ray swore inwardly, fearing a sermon. "The Inupiat believe that Raven created everything: the sun, the moon, the stars."

"Same with Yupik," Glen said. "All of the Native creation myths are remarkably similar."

Glad that the distraction had worked, Ray wondered, "Why do you think that is?"

"They're all a shadow of the truth, which is that—"

"There he is," Ray interrupted. He gestured at the head sticking out the window of the midway house.

When they dismounted from the lift, the kid admonished, "Hey, man . . . What are you dudes doing? You're not supposed to dismount here—"

Ray and Glen displayed their ID badges in unison. The kid's pinprick pupils reflected panic. He retracted his head and there was a thrashing noise inside the shack.

Ray opened the door and peered inside. The kid was on his knees, frantically stuffing wads of dope into his mouth.

"It's Gary, right?" Ray said, trying to keep a straight face. "Gary Bond?"

The kid nodded, still choking down his stash. He had tears in his eyes from the effort. "Aw . . . man!" he mumbled through the mouthful. "You're gonna bust me!"

"No, Gary," Ray said, smirking. He guessed that the "product" the kid was chowing down on amounted to a full week of sitting in this little outhouse. "Actually we just want to ask you a few questions. But we can wait until after your snack."

►►► SIXTEEN ◄◄◄

GARY SPEWED MARIJUANA like a horse choking on hay. After raking his tongue clean, he glared up at Ray and cursed. "Yer the dude who made the dead guy."

Ray nodded. "I'm the *dude*. And I warned you about smoking dope up here."

"I wasn't smoking it," he pleaded. "I been on shift since you rousted me, man. You dudes spooked me so I just . . . you know . . . started chowin' down, to ditch my stash."

"Uh-huh." It wasn't a bad lie. The problem was the shack reeked of dope. Burnt dope, not the kind in a plastic sack. "You were working last night, weren't you?"

Gary squinted as he considered this. "Uh . . . yeah. I think so."

"You were on when the lift closed?"

He consulted a schedule affixed to the wall next to the door of the hut. "Yeah. I was here." He winced and bent forward, cradling his stomach. "I'm feelin' sour."

"Do you remember seeing a man come up just before closing?"

Gary's face was ashen. "Um . . . A man?"

"Right. About six foot. Light brown hair. Wearing a blue jacket and tan chinos."

"Chinos? What're chinos?"

Glen flashed Ray's sketch at him. "This is the man."

Gary's eyelids fluttered as he attempted to focus on the image.

"Came up right before closing," Ray reminded. "Did you see him?"

"Maybe . . ." He belched. "Is he the stiff?"

Ray ignored this. "Did you see this man come up here last night?"

"I don't know. I was a little under the weather," he complained.

The phone rang, but Gary didn't even glance at the device. Ray picked it up on the fourth ring. "Midway."

"Gary?" a German voice asked.

"No, Hans. This is Ray Attla. Hang on." He extended the phone, but Gary was suffering from the dry heaves. "He's a little indisposed. I'll have him call you back."

"Don't bodder. I'm coming up!"

Ray hung up.

"Was that Hans?" Gary panted, wiping at his mouth with a shirt sleeve.

"Yeah. He's headed this direction, to have a little talk with you."

Gary swore. "Dude, I can't lose this job."

"Maybe you should have thought about that when you were getting high."

"My smokes don't impair my ability to perform my job," he slurred.

"Addictions never do," Ray shot back sarcastically. He gestured to Glen and they positioned themselves to catch a chair bound for the base.

As they started down, Gary called from the hut, "Thanks for not bustin' me, man."

"Why didn't we?" Glen asked as the chair collected them.

Ray shrugged. "Possession is a misdemeanor. He'd get probation. I'm not sure that would faze him. But Hans is peeved. He'll probably fire him."

"Maybe that'll get his attention."

"Maybe," Ray grunted. It was his experience that most dope addicts and alcoholics were unwilling to admit their problem and seek help, no matter what they lost.

Below them, a trio of brave souls were testing their skills and their bikes on a steep, rock face that looked like a challenge to scramble, much less ride.

"Life is like that," Glen observed. He pointed at the bikers.

After watching the first one roll over the edge of the precipice, only to leap off his bike and hug a tree, Ray said, "I thought life was like a box of chocolates."

Glen shook his head and smiled. "You're one of the most sarcastic people I've met."

"Thanks." Ray gestured at a concrete half pipe that snaked down the bunny slope. "What's that?"

"The alpine slide. You should try it. If you get a fast sled, it's pretty fun."

As Glen began to explain the ride, Ray noticed a couple standing at the edge of the parking area. Even from this distance, he could tell that one was a woman, the other a man. They were wearing dark blue clothing, sunglasses, leaning against a white Ford, peering up the mountain.

"Great . . ."

Glen paused in mid-sentence. He followed Ray's gaze. "Know those people?"

"They're not people. They're federal agents."

Glen squinted at them. "You can tell that from here?"

"They've got the look: the car, the clothes . . . the Ray-Bans are a dead giveaway."

"FBI . . . ?" Glen said, making the letters sound like an acronym for something particularly distasteful. "What do they want?"

Ray shrugged. "Probably want to ask us about Cox."

"Why would they care about him?"

"Good question. If they try to drill us for information, keep that in mind. See if we can figure out what the heck they're up to and why this is any of their business."

"Can't we just ask them?" Glen wondered.

Ray laughed at this. "We can." He watched the agents watching them. "But they won't give us a straight answer. They're Fibbies and we're lowly local law enforcement officers. Whatever they're investigating is, by nature, far, far above our comprehension, intelligence, and security level."

The agents stirred as the chair floated toward the lower house: standing at attention, buttoning their jackets, adjusting their shades.

Hans emerged from the lift shack below them. Stepping backward toward a chair, he was jabbing his finger at the attendant. Still railing, he hopped aboard a bench.

Ray waved as the chairs passed each other. "Go get 'em, Hans."

By the time he and Glen had alighted on the platform and trotted down the ramp, the Feds were there to greet them.

"Agent Randolph," the man grunted, giving them a full quarter second to examine and appreciate his impressive badge before pocketing it.

"Agent Moore," the woman chimed with a humorless expression. She waved her badge at them and declared, "We're with the Federal Bureau of Investigation."

"Really?" Ray asked, as if this were a complete surprise.

"Which one of you is Attila?" she asked, reading from a miniature notepad.

"*Attla*," Ray corrected.

"We understand that you found a body up on the mountain this morning," the man said. Randolph was husky, about five-ten and walked the line between downright homely and ruggedly handsome: short, dishwater-blond hair, large ears, crusty cheeks . . .

Ray found it difficult not to stare at the man's mouth. His lips were thick, and the pencil-thin mustache above them almost looked drawn on.

"And we need to ask you a few questions," Moore said, completing her partner's statement. She was blond, fit, her face as hard and brittle as a mask. "First of all, there's the matter of—"

"The time," Randolph said without emotion. "When did you—"

"Find him," Moore said.

"Find who?" he asked.

After glancing at each other, Randolph said, "The body."

"Oh, *that* him," Ray said. "The him that's now missing?"

"Missing?" Moore's face shrunk into a grimace.

"I handed him over to the State Police," Glen interjected. "And they lost him."

Moore consulted her notepad. "You must be . . . Redfern."

"He's the Girdwood sheriff," Ray informed. "And the local chaplain."

After flipping pages in her notebook, Moore said, "We know."

"Back to the time frame . . ." Randolph said.

"When did you find him?" Moore asked.

Ray rubbed his chin and adopted an expression of deep thought. "Around . . . Oh, I'd say . . . about seven-forty, seven-forty-five . . . Right in there."

Moore dutifully recorded this.

"And what was his condition at that time?" Randolph asked.

"Dead."

"You're sure?" Moore pressed.

Ray nodded. "He had a broken neck, from falling off the chair lift."

"We know," they chimed. Moore continued to scribble on her pad.

"Why's the FBI in on this?" Glen wondered aloud.

Ray glared at him. Nothing like the subtle approach.

Randolph sighed. "The . . . uh . . . man in question . . . the deceased . . . was . . ."

"The body you located," Moore said, nostrils flared, "belonged to a man who was part of a federal investigation."

"Is that right?" Ray said. "What kind of investigation?"

"We're not at liberty—" Randolph said, but ran out of words.

"To discuss the matter," Moore added.

"Of course not," Ray said. "I understand."

"So if you could just—" Moore said.

"Tell us where you found the body," Randolph said.

"Under tower forty-two," Ray answered matter-of-factly. "That should be in the State Police report. Right, Glen?"

Glen nodded.

"And what were you—" Randolph said.

"Doing up there?" Moore finished.

"Mountain biking. I was coming down and I happened to see him in a clearing. I checked for vital signs. There were none. Then I went for help."

"Is that it?" Randolph asked.

"Is that all you know about the matter?" Moore pressed.

Ray shrugged. "Pretty much." He paused before dropping the bomb. "Oh, there was one other thing."

The two agents leaned forward expectantly.

"I checked his ID."

➤➤ SEVENTEEN ◄◄

THE RESPONSE WAS exactly what Ray was hoping for: Randolph cursed the sky and Moore glared at her pad as though it had just reached up and slapped her in the face.

"Seems his name was Richard Gleary," Ray continued, certain that they already possessed this information. He spelled the last name for Moore and she pretended to write it down. "Except his real name was Michael Cox. With an X."

This time Randolph kicked the ground like an anxious horse.

"He had a driver's license that read Gleary. And a passport. Oh, and get this, he had reservations on the red-eye to Japan last night. In the name of Gleary."

Another curse fell from Randolph's frozen mouth. Moore's shoulders slumped.

"So who was this guy, anyway?" Glen asked.

"We're not at liberty—" Moore began.

"To discuss it." Ray frowned. "So you said."

"And we'll have to ask you not to discuss it with anyone," Randolph told him.

"It's classified," Moore assured him. "As for your role in the investigation . . ."

"You'll have to step aside," Randolph said. "We'll handle it from here."

"Fair enough," Ray said. The sentiment was genuine. Though the double-identity aspect of the case was mildly interesting, he was nevertheless ready to wash his hands of the whole thing. He would be happy to leave this headache to the Feds, to bid Glen farewell, and to go have that picnic with Keera.

"Please refrain from involving yourselves further," Moore warned.

Randolph dug something out of a jacket pocket: a business card with the emblem of the FBI. "If you think of anything else, give us a call."

"Day or night," Moore added.

They were turning to leave when Moore whirled back around. "You said you found ID. Did you find anything else?"

"On the body itself," Randolph clarified.

Ray realized what they were fishing for: the manila envelope. He searched their faces, wondering why they didn't just ask about it. Why beat around the bush? Was there something important inside? It would have to be pretty darn important to warrant a visit from the Feds. He volleyed back, "Like what?"

"Anything at all," Moore said.

"Nothing I can think of," Ray said. "But if I remember something . . ." He tapped the business card. "I'll give you a call, day or night."

"Thank you," Moore grunted. She holstered her notepad with a sniff.

"Thank you for your cooperation," Randolph agreed sternly.

Ray and Glen watched as the agents walked crisply back to their Ford.

"What was that?" Glen said.

"Our tax dollars at work."

"How did they find out about Cox so fast?" Glen glanced at his watch. "The state patrol only took the body a few hours ago. I doubt they've finished writing the report. And those two didn't seem to care that the body has been misplaced."

"I think they already knew. Which means it probably wasn't misplaced. My guess is they hijacked the entire case, corpse and all, and told the state cops not to talk about it."

"But how . . . ?"

"Maybe having Betty do background into Cox alerted them," Ray proposed.

Glen produced his cellular and handed it to him. "See what she found out."

Ray lifted his hands away from the phone as if it might burn him. "Weren't you here just a minute ago when those two Fibbies told us to back off?"

"They just said not to discuss the case or get in the way."

"And the background check does both."

Glen shrugged, unable to see the conflict. "We're all in this together."

"No. We're not in this together. The FBI is in this. We're not. They want us to butt out. Which is exactly what I plan to do." He started for the Jeep.

"What harm will one phone call do?" Glen asked. When Ray didn't answer, he dialed directory assistance. "Barrow . . . The Barrow Police Department . . ."

"Give me that." Ray stole the phone and pressed the end button.

"Come on," Glen begged. "Just one call. Then I promise to stop bugging you. I'll take you back to my place. We can pick up Keera. I'll drive you two back to your condo. How's that sound?"

"Unbelievable," Ray deadpanned. He scowled at the phone, flipped it back open, and dialed. "Betty? Ray. What's the scoop?" He listened for a minute. "Really? . . . What?!" He swore before thanking Betty and hanging up. Ray handed the phone back. "Can you unlock the door?" he asked impatiently.

Glen complied, leaping into the cab beside Ray. "Well . . . ?"

"Betty did some digging. She had a friend in Seattle run Cox and Gleary through the bureau computers. Cox wasn't in the system."

"What about Gleary?"

"I'm getting to that." Ray took a deep breath. "According to Betty's friend, Richard Gleary was employed by the State Department. Or at least, his name turned up in that branch of the system."

"You mean he worked in Juneau?"

"Not the state of Alaska. The U.S. State Department."

For the first time since Ray had met him, Glen looked capable of swearing. Instead, he asked, "What did he do for the State Department?"

"The file was locked and Betty's contact didn't have the security to access it."

"So . . . what was he . . . some sort of a spy?"

"I seriously doubt it," Ray said.

"The State Department has spies," Glen pointed out.

"Start the car."

Glen tried, but the Wagoneer objected. Behind them a cloud of blue smoke drifted from right to left, partially obscuring the slope.

"Doesn't Girdwood have emissions standards?" Ray wondered.

"If he was a spook, that would explain why the FBI was so interested and why it was a top-secret matter." The second attempt at ignition sent more smoke into the sky. The third ended in a backfire that shook the entire Jeep.

Ray climbed out. "Pop the hood."

Glen reached to pull the latch, then rolled down his window to continue his assessment of Gleary. "Maybe he was selling secrets to the Russians or something."

"Uh-huh," Ray muttered as he eyed the engine. It was filthy, encased in decades' worth of oily sludge. Toggling the throttle, he called, "Give it another try."

"Or maybe to the Iraqis. Saddam Hussein would probably pay big money for inside information."

"Give it a try," Ray insisted.

"Huh? Oh." A second later the Jeep sputtered and coughed before falling silent.

"Okay. Hold it." Ray frowned at the carburetor. "Got a wrench?"

"And I read how the Israelis . . . A wrench? Uh . . . No. Back at the house, but . . ."

Ray crouched and considered sliding under the front end. The asphalt under the engine was speckled with wet droplets. The Jeep not only ran poorly and was having trouble starting, it leaked. He crawled under carefully, doing his best to avoid the oil spots. Lying beneath the vehicle, he was glancing around, trying to get his bearings when something dripped on his crotch. He dabbed at it and sniffed his finger: brake fluid. So much for these slacks. Repositioning himself to avoid the leak, he felt something soak through the back of his right pants leg. A blind hand told him that it was a miniature lake of liquid. Moving in the opposite direction, his left shoulder found another pool.

Staring up at the engine block, he realized that Margaret had given him this shirt for his birthday. Great. That's when he noticed the brake lines. Severed. Broken off. He examined them, rubbing his thumb across the broken ends. Not broken. Cut.

The rod connected to the pedal pumped twice and the entire chassis trembled as Glen gave it the old college try. The Jeep lurched and spewed smoke.

Ray scrambled out, catching his pants pocket in the process. Hauling himself up on Glen's open window, he glared at the tear before muttering, "Don't bother."

"Just be patient. It'll start here in a second. It always does." He tried to turn the key again, but Ray reached in and yanked it away. "What are you doing?"

"You don't have any brakes."

"The pads are pretty worn, but last time I had it in the garage, they said—"

"No. I mean you don't have any brakes. Someone cut the lines."

"Cut them?" Blinking at this, Glen said, "But without brakes. . . . We might have . . . we could have . . . Who would . . . ?"

Ray shrugged. "Beats me. Got any enemies?"

"Not that I know of."

"Call that garage of yours," Ray suggested. He started across the parking lot. "In the meantime, I'm going back to your place to get Keera."

"Shouldn't we report this?" Glen called.

Ray laughed. "Yeah. Contact your local sheriff right away."

➤ EIGHTEEN ◄

"SEE YOU LATER," Ray called. He was ready to spend some time away from Glen. His heart sank when he heard the car door slam, footsteps running to catch up.

"I'll call Jean and have her pick us up," Glen said, phone in hand.

"I don't mind walking," Ray grunted.

"It's a ways. Maybe two miles. But I guess we can walk it."

"*We?* Shouldn't you wait for a tow truck?"

Glen shook his head. "I know the guys at the garage.

They know me. I left the keys in it." As they started down the road, he dialed the garage, made the arrangements, then called Jean. Hanging up, he said, "She'll pick us up in about twenty minutes."

They walked for a quarter mile. Tour buses rumbled past, cars streaked by. Breaks in the traffic were peaceful: cottonwood leaves rustling in the breeze, streams gurgling down the valley toward the ocean, the distant calls of hawks and loons. It was time to get the vacation back on track, Ray decided.

Glen gestured toward a long, double-story building nestled in a grove of alders. "That's where the other lift attendant lives. The one working base last night."

Ray didn't say anything.

"What I'm wondering is, did the brake job have anything to do with this case?"

"Doubtful," Ray grunted.

"Think about it though. A man dies up on the hill. Turns out he has two identities. The FBI's interested. The guy worked for the State Department."

"What does any of that have to do with your brakes? So Mr. Cox/Gleary falls, or purposely leaps, from the lift. That has no relation to your Wagoneer."

"Then who cut the lines?"

Ray sighed wearily. "An irate parishioner?" He was about to make another smart-alecky comment when he realized that Glen had stopped. "What's the matter?"

He gestured toward the apartments. "Why don't we just see if he's home? He could know something." Glen shrugged. "No harm in asking."

"Unless we get arrested."

"For what?"

"Obstruction of justice, compromising a witness, interfering with a federal investigation. . . . The Feds don't need much of an excuse."

"Just a few questions. We'll be in and out in ten minutes."

"Five minutes. If he does know something, we put him in touch with the Fibbies."

"Deal." Glen grunted as he strode toward the building.

The small parking area in front of the apartments held only two cars: a tireless, lime-green Volkswagen bug held aloft by concrete blocks, and a black Malibu with a dull, oily cam jutting up from a rusting hood. The building fit the vehicles. It was old, probably constructed in the seventies, and looked as though it hadn't been painted since. Turquoise-blue paint was peeling in long chips, the wood beneath it worn chocolate.

Ray followed Glen up a set of stairs attached to the right end of the structure. The steps creaked mournfully, the railing quivered, and the entire building seemed to shudder.

"Nice place," Ray said.

"Running the lift doesn't exactly pay the big bucks," Glen explained. "Most of these kids are taking a break from college, or just bumming around."

They found a door marked 7. Glen rapped on it, waited, tried again.

"Not in." Ray was halfway to the stairs when he heard the bolt slide back. The door cracked open and two bleary eyes peeked out.

"Jason Simms?" Glen asked.

"Yeah?" The door remained steady, the eyes riddled with red veins.

As Ray returned to his post next to Glen, he noticed a gold chain: the safety latch.

"I'm Sheriff Redfern and I was wondering if we could ask you some questions."

The eyes blinked. "About what?"

"Do you mind if we come in?"

Jason glanced at Glen, then Ray, back to Glen. "You got ID?"

Glen politely waved his badge at the door. Ray did the same.

After a brief hesitation, Jason unfastened the chain

and opened the door. He was smaller than Ray expected. And younger. Despite the two-day growth on his face and the shoulder length blond hair, Jason couldn't have been much more than twenty. He turned his back and grunted, "Try to hold it down. My roommates are still crashed."

The small studio was a study in clutter. A half dozen snow boards hung on the wall, a heap of boots piled below them. Skis adorned another wall, forming a fiberglass partition that led to the kitchen. It was cramped and dirty, every flat surface bearing a stack of dishes or pots or pizza boxes. The sofa was folded out in the middle of the room. Ray could make out two lumps in the tangle of sheets and blankets. Roommates.

Ray had decided that Jason must share the fold-out with his buddies when he noticed another door beyond the bed. It was partially hidden by an avalanche of dirty laundry that was half as tall as Jason. He glanced through the opening and realized that it was a closet. A down sleeping bag had been spread on the floor.

Jason jerked open cabinet doors in the kitchenette. "Want some coffee?"

"No thanks," Ray said.

"Good, 'Cause . . . I think we're out."

"We are," a voice assured him. It was female and belonged to one of the lumps in the bed. "You forgot to go to the store." The covers stirred and a girl in her early twenties gazed up at them. Her unruly hair was brown with a slight greenish tint, longer than Ray's. Sniffing, she threw back the covers and stretched, apparently unaware, or unconcerned, that she was completely naked. She rose and padded into the bathroom.

"That's my sister," Jason told them casually. "Brenda."

Ray nodded. Whatever. "Were you working the lift last night?"

Jason knelt and found a container of Tang in the lower cabinet. "Yeah."

"Did you happen to see a man go up, near closing time?"

Spooning a generous amount of drink mix into a coffee mug, he grimaced. "Yesterday?" He turned on the faucet and waited as it hissed. "Maybe."

"Blue jacket, tan pants," Glen said helpfully.

Stirring, Jason pursed his lips. "Yeah. I think so."

"Do you remember anything unusual about him?" Glen asked. "Did he act funny?"

After downing the entire mug of Tang, Jason said, "No. Except he was in a hurry. We were just about to shut down."

"So he seemed intent on getting up the lift?" Glen asked.

"I guess."

Glen glanced at Ray as though it was now his turn to lead the questioning. When Ray refused to step up, Glen said, "There was nothing else unusual about him?"

"Huh-uh." Jason began to concoct another shot of Tang.

Sighing, Ray said, "Did anyone go up after him?"

Jason shook his head.

"How about before him?" Ray wondered. "How many riders after . . . say . . . six?"

"I don't know. Maybe . . . five."

"Do you recall who went up right before the man did at closing?"

Jason stirred, tested his drink, added more instant mix. "Not really."

"Thanks for your help," Ray said. "Sorry to bother you."

"There were a couple of hotties though. You know, babes. Maybe not right before Mr. Dockers, but they went up. I don't forget hotties."

"What did they look like?" Ray asked from rote.

"One had black hair . . . about the color of yours," he said, pointing to Ray. "The other had blond hair. Both of them were cherry. We're talking brick houses," Jason explained. "We don't get many in off season. The babe-watch is pretty slow till ski time."

Brenda emerged from the bathroom, still void of clothing. "You wouldn't know a babe if you fell over one, Jass," she remarked before sliding beneath the covers again.

"Shut up!" Jason responded in brotherly fashion.

"This guy who went up last, he wasn't with the 'hotties'?" Ray clarified.

"Nope."

Ray sighed. "Thanks."

Jason started a third batch of Tang as Ray and Glen showed themselves to the door. Outside, Ray said, "Are you satisfied?"

Glen nodded.

"And you understand that we've more than fulfilled our obligation, that we've stepped over the line, going above and beyond our duty?"

Another nod, this one accompanied by a vacant stare.

"It's time to hang it up and let the Feds do their thing," Ray said. "Are you listening to me?"

"Right," Glen grunted. When they reached the bottom of the stairs, he said, "So I guess our next step is to find the 'hotties.' "

➤➤ NINETEEN ◄◄

RAY IGNORED THE remark. Striding toward the main road like a soldier on a forced march, he began mentally planning the picnic he and Keera would be taking: Rent a bike trailer at the shop by the condo; pick up sandwiches, chips, and pop at the deli . . .

"Maybe they saw something," Glen suggested.

A bus growled past, spewing a cloud of diesel exhaust. The trail that went north, into the Alyeska valley, was the best bet, Ray decided. Motorized vehicles weren't permitted beyond the hotel. No smelly buses or noisy trucks. Just hikers and bikers.

"They could have seen something," Glen repeated.

Kicking at a rock, Ray watched it skitter along the shoulder, then roll down the embankment and drop with a thunk into a shallow brook that ran parallel to the road. If he had thought about it, Ray would have packed his fishing gear on this trip.

"It's possible. Isn't it?" Glen huffed at him. "Hey, a lead's a lead. The least we can do is check into it."

Ray fought off a curse. "Check into what?"

"Those women. They could be witnesses."

"So what if they are?" Ray asked. He scanned the road for Jean.

"They may have information that—" Glen started to say.

Ray cut him off. "Cox is dead. The Feds are handling it. End of story."

They walked the next hundred yards in silence. A dairy truck labored up the hill. In its wake, a line of cars impatiently observed the no-pass zone.

"What if Cox was going up to meet them?" Glen hypothesized.

Ray laughed at this. "Oh, yeah . . . Sure. That makes sense. He went up to have a rendezvous with a couple of 'hotties,' and on the way back down, jumped to his death."

Their shoes scratched against the gravel in a steady cadence for a full minute. A motorcycle club rumbled by en route to the lodge.

"That kind of bothers me. Doesn't it bother you?" Glen asked.

"What? Hell's Angels who belong to AARP?"

"The whole suicide business. What if . . . What if Cox didn't jump?"

"We found a note," Ray reminded him. He squinted but saw no sign of Jean.

"Yeah," Glen agreed, "but it didn't say he was going to kill himself. Not in so many words. Maybe he was just running out on his wife."

Ray shrugged. "Okay. So he didn't kill himself. He fell. Dead is dead."

"How do you explain the airline reservation?"

"I can't. But that doesn't mean—"

"And why would a man who had just sealed a big business deal kill himself?"

"I don't know." Ray groaned, ready to admit defeat. "What I do know is that this is not our case. You want my advice? Forget about it."

A horn tooted and they turned to see a tow truck dragging the wounded Wagoneer down the hill. The driver waved cheerfully, never slowing to ask if they needed a ride. The truck had just rounded the bend when a green Camry appeared, coming toward them. It veered onto the shoulder and stopped a dozen yards away. The driver's window came down and Jean yelled, "Girdwood Taxi Service."

Glen ushered Ray into the front, then slid into the backseat. "Hello, ladies."

Keera and Ruby giggled but never looked away from their dolls. They continued performing ventriloquism tricks, oblivious to the fact that their fathers were now aboard.

"I saw your baby being hauled away," Jean said. "That car . . ." She shook her head as though the Jeep were a disobedient child. "It's been nothing but trouble since it topped two hundred thousand miles. What was it this time? The carburetor finally give up?"

"Not yet," Glen answered. "But Ray says it's about to."

"The clutch again?" Jean guessed. She did a head check, surveying the traffic.

"Huh-uh. Brakes."

"Brakes?" Jean shifted into reverse and backed further onto the shoulder. "Didn't you have it in for brakes just a couple of months ago?"

"It was more like a couple years ago," Glen said.

"Still . . ." She shifted into first and eased forward, waiting for a tour bus to pass.

"Somebody cut the brake lines."

An opening presented itself but Jean wasn't paying attention. Craning to look into the backseat, she said, "*Cut?* You mean . . . on purpose?"

Glen frowned. "Looks that way."

Blinking, Jean's face slowly contorted into a grimace. "Why?" She looked to Ray.

"Maybe they got tired of listening to Glen's sermons," he offered.

Jean failed to appreciate this. "Are you both all right?"

"We're fine, honey," Glen assured.

She glared at the steering wheel. "What are you guys getting yourselves into?"

"Nothing," Ray said. "The Feds are handling it now. It's their show."

Jean didn't seem to hear this. "Glen . . . I don't like this."

Before Ray could respond to Jean's paranoia, Keera blurted, "Raven got him 'cause of the package."

Package? Ray saw a picture in his mind: the envelope from Cox's jacket pocket with what felt like a computer disk inside. Weird. How could Keera possibly—

"What package?" Glen asked.

"Nothing," Ray told him. He glanced at his watch: 1:18. The idea of a picnic was fading. It was already past Keera's usual lunchtime. By the time they made the necessary arrangements and pedaled down the trail, it would be mid-afternoon. "We need to get back to our condo."

"Why don't you come back to our place for lunch?" Glen invited.

"No, thanks."

"It's already fixed," Jean said. "Seafood quiche."

Ray felt his stomach rumble at the words. "Sounds delicious, but—"

"Mommy! You said we could have hot dogs! You said Keera could stay!" a shrill voice whined from the back.

"I'll make you a hot dog," Jean promised.

"But Keera wants one too!"

"Dad-dy!" Keera pleaded at an even higher pitch. "I wanna hot dog! Pleeeze?!"

"What about our picnic?" Ray tried. "Remember? We're going biking. You get to ride behind Daddy in a private carriage." He wiggled his eyebrows at her hopefully.

"Can't we do that tomorrow?" she moaned. "I wanna hot dog. Pleeze?!"

Ray wanted to throttle her.

"The quiche is warming in the oven," Jean said.

"I'll run you back to your condo as soon as we have a bite," Glen said.

"Pleeze, Daddy!"

"Okay . . ."

The girls celebrated with ear-splitting shrieks and Jean took advantage of a break in the traffic, jerking the Toyota around and accelerating down the hill.

They were approaching the turnoff before Jean asked, "Why does the FBI care about a man falling off a ski lift?"

"No telling," Ray answered. He was already working on his escape. Thanks to Keera, they had been roped into lunch. But as soon as she finished that wiener . . .

They turned onto the dirt road and Ray gazed out the window at the A-frames scattered about the hillside, rooflines rising like sails on a sea of dense green foliage.

"Property must be pretty pricey up here," he observed.

Jean nodded. "Too pricey for us. We rent."

"But we're saving up for a place," Glen said. "Five acres or so. Up the valley."

"Sounds nice."

Glen began describing their dream home and was still going strong when they pulled into the driveway.

"Sounds nice," Ray repeated politely.

Disembarking, they entered the house and were met by a wonderful aroma. If Jean's quiche was anything like her sticky buns, it would be scrumptious.

After washing up, they all took seats at the cramped table wedged into the kitchen nook. Keera and Ruby sat on stools that placed them a head above the adults. Jean served up their meal first, then put plates of quiche and salad in front of Ray and Glen. After a brief prayer of thanks, they began eating.

Almost immediately, the phone rang. Glen rose to answer it. Standing at the bar, he muttered and nodded. Ray was finishing up his quiche when Glen returned to the table.

"The plot thickens," he said gravely.

Ray didn't respond. Keera had already gobbled a hot dog and a half, drained her milk, and was climbing down to play with Ruby. He was two bites away from free-dom.

"That was Bob Baker, a buddy of mine in Anchor-age."

Ray took a forkful of quiche. One bite left!

"He's with the medical examiner's office."

Ray took a sip of iced tea and downed the last bite.

"A John Doe/DOA showed up there about two hours ago, in the company of a couple of FBI agents. Broken neck, crushed face. No explanation other than he'd been found in Girdwood. That's why Bob called." When this drew no response, Glen added, "They ordered a rush autopsy."

Chewing, Ray dabbed at his mouth with a napkin. Done.

"Bob performed it, with the Feds in the room, looking over his shoulders the whole time."

"That was great, Jean," Ray said, pushing his chair back. "Thanks for lunch. And thanks for watching Keera."

"You're welcome."

"He found something interesting." Glen waited. "Don't you even want to know what it was?"

After a deep breath, Ray said, "What?"

Glen consulted a scrap of paper. "As_2O_3 in the blood-stream."

"What's that?"

"Pentavalent trioxide," he read from the note. "According to Bob, it's an especially potent form of ar-senic."

⟫⟩ TWENTY ⟨⟪

"ARSENIC?!" JEAN GLANCED at the hallway, as if this might somehow put the girls at risk. "You mean . . . someone . . ." Her expression intensified. "Someone purposely . . . they poisoned him . . . and then . . . he *expired* . . . and . . . fell . . . ?"

Glen shrugged.

"Who on earth would . . . ?" Jean asked.

"The funny thing is that the FBI wouldn't let Bob file a report. Apparently the state and city cops are out of the loop. And after the autopsy, they hustled the body off to the airport before Bob even had a chance to clean up the mess."

"Clean up what mess, Daddy?" Ruby wanted to know. She and Keera were standing in the doorway, dolls in hand.

Jean asked brightly, "How about a cookie, girls? Chocolate chip."

The ruse worked. "Yeah!!!"

As Jean arranged cookies on a plate, Glen gestured toward the living room. Ray followed him grudgingly. It was becoming obvious that Glen was right. Something was amiss. Maybe several somethings. A man with dual identities who worked for a high-tech corporation, and possibly the State Department, committing suicide . . . That was strange enough. But having Feds descend like scavenger birds, taking control of the matter, seemingly doing their best to keep a lid on things . . . That was downright suspicious. Factor in an express autopsy and a victim with toxin coursing through his veins . . . This thing had the makings not only of a true puzzle but of a jurisdictional nightmare.

Safely out of the children's earshot, Glen whispered, "You thinking homicide?"

"Maybe. Or maybe he took the poison voluntarily. To make sure the suicide attempt worked. Think about it," Ray said. "What if the fall didn't kill him? What if it left him in a wheelchair for the rest of his life? He wanted to make sure that didn't happen. So he downed some poison."

Glen scowled at this. "That's a lot of trouble, just to die. Why not go back to your hotel room and take the poison? You could pass away in bed."

It was a valid point. Cox's means of killing himself didn't make much sense.

"I never did like the suicide idea," Glen confessed. "A man doesn't do that right after landing a big deal. He celebrates by getting blasted maybe. Not by bidding the cold cruel world goodbye from a chair lift." He shook his head at the mental image. "That must have been a Dear John letter we found. And the plane reservations . . . I'd say he was planning to make a speedy exit when someone stopped him. Either that or—"

Ray raised a hand in surrender. "You sold me already." After a pause, he asked, "So who would want to murder Cox?"

"His wife?" Glen shot back with a smug grin. "He was about to run out on her. And according to Ehrlich, he wasn't exactly a candidate for husband of the year."

"She may well have wanted to put arsenic in his coffee on numerous occasions. But, seriously, who would actually do it, and why?"

In the absence of an answer, they both stared at the carpet. Down the hall, Jean was explaining the rules to a junior version of Monopoly to the girls. Ray's heart sunk. Monopoly? The game that lasted forever? Keera would never want to leave.

"Maybe it has something to do with the agreement they just signed," Glen said.

"Maybe. Or the fact that Cox was working for the State Department under another name." Ray closed his eyes and massaged the lids. "If he's even the right guy."

"What do you mean?"

"The State Department has zillions of employees. Their Richard Gleary might not be our Richard Gleary."

"How can we find out?"

"I doubt that we can, especially now that the Feds are in a frenzy. The files are probably locked up tight."

"Then that leaves us with the Suntron/Fukutomi agreement." Glen stroked his face as if he had a beard. "Let's have a talk with them."

"With who?"

"Fukutomi. See if they can help us fill in the gaps."

Gaps, Ray thought, was a bit of an understatement. More like canyons. "The Feds have probably already questioned them and instructed them not to discuss the case."

Ignoring this bit of pessimism, Glen said, "At the very least they can explain what their company does and what this contract means. That could be important."

"Only to someone working the case. And we're not."

Glen slumped at this. "We should be. I am the sheriff of Girdwood. As such, I feel a certain responsibility to look into a possible homicide in my own backyard. As a law enforcement officer, I feel a responsibility to get at the truth. Don't you?"

"No. I'm on vacation."

Laughing, Glen linked his fingers together. "As a personal favor, go with me to talk to Fukutomi. It won't take long. And seriously, Ray, I really think we're supposed to do this. I've got this feeling." He tapped his chest.

"Heartburn?"

"Come on . . ."

Sighing, Ray asked, "What makes you think they'll bare their souls to us? We're American cops. *Native* American cops. They're Japanese nationals."

"I've just got this sense. Call it a gut instinct. They'll talk."

Ray almost laughed. Glen had never worked a bona fide police investigation, yet he had a gut instinct about how this one would go down. In a last ditch effort to weasel out, Ray added, "You know, I did promise Keera a bike ride this afternoon."

"Hey, no problem. I understand completely," Glen sympathized. "Being a father has to come before being a policeman. You get those priorities out of line and you pay a terrific price." He started for the kitchen. "I can talk to Fukutomi myself, I guess."

They found Keera, Ruby, and Jean at the table, hunched over the colorful board game. Keera rolled and advanced her piece a space farther than the dots on the die.

"You got a three, Keera," Jean told her helpfully. "One, two, three . . ."

"What do I win?"

"You got a Chance card." Jean glanced at Ray and Glen. "What's up?"

"Keera," Ray said gently. "About our bike ride . . ."

"I don't wanna do that right now, Daddy," she said in a very grown-up tone.

"I have some work to do," Ray tried again, "but if you don't want me to—"

"It's okay, Daddy." She proudly set a miniature building on the square marked Video Arcade. "I'm not ready to go yet. I'm having fun."

"You're sure? Because I promised you that ride and—"

"If you fall on my space," she told Ruby, "you have to pay me money!"

"I know," Ruby said glumly.

"We'll be fine," Jean assured them.

"I'll get my keys," Glen said, obviously pleased.

Ray checked his watch: 2:27. His vacation was racing past unchecked and he seemed impotent to stop it. He could have stayed in Barrow and had this much fun. At least back home there weren't many deaths. No false IDs, circling Fibbies, high-tech corporations, closed files, poison . . . What a headache.

"Okay . . ." Glen called from the living room.

"See you in a little while," Ray said.

Keera didn't respond. She was busy trying to figure out who got what when she passed Go *and* landed on Ruby's square.

"Have fun," Ray told them, certain that he would not be missed.

As he and Glen stepped out the front door, they encountered a cool, damp afternoon. The bright sun had been eclipsed by a bank of clouds that cut the sky in two. The eastern half was a pale, anemic blue, the western half shrouded in a silvery gray bunting that promised rain. Awakened by the change in weather, mosquitoes swarmed the porch in a thick fog.

They trotted to the Camry and Glen fumbled with the keys, trying to hurry. "I don't know why Jean locks it out here."

Ray slapped at mosquitoes with one hand, shooed them away with the other. When the locks finally popped, he scrambled inside.

"You think they're thick now," Glen said, "wait till later, when it starts to drizzle." He twisted the key and the Toyota purred. Backing out, they started for the main road. "I never could understand how those things make it through the winter."

Shaking his head, Ray grunted, "You got me."

They slowed at the road and Glen waited for a break. The stream of traffic, both up and down the hill, was unbroken for a half mile: cars, campers, pickups, RVs . . .

Thirty seconds later, Glen punched the pedal and the Camry darted across a narrow gap in the highway-bound vehicles. A horn sounded and one of the drivers waved a single digit at them.

Glen waved back, smiling broadly. "Bless you too."

"I don't think those were blessings he was grumbling at us," Ray said.

Glen laughed at this. "How a person acts when he's behind the wheel of a car reflects the condition of his heart."

"So your heart is . . . crazy?"

Another laugh. "Basically. Jean says I'm a nut. I take that as a compliment."

You would, Ray thought.

The parking area at the lodge was overflowing: cars parked along the shoulder of the main road, newcomers trolling the lot for spaces.

"Can I use your phone?" Ray asked.

Glen produced it from a jacket pocket. "Calling Barrow?"

Ray dialed the number and pushed send.

"I was going to suggest that you ask your people to do a little more digging for us."

Ray frowned at this. It was precisely what he had in mind. Which was frightening. He and Glen were starting to think alike.

"Barrow Po-lice," a male voice answered.

"Billy Bob? It's Ray."

"Wall, howdy there, partner. How's yer vacation goin'?"

"Great . . ." Ray groaned. "Listen, is Betty around?"

"Naw. She's off this afternoon. Thank she had herself some kinda appoint-ment."

"How about the captain?"

"Sure thang. Hold on."

There was a clank. Apparently Billy Bob still hadn't

mastered the hold button. Ray could hear boots clomping down the tiled hallway, toward the captain's office.

Rounding a bend in the road, Glen slowed. Cars were parked at odd angles along the shoulder and on the road itself, leaving only a single lane to pass through. "What the . . . Oh . . . the Bullwinkle Show." A dozen people were congregated on the west side of the road, many bearing Instamatics and camcorders. Fifty yards away, across a flooded marsh, a pair of moose were assaulting a willow tree, stripping leaves from the branches and chewing contentedly. A trio of kids had started wading in their direction.

Rolling down the window, Glen warned them off. "Hey! Get back from there."

The kids looked at him for a long moment before continuing on their quest.

"Get out of there!" Glen yelled. He fished his badge out.

Ray was about to make a snide comment when someone picked up the phone. "Who dis?"

"Lewis? It's Ray. I'm holding for the captain."

The line erupted in laughter. "You wanna be punish?"

"Huh?" Ray had known Lewis most of his life, yet still had trouble with the guy's thick, sometimes unintelligible pidgin English.

"Captain's bear-mad with you, Ray."

"Mad? Why?"

"He gots da Fed cops on his back. Day be gettin' upset with you."

"The Feds have been in touch with the captain?"

"Some a-kinda obstrusion a-jus-tees. And da captain, he . . . Uh-oh . . ." There was a clatter as the phone hit something. Ray could hear urgent footsteps approaching.

"Attla?!" a voice bellowed.

"Yes, sir?"

"What in blazes are you doing down there? I thought you were on holiday?"

"I thought so too, sir."

➤➤ TWENTY-ONE ◄◄

"WHAT DID YOU do to get the Fibbies so hot and bothered?" the captain demanded.

"You got me."

"Those idiots," Glen muttered. He hopped out of the Jeep and started toward the tourists. The moose, distracted from their meal, were eyeballing the kids:

" 'You got me' doesn't cut it, Attla. What's going on?"

Ray watched as Glen urged the children back to their cars. "A man died down here yesterday. And I happened to find the body when I was mountain biking this morning."

Glen was shouting now, gesturing wildly, insistent that the kids get out of the marsh.

"What's the Federal angle?" the captain wanted to know.

"We don't know for sure."

"*We?*"

"I'm tethered to the local law down here. A sheriff named Redfern."

"Well, whoever he is and whatever it is you two have been doing, it's sure ticking off the folks at the Bureau. I'm in bed asleep this morning when I get this call from Anchorage. Some suit is busting his buttons, wanting an exhaustive report on Raymond Attla: where he lives, how long he's been on the force, whether or not he's trustworthy—"

"Trustworthy?"

"He made it sound like you were a fugitive, a featured perp on *America's Most Wanted*." The captain grunted. "My first response was to chew you out for sticking your nose where it shouldn't be. Except you're not like that. If this were Lewis we were talking about, or even Billy Bob. . . . But you know better than to mess with the Feds."

"Yes, sir," Ray acknowledged.

"My second response was to tell the Bureau where they could stick their attitude. This is Alaska, not D.C. Who do they think they are pulling rank on a local case, waking people up, asking all sorts of intrusive questions?" After denouncing the Bureau, he said, "I want to know what the heck this is all about."

Ray spent the next two minutes offering a thumbnail sketch of the case: the body, the suicide/Dear John note, the agreement with the Japanese, the presence of the FBI and of a big wheel in the mob, the airline tickets to Tokyo, the lab report revealing rat poison in the blood, the double ID, Richard Gleary connected to the State Department . . .

When he paused, the captain swore at the tangle of seemingly unrelated facts.

Outside, Glen had the kids back by the cars and was giving them and their parents a tongue-lashing, lecturing them on the dangers of approaching large mammals.

"Why is the FBI in on this?" the captain wanted to know. "Any theories?"

"Not really. Except that maybe it has something to do with Gleary working with the State Department. Or maybe with the agreement with Fukutomi."

"Elaborate."

Ray sighed and made an attempt, watching as one moose ambled over and held five cars and a dozen tourists at bay by standing on the shoulder of the road and blinking.

"Sounds like one heck of a mess," the captain summarized. "You think maybe this guy was some sort of spy?"

"No idea. It's possible . . . I guess. But at this point, just about anything is possible. We have nothing even resembling hard evidence. Not even any strong leads."

"Except for the autopsy report," the captain pointed out.

"Which we may never see and the Feds could deny even exists."

"This stinks," the captain mumbled. "It smells like a cover-up."

Ray agreed. It all seemed rather clandestine. The sudden appearance of Federal agents, phone calls checking into Ray's background, a closed-loop investigation . . . Who exactly was Michael Cox and why were the Feds swarming over his corpse?

No longer interested in the intruders, the moose moseyed back toward its partner, hooves sloshing through the bog.

"Does sound like a Federal matter though," the captain confessed. "Especially if it involves the State Department. Still, I don't like being kept in the dark."

"Join the club."

"It's bad enough having the naluaqmiut city cops in Anchorage and Fairbanks put us down. But the Feds. . . . They act like we're a bunch of aborigines."

"We are aborigines," Ray said. "Technically speaking."

This sent the captain into a profane diatribe about the evils of white society.

Glen returned to the Jeep, shaking his head. "Idiots. Lucky they didn't get killed."

Losing steam, the captain sighed heavily. "You were the first one on the scene, right? The first person to get a look at the body?"

"Yeah."

"Must be why they're interested in you. Did you pat the guy for personal effects?"

"Yeah. That's how I learned he had two identities."

"Was there anything else?" the captain wondered. "Money? Drugs? Documents dealing with national security?"

Ray paused, recalling the envelope and the square, thin object it held.

"The Fibby that got me out of bed wanted to know whether you'd filed a report and whether you recovered anything from the body. He seemed pretty focused. I got the feeling he was after something specific."

"I did find . . ." Ray felt a knot form in his throat. He pulled the cellular away from his ear and examined it critically. Was it possible that a van full of FBI agents was parked nearby, the inhabitants sipping bad coffee as they recorded and took notes on this conversation? Probably not. Still, he had just blabbed everything he knew about a Federal investigation on an open, cellular line that any jerk with a radio scanner could pick up.

"What? What did you find?!" the captain's tinny voice demanded.

"Nothing. That's it. Just the ID. Did I mention I'm in Glen's Toyota? It's his wife's car, and I'm using her flip phone. Her *cellular*."

"What? Who gives a rat's—Oh . . . Oh . . . ! Okay." His tone implied that he understood the problem. After another sigh, he said, "Okay . . . Here's the deal. This is a Federal case. Plain and simple. You stay out of it. Got that?"

"Yes, sir."

"That's an order. The Barrow PD would never dream of obstructing an FBI investigation. They can handle it without any help from the peanut gallery."

"Right." Ray sighed. The about-face was abrupt, wholly unbelievable. Even the most inattentive eavesdropping ears would catch the shift. The captain was a lousy liar.

After another thirty seconds of faint praise for the Bureau, the captain said in a tone of friendly greeting, "Talk to you later. Paqitichit."

"Paqitichit," Ray replied, letting the captain know that he understood. In Inupiaq, paqitichit meant to find out or to discover something hidden, especially someone's guilt.

"What's the story?" Glen asked. "Are we in trouble?"

Ray hesitated, unsure whether to tell Glen that they had just been issued a coded mandate to pursue the case in earnest. "Not exactly. But we're supposed to butt out," he said, for the benefit of any listeners. If someone could cut the brakes on the Wagoneer, why not bug the Camry? When Glen started to object, Ray waved him off and put a finger to his lips. He found a pad in the glove compartment and used a short pencil to scribble a note: *We're on the job. Car could be bugged.* "Understand?"

Glen nodded, mouth agape. He scrutinized the interior of the Camry, squinting at the roof, dash, floorboard . . . as if a microphone planted by the FBI would be easy to spot. Finally he shifted into gear and they rolled through the vehicles that were still littering the edge of the road. The moose had retreated into the brush and a half-dozen camera-clad nature lovers were plodding into the marsh. Glen snorted at them. "I'll probably get a call in a few minutes to come back and scoop some flattened tourist off the tundra."

The phone buzzed and Ray flipped it open. "Sheriff Redfern's office."

"Raymond?"

"Betty? How'd you get this number?"

A deep laugh betrayed her husky Athabascan frame. "I try to keep my eye on you, Raymond Attla. I called the number you left and got Jean. She sounds like a nice lady."

"She is," Ray agreed. "What's up?"

"I'm worried about you, Raymond." Her tone had shifted radically to one of grave concern. "I talked to my friend in Seattle."

"Yeah. I know," Ray said. "Thanks. That was a big help."

"No. I mean I talked to her again. This time she called me. From a pay phone."

Ray sighed, trying to figure out a way to tell Betty their conversation might not be confidential, without actually saying as much. "Is that right?"

"To warn me."

"Warn you? About what?"

"About this Richard Gleary business. Somehow her supervisor found out that she was checking into it and she nearly lost her job. And he knew that she had talked to me. She thinks they're tracing all outgoing calls. Pretty crazy, huh?"

Almost as crazy as bugging a sheriff's wife's car. "Yeah."

"The worst part is that you're the man of the hour. According to my friend, your name is on the lips of every federal agent from here to the State Department."

Ray stared out the window, considering this. They were approaching the hotel. In his present mood, the structure seemed threatening, out of tune with its environment: glaring metal and glass, harsh slabs of concrete.

"She also told me . . . Now you need to keep this under your hat . . ."

Right, he thought. On an unsecured line. "Betty, we're not working this case. It's Federal. I just talked to the captain about it. We washed our hands of the whole mess."

"You still need to know this, honey."

"Can I call you back?" he tried. "From *another* phone?"

"It's about an envelope," she continued. "Apparently the FBI is looking for—"

"Betty, can't this wait?"

"No. This envelope is very important. My friend wasn't sure why, but—"

"Listen, I gotta go—"

"And they think this Gleary might have had the envelope with him when he died."

"Hmph . . ." Ray grunted. There seemed to be no point in trying to head her off.

"*And,* it wasn't on the body when the FBI took possession in Anchorage. *And,* since you were the first one on the scene, they think—"

"Oh, you gotta be kidding."

"I'm serious, Raymond. You could be in some trouble."

Since Betty hadn't taken any of his hints, he decided that this was an opportune time to relay some misinformation to any and all eavesdroppers. "When I found the body, I checked for vitals, then frisked it. All I found was ID. Thanks to your friend, that's been ironed out. This Gleary has something to do with the State Department. Now it's up to the Feds to untangle things. As far as I'm concerned, the entire matter is ancient history."

"Whatever you say, Raymond. But you watch yourself. You hear me?"

"Yes, ma'am."

"See you back here on Monday, okay?"

"Yes, ma'am."

When he hung up, Glen asked him, "Who was that? Your mother?"

"Basically," Ray said. Though only fifteen years his senior, Betty was the maternal type, mother to five children of her own, as well as to the entire Barrow Police Department. Like most mothers, Betty worried too much. Unfortunately, like most mothers, she was right a good deal of the time. And this was one of those times, Ray decided. The Feds were a rough bunch, especially when they were racing to contain something or cover someone's tracks. Or find a missing envelope.

Glen found a spot near the hotel entrance and they climbed out of the Camry. Slamming the driver's door, he activated the alarm system. When it had chirped happily, he stepped to Ray's side, leaned toward him, and whispered confidentially, "What's going on?"

"I wish I knew." This obviously didn't satisfy the sheriff. "Let's go find out." They walked along the sidewalk and under the carport, toward the entrance. They were ten yards away when two doormen sprang from chairs hidden in matching alcoves and hurried to welcome them.

Ray watched, studying the smiling faces as the men pulled the brass-handled doors back in perfect unison. Could these guys be FBI? Informants? Snitches? Spies? He blew air at the outlandish idea and shook it off. Talk about paranoid.

➤➤ TWENTY-TWO ◄◄

"How should we handle this?" Glen asked as they started across the lobby.

"Hey, this was your idea, Sheriff."

Glen sighed. "What's our authority? I mean, we can't say we're involved in a Federal investigation. What if they won't talk to us?"

Without commenting, Ray paused to pluck a courtesy phone from its wall mount.

"What are you doing?"

Ray asked the receiver, "Could you tell me what room Jack Ehrlich is staying in, please." A moment later he grimaced at the floor. "He did? Are you sure? What time?"

"What?" Glen wanted to know.

"He checked out," Ray whispered. "Two-thirty?" Ray glanced at his watch. "But it's just now two-thirty . . ." His voice trailed off as he gazed across the lobby and spotted Ehrlich. He was standing near the counter, hemmed in by suitcases, an overcoat slung over his shoulder. Though facing the main entrance, his path had been blocked by two men. Ray recognized the dark blue suits. Fibbies.

Replacing the phone, he directed Glen's attention with a thumb.

"Wonder where he thinks he's going?" Glen asked.

"Let's find out."

As they approached, Glen noted, "He looks nervous."

Actually, Ray thought, he looked guilty, like a perp who had been caught red-handed and would now be facing a long prison term.

When Ehrlich saw them, an expression of relief swept his face. "Hey, guys!"

The Fibbies turned in unison and regarded them with noncommittal stares. The taller of the two was fit, in his early fifties, with silver hair and a leathered face that implied wisdom. The other, a young, husky blond, was clutching a notepad.

"These are the guys you need to talk to," Ehrlich told them excitedly. "This guy," he said, patting Ray on the shoulder as if he were a long-lost pal, "he found the body. And this guy," he added, giving Glen's shoulder a squeeze, "he handled the recovery."

The blond recorded this dutifully as his partner asked, "Officer Raymond Attla?"

"Yes."

"We've been looking for you. We stopped by your condo twice."

"I've been out most of the day," Ray replied. The elder agent reminded him a little of Clint Eastwood. "As long as we're getting acquainted, mind telling me who you are?"

They produced badges mechanically and presented them at eye level.

"Special Agent Bailey," the blond said. He was a lefty, Ray realized, the outer edge of his hand black from being dragged through pencil lead.

"Special Agent in Charge Pool," the Eastwood look-alike said.

"FBI," Glen read. "We met some of your friends this morning."

The agents cut their eyes at each other. "*Our* friends?"

"Other FBI agents," Glen said. "But don't worry. We're minding our own business, just like you told us to."

Ray cringed. The line sounded canned, an obvious falsehood.

"Who did you talk to?" Pool asked. "What were their names?"

"Agents Randolph and Moore," Ray said.

After another puzzled glance at his partner, Pool asked, "Can you describe them?"

Bailey flipped to a new page and waited, pencil poised.

Shrugging, Ray said, "The man, Randolph, was about five-ten. Two hundred pounds. Brown hair. And the woman . . . She was maybe five-four, blond hair."

Pool shook his head. "The man doesn't ring a bell. And the woman . . . We don't have a female agent assigned to this case."

"What are you saying?" Ray wondered. "They weren't FBI?"

"We saw their ID," Glen testified. "It was real. Or, at least, it looked real."

"We'll look into it," Pool assured them. In a hushed, secretive tone, he told Bailey, "Make a note of that. Maybe State's playing games again."

Bailey nodded and scribbled.

"Officer Attla," Pool said, "you found the body. Is that correct?"

"Right."

"And the man was already dead, correct?"

"Right."

"I took the body down to the State Police," Glen volunteered.

"And you are?" Pool asked, as Bailey hurried to flip to a fresh page.

"Glen Redfern, sheriff of Girdwood."

Pool snorted at this. "They didn't tell us anything about a sheriff." He whispered to Bailey, "Make a note of that." He sniffed at Glen. "And you transported the body?"

Glen nodded. "And released it to the custody of the State Police."

Pool pursed his lips and nodded. Bailey wrote with renewed fury.

"We told all of this to your *partners* this morning," Ray said.

"In cases like this, we have to go over the facts again and again," Pool explained, as if Ray had never taken part in a police investigation. "It gets redundant."

And laborious, Ray thought.

"When you found the body," Pool asked, "could you tell if it had been . . . uh . . ." He paused, searching for the right word. "Compromised?"

"What do you mean?"

"What condition was it in?"

"He was dead. And had been for a while."

"Right, but had the body been moved or disturbed, that you could tell?"

Ray shook his head. "I'm not a medical examiner, but it looked to me like the guy had fallen, hit the ground, and stayed put until I found him."

"No sign of animal tracks or . . . footprints?"

"No."

"I assume you checked for ID."

"Yeah," Ray sighed. "He had a wallet: driver's license, family photos, a little cash, credit cards . . . The ID was all in the name of Gleary. Richard Gleary."

Pool nodded slowly. Next to him, Bailey scrambled to keep up.

"Anything else on the body? Watch, passport, keys . . ."

"Yes, yes, and no," Ray answered.

"Anything else?"

Anything, Ray decided, meant the envelope. He hesitated. If the last set of Fibbies had been bogus, why not these jokers? Until he knew the players and the rules of the game, it seemed safer to feign ignorance. "Not that I recall."

"No papers or letters on . . ."

Ray shook his head. "And everything I did find, I left on the body." He paused, then emphasized, "*Everything.*" If they already knew about the envelope, he wanted to make certain they also knew that he hadn't lifted it.

"We did find a letter in his room," Glen said.

Pool reached into his coat pocket and produced an envelope. "This one?" He handed it to Ray.

After examining the hotel logo on the envelope, he dug out a single-page letter and nodded.

"We assumed it was a suicide note," Glen said.

"Maybe." Pool grunted. Reclaiming the letter, he slid it into his suit coat.

Until we found out about the poison, Ray thought. Did these guys know about that? Surely they did. The Bureau had snatched the coroner's report and buried it in a hole somewhere. The Bureau or some other government agency masquerading as Fibbies. Who else would be interested? The State Department? If Gleary was on the payroll, especially if he was involved in something less than scrupulous, they might have a vested interest in keeping his death as quiet as possible.

"So you've been in Michael Cox's room," Pool said. It wasn't a question, it was an observation, and Bailey entered this fact into the transcript of the meeting.

Watching him attack the paper with the mechanical pencil, Ray wondered if they were also taping the conversation. Probably not. Otherwise, why would this kid be knocking himself out to catch every word?

"When were you there?"

"This morning," Ray reported. "Around . . . ten?"

"Were you with them?" Pool asked Ehrlich.

Ehrlich, who had been standing there with the stupid, blank expression of someone under hypnosis, flinched when he realized the question was addressed to him. "Uh . . . Yeah. But . . . I didn't break in or anything. If that's what you mean. It was their idea," he said, accusing Ray and Glen with an index finger.

Pool frowned, as if he wasn't convinced. Looking to Glen, he asked, "Did you write up a report on his room?"

"Not yet. There really hasn't been time."

"Your buddies warned us off before we had a chance," Ray said. "And they didn't seem too interested in being brought up to speed, especially by two lowly local cops."

This drew another sniff from Pool. Bailey never missed a word.

"We went by standard procedures," Ray said. "We looked around, rummaged through his luggage, played with his computer, but didn't take anything out of the room."

"Nothing?"

"Oh, except for that file full of top-secret documents," Ray told them sarcastically.

Pool blinked sleepily at this and nudged Bailey, who was writing like mad. He then reached into an outer jacket pocket and withdrew a business card. "The number on here is our Seattle office. They'll page me."

Ray accepted it and stuck it into his wallet.

"Thanks for your help," Pool said without sincerity. "From here on out, this is a Federal case. Please respect that. Stick around. We may need you. Call if you remember anything else."

Ray nodded. These two weren't as bad as the first pair, but they were still Feds.

Pool turned abruptly and started for the exit. Bailey followed, bent over his pad.

When they had disappeared through the revolving door, Ehrlich gushed, "Thanks guys! You saved me. Those two were really putting the pressure on. They thought I had something to do with Mike's death. Or at least they made it seem that way."

Ray reached over and flicked an airline ticket protruding from Ehrlich's breast pocket. "Where you headed?"

His face flushed. "Back to San Francisco."

"I thought you said you'd be hanging around until we got this sorted out."

"Yeah . . . I know . . . But I got a call from the home office. From my boss."

"I thought Cox was your boss," Ray prodded.

"From my *new* boss. There's this big meeting he wants me to attend . . ." Ehrlich sighed heavily. "Listen, I'm as broken up over this as anyone. Mike was my friend. But . . . Life goes on. You know?" He shrugged. "Business is business. I have to disregard personal problems and do the job they pay me for."

"How noble of you," Ray observed.

"And right now, I'm being summoned back to San Francisco."

"I don't think that's such a good idea," Glen said.

"There's nothing I can do about it," Ehrlich concluded. He reached for his bags.

"Sure there is," Glen said. He deftly snatched the ticket from Ehrlich's pocket.

"Hey!"

"Just relax. I'm a chaplain. I specialize in dealing with people in crisis, grieving, on the verge of spiritual and emotional breakdowns."

Ehrlich made an awkward attempt to retrieve his ticket.

Dodging, Glen added, "And it's my professional opinion that you're unstable and should stay put for at least twenty-four hours."

When Ehrlich lunged again, Glen said, "Forty-eight hours? I can talk to your boss, give him my evaluation. Tell him you're reeling from the tragedy, in desperate need of a break."

Ehrlich sagged. After consulting his watch and swearing softly at the marble floor, he conceded. "I guess I could catch a flight in the morning. Maybe they could push the meeting back a day." He cursed again.

"Maybe you could watch your language," Glen said.

Swallowing another four-letter word, Ehrlich shook his head and waddled to the front desk to procure a room.

"I like the way you handled that," Ray said. "You really think he's losing it?"

Glen laughed. "No. But the way he's acting . . . mourning the loss of a close friend one minute, bugging out as if the hotel was on fire the next? Something's not right."

For the first time, Ray held out hope that Glen might one day evolve into a competent law enforcement officer. In this exchange he had displayed a certain knack, the kind good cops cultivate: an intuitive appreciation of human nature, for knowing when people are telling the truth, lying, hiding things . . .

"Besides," Glen added, "I still think I can get the guy to church."

So much for hope.

➤➤ TWENTY-THREE ➤➤

RAY WALKED TO an alcove of pay phones. He lifted one of the receivers and began fishing through his wallet. His long distance card was in there somewhere. After two front-to-back searches, he discovered it wedged between his Visa and a business card.

"Who're you calling?" Glen asked.

Ray ignored him. As he extracted the AT&T card, the business card followed, disengaged, and fluttered to the floor. He entered his code from the back of the card before bending to retrieve the card. Glen beat him to it.

"Why didn't you give this to those agents?" He handed it back.

Ray examined the card that the first pair of FBI agents had given him, then hung up the phone. "I forgot about it." It looked genuine: nice, crisp cardstock, embossed insignia, raised letters. He rummaged through his wallet until he found the card he had just received from Agent Pool. It was almost identical. Same seal, same font style, same layout, same Seattle address. But there was a name on one of the cards: Arbugus J. Pool. The other bore only a phone number.

Lifting the phone again, Ray reentered his long distance code and tried the number from the card the mystery agents had given them. He got a recording: "You have reached a number that has been disconnected or is no longer in service . . ."

"Since when does the Bureau have its lines disconnected?"

Glen shrugged. "Maybe it's an old card with an old number."

"Or maybe it's fake." He toggled the button until he got a dial tone, punched in his code again, and tried the number on Arbugus Pool's card. A monotone female voice answered. "Seattle office of the FBI. How may I direct your call?"

"I'm trying to reach Agent Moore."

"Moore?" After a brief pause, the woman replied curtly, "I'm sorry, but there's no one here by that name." She didn't sound sorry.

"How about Agent Randolph?"

Before he could tell her that he was calling from Girdwood, Alaska, she had him on hold and he was being treated to a bland, instrumental version of "I Write the Songs."

When the woman finally came back on the line, she was suddenly personable. "No, I'm sorry, sir. There's no one here by that name either. Are you certain they're based out of this office?"

"Actually, I'm not. Is there any way that you could track them down for me?"

"Certainly. Let me have your name and a number where you can be reached."

Ray considered this. He had already learned that the agents were not based in Seattle, as their card claimed. Leaving his name would only stir things up. Especially if the office was as nervous as Betty's friend claimed they were. "Uh . . . No. Thanks."

"It's no trouble!" the woman said with too much enthusiasm. "Just give me—"

He hung up on her.

"What did you find out?" Glen asked.

"That those two that gave us a hard time this morning

don't work for the FBI. At least not in Seattle." He frowned at his watch. "How long was that call?"

"Don't worry," Glen consoled. "It's Saturday. Weekend rates."

"I don't care how much it costs. I was wondering if they had time to trace it."

"Trace it?"

"When I mentioned those names, the receptionist put me on hold and when she came back, she sounded . . . different."

Glen squinted at him. "What do you mean?"

"She was friendlier. Glad to help. Maybe we spooked somebody."

"With the names?"

Ray shrugged. "Maybe they're trying to figure out who Moore and Randolph are too. I don't know." He shook his head and picked the phone back up.

"Now who are you calling? The State Department?"

"Why don't you go and see if you can set up a meeting with the folks from Fukutomi. Talk to the desk. Maybe they'll let us use one of the conference rooms."

Glen nodded and left to attend to the task.

On the line, an answering machine picked up. Betty's recorded voice informed him that she was unable to come to the phone. Which probably meant that she was over at her daughter's house, Ray guessed. Betty had become a grandmother just a month earlier.

He called information and got the number. When he dialed, a tired voice answered, "Hello?"

"Abby?"

"Yes?" She sounded dazed, as though she had just woken up.

"This is Ray Attla. I hope I didn't get you out of bed."

"Hi, Ray. No. You didn't. Little Jimmy has been doing that for you."

"Is that right?"

"How did you and Margaret ever survive?"

"It gets better," he promised. In truth, Keera had been

an easy baby, sleeping through the night at just two weeks and taking nice long naps during the day. "You'll make it. Hang in there. Is your mother there?"

"Yeah. Just a second." There was a clunk as she set the phone down. After another clunk, Betty said, "Raymond? What's wrong?"

"Nothing. I'm sorry to bother you again, but . . . I need another favor. I need you to call your friend in Seattle one more time to—"

"Huh-uh. I can't do that."

"Why not?"

"I told you already, honey. They're tightening the screws down there. She already put her job at risk by talking to me. I can't ask her to do that again."

"But, Betty, I just need to run a couple of names."

"What kind of names?" she asked suspiciously.

"Agents. Or . . . at least we thought they were agents. Now we're not sure. Just four names. It'll only take five minutes."

There was a long pause. "Tell you what I'll do," she groaned. "I'll access the Bureau's on-line system from the terminal here in Barrow. It's not exactly protocol, but . . . It's not illegal either. I can run the names for you myself. But if they don't turn up in the main file, end of the line. Got that?"

"Yes, ma'am."

"And if they somehow manage to follow my trail and figure out where the search originated, I won't hesitate to tell the captain that you requested it. Understand?"

"Yes, ma'am." He read her the names. "Call me when you're done. All right?"

"Okay."

"Thanks, Betty. I owe you."

"Big time." Her inflection changed. "Be careful, Raymond."

"I will."

He hung up just as Glen was returning from the desk.

"We can use Conference Room Two," he told Ray. "It's open until five."

"Great. What about Fukutomi?"

Glen nodded at the check-in desk where Ehrlich was leaning on an elbow, courtesy phone to his ear. "He's talking to them now."

Ray took a deep breath and let it out slowly. What an ordeal. Instead of spending time with his daughter, here he was working: investigating a death, jousting with the FBI, arranging an interrogative meeting with a Japanese corporation.

As they started for the desk, Ray caught a whiff of something. Coffee! For the first time he noticed a cart nestled in the bank of ferns that lined the fountain. A woman was standing behind it, working a machine that sent steam into the air. Ray veered toward the cart. If a bike ride was out, at least he could drown his sorrows in a cup of java.

The woman was just finishing with a man in a suit, handing him his change, as they reached the cart. "What'll it be, fellows?"

"One large coffee," Ray told her.

"Just plain coffee?" She seemed offended. The woman pointed across the atrium, toward a glass walkway. "You'll have to go to the restaurant."

Ray blinked at her, confused. "Don't you sell coffee here?"

"Espresso."

"I'll take a grande mocha valencia," Glen told her. "He'll have the same."

"Two grande mocha valencias," she repeated enthusiastically, setting to work. She emptied a plunger full of finely ground coffee, reloaded it. "Whipped cream?"

"No thanks." Glen looked to Ray.

"I just want a cup of black coffee."

"No whipped cream," Glen answered.

The woman poured milk into a steel pitcher, seated it beneath a narrow steel pipe.

"I assume you've had espresso?" Glen wondered as he watched her.

Ray nodded. "It's fine. But I like plain old coffee."

When the milk had been drawn to a thick froth, the woman pushed another button and the machine shrieked, spitting streams of black liquid into a pair of shot glasses. After pouring the shots into paper cups, she squirted them with chocolate and orange syrup, then spooned in the milk.

"Perfect," Glen remarked, handing her a ten-dollar bill. "Lots of calf slobber."

"Calf slobber . . . ?" Ray gazed at the foam over-flowing from the cup.

The woman was still making change when she looked over their shoulders and asked, "What'll it be, sir?"

"One Americana, one nonfat latte," a voice hissed.

The accent was heavy. New York, Ray guessed. He glanced back and found himself staring into the big, sad eyes of Ron Mancini.

"How's it going?" Mancini grunted. It was obvious that he didn't remember Ray.

"Hi." Ray turned back around and stepped aside, wait-ing as Glen counted and pocketed his change. Before he could finish, a rhythmic clicking echoed across the mar-ble floor and an instant later they were enveloped in a cloud of perfume.

"Did you miss me?" a shrill voice whined.

"You bet I did, baby."

Ray snuck another look and caught Mancini planting a long, wet one on his wife. She was wearing heavy makeup, spike heels, a different dress, this one so min-uscule as to border on obscene.

"If we can make this happen, baby," Mancini said in a throaty whisper, "you and me, we are gonna do some serious partying . . . all night long."

She giggled at this and slung a leg up around him like a contortionist. Mancini growled and pushed her long dark hair aside to nip at her neck. If these two didn't get to their room soon, Ray thought, the lobby would become the site of an X-rated porn show.

Mancini's hand moved south, giving his wife's derriere a massage. Ray was gawking at this when Glen chimed, "Like it?"

"Huh?"

"Your espresso."

"Oh . . ." Ray took a sip and grimaced as he burned his mouth. The "valencia" was too hot, too thick, too sweet, and suffered from a citrus aftertaste. "Yeah, it's great."

They left the lovers and met Ehrlich by the main desk.

"Conference Room Two. Ten minutes," he grumbled at them. "Do I have to be there?" His expression was pained, as if attending would be an especially painful form of torture.

"We'd appreciate it," Ray said.

Ehrlich muttered something under his breath, then sighed, "I gotta put my bags back in my room." He lifted them with exaggerated effort.

"How many of them are we meeting with?" Glen asked.

"Just one."

"Who is it?" Ray asked.

"Edward Fukutomi," Ehrlich told them as he started for the elevator. "The big kahuna himself."

➤➤ TWENTY-FOUR ◄◄

ACCORDING TO A young lady at the desk, the conference center was located on the north side of the hotel in a wing dedicated to special meetings and seminars. She described the complex in glowing terms, boasting that it had its own kitchen, library, theater, restaurant, copy services, video, computer, and teleconferencing equipment.

As they began the trek to the center, Ray decided that the entire hotel was an attempt to replicate the heavenly: a sort of rich-man's nirvana that bordered on gaudy opulence. Marble floors and expensive-looking paintings were one thing. But this: massive bronze sculptures, Oriental rugs, textured walls, stone columns, attendants stationed at every turn, and fountains . . . Ray had already counted four.

Nearing the nucleus of the building, he spotted another. This way by far the largest, spraying water twenty feet into the air in varying patterns. Above the mist was an expansive, circular opening that reached to a glass roof twenty-two stories above. Lined by hundreds of ornate, rod iron balconies, it made Ray feel woozy.

Spokelike halls ran away from the fountain bearing tasteful storefronts: furriers, jewelry, travel agent, salon . . .

A number of people were patronizing the businesses and the hall was thick with window shoppers. It was disorienting. Here in the bowels of the building, they could have been in New York or London or Rome.

They slowed at the intersection to allow a cart of mink coats to wheel past, then fell into a steady flow of foot traffic, all heading in the general direction of the conference center. As they neared the entrance, a grating laugh rose from somewhere ahead of them: a dull saw assaulting hardwood. Mrs. Mancini.

They passed beneath a tall arch that announced in huge, silver letters, their arrival at the Prince Hotel Conference Center. The woman cackled again. By walking on tiptoes, Ray managed to catch a glimpse of her hair swishing against her husband's shoulder. Positioned twenty yards ahead, they were mostly concealed by a cluster of businessmen.

At Conference Room One, the flow split: Asians entering the room off the rest, composed mostly of naluaqmiut, continuing on. Ray paused as they reached the first meeting room and stuck his head inside. Plush chairs had been set up in rows, facing a small, raised stage. A banner behind the podium read: FUKUTOMI ENTERPRISES—TOOLS FOR A NEW MILLENNIUM. There were about fifty people milling around.

"This is Room One," Glen pointed out helpfully.

Ray watched as the Mancinis greeted an elderly Asian man. The three of them seemed well acquainted: exchanging smiles, handshakes, the mood almost celebratory.

"We're in Room Two," Glen added.

"I know." The Asian man, a high-ranking executive, Ray guessed, ushered Ron and his lovely wife to a pair of seats on the stage itself. A man mounted the stage after them and took up position directly behind their chairs. It was Hat Trick Benny.

"What are you doing?" Glen asked impatiently.

Ray shook his head and started down the hall. "Trying

to figure out why Ron the Don Mancini is attending a Fukutomi meeting."

"Maybe he's a shareholder," Glen suggested.

"Maybe . . . But why would he be up on the stage like the guest of honor?"

"Why don't we ask Mr. Fukutomi?"

They separated themselves from the current of white males and stepped through the open door of Conference Room Two. It seemed larger than the first room. Probably because it was mostly empty: an expanse of open, low-pile gray carpet. Crooked towers of chairs were stacked along the back wall and less than half of the overhead lights were operating. Two men in coveralls and baseball caps were setting up a table on the darkened stage. Another man was kneeling in front of the riser, plugging cables into a panel of outlets.

Glancing to his left, Ray saw three chairs lined up in the shadows. Squinting, he realized that one of them was occupied. A figure sprang up to greet them. A young man. No. Not a young man, Ray thought, as the fellow hurried toward them, an enthusiastic smile plastered on his face. A kid. Some gofer sent to tell them that Mr. Fukutomi would be late or couldn't make it altogether. Fukutomi had probably been the guy back there palling it up with Mancini.

"Officer Attla? Sheriff Redfern?"

Frowning, Ray accepted the kid's hand, sizing him up. He was Asian, wearing a black, double-breasted suit. A little overdressed for a gofer. "Where's Mr. Fukutomi?"

"You're looking at him."

Ray almost laughed out loud. "Right . . . Where is he?"

The fresh young face bent into a mischievous grin. "Eddie Fukutomi." When neither of them responded to this, he added, "*Edward* Fukutomi, CEO of Fukutomi Enterprises, is my grandfather."

"Oh . . . okay . . ." Ray sighed. "When will your grandfather . . . ?"

"He's running a shareholders meeting down the hall. So . . . I'm it. But I'm the vice president of research and development." He glanced at Ray, then Glen, back to Ray. "I'm twenty-seven, and I've got a doctorate in artificial intelligence from MIT."

"Wow." Ray was impressed. Not so much at the degree, as at Eddie's age. He didn't look a day over twenty-one. His English was impressive too, no trace of an accent.

"I assume you're here about the . . . mishap."

Ray nodded, wondering about the kid's choice of words. *Mishap* . . . In his mind, a mishap was usually a minor accident, a fender bender at an intersection. Death—self-inflicted, accidental, or purposely imposed—seemed well beyond "mishap" territory.

"Such a tragedy," Eddie lamented.

Ray nodded again. *Tragedy* . . . That was more like it.

"Show him the sketch," Glen suggested.

Digging the drawing out of his pocket, Ray presented it to Eddie. "Is this him?"

Sighing, Eddie whispered, "Yes."

"How well did you know Mr. Cox?" Ray asked as he folded the sketch.

"Mike?" He laughed sadly. "He and I were like this for eight months." He crossed his fingers. "We talked a dozen times a day, e-mailed each other silly."

"What was it you were working on?"

"Mike and I made this deal happen," Eddie boasted. "My people came up with the technology, Mike's people came up with the marketing strategy. He pushed it through Suntron. I green-lighted it for Fukutomi."

"So you have the power to approve contracts and agreements?"

"I have the power to do anything I please," Eddie admitted.

"What about Mr. Fukutomi?"

"Grandfather?" Eddie rolled his eyes. "I respect him very much. He is an honorable man. A great man. He built our company with nothing but small change, lofty ideas, and hard work. He is highly revered in our country and around the world. But his time is passing. And he knows this. That's why he puts such trust in me. He knows that I belong to the new breed and he gives me the authority to do what must be done."

"Which is?"

"We must look to the future. We cannot be satisfied with past success. We must set our eyes on the horizon and march boldly into the next millennium. Our company holds the keys to the world marketplace in the palm of its hand."

Eddie reminded Ray of a motivational speaker who had once visited Barrow to convince the borough council to modernize the sewage system: lots of energy, enthusiasm, and vague, inspirational language. Why wasn't this guy down the hall, giving a rousing speech to the stockholders?

"Forgive me." Eddie blushed. "I'm very excited about this project."

"What exactly is the project?" Ray asked.

Eddie dug into a suit pocket and produced a gold square the size of a postage stamp. "This." He gazed at it longingly before tossing it to Ray.

Catching it, Ray held it up to the light. "What is it?"

"A computer chip," Glen told him.

"Not just any computer chip." Eddie beamed.

Taking the chip, Glen squinted at it. "A Pentium Pro?"

Eddie laughed. "It is to a Pentium what a Cray is to a slide ruler."

"Is that right?" Ray took the chip back from Glen, hoping someone would explain what a Cray was. It sounded like a type of fish.

"The microchip you are holding is going to revolutionize the world."

Turning it over in his palm, Ray grunted. "Really?" It didn't look revolutionary. It looked like a cheap piece of gold aluminum foil. "What makes it so special?"

Eddie's eyes lit up. "Ah . . . that is our secret." He smiled like the Cheshire Cat. "But I can tell you that this microchip, the NVSC, will enable a single mainframe to perform in excess of two trillion calculations per second." He paused, allowing this to sink in. "We are talking about massive parallel computing, petaflop operations, at a tenth of the cost of Intel's supercomputer speed record holder. You can imagine the implications."

Actually, Ray couldn't. "What would those be, in layman's terms?"

Eddie leaned toward them and in a conspiratorial tone said, "*Star Trek.*"

"You mean like the holodeck?" Glen asked.

Eddie's smile, already straining his cheeks, somehow grew. "Exactly."

"What's a holodeck?" Ray finally asked.

"The advanced computer on the *Enterprise,*" Eddie explained. "It could speak, make complex calculations, even learn."

Glen took the chip back. "This thing will do all that?"

"Eventually," Eddie assured them. "Basically, it will enable us to do real simulations of the physical world for the first time, a quadrillion operations per second." Staring at the ceiling, he told them, "Simulations of nuclear reactions and explosions . . . Analysis of DNA strands . . . The applications to scientific research will be unlimited. The Internet will undergo a full-blown renaissance. All current methods of recording, communication, and presentation will be rendered obsolete. At long last, AI will be a reality."

"AI?" Ray asked.

"Artificial intelligence," Glen translated. He shrugged in response to Ray's puzzled look. "Jean and I watch *Deep Space Nine.*"

"I have dreamed of constructing smart-robotic droids

since I was a child," Eddie said. "Finally, after a decade of research and development, I am being afforded that chance." Closing his eyes, he announced, "Life on planet Earth will never be the same. From this point forward, machines will supplant man."

"Like the *Terminator* movies?" Glen wondered.

"Exactly!" Eddie shouted. "Except instead of fighting the machines, we will be using them to fight for us. Several governments have already recognized the potential: AI bombs that learn and react in flight, AI aircraft that can engage in strikes without human pilots, AI tanks rolling across the battlefield, AI soldiers manning the bunkers . . . In the next half century, battles will be waged without risk to human lives." Sighing, he retrieved the chip. "This, gentlemen, represents a major shift, a quantum leap forward. It will radically alter the nature of science, industry, entertainment, and warfare. In other words, it will change civilization forever."

Eddie, Ray decided, was nothing if not high-minded. Change civilization forever? "Getting back to Mr. Cox . . ."

"Right . . ." Eddie's countenance fell. "Tragic . . ."

"Did you see him last night?"

"We sat at a table down the hall here and signed an agreement."

"What sort of agreement?" Ray was curious to hear Eddie's version.

"Suntron will be handling the licensing agreements with American companies. For instance, they'll be working out deals with Hewlett Packard, MCI, AT&T . . . And believe me, deals will be forthcoming. As soon as this jewel hits the World Computer-Tech Exposition next month, the frenzy will begin. Suntron will be setting up additional factories here in the States to produce the chip. We predict that it will take five to seven years at full manufacturing capacity just to fill the orders we receive in the next six weeks. We already have contracts with IBM, Microsoft, Apple, and a dozen others."

"What about the U.S. government?" Ray asked.

"Uh . . . I'm not at liberty to discuss that at this time."

"I see." Ray considered this. Was the State Department a customer too?

"Research and development on something like this is extremely cost-intensive," Eddie explained. "It requires not only private funding, but grants."

"U.S. grants?" Ray pushed.

"I am not at liberty to divulge the identities of our investors."

"I understand." Was the American government helping fund Eddie's little chip? If so, why? Why would the Feds pour money into a Japanese corporation? Why not support a home-grown company and try to beat them to the punch? Maybe Fukutomi was too far ahead. "What's the return?"

"The satisfaction of contributing to a technological breakthrough," Eddie explained. "Helping to make a better tomorrow."

"And making big bucks in the process?" Ray asked.

"That too."

"How big?"

"Again, I am not at liberty to discuss the details."

The line reminded Ray of the FBI's handy-dandy "national security" catch-all. "What about Ronald Mancini? What does he have to do with all of this?"

"Ron?" Eddie grinned. "That's a funny story."

Ray waited, not convinced that the punch line would be all that humorous.

"I never heard of the guy until two weeks ago. Out of the blue, he called Grandfather. He asked a few questions. The conversation lasted maybe twenty minutes. The next day, he snatches up thirty percent of Fukutomi's stock."

"Thirty percent?" Ray thought aloud.

"That's right," Eddie told them. "Aside from Grandfather and myself, Mr. Mancini is now our largest stockholder."

➤➤ TWENTY-FIVE ◀◀

"YOU DO KNOW that Mancini has ties to organized crime," Ray pointed out. Ties was the nicest word he could think of to describe the mobster's relationship to the Mafia.

"Sure," Eddie said, nodding. "We know about his past. But he's a legitimate businessman now. Which is why this project is perfect for him. It affords him the opportunity to contribute to society rather than take from it."

Ray squinted at this. Ron the Don turning over a new leaf? A known Family man investing in high-tech R&D? What next? A Web site: www.cosanostra.com?

"Stranger things have happened," Glen said.

"Getting back to Mr. Cox . . ." Ray said. "You were at the meeting with him last night? Is that right?"

Eddie nodded, frowning.

"Did you notice anything odd about his behavior?"

"No. We signed the contract and adjourned to celebrate."

"But Cox didn't celebrate with you?"

"No. He went to his room. I think he was drained. We all were."

"And that's the last time you saw him?"

Another nod. "Tragic . . ."

"Would you say that Cox had been depressed?"

"Not that I noticed. Mike was a player. Always coming up with new angles."

"Did he have any enemies, that you're aware of?"

Eddie shook his head. "Everybody liked Mike. Especially the ladies."

"Did Mr. Cox have one of those?" Ray asked, pointing at the chip in Eddie's hand.

"Mike? No. He had all the literature and test results. But he didn't need a prototype. Outside of myself and maybe three of my lab rats, no one has access to these. And this one is just for show. It isn't real. The microchips don't leave our complex in Osaka until we ship. Except for trade shows and demos. And then only under tight security."

Pocketing the faux chip, Eddie checked his watch. "Now, if you'll excuse me, gentlemen, I'm due at the stockholders meeting." He shook their hands energetically. As he was turning to leave, Ehrlich wandered through the door looking lost.

"Mr. Fukutomi," he grunted.

"Ehrlich." Eddie paused and sighed, "A real tragedy. We're all at a loss. Mike will be missed." Before Ehrlich could respond, Eddie fled the room.

"How'd it go?" Ehrlich asked.

"What happened to you?" Ray wanted to know. Ehrlich not only reeked of alcohol, but seemed to have aged ten years since the lobby.

"I stopped off for a quick one." He closed his eyes to Ray's glare. "Don't start with me. I've had a tough day."

"Join the club," Ray grumbled. "What's the problem?"

"*Problems.* Plural."

"Want to talk about it?" Glen asked, sounding more like a chaplain than a sheriff.

"It's . . . complicated." After a pause, he said, "Fukutomi is threatening to walk."

"They are?" Ray said. "Eddie sounded pretty happy with the arrangement."

"He always puts a good spin on things," Ehrlich said gloomily. "He's a smooth operator. But this business with Mike . . . The contract is still binding, but . . ."

"But what?"

"But Mike was our go-to man on this deal. He had an inside track with the Fukutomi people. He and little Eddie were tight. As close to being friends as you can get in a multinational trade agreement. Without Mike . . ." He sank into one of the chairs. "Fukutomi can sit on the deal until it expires, if they want to. It would delay release in some markets for up to a year. But they could definitely cut us out of the loop."

"It'll work out," Glen consoled, placing a hand on his shoulder. "You just have to be patient. And have faith." The buzz of Glen's cellular cut the sermonette short. He fumbled to answer it, then handed the phone to Ray. "It's for you."

"Hello?"

"Raymond, what have you gotten yourself into?" Betty's motherly voice asked.

"I'm not sure, Betty. But I get the feeling you're about to tell me."

"First you're interested in some State Department guy. Now you've got me tracking down spooks."

"Hang on, Betty," he said, cutting her off. "Let me call you right back." Ray flipped the phone shut and started into the hall, searching for a pay phone. There was something called a "communications center" right next door to the conference room: fax machines, e-mail access, scanners, copiers . . . "Got any phones?" he asked the attendant.

The young woman motioned toward a bank of stalls. Ray sank into a padded chair and dialed Betty's daughter.

Betty picked up on the first ring. "You got me chasing spooks," she blurted. "The names you gave me, the first two—Pool and Bailey—they're FBI out of Seattle. I tracked them down with no problem. But the other two, they don't work for the Bureau."

"I assumed that much."

"When I ran those names, I didn't get anything. So, despite my better judgment, I called my friend in Seattle. I shouldn't have. But . . . Anyway, she came up with zip too. Until she tried linking them with your Mr. Gleary. Then she hit a security block."

"Great . . ." Ray groaned.

"A block at the interface with the Langley databank."

"The what?"

"Langley. As in the home of the Central Intelligence Agency."

"What are you saying, Betty? The names I gave you belong to CIA agents?"

"Or spies, international terrorists, desk clerks, intelligence officers, parking attendants . . . I'm just telling you they're in the CIA database. And I don't know about you, honey, but that makes me a little nervous."

In the absence of any more appropriate response, Ray cursed.

"You got that right, honey. And my friend in Seattle could be in it deep. She was careful not to break any rules, but if someone finds out, especially given the current climate of paranoia . . . You just better watch yourself, Raymond."

"Thanks, Betty. I will. Talk to you later." He hung the phone up and went back to the conference room. Glen had one hand on Ehrlich's back and was praying for him.

Ray had half a mind to join in. With the FBI watching his every move, or at least, looming in the background, and now the suggestion that the CIA might somehow be involved, he felt the sudden urge to elicit protection from on high. Factor in a mobster who was cozying up to a high-tech company that was at least remotely involved in a death, and you had the makings of a mess. A dangerous, quite possibly life-threatening mess. He wasn't sure who intimidated him the most: the Feds, the secret agents from Langley, Hat Trick Benny . . .

Instead of falling to his knees, Ray nudged Glen. "You about done?"

Glen nodded and gently removed his hand. "Amen."

Ehrlich raised his head. "I feel . . . better."

"Never fails," Glen explained. He turned to Ray. "What's next?"

"Good question."

"Should we have a talk with this Mancini guy?" Glen wondered. "It does sound a little strange: a mafioso type getting into bed with a computer company."

"Happens all the time," Ehrlich reported. "You'd be surprised at who invests in what. There's dirty money all over corporate America."

"Still, since he's here," Glen said, "and Cox was the go-to man in the deal with Fukutomi . . . Maybe there's some connection. The least we could do is—"

"No." Ray grunted. "First of all, we haven't ruled out suicide."

"It could have been . . ." Glen objected.

Before he could say "murder," Ray affirmed, "*Could have been*. But we don't know. Second, no matter how strange it seems, Mancini is a bona fide stockholder. We don't have just cause to interrogate."

"I'm not suggesting grilling him in a smoke-filled room. Just a talk."

"If it's in an official capacity, no matter how casual, we'll be crucified," Ray assured him. "Mancini has a whole gallery of lawyers who would like nothing better than to slap us with harassment."

"Harassment? For talking to the guy?"

"He'll decline comment," Ray said. "Then he'll call his people. Next thing you know, we'll be in court trying to explain to a judge why we were interrogating Mancini in a death-by-suicide case. A Federal case, no less. And his lawyers will be right. There is no justification, no link. He wasn't a witness and isn't a suspect. Our only reason for singling him out is that he's a mobster." He shook his head. "They'll kick our butts, maybe even take our badges."

Glen scoffed at this. "What are you, a Mancini expert or something?"

"I saw an exposé about him on *Dateline*. It was about how a couple of New York beat officers lost their jobs for asking Mancini to move his car out of a fire lane."

"I saw that!" Ehrlich said, rising. "Yeah . . . These two poor cops were fired because Mancini's lawyers proved that they were harassing him. Lost their pensions too."

"Still want to talk to him, Sheriff?" Ray asked.

"I guess we could get by without it." Glen paused. "What about Sheri? The girl who was working the top of the lift. We should talk to her, for sure."

Ray frowned. "Hans said she was off somewhere competing in a race."

"The Bird. It's tonight. At nine."

Ray glared at his watch. It was after four and he couldn't think of any other people to talk to or places they needed to visit. The major players had been questioned, the puzzle pieces shuffled and reshuffled, to no avail. The case was on hold until something significant broke. And there was a good chance that nothing would. In the meantime, if he could convince Glen to take him and Keera back to the condo, they could spend the evening playing, relaxing . . . engaged in activities that were conspicuously absent from their vacation thus far. Later he and Glen could drop in on that race. After that, he hoped, the whole matter could be left in the capable hands of the FBI, and the rather suspicious death of Michael Cox, aka Richard Gleary, would quickly fade to an unpleasant memory.

"Whatever shall we do till then?" Ray jokingly asked.

"Actually, I've got something," Glen submitted.

Ray started for the door before the sheriff could share his idea. A half dozen more workers clad in khaki coveralls were filing in with carts of extra chairs.

"Got any plans for dinner?" Glen asked.

Ray glanced back, hoping the invitation was directed toward Ehrlich. But Glen was looking squarely at him. "Uh . . . I'm . . . I'm not sure. Margaret won't be done until five. And . . . She'll probably be tired. I doubt she'll want to—"

"Bother with dinner," Glen nodded. "I understand. So why don't the two of you come over to our place? You don't need to bring anything. Just yourselves."

When Ray didn't answer, Glen broadened the invitation to include Ehrlich, who was trailing several steps behind. "You too, Jack. I'd especially like you to come."

"Well . . . I . . . I have a lot of . . . work . . ." Ehrlich said, struggling for an excuse of his own. He slowed his pace to a plod, as if he could deter Glen by sheer sluggishness. "I just . . . I have to . . ."

"You have to slow down before you break down," Glen warned. "With the stress you've been under the last couple of days, a little R&R will do you good. Change out of that suit. We'll wait for you in the lobby."

Ehrlich moaned something, but offered no further resistance. He waddled toward the elevator with the stiffness of an arthritic old man.

"I'll have to ask Margaret," Ray stipulated. He hadn't conceded defeat yet.

Glen didn't seem to hear this. As they wove their way through the hotel's inner wheel of shops and fountains, he offered a glowing report of Jean's cooking and informed Ray that tonight's featured entrees included taco salad and hamburgers.

Taco salad was one of Ray's favorites. But he wasn't about to tell that to Glen. Instead he summoned all of his powers of ESP to communicate a message to Margaret: *Please be too tired Please!*

➤➤ TWENTY-SIX ◄◄

IN THE LOBBY, they found a spongy, overstuffed couch near the espresso cart that offered a view of the front desk, and, across the vast, flawless sea of green marble, the entrance. The revolving doors were spinning now, the glass-roofed atrium a hive of activity as guests surged in and out.

"Jean loves to cook," Glen was saying, his mouth still running over with words. "So we have people over a lot. Especially on Saturdays."

Ray watched a couple march toward the door. They looked like models from a Land's End catalog: Dockers, polo shirts, sweaters over their shoulders, boat shoes . . .

"It's gotten to be a regular thing. Folks just sort of naturally congregate at our place on Saturday night."

As the couple disappeared through one door, a pair of men emerged from the other: blue suits, black shoes, dull ties, sunglasses . . . Agents Pool and Bailey, Ray realized before they had taken two steps inside the building. He considered hailing them, asking if anything new had turned up, but decided against it. Instead, he sank into the couch.

"One time we had twenty-seven," Glen laughed. "Last week, I counted twelve."

"Twelve what?" Ray asked, eyes still on the Fibbies. They had cut straight across the lobby and were now conferring with the woman at the desk.

"Twelve wolverines," Glen answered facetiously. "You're not listening, are you?"

The Feds moved further into the hotel and out of sight. A half-dozen businessmen strolled in from the hall: three-piece suits, slightly overweight, balding . . . Club Rogaine.

Ray checked his watch without noting the time and wondered what was taking Ehrlich so long. How much time did it take to change clothes?

"After we eat, we usually have a sort of impromptu church meeting."

The word church was like a cattle prod, rudely waking Ray from his daze. "You what?!"

"Tonight, we're getting ready for cauyaq. Practicing our dances, getting the music lined up . . ."

Before Ray could ask what a Native drum festival had to do with church, Amy Yasaka emerged from the ferns. "Gentlemen. How goes the investigation?"

Ray and Glen fought their way out of the man-eating cushions. "It's progressing," Ray told her. It was amazing how beautiful this woman was and how her appearance intimidated him.

"We're stymied," Glen confessed. "Turns out Mr. Cox didn't kill himself."

"Glen . . ." Ray warned.

"He didn't?" Her eyes somehow grew larger.

Glen leaned toward her and whispered, "He may have been murdered."

"Glen . . ."

"Murdered?!" Yasaka registered her shock by blinking rapidly.

"Poisoned."

Yasaka gasped, a reflex that made her appear all the more innocent—and attractive.

"Glen!" Ray repeated in the disapproving tone of an angry parent. The details concerning the death of Michael Cox were not public knowledge. In fact, Ray and Glen weren't even supposed to be privy to all of them. It was an open case. An open *Federal* case. Sharing this confidential information was unprofessional. And yet, Ray couldn't really blame him. Yasaka had a certain mesmerizing effect that short-circuited male brain connections.

"Any idea who . . . ?" she asked, eyebrows raised above a grimace.

"We're looking into it," Ray answered diplomatically.

"Should we warn our guests?" she asked. "Is there a killer running loose?"

"It wasn't random," Glen told her. "But that's all we can say right now."

Yasaka thought over the information. "What an ugly business."

"Murder always is," Glen said with the grim authority of a seasoned television private eye. "On a different subject, what would it take to get you to church tomorrow?"

"A miracle," she replied without hesitation.

Ray smiled. No wonder he liked this woman.

Undaunted, Glen asked, "What if we could arrange that?"

Yasaka laughed. "Sounds interesting. But I'm Buddhist."

"So you said. But that's okay. Remember? My mother's Buddhist."

"And I have to work at ten," she added.

"No problem. We've got an eight o'clock service. It's over by nine-fifteen." When Yasaka hesitated, he said, "Starbucks coffee and homemade sticky buns afterward . . . regardless of what you think of my sermon."

Yasaka turned to Ray. "Are you going?"

The question caught Ray off-guard. "To church?"

"Sure, he's going," Glen said. "He wouldn't miss it for the world. Right, Ray?"

Yasaka looked at him in surprise. "Really? Well . . . I guess, just this once."

"Great!" Glen was beaming.

"I'd better get back to work," Yasaka said.

"See you tomorrow, eight A.M. Girdwood Chapel," Glen said.

"Okay." She aimed a finger at Ray, eyes narrowing. "You better be there."

"I will be," Ray heard himself say. As she strode across the lobby, Ray shot Glen a dirty look. "You should be ashamed of yourself. Luring women to church with the promise of free refreshments, using her to get me to come and vice versa . . ."

"Hey . . . You gotta use whatever the fish are biting on."

Ray ignored the nonsensical remark, since asking would only encourage Glen, and nodded in the direction of the front desk, where the Amazon-like security guard and her husky male sidekick were waiting for Ms. Yasaka. "The bookends are back."

"Wonder if I should ask them to come tomorrow?" Glen thought aloud.

"Why? Does your church need bouncers?"

A short, round figure emerged from the elevator and plodded past Yasaka and her security team. Wearing green, cuffed chinos, gleaming white Reeboks, and a brushed Yale sweater, Ehrlich looked like a professor on holiday. He wandered in their direction without enthusiasm, like a beast of burden being driven to market.

"I really have a lot of paperwork to catch up on," he complained in greeting, still trying to weasel out of dinner. His nose was pink and slightly swollen. He had either hit the lounge on his way down or raided the mini-bar in his room. Or both.

"It'll be there when you get back," Glen promised.

"That's the problem . . ." Ehrlich muttered. He belched and Ray detected the delicate bouquet of Kentucky whiskey.

Falling into line, they made their way through the revolving door. Ehrlich navigated through the disorienting

passage successfully, but tripped on the curb outside and
sprawled to the pavement. Attendants rushed to his aid.

"Thanks," he told them, staggering to his feet. "I'm
fine. Just a little dizzy." When they reached the Camry,
he leaned against the roof. Ray poured him into the
backseat.

"He's smashed," Ray whispered as he and Glen
strapped in.

"Another good reason to take him home for dinner,"
Glen responded, unfazed. When he turned a tight circle
and accelerated out of the lot, Ehrlich moaned a curse.

The road was quiet, traffic light. The moose had va-
cated the meadow and the cars that had been lined up
on the shoulder were gone. As Glen slowed for a curve,
fiery rays streamed in from the southern horizon. The
sun seemed determined to break through a layer of dense
clouds, but another bank of soupy gray was descending
from the east. On this, the longest day, the Midnight Sun
would be obscured, Ray decided. The night would not
know darkness, but it would be dull and, most likely,
damp.

As they approached the resort area, a sign specified
that a square, squat structure housed the Alyeska Conference Association and the local YMCA. A dozen people were exiting through the glass doors, making their
way down the concrete steps.

"That's where my wife—" he started to say when he
spotted a trio of women marching across the lot. "There
she is." He checked his watch. She was out early.

As if guided by telepathy, Glen swung into the parking area and drove up beside them. Rolling down his
window, he adopted a winning smile and chimed, "Ladies."

They stopped in their tracks and glared at him. Ray
could see the wheels turning as they tried to decide
whether this unwelcome stranger was a pervert or a
salesman.

"Glen Redfern," he told them. When the wary expressions remained in place, he added, "Sheriff of Gird-wood. And the local chaplain." Glen flashed his badge.

This had a calming effect. The ladies nodded, no longer alarmed, simply puzzled.

Ray leaned forward. "Margaret!"

"Ray?" She blinked at him, clearly confused. "What are you doing?"

"It's a long story," he explained, without explaining. "Are you done?"

"For today. They let us out early." All three ladies tittered, as if it were part of some inside joke. "And we don't have to be back tomorrow until ten." More giggling. Then Margaret glanced into the back seat of the Camry. "Where's Keera?"

"She's over at Glen's." Before she could ask, he said, "It's part of the long story."

"We're headed over there now," Glen told her. "For dinner. Hop in."

Margaret looked at Glen, then at her husband.

Ray shrugged. "I told him you'd probably be too tired. It's fine with me if we just—"

"My wife's dying to meet you," Glen countered. "And you should see Keera and Ruby. That's my daughter. She's four years old too. They've been having a great time."

Ray clenched his teeth. Appealing to Margaret's desire for social interaction was unfair. Unlike Ray, she loved to be around other people and enjoyed conversation more than almost anything. She was a lawyer, for pete's sake. "If you're too tired . . ." he tried.

"No. Actually, that sounds fun. We've been cooped up all day. I'd like to get out for a while. Let me put my books up." She hurried off toward the condo, then turned and shouted to her fellow conference-goers, "See you guys in the morning!"

"You ladies are welcome too," Glen offered. "Taco salad . . . burgers . . ."

The women shook their heads in unison and politely muttered, "No, thank you."

Glen rolled the Camry to the curb next to the unit Margaret had entered and left it idling. "I know what you're thinking."

"I doubt that."

"You're thinking that you'd rather kick back and spend the evening watching the boob tube."

"You're psychic," Ray admitted.

"But believe me," Glen said, "tonight will be something you'll never forget."

"I'll just bet."

➤➤ TWENTY-SEVEN ◄◄

MARGARET JOGGED OUT of the condo carrying a large Tupperware container with a blue top. She had changed out of her blazer and skirt, into a pair of jeans and a bulky sweater. Ray got out and opened the back door for her. Despite encounters with Mrs. Mancini and Amy Yasaka, Margaret was still the most attractive woman he had seen all day . . . all year . . . in his entire life. Watching her approach, he recalled the poet's line, *she walks in beauty like the night,* and wished again that they weren't going out for the evening.

"Here." She handed him the tub.

He glanced down and realized that it held chocolate chip cookies. The ones Margaret had made yesterday and packed from home. The ones he had yet to sample.

She bent and scooted into the backseat, freezing halfway inside. "Who's this?"

"Jack Ehrlich," Ray informed. He waited as she pulled her legs in, then shut the door and climbed into the front.

"He's a friend," Glen explained.

Margaret sniffed the air. "I think your friend has been knocking back a few."

As if sensing that his drinking habits were being discussed, Ehrlich belched, twisted in the seat, and flopped toward Margaret, head rolling against her shoulder.

Pushing him away, Margaret leaned forward and offered Glen her hand. "We haven't really been introduced. I'm Margaret."

Glen twisted to shake her hand. "Glen Redfern. It's a pleasure. I recognized you the moment I saw you. Ray's told me a lot about you."

"How was the conference?" Ray asked, hoping to change the subject.

"Long," she lamented in a weary tone. "And boring. Tomorrow should be better."

Ray nodded, hoping tomorrow would, in fact, be better. Today had been—

"What have you guys been up to?"

"Investigating a murder," Glen reported.

"A what?!"

"Ray discovered a body."

Leaning forward, she frowned at the side of Ray's head. "A body?"

"Up on the mountain," Glen said energetically.

"Where was Keera?" Margaret wanted to know.

"With you. It was this morning, when I was biking."

Margaret sighed, then whispered, "Why didn't you tell me?"

Ray was opening his mouth to reply when Glen's cellular buzzed. In the backseat, Ehrlich muttered something about feeling sick.

Still in possession of the phone, Ray answered it. "Attla here." A faraway voice started talking. Only pieces of sentences survived the pulsing static. He managed to discern that the caller was with the Anchorage "something-something" office.

"That's how we got hooked up," Glen was telling Margaret. "We decided that it was an accident, until we found a suicide note. Or at least what looked like a suicide note."

Ray put a finger in his free ear and pressed the other against the phone. "I can hardly hear you. Could you repeat that?" The caller did, recycling the message. A name reached Ray's ear: Bob Gifford, Glen's contact. And something about a report.

". . . and that's when the FBI showed up . . ."

"Shhh!" Ray ordered. He closed his eyes and listened, catching the words lab . . . autopsy . . . fax? The latter took the form of a question. "Have you got a fax machine?" he asked Glen.

Glen nodded and recited the number.

Ray repeated it into the receiver. "Got that?" The response was an audio wind sheer followed by a dial tone. "Call your buddy at the medical examiner's office when we get to your place." A tiny red light was blinking on the phone. "What's that mean?"

Taking the phone, Glen squinted at the light. "Low battery. I need to charge it."

"What does the FBI have to do with—?" Margaret started to ask.

"Ooh . . . !" Ehrlich interrupted. He lurched forward and gagged. "Pull over!"

Glen braked and edged onto the shoulder. With the car still rolling, Ehrlich popped the door open and jumped out. Sprawling to his knees in the gravel, he retched and swore.

"So you're a sheriff *and* a chaplain?" Margaret asked.

"That's right. In fact, I'm the sheriff of Girdwood, the chaplain of Alyeska, *and* the rector of Girdwood Chapel. Oh, and I'm filling in for the local Catholic priest until the diocese sends a replacement." He cleared his throat, proud of his résumé.

"You okay out there?" Ray called.

Ehrlich groaned, vomited again, then cursed in a voice loud enough to put any wildlife in the vicinity on alert. He spit and coughed before finally climbing back inside.

"You gonna live?" Ray asked him.

He dabbed his face with a shirt sleeve. "Must have been something I ate."

Glen drove on and turned into a dirt road. When Ehrlich made an uncertain sound, he said, "My wife would appreciate it if you didn't soil her car."

"I'd appreciate if you didn't soil me," Margaret said.

Turning his head, Ehrlich regarded her with bloodshot eyes. "Who are you?"

"This is Margaret," Ray said. "My wife."

"Nice to meet you." He extended his hand. "I think I may have a touch of the flu."

"The virulent Jim Beam strain," Ray said under his breath.

They turned another corner and Glen's house came into view. A tow truck was sitting in front, lights blinking as an attendant in oil-stained coveralls unhooked cables and chains from the Wagoneer.

"There she is," Glen announced proudly. "Good as new." He slowed and toggled the window down. "Hey, Fred!"

The man in coveralls turned, squinted, then waved. He trotted over and leaned on the door. "Got you fixed up, Glen."

"Great!" Glen was exuberant, acting as though the man had just delivered a new BMW.

Pulling a slip of yellow paper from his breast pocket, Fred said, "Here's the damage." He handed the bill to Glen. "The boss didn't charge for labor, only parts."

"Great," Glen repeated. He accepted the receipt without looking at it.

"While we had it on the rack, we noticed your struts were shot."

Glen nodded. "That'll have to wait. Say, when do you get off?"

"I'm off as soon as I'm done here."

"Why don't you join us for dinner?"

The mechanic looked down at his coveralls, frowning.

"We don't mind if you don't."

Shrugging, he grunted, "Sure. Let me cut you loose and give the boss a call."

Glen pulled into the driveway and they all got out. Except for Ehrlich, who remained in the backseat, sighing like an ailing cow.

"Come on, Jack," Glen coaxed. "Once you get a little food in you, you'll be fine."

He sighed heavily. "Maybe you should take me back to the hotel."

"Oh, come on." Glen pulled him out and led him to the front door.

Filing inside, they were met by the buttery aroma of fresh bread, the sweet, warm smell of chocolate and cinnamon. It was like entering a bakery. Ray's stomach growled and he realized that he was famished.

Jean emerged from the kitchen, still in her apron, and smiled pleasantly as Glen made the introductions. Ehrlich got a handshake and a nod, Margaret an enthusiastic hug, as if she were a long-lost sorority sister. Before Ray could escape, Jean turned on him and he found himself trapped in her brief but firm embrace.

"Mommy!" Keera bolted down the hallway and wrapped herself around Margaret's legs like a boa constrictor. "Mommy, I have a new friend!" She motioned to Ruby, who had followed her at a more cautious pace. "This is Ruby."

"Hello, Ruby." Margaret shook her hand. "What have you two been up to?"

It was as if the little Dutch boy had just removed his finger from the dam. Keera began babbling, describing in stuttering detail every facet of their time together. Ruby nodded with wide eyes and jabbered her own comments whenever Keera took a breath.

"Dinner's ready," Jean said, starting for the kitchen. "Girls, get cleaned up. You too, Glen."

The door opened behind them and a second wave of visitors entered: Fred from the garage; two young women whom Ray guessed were in college; a tiny, elderly Native woman in a wheelchair being pushed by Jerry Garcia. Or at least it looked like the late great leader of the Grateful Dead. He was more muscular than Jerry, but wore the same round, wire-rim glasses and sported the same graying beard and bushy out-of-control hair.

"You guys are just in time!" Jean called without looking back.

After introducing everyone, Glen made the rounds, greeting the newcomers. Ray took Margaret's hand and pulled her toward the kitchen, already brainstorming for an excuse to leave immediately after dinner.

In the kitchen, Keera and Ruby were seated at the bar. Balanced atop swiveling stools, they were feeding two dolls from a set of empty plastic dishes and cups. The table had been pushed back into the nook, the chairs positioned along the opposite wall. Jean had laid out paper plates, napkins, and plastic utensils. A half-dozen glass serving bowls were arranged in a circle on the table: tortilla chips, taco salad, hot dogs, hamburgers, ice. A trio of two-liter soda bottles sat at the far edge, next to a stack of red plastic cups.

"Grab a plate and serve yourself," Jean encouraged. She bent and pulled a cookie sheet out of the oven. It was littered with fat snickerdoodles. "For dessert."

The girls hopped down and snatched up paper plates, chattering "Mommy, can I have . . . ? Do I have to have . . . ? How many of these . . . ?"

When they were satisfied and had reclaimed their

perches at the bar, the adults descended on the table like famished birds.

Turning his nose up at the food, Ehrlich poured himself a cup of Sprite and took a seat in the corner. His cheeks and forehead were still pale, his eyes pinpricks of distress.

Before reaching the table, Glen raised a hand and whistled. The din of conversation fell away and all eyes turned toward him. "Glad you could all come tonight. We've got plenty of food here, don't be afraid to get seconds and thirds." He glared at the hippie. "Or in your case, John, thirds and fourths."

John chuckled at this, his substantial frame rocking.

"First," Glen said with a mock flourish, "let's give kudos where kudos are due." He turned to Jean. "To my beautiful wife who has slaved in the kitchen the entire day."

Jean wiped her brow with the back of a hand and sagged, as though exhausted.

"And let's give thanks to the Big Guy by saying grace," Glen exhorted.

Ray swallowed a groan. Bowing his head, he realized that this had the makings of a long evening. Excruciatingly long.

TWENTY-EIGHT

MERCIFULLY, GLEN'S GRACE over the meal was short and sweet. When he finished, the group chimed a hearty "Amen," and dug into the food.

Having filled his plate, Ray surveyed the room for a place to sit. He turned to consult Margaret, but she had abandoned him. Leaning against a cabinet next to the stove, she was engrossed in conversation with Jean.

"Have a seat!" John implored. He was grinning like a madman, patting the chair next to him. "Don't worry. I don't bite!"

Ray sat down and picked up his burger. Like everything else that Jean cooked, it was excellent.

"Can Jean cook? Or what?" John asked.

"Or what . . ." Ray agreed, chewing. He could feel his mood turning sour. Already tired from a lousy day, a vacation day hijacked by an irritatingly complicated, genuinely confusing series of events, he was finding it difficult to be polite to people he didn't know and didn't want to be around. He cut his eyes to Ehrlich. Still nursing his Sprite, the man looked about like Ray felt: a cross between serious boredom and seasickness.

"Ain't life good?" John asked, eyes on the wiener protruding from his mustard- and kraut-laden bun.

Ray worked on his burger, hoping it was a rhetorical question. He glanced into the kitchen. Margaret happened to be facing in his direction. She waved, smiled, continued her conversation, chuckling about something Jean was saying. Ray frowned back at her and tried the potato salad. It was delicious.

The doorbell rang and a moment later three Native teenagers entered, all carrying skateboards. The noise level jumped as a chain reaction of hugs and handshakes broke out.

Setting the heaping second-helping plate on his seat, John made the rounds, handing out embraces like an overexcited grizzly. When he ran out of people to hug, he returned to his seat. Elbowing Ray, he asked, "How do you know Glen?"

Ray sighed at the question. "Actually, I just met him this morning."

"Is that right?" John was doing damage to a burger, relish escaping from the sides with each bite. "He's something, ain't he?"

"Oh, yeah. He's something all right."

"I met him two years ago."

Ray picked at the potato salad and eyed the kitchen. Margaret was now sitting on the counter, shaking with laughter. Apparently she and Jean were hitting it off.

"Two years, one month, and thirteen days ago, to be exact."

"He obviously made an impression." Giving up on the salad, Ray sampled the cookie. It was wonderful: packed with chocolate chips and macadamia nuts.

"Glen saved my life." John paused, stared at Ray, then pushed the remainder of his burger into his mouth. He chewed, swallowed hard, and sucked in an unsteady breath of air.

Great, Ray thought. Not only was he stuck at a dinner party with a bunch of oddballs, now this graying hippie was going to start bawling. Just when he was wondering if things could get worse, he saw Keera poke her head in from the hallway. He motioned her over with a finger.

"Glen . . . he . . . He's the reason . . . I'm alive today and not in prison or dead from doing drugs or something." A tear trickled down his round, formerly jolly cheek.

When Keera hopped into his lap, Ray said, "John, this is my little girl."

Wiping his eyes with a shirt sleeve, John sniffed once and magically retrieved his happy-as-a-clam attitude. "Well, hi there. What's your name?"

Keera looked at Ray. He nodded. "It's okay, honey."

Satisfied that John wasn't the bogeyman, she peeped, "Keera."

"Keera? What a beautiful name! How old are you, Keera."

After another quick glance at her father, she timidly held up four fingers.

"Four? Why, what a big girl."

At this point, Keera lost interest in John. Yawning, she asked, "Can we go home?"

Ray smiled. There was nothing he wanted more in all the world.

"You folks live around here?" John asked.

"No. She means the condo. We're just here for my wife's conference. We're from Barrow."

"Barrow?! Way up at the top of the world?" His jaw fell open as he scrutinized Ray, then Keera. "Are you folks . . . Eskimos?"

Ray nodded. The man was brilliant.

"Wow . . ." John was clearly impressed. "Do you, like, live in igloos and travel by dogsled?"

Keera giggled at this.

"No," Ray said, frowning.

"What about whale blubber?" John asked. "That's pretty much all you eat up there, ain't it?"

Glen stood up and quelled the din of conversation with a shrill whistle. "If everybody's about done with dinner, why don't we start migrating into the living room?"

Ray could think of several good reasons. But the most

compelling was that Keera was tired and wanted to go home. He kissed her on the head.

Producing a garbage bag, Glen accepted plates and utensils as people filed by en route to the living room. When Ray reached him, he deposited his trash and was about to excuse himself and his family. Before he could, Glen whispered. "The fax came."

"Fax?" It took Ray a moment to recall what he was talking about. "Oh . . ."

Glen nodded toward the hall. "It's in my study. Second door on the right."

"Okay." Bending, Ray told Keera, "Go with Mommy. I'll be right back."

"I'm tired, Daddy," she said, whining.

"I know." He looked at Glen. "We'll leave in just a few minutes."

She turned and staggered toward Margaret. Ray started down the hall. A quick look at that fax and they'd be in the car, headed for the condo.

Glen's study was a small room made to seem even more cramped by the presence of hundreds of books. Cinder blocks and pine shelves hid two walls. In front of the shelves and around the desk more books, file folders, and magazines sat in neat stacks. The desk was more of a table, Ray realized. No drawers. A free-standing wooden file cabinet on wheels had been positioned beneath it, and the desktop itself held an array of equipment: computer, phone with answering machine, fax machine, lamp.

At the center of the desk, accentuated by a pool of white lamplight, a collection of paper glowed like the Holy Grail. The ends were curling up, the printing tiny and smudged—dot matrix. The fax. Ray picked it up and scanned it.

There were four pages. A cover page written by the State Troopers. A short section by the Anchorage Police. Two pages from the ME's office. Nothing earthshaking: A body had been recovered from Mount Alyeska at three minutes after nine on Saturday morning. The State Troopers had transported the corpse to the Anchorage Police, who had then handed it over to the morgue. The autopsy was brief and succinct, listing the cause of death as a broken neck. The ME was quoted as saying that the victim had fallen "some distance." There was no mention of poison in the bloodstream.

Ray found his own name in the troopers' report. He was referred to as the FOS—"first on sight." Hans had made the form, along with Glen.

Cox's age, weight, hair color, and other physical traits had been typed into the appropriate slots, along with information concerning his next of kin. His personal effects were described as a Rolex, a wedding band, a wallet, several receipts, $256 in cash.

A single sentence closed the report with the warning: *This has been deemed a Federal investigation and is currently being worked by the FBI*. This was followed by the date and two lowercase letters wrapped in parenthesis—(ap).

Arbugus Pool? Ray wondered.

Along the bottom margin of the last page a handwritten note said: *Glen, this is the "official" report. The one we filed, with the details of the poison, may or may not ever see the light of day. The Feds are railroading this thing, Good luck. Watch your back. Bob.*

"Watch your back . . ." Ray mumbled aloud as he stared at the fax. While he appreciated the warning, Glen's buddy hadn't given them anything to go on. They already knew that the Fibbies were railroading the case. That the real cause of death wasn't listed didn't really surprise him. Not with the FBI in a panic. If Cox had worked for the State Department and was involved in some sort of scandal, they would do everything within their power to bury the autopsy report.

Despite the lack of any new information, the fax did confirm two things. First, that the case was imploding, spiraling in on itself to form a black hole. No leads. No suspects. Just a tangle of unrelated events and clandestine attempts to cover them up. Second, he might soon be rid of it. No more headaches, no more working on vacation, no more Glen! And it wasn't as if he hadn't made an effort. Even the captain would agree that he had given it the old college try. And he had turned up zip. After wasting an entire day, he was quite possibly standing at the gates of freedom. All they had to do was question the lift operator, the one in the midnight race, and the whole mess would be over.

This encouraging thought evaporated as he started to set the fax down on Glen's desk and a bold demarcation on page one caught his eye: *Personal Effects.* For a reason that he couldn't explain, the words seemed to shout at him, demanding his attention. He scanned the list again wondering what it was about the items that bothered him: watch, ring, cash . . . So? It was exactly what you would expect to find on almost any man's body if he died in public. Nothing out of the ordinary.

He was turning to leave the study when it struck him and he picked the fax up again. It wasn't what the list contained. It was what it didn't contain. No credit cards. No driver's license. No passport. No ID whatsoever.

Ray checked the heading of the cover page and then leafed through the fax. No mention of Cox's name. He was listed as a John Doe.

And no envelope. Where was the manila envelope?

➤➤ TWENTY-NINE ➤➤

THE ANSWER SEEMED obvious: The FBI had it. They had barged in, hijacked the case, and were running things their way, telling the local authorities to back off, issuing censored reports, suppressing any and all evidence they deemed necessary. The poison, for instance. And Cox's identity. So why not bury the envelope? Except . . .

Music filtered in from down the hall: wordless chanting accompanied by a thumping sound. Either someone was trapped in a cardboard box, trying to punch his way out, or Glen had broken out the seal-gut drums.

Ray glared at the fax without seeing it. If the Feds were in possession of the envelope, why had they asked him about it? They hadn't mentioned it by name. But the implication was there. Pool and Bailey had been fishing for something specific. For that matter, so had the fake agents. Everyone and his dog seemed interested in something Cox was supposed to be carrying: a manila envelope that had magically disappeared.

Voices rose, and the person trapped in the box continued to struggle for freedom.

If the Fibbies hadn't recovered the envelope, Ray thought, ignoring the concert, who had? He leaned against Glen's desk chair and mentally mapped the trail the body had taken: himself, Glen, State Troopers, Anchorage PD, the ME's office. Somewhere in there, the FBI had forced its way in. That brought the number of contacts to ten . . . twelve?

The troopers had signed off on the report. And they didn't mention any envelope. Unless the Bureau had ordered them to falsify their report, the envelope had presumably "walked off" prior to Cox's arrival in Anchorage. Working backward, that left the troopers themselves and Glen. Glen . . . ? Yeah, sure. Chaplain Glen had stolen it.

What about Hans? That was another possibility. Though Ray couldn't imagine why the head of the ski school would care about something in the pocket of a corpse.

In the living room, one song faded and another rose in its place, the drummers never missing a beat.

Ray shook his head at the ridiculous scenarios his brain was submitting: Glen the shallow-grave robber, Hans the bloodthirsty resort manager . . . Next he would be coming up with a theory for fitting Amy Yasaka, Ehrlich, and John the hippie into the plot. A huge conspiracy, that's what it was. Carried out specifically to drive Ray batty. And it was working.

He sank into the desk chair and stared at the blank, greenish screen of the deactivated computer. His own image stared back, mouth bent into a frown. Several locks of long black hair had escaped from his ponytail and hung limply in front of his ears.

The choir down the hall was singing what sounded like a sixties folk song, the percussion section doing a convincing imitation of an old *Tarzan* movie in which the natives had grown restless.

Closing his eyes, Ray visualized the envelope: manila, six-by-nine, folded in half, no address . . . Assuming he wasn't losing his mind and hadn't imagined it, and assuming it hadn't been lost or misplaced somewhere between Alyeska and Anchorage, why would someone take it? What had been inside that envelope? Eyes still closed, Ray gazed at the image in his mind and tried to recall the weight and feel. The edges of the envelope were flimsy. A third, or perhaps a half was stiff and heavy. At least, heavier than mere paper. His thought at the time had been that it held a cassette tape. Not a tape, necessarily, but a square plastic box. Square . . . Cassettes weren't square. They were rectangular. And the envelope hadn't bulged. Whatever was inside was slim. A CD?

Rising, he scanned the shelves. On the end closest to the desk, he found a disk file overflowing with CDs. He picked one at random and glanced around for an envelope. There was a stack of old mail on the shelf below. He drew out an oversized letter of about the right size and held it against the disk. Nope. The disk was too big.

He put the CD back and picked a floppy disk from another roll-top file. Better. But still not quite right. Next to the mail was a microcassette recorder. He popped it open and stuffed the tape into the envelope. It fit, but . . . Too thick.

As he replaced the tape and the letter, Ray tried to imagine something square, hard . . . bigger and weightier than a credit card, smaller and lighter than most pocket calculators. About the size of a . . . a . . . what . . . ?

Falling back into the chair, he closed his eyes again and sighed as the envelope appeared, ghostlike, in his mind. What else would fit the criteria?

He swore softly. The envelope could have contained just about anything: a tightly folded letter, a box top for a free decoder ring, a Gameboy cartridge . . . Maybe Cox had been carrying around the latest version of Donkey Kong. That would explain why the FBI was so hot and bothered. Imagine what could happen if that fell into the wrong hands.

Voices in the other room were belting out another song, this one involving the word cauyaq.

Opening his eyes, Ray extracted his calling card from his wallet, lifted the phone, and dialed. As he waited, he heard the drum corps shift to double time. Now instead of African cannibals, they sounded like the band from *Hawaii 5-0*.

"Anchorage PD," a voice answered.

"This is officer Ray Attla. I'm calling for Dan Meets." He and Meets had studied criminal justice together at U. of A. Meets probably didn't even know about Cox's death, but Ray was running out of options. Time to grasp at any and all straws.

"Sure, I'll hold," Ray said.

Thirty seconds later, a voice said, "Officer Attla? Lieutenant Meets has left for the day."

"Thanks." Ray hung up and consulted his wallet. Somewhere among the various business cards and scraps of paper, he was pretty sure that he had Meets's home number. He extracted the stash and fanned through them like playing cards. There was a whoop, John the hippie, Ray guessed, and suddenly the floor began to shake. The dancing had begun.

He discovered Meets's number on the back of a ticket stub, dialed, and waited.

"Hello?"

"Meets?"

"Yeah . . ."

"This is Ray. Ray Attla."

"Hey, Ray, how are—? Hang on." There was a rustling noise and in the distance, Meets said, "Both of you go brush your teeth." Then, "How's it feel to be famous?"

"Huh?"

"You found the diver in Girdwood, right?"

"*Diver?* Oh . . . yeah . . . How'd you—?"

"The FBI briefed us, threatened to prosecute if we breathed a word."

"You're kidding?"

"No. They're doing a heavy-duty song and dance. So what's the deal? Was the John Doe a spook or something?"

John Doe? The FBI had told the Anchorage Police

that Cox was a John Doe? "It's a long story," Ray admitted.

"You sound tired. Are the Feds giving you fits?"

"No. But only because they don't know we're actively working this thing."

"We?"

"Me and the local sheriff."

"I didn't know Girdwood had a sheriff," Meets said.

"Me either. Listen, I just read the report on this guy." Ray picked up the fax. "Were any other personal effects found on the body?"

"You're asking me? You're the one who found him."

"I know. But I'm sitting here looking at the list, wondering if it's complete."

"I don't have it in front of me," Meets said. "But I was there when the troopers showed up and did the log. I think they got it all."

Ray read the list to him.

"Yeah, that's it. No ID. No car keys. Why?"

"I don't know . . ."

"Is there something wrong?" Meets asked. When Ray didn't answer, he said, "There is, isn't there? You found something else, something that never made it to Anchorage." After another span of silence, he asked, "Did you tell the FBI?"

"This is off the record, right?"

"Buddy to buddy."

"There was something," Ray confessed. "And no, I didn't tell the Feds about it. But I get the feeling they already knew. The problem is, it's missing."

"What is it?"

Ray considered the question and the implications of his answer. Meets was an old friend. They had attended classes together, played on the same intramural football squad. Dan was a good guy. But somehow the idea of telling him about the envelope didn't set right with Ray. For one thing, it served no real purpose. Meets wasn't actively involved in the case. He didn't *need* to know.

For another, Meets might be working with the FBI. Probably not. But maybe. Back to the conspiracy theory run amok. Still, better safe than sorry. Furthermore, Ray had used Glen's phone to place this call. What if, by some stretch, the FBI had bugged it? It was a crazy idea. And yet . . . Brake lines didn't cut themselves. ID didn't disappear into thin air. Envelopes didn't just get up and walk away.

"I've already said too much," he finally told him.

"No problemo," Meets replied. "I understand. You need anything, just call."

"Okay. Thanks for your help."

"And Ray . . . be careful. I don't know what's going on, but . . . Watch yourself."

"I will," Ray said. "Talk to you later." Folding the fax, he slipped it into his pocket and started down the hall, toward the now frantic drummers.

He slowed as he reached the living room and peeked around the corner. Three "performers" were hopping about in the middle of the room, their faces obscured by traditional masks. Yupik, Ray guessed. Kneeling on the floor in a semicircle around them were the percussionists—the two college girls and a member of the skateboarding crew, madly beating their seal-gut instruments. Margaret was on the other couch, wedged between the tow truck driver and Jean. Keera was in her lap, head cocked to one side, asleep. Ray motioned toward the door with a finger and mouthed, "Ready?"

She smiled down at Keera, then mouthed back, "In a little bit."

He offered her his most pitiful expression, clasped his hands together, and was about to mime, "Please?" when an elbow caught him and he looked up into the cartoonish face of a giant spirit mask.

"Ain't this cool?" John whispered from behind it. "I get off on all this tribal stuff."

Ray just blinked at him, unable to fathom the purpose

behind having naluaqmiut dress up in ceremonial garb. It was idiotic, if not sacrilegious.

When the song ended, one of the dancers removed his wooden mask. It was Glen. Panting, he offered the mask to Ehrlich. When Ehrlich shook his head, Glen insisted.

"Come on. Dancing's good for the soul."

"He's right," John bellowed. Sidling over to Ehrlich, he gripped him with two beefy paws and dragged him to center stage, then slung Glen's mask over his face.

"Let's try the 'Song of Summer' again," Glen instructed. "From the top."

As the other dancers took their places, and the drums struggled to find a common cadence, Ehrlich sagged and stood there like the ancient spirit of the party poop.

Ray was reminded of the many festivals Grandfather had forced him to attend and felt a tinge of sympathy for the man. For the most part, however, he was simply glad that he hadn't been chosen to be the fool of the dance.

THIRTY

STRANGELY, GLEN'S PRESCRIPTION for improved mental health actually seemed to work. For a full minute, Ehrlich remained motionless, a statue around which the other dancers pranced and twirled. But slowly he began to loosen up. Prodded by Glen and the others, he finally began to move. Clumsily at first, then with what almost could have passed as rhythm. Almost.

By the time the song ended, Ehrlich seemed to be enjoying himself. At least from the look of his body language: arms waving, hips swaying in a sort of awkward hula. When he removed his mask, his face was sweaty, the expression communicating fatigue more than amusement.

"Now see," Glen said, trying to catch his breath. "Don't you feel better?"

Ehrlich nodded without conviction, handed back the mask, and quickly retook his place along the wall, away from the spotlight of attention.

Ray looked to Margaret, determined to impress upon her the urgent need to leave. He caught her eyes and aimed a thumb at the door. Before he could punctuate this with a stern "Let's go!" Glen had him by the arm. Pulling him into the center of the room, he said, "You've all met Ray." Smiles greeted him. "He's a full-blood Inupiat from Barrow."

"A big one," someone murmured.

"I'll bet he can dance circles around us southern folk."

"Speak for yourself," John said, feigning offense. He did a little soft-shoe and the onlookers hooted.

Glen signaled the musicians and they began thumping their hoop drums. "Come on, Ray." He thrust the wooden mask into Ray's hand.

"No. Thanks, but . . . I'm tired and . . . it's been a long day . . ."

Glen donned his mask. "Just a quick one." He and the others began bouncing and jerking around him.

"I really don't want to." He was getting irritated now.

"It's good for what ails you. Just ask Jack."

Ray glanced at Ehrlich. Eyes closed, hand on his forehead, he looked ill again.

"Put the mask on," Glen urged.

When Glen reached for him, Ray pulled away. He lost his grip on the mask and it flew toward the couch, landing in Keera's lap. She awoke suddenly, blinked at it, grinned, and put it on. The group cheered at this. Margaret helped her stand up and she made her way toward the other dancers.

"At least someone in the family knows how to have a good time," Glen said.

Ignoring this, Ray went to help Ehrlich hold up the wall. He glared at Margaret, but found her watching Keera, clapping and laughing as the four-year-old did an energetic, high-stepping jig.

Glen and the others began clapping too, linking arms to perform something of a hoe-down. It wasn't graceful, but it was amusing to watch, Ray had to admit. After a couple of minutes, the dance ran out of gas and the drummers finally gave up on their instruments. The audience applauded their efforts nonetheless.

"Now that was fun," Glen said, shedding his mask.

The others did likewise, bending in half to try and catch their breath. Except for Keera. She kept at it, bounding about the carpet on fresh legs.

"You've got a dancer on your hands, Ray."

He nodded politely. Keera had been to several festivals and had even danced at a Messenger Feast. But by her own choice. Ray wasn't going to force her. Knowing about your heritage and actually practicing it were two different things, the latter being a matter of preference.

He waved subtly at Margaret. When she squinted back at him, he mouthed, "Let's go!" She nodded and he was about to excuse himself, thanking Glen and Jean for their hospitality, when Ehrlich nudged him. "There's something else you should know about Mike."

"Mike? You mean Cox?" Ray asked.

Ehrlich replied with a single, curt nod. "He was having an affair."

"Daddy, what's a a-ffair?" Keera asked. She had stopped dancing and was looking up at him.

"It's a grown-up thing," Ray assured her. He pointed in the direction of Glen's study, and told Ehrlich, "Let's talk about it back it here." He motioned for Glen to join them.

"We'll be right back," Glen told everyone as they ushered Ehrlich down the hall.

Behind them, Jean said, "Let's call it a night and break for coffee."

"And cake!" John chimed.

By the time they reached the study, Ehrlich looked as though he had changed his mind and wasn't interested in discussing the matter.

"Well . . ." Ray prodded.

He sighed, shook his head. "Mike was having an affair . . ."

"You said he had lots of them," Glen pointed out.

"He had lots of women. Lots of one-night stands. But . . . well . . . I wouldn't even mention this except while I was dancing in there . . ." He paused and blew out air. "For some reason I got to thinking of a business trip Mike and I took to New York about six months ago. While we were there, he dragged me to this dance club that was supposed to be really popular. You know, exclusive and all. I hate dancing, so I just sat at a table, nursing drinks while he went wild out on the floor with some of the Big Apple's hottest babes." Ehrlich shook his head at the memory. "Anyway, right before closing, he met this lady." He sighed again. "A married lady. And that's when the affair started."

Ray leaned against the desk, hoping the punch line was coming soon.

"Is that who the second ticket to Tokyo was for?"

Ehrlich shrugged again. "I don't know. Maybe. I don't know."

"Who was it?"

"It's kind of a sticky situation," Ehrlich explained. "I mean . . . this lady . . . Her husband . . . I could get in trouble. Or worse."

"Who was it?" Ray demanded.

After a deep breath, he confessed, "Louise Mancini."

Ray assumed he had heard wrong. Either that or this was another Mancini. "You don't mean Ron the Don's wife."

Ehrlich's eyebrows rose.

"Only a fool would mess with Mrs. Mancini."

"When it came to women," Ehrlich said, "Mike could be pretty stupid."

Ray's mind raced. Cox was having an affair with Mrs. Ron the Don? If it was true, the question of who had murdered him was no longer a mystery. Ron Mancini was a violent man: ruthless, cruel, volatile. If he suspected that someone was messing around with his wife . . . Ray imagined Ron dispatching Hat Trick Benny to have a little talk with the overamorous Casanova to ensure that he would forever regret the indiscretion. Poisoning Cox was actually rather lenient on the scale of Mancini-worthy methods of vengeance.

"Why didn't you tell us?" Ray wondered.

Ehrlich shrugged. "I didn't think it was important."

"You didn't think it was—" Ray cursed softly. "No, it's not important. It just gives us motive and a prime suspect in Cox's murder. That's not important."

Ehrlich swore back at him. "I was scared, okay? I knew that Mike was playing with fire. And when he turned up dead . . ." He emphasized his fear by drawing out a four-letter-word. Glancing at Glen, he said, "Sorry, chaplain. But I just . . . I freaked. I kept thinking Hat Trick Benny would come after me too."

"Is that why you were trying to bug out?" Ray asked.

"You bet it is."

"You should have told us."

"I know." Ehrlich hung his head.

"Any other bombshells?" Ray asked sarcastically. "Was he embezzling from Suntron, cheating on his taxes, going out of his way to be cruel to animals and small children?"

Ehrlich balked, his face draining of color. "No," he

managed. "Mike wasn't cruel. And as far as I know, he didn't cheat on his taxes."

Ray covered his eyes with a hand. "Don't say it."

But Ehrlich did. "I think he may have been doing some *creative* accounting. I'm not sure it actually constituted embezzling—per se."

Swearing, Ray sighed, "Is there anything else?"

Ehrlich squinted as he considered the question. "There was one thing. It was a couple of months back, when Mike was putting together the deal with Fukutomi. He had this totally outrageous idea. I thought he was just joking, you know. But now . . . I'm not so sure."

"What was it?"

Ehrlich frowned. "He said something about getting his hands on a prototype of the NVSC: the Fukutomi super chip."

➤➤ THIRTY-ONE ◄◄

RAY FELT LIKE crying. In the span of a few short minutes, Ehrlich had turned an already tangled investigation into a nightmare: Cox, the executive with a strange Federal tie but no outstanding enemies, was now Cox, the scoundrel and industrial thief. A virtual myriad of interested parties would cheer if this louse performed a nose dive from a chair lift.

He glared at Ehrlich. "Did you know Cox was employed by the State Department?"

"That what?!"

"The State Department."

"Mike?" Ehrlich shook his head. "Are you sure?"

"We think that's why the FBI's circling." Ray leaned back against the wall and stared at the ceiling as he considered the possibilities. If Cox was working for or with the State Department, perhaps he had betrayed them.

"Why would Mike be working for the State Department?" Ehrlich wondered aloud.

Ray ignored this, turning his attention to Mancini. Ron was still the best bet for a culprit in Cox's death. He would have been insanely jealous if he had found out about the affair. Insane to the point of murder. Maybe Cox had done something especially dumb, like trying to see Louise while they were all here at Alyeska. And Ron had walked in on them. No. That would have brought a sure and sudden response: gunshot to the back of the head.

"What are you thinking?" Glen asked.

Shaking his head, Ray continued down the trail of suspects. Ehrlich's disclosure had dumped Suntron and Fukutomi into the mix of those who would have celebrated the demise of Cox. Embezzling didn't usually warrant execution. A pink slip. Prosecution. Even a jail sentence. But not murder. Stealing a chip, on the other hand . . . If the NVSC chip was all that Eddie Fukutomi built it up to be, lifting it would be a serious offense. Yes, Ray could see a foreign company knocking off an industrial spy. To the Japanese, business was war, and Cox was merely a soldier in the battle.

Ray massaged his temples, fighting off a fresh headache. All day he had been frustrated by the lack of suspects and motives. Now there were so many that his head was swimming.

"You okay?" Glen asked.

"No," Ray grunted. The answer to the puzzle wasn't with the menu of interested parties so much as with the victim himself. Michael Cox was the key. What had his game been? Which of his angles was the one that had resulted in his death?

"Do you think that he actually stole a chip?" Ray asked.

Ehrlich blew out a maudlin laugh. "I doubt it. He was working on the contract, reading all the test reports and the production estimates. The thing's a gold mine. It would make anybody a little drunk with envy. He was just dreaming about winning the lottery."

Winning the lottery and planning to steal a valuable technological breakthrough didn't occupy the same plane in Ray's mind. "Any idea why he went to the top of Alyeska last night?"

"You already asked me that," Ehrlich answered rather defensively. "I have no earthly idea. I mean, I could speculate, but—"

"Speculate," Ray encouraged.

"To meet someone?"

"Who?"

Ehrlich didn't know and said so with a shrug.

Ray considered asking about the envelope, but couldn't think of a way to do it without revealing its existence.

"Sounds to me like Mancini is our man," Glen said. "Cox was having an affair with his wife. Mancini killed him."

"Maybe," Ray said.

"So let's go."

"Where?"

"To arrest Mancini."

"Right. Except we don't have any evidence." Ray rubbed his eyes. "If Cox and Mrs. Mancini were having an affair, that gives Ron a motive. That's a start. But motive alone isn't enough. He might not have even known about the affair. If we haul him off in cuffs without a witness, without opportunity, without a murder weapon . . ." He shook his head. "He'll be out within the hour, and he'll be ticked. At us. Our careers, possibly even our lives, will be in jeopardy."

"Are you saying we should let him get away, because he's powerful?"

"I'm saying we have to handle this the right way," Ray explained. "Otherwise, guilty or not, he'll eat us alive."

Sighing, Glen asked, "Then what are we supposed to do?"

Ray didn't have an answer. He knew what he wanted to do: go back to the condo and forget Cox, Mancini, Glen, Ehrlich and all things remotely related to law enforcement. He glanced at his watch. "What time is that race?"

Glen checked his own watch. "It starts at nine. We better get going."

"What kind of race are you talking about?" Ehrlich wanted to know.

"A running race," Glen told him. "The girl operating the lift last night is in it."

"You think she saw something?" Ehrlich asked.

"Maybe." Ray sighed. He wasn't exactly holding his breath. In fact, he doubted that the lift operator would be of any help at all. She probably wouldn't even remember seeing Cox, much less seeing Mancini or Hat Trick Benny up there chasing him around, trying to pour poison down his throat. The scene didn't make sense. The more Ray thought about it, the less likely it seemed that Mancini would poison Cox. Affair or no affair, it wasn't his style. Cement boots and an express trip to the bottom of Turnagain Arm maybe. Bullet to the brain and a shallow grave in a gully somewhere in the Chugach foothills. Something swift, brutal, merciless. But poison at the top of a ski resort?

"I'll get my keys," Glen said.

"What about me?" Ehrlich wondered.

"You want to come?" Glen asked.

Before Ray could retract the offer, Ehrlich was nodding. "Sure. Why not?"

"It won't be very interesting," Ray assured him. "We're just going to ask her questions."

"Sounds interesting to me," Ehrlich said. "Especially if it can help us find Mike's killer."

Us? "It's a long drive," Ray warned.

"Twenty minutes," Glen corrected.

"And you're not feeling well . . ." Ray tried.

"I feel great now. Ever since that dance . . . I'm as good as new."

Ray sighed, wondering why Ehrlich was suddenly attracted to the case.

Moving back down the hall, they heard what sounded like a man being tortured in the kitchen: yelps of pain. It turned out to be John laughing at the antics of the skateboard trio, who were performing a human juggling stunt.

Keera was grinning, pointing and yelling, "Froggies!"

When the boarders skid to a halt, the audience applauded enthusiastically.

This seemed to signal the end of the meeting. The skateboarders hurried out as though they were late for another engagement. The others filed out behind them. Everyone made a point of saying goodbye to Ray and Margaret. Part of the proselytizing process, Ray decided as he smiled back.

John brought up the rear, pushing the man in the wheelchair. "Love you, man," he bellowed, patting Ray on the back.

Before the front door had closed, Glen told Jean, "We're headed to Bird Creek. Can you take Margaret and Keera home?"

"Sure."

"Why are you going to Bird Creek?" Margaret asked with a curious expression.

"Part of the investigation," Ray explained glumly.

"When will you be back?"

He shrugged. "We'll try to make it as quick as possible."

"That means late, Mommy," Keera translated.

Ray kissed her, then kissed Margaret. "See you guys in a little while."

"A *long* while," Keera said.

"You be good for Mommy," Ray told her as they started for the door.

Outside, the clouds had converged, eclipsing the sun and filling the air with moisture only. A trace of drizzle was making it to the ground.

"I'll grab some coats," Glen said.

Ray and Ehrlich got into the Camry. When Glen returned with an armload of Gor-tex, he shook his head and pointed down the driveway at the Jeep. "Jean needs her car to take your family home."

They got out of the Toyota and were climbing into the truck when Ehrlich said, "You sure this thing will get us there?"

"No," Glen replied. He tried to start the sickly Wagoneer, pumping the gas and working the ignition key. The truck lurched, coughed, and finally caught, jerking to life.

"Might want to try the brakes a few times to make sure they work," Ray suggested.

"If Jim's Garage fixed them," Glen said, "they work."

"What's wrong with the brakes?" Ehrlich wondered.

"Nothing," Glen assured him.

"Anymore," Ray added. "We hope."

"Maybe you *should* take me to the hotel," Ehrlich said. "I have a lot of work."

"Just relax," Glen said. "The brakes are fine." When they reached the corner, he tapped the pedal and the wheels locked. The Jeep shuddered, skidding sideways. "They're just a little touchy. That's all."

Ehrlich whispered, "I need a drink."

Ray gripped the armrest as they raced toward the inlet. The road was empty and wet, a shiny black ribbon dividing the emerald hillsides into two sparkling halves.

"I can't believe it stays light like this," Ehrlich said.

"Takes some getting used to," Glen responded. He flipped on the windshield wipers and they began streaking the windows at a jerky tempo. "You think it's light here? You should see it in Barrow. The sun stays up for three months."

"Eighty-two days," Ray muttered. "In the winter it doesn't rise for sixty-six days."

"How do you stand it?" Ehrlich wondered. "I'd probably eat myself to obesity."

And drink yourself to death, Ray thought. The darkness above the Arctic Circle could be debilitating, especially for Outsiders. "You get used to it. Or you don't."

"I don't think I would." Ehrlich sighed. "Man was not made to live without light."

"Amen," Glen chimed. "Which is why God gives us his Light."

Ray stifled a groan. "How far is Bird Creek?"

"About ten miles," Glen estimated. He waited as a Winnebago hissed by, then punched the pedal. When they had successfully achieved a cruising speed of sixty-two, Glen launched into a Sunday school lesson on the theme: light in the darkness.

Ten miles? Ray thought. On this winding road? In this weather? With Glen assailing them with Bible verses? He wasn't sure he could survive for ten whole miles.

➤➤ THIRTY-TWO ◄◄

GLEN'S SERMONETTE LASTED for six of the ten miles. It would have stretched all the way to Bird Creek, Ray felt sure, had they not come up behind a slow-moving beer truck. Glen pulled around to pass it just as a string of oncoming traffic appeared from around the next curve. The Jeep hesitated slightly. The truck gained on them. Glen goosed the pedal, determined to pass.

"You'll never make it," Ray said, hoping Glen would pull in behind the truck.

"Sure I will." Shifting, Glen pushed the accelerator to the floor.

The beer truck lumbered along without breaking pace. The driver was either unwilling to let them by or simply hadn't noticed them.

The leader in the string of southbound cars, a Taurus, flashed its lights at them.

"Glen . . ." Ray warned.

"We're okay."

"Glen . . . !"

In the backseat, Ehrlich swore and struggled to fasten his seat belt.

The Taurus, now just an eighth of a mile ahead, sounded its horn and flashed its lights again. Ray hooked his own safety belt. Suddenly the Jeep found a hidden reserve of power and the Coors distributor took pity on them. The truck fell back and Glen slid neatly in front of it, beating the Taurus by a full twenty yards.

"You're insane!" Ehrlich exclaimed.

"So I've been told," Glen said. He looked pleased with himself.

They caught the Winnebago and Ray eyed the speedometer. The needle was on sixty-seven and the Jeep felt as though it was about to break apart. He could tell that Glen was planning to make a move. "Don't even think about it. We're not in that big of a hurry."

"Agreed," Ehrlich grunted from the backseat.

Glen grinned. "You boys afraid to die?"

"If I say yes, will you slow down?" Ray asked.

"I'm not. You know why?"

"Because you're nutty as a fruitcake," Ray tried.

"No. Because I've got insurance. Eternal insurance."

A sign flashed past: BIRD CREEK 3 MILES. Thank God! Ray thought: 7040 yards; 21,120 feet. He committed all his mental powers to willing the Jeep forward.

Glen was describing his "insurance policy" at length when Ray saw the sign for the Bird Creek turnoff. He waved at it, but Glen was engrossed in his own story.

"This is it," Ray told him. "The turn off." Ahead of them the Winnebago signaled and made a right. "Glen . . ."

Sheering down on the brakes, Glen veered onto the gravel shoulder. The tires locked and they went into a wide skid. The Winnebago had stopped at a check-in point just off the road and Glen had to spin the wheel to avoid sideswiping it. The Wagoneer took out a plastic garbage can and bumped to a clumsy halt inches from a metal placard: SOLSTICE MOUNTAIN RACE—9:00 P.M.

A shiny hooded parka materialized on the driver's side and a wax pencil tapped on the window. When Glen rolled it down, a frowning woman grunted, "Nice stop." Water dripped from her nose. She looked cold and miserable. "Welcome to the Solstice Mountain Run. Name and race number?" She glanced down at a soggy clip-board.

"We're not here to race," Glen said. "We just want to talk to one of the entrants."

"Fine. Park in the lot." She left to attend to another arrival.

"Thanks." Glen rolled up his window and pulled into the parking area.

The rain was blowing sideways, creating an uneven, ticking percussion as it assaulted the Jeep. The gray ceiling of clouds had dipped to kiss the ground in thick, ghostlike whirls, transforming the "midnight sun" into a colorless "midnight haze."

"People race in this weather?" Ehrlich wondered.

"Alaskans race in anything," Glen boasted as he slipped the Wagoneer between an Explorer and a Fore-runner. "You should see the Yukon Polar Express. It's a hundred miles on hard-packed snow in temperatures anywhere from twenty above to sixty below. This is nothing. Right, Ray?"

"Nothing," Ray agreed in a flat tone. He zipped his borrowed parka and pulled up the hood.

"Looks wet to me," Ehrlich observed.

"You want to stay in the car?" Glen asked. "We probably won't be that long."

"If we can find this girl," Ray reminded, "in the drizzle and fog."

"I'll come," Ehrlich said gloomily.

They got out and started across the lot. It was un-paved, a collection of potholes that were now small ponds. A wilted cardboard sign with a blurred arrow directed them forward. Beneath the arrow, the letters R-A-C-E had deteriorated, permanent marker running like cheap mascara to create a macabre ink blot.

The trail led up a steep knoll to a ledge of granite. Here the wind was blowing in earnest, pushing them away, as though the gods of Bird Creek were opposed to their presence. The starting line of the race was fifty yards below: a small encampment of tents, umbrellas, portable toilets, and pennants. The banner stretched across the starting line billowed like the sail of a tall ship, its message round and plump: SOLSTICE MOUNTAIN RUN. A huge digital clock next to the banner clicked off a countdown: 22:27 . . . 22:26 . . . 22:25 . . .

Hunched against gusts of horizontal pellets, hoods pulled snug, they descended the knoll. Ray was reminded of a movie he had seen in which a trio of penitent monks had endured similarly adverse weather in their pilgrimage to a remote Himalayan temple. Ahead of him, Ehrlich tripped, scrambled to keep his footing, then sat down hard. He cursed the stone that he considered responsible for the mishap.

Ray helped him up. "You okay?"

"Just swell," Ehrlich grumbled. His chinos were stained dark brown in the seat and there was a dime-sized tear in the rear pocket. The soles of the Reeboks bore an inch of muck, and the tops were watermarked and scuffed.

A deep, resonating voice proclaimed, "Twenty minutes until start time. Twenty minutes." The massive clock winked in agreement: 20:00.

The announcement caused the umbrellas lined up at the Porta-Pottys to waggle. Several entrants tossed off ponchos and began stretching as though there were only twenty *seconds* to go before the gun. A pair of Gor-tex-clad racers swept past Ray, leaping down the trail like startled mountain goats.

A thin, elderly man with a red, chapped face was standing at the bottom of the trail, directing foot traffic with one hand, speaking into a walkie-talkie with the other. A reflective apron tied around his rain parka designated him as a "Race Official."

"Registration tent?" Ray asked as they approached.

Bending forward, radio clutched to his ear, he gestured. "Next to the cans."

The Porta-Pottys were set up in ragged, parallel rows,

forming a wide aisle that ended at the starting line itself. There were two tents behind the left row, two behind the right. All were leaning slightly, rain flies flapping madly.

Runners were emerging from the first tent carrying manila envelopes, pinning on white squares of paper with large, red numbers.

Stepping inside, they found themselves at the back of a wide, unorganized line. Tables had been set up along the rear wall and the crowd was inching its way toward them.

When Glen pushed his way into the mob, a chorus of objections rang out. Ray raised his ID. "Police."

"Uh-oh . . ." someone said. "Busted." The entire tent rocked with laughter.

They squeezed to the front and waited as a lithe gray-haired woman seated behind the table paged through a list, marked off a name, and handed a serious-looking man in his early forties a race packet.

"Preregistered?" she asked them without looking up.

"No, we're looking for—" Ray started to say.

"Day of race is thirty dollars. Fill this out." She slid an entry form across to them.

"No," Ray said, returning the application. "We're looking for someone."

She squinted at him through her bifocals. "Try the lost and found tent."

Ray displayed his badge. "We're looking for someone. Sheri Groves. We need to know if she's checked in yet."

"Why didn't you say so," the woman muttered. She began paging through her list. "Groves . . . Groves . . . She's registered all right. All set to go."

"So she's here?" Ray asked.

"I didn't say that. I said she's checked in. I have no idea where she is."

"Do you have to check in personally? Or can you have a friend do it?"

"You're supposed to do it yourself, but this isn't the army. It's a fun run."

"Fun?!" someone shouted. "More like torture." The crowd hooted.

"Thanks," Ray told her.

Outside, the storm was getting serious, sheets of rain thrown with violent fury, whipped in unexpected directions. Visibility was reduced to a quarter mile. Ray wondered if there was a point at which the event would be called off. Running in this squall would be worse than difficult. It would be dangerous.

On cue, the booming voice assured everyone that the race would start in fifteen minutes.

Ray stuck his head into the second tent. It contained three stretchers, several sets of crutches, and a table of medical equipment. There was only one person in the tent, a young man in a sweatshirt marked "Race Aid." He looked at Ray skeptically, "Can I help you?"

Ray shook his head. He turned and walked along the rank of Porta-Pottys, straining to make out the faces in line. "See her anywhere?" he asked Glen.

"Who are we looking for?" Ehrlich wondered stupidly.

"Let's try the other tents," Glen suggested.

They traversed the "can" gauntlet and discovered a tent stocked with running shoes, running tights, T-shirts with running slogans, hats, Gor-tex jackets . . . A banner declared that all items were 50 percent off. Except for being housed within wavering nylon walls, it could have been a department in a sporting goods store. Waterlogged runners fished through the racks, fingering products.

Leading the way to the final tent, Ray surveyed the swelling throng and did his best to avoid the mud holes. Behind him, Ehrlich swore and said something about his shoes being ruined for life.

The voice told the congregated athletes that the competition would begin in thirteen minutes. This for those who couldn't read the giant digital clock.

"Maybe she's not here," Ehrlich said.

Ray poked his head into the last tent. It was full of people and food. He stepped inside and stood on his tiptoes, not at all sure that he would recognize Sheri if he saw her. Especially in rain garb.

He was about to declare the expedition a failure and suggest that they return to the Wagoneer when a cheery voice said, "Hey you! How's the cheek?"

➤➤ THIRTY-THREE ⬅⬅

"SHERI." RAY INSTINCTIVELY reached up to touch his face.

Sheri was smiling, perfectly straight, white teeth gleaming, blue eyes sparkling. Holding a paper cup with the logo "Just Do It," and decked out in purple and black, she looked like an advertisement for Nike.

"What are you doing here?" she asked. Then she noticed Glen. "Hey, Glen. You guys racing?"

"Not hardly," Ray told her. "We're here to—"

"Investigate a murder," Glen informed.

"A murder?" She blinked at them, large eyes swelling.

"Possibly," Ray admitted. "We were hoping that you could help us. Last night at about closing time a man rode the lift up."

"Oh, you mean the guy who fell? That was horrible."

"You were probably the last person to see him alive. So anything you remember could be useful."

She shrugged at them. "I didn't see it happen."

"But you saw him come up and ride back down, right? Did you notice anything strange? Was he acting funny? Did he seem nervous? Depressed?"

"I wasn't really paying attention."

"Show her the sketch," Glen prompted.

Ray withdrew the drawing from his pants pocket. It was heavily creased, the picture itself smeared. "Is this the guy?"

Sighing, she grunted, "Yep. That's him."

"Do you remember anything else?"

After thinking for a moment, she said, "Just that he was a last run. That's what we call the stragglers who ride the lift at closing."

The voice bellowed, "Six minutes. Six minutes until start time."

Sheri gulped down the rest of her drink, turned, and shot it into a trash can.

"Did you see what he did at the top? Did he meet anyone?" Ray asked.

"He got off. Went into the lodge. He came out maybe . . . ten minutes later with some woman. Got back on the lift."

"*With* the woman?"

"Well, I don't mean *with*, necessarily."

The voice told the world that there were only five minutes remaining and Sheri hurriedly snatched up another Nike cup.

"Could you describe the woman?" Ray asked, struggling to remain patient.

"Long dark hair. City clothes: short skirt, heels . . . Attractive. But like I said, they might not have been together."

"Were they talking?"

"Four minutes!" the voice boomed. "Racers please assemble at the starting line!"

"Were they talking?" Ray repeated.

"I gotta go," Sheri said.

"Were they talking?"

"Yeah."

The other runners were abandoning the refreshment tent as though it had caught fire. Sheri was clearly anxious to leave too.

"Can you tell us anything else about the woman?"

She started for the door. "I only saw her from a distance."

"You must have seen her get off the lift."

Pausing at the door, Sheri shook her head. "No. At least, I don't remember her."

"What about going down?" Ray wondered, following her outside. "She had to ride back down."

"Three minutes," the voice said. "Racers should be at the starting line." The wind responded to this by howling and tearing the fly from the first aid tent.

"I gotta go," Sheri apologized. She began pushing her way through the bodies. Ray stayed behind her.

"Did you see the woman ride down?"

"No. I don't think she got on the lift."

"Then how did she get to the bottom?"

"I don't know. Maybe she biked."

They passed a waterlogged placard bearing the numbers 8:00.

"I thought you said she was wearing nice clothes."

"Yeah." Sheri was bullying her way forward like a football lineman, creating a path where there wasn't one. They passed a sign that said 7:00.

"If she was wearing nice clothes," Ray said, fighting to keep up, "she wouldn't have been riding a bike."

"You're right," Sheri admitted. She finally stopped beneath the 6:00 sign.

Ray was breathing hard, thankful that he wasn't about to sprint up a muddy mountain in the rain. "Do you think she could have been Italian?"

"The woman?"

Ray nodded. It was a leading question, he realized, but there wasn't time to beat around the bush.

"Could've been," Sheri said. She bent over, stretching her hamstrings, then began to hop like a startled rabbit. "I'm not sure."

"When you say attractive . . ."

"She wasn't fat," Sheri said, bouncing.

"Was she thin? Was she . . . well endowed?"

"I saw her from a hundred yards away. I'd only be guessing."

"Guess," Ray implored.

"I don't know . . ." Sheri said, pausing to stretch. "Barbie doll figure."

The one-minute mark was signaled and the runners went into a frenzy, stamping their feet and twitching like anxious race horses. "You'd better head for high ground," Sheri warned. "Otherwise you'll be trampled. These people are animals."

"Okay. Thanks for your help. If you think of anything else, you can reach me through Glen." Ray retreated, slogging awkwardly through the human forest. He was approaching the Porta-Potty when the loudspeaker started the countdown: "Ten, nine, eight . . ." Frantic runners pushed past him. "Seven, six, five . . ." A Porta-Potty door flew open and a man tripped out, yanking up his running tights. "Four, three, two . . ."

At the crisp retort of the starter's pistol, the living mass of Gor-tex exploded into motion: legs churning, feet fighting for traction, arms swinging wildly, bodies bumping and jostling, steam rising from overexcited lungs. In thirty seconds, the group had disappeared into the fog like an army of specters.

"Well?" Ehrlich asked. "What did you find out?"

He glanced at Ehrlich, wondering why he cared, wondering for at least the third time why he had agreed to come along. Cox had been his friend, his colleague. Was that reason enough? "She saw a woman."

Ehrlich cursed. "Louise Mancini?"

"Maybe. Sheri didn't get a good look at her. She just said that she was attractive: quote 'a Barbie doll figure.' "

"Louise Mancini," Ehrlich repeated. "I knew it. Ron the Don killed Mike."

"Maybe."

"Who else?" Ehrlich demanded. He swore again, then argued, "Mike was sleeping with Louise. Ron found out and had him iced."

As they started back to the car, Ray tried to make sense of this. It seemed logical on the surface: a simple case of jealousy. But practically speaking, how could Ron have done the job? Say he had learned of his wife's affair, how could he manage to poison Cox in such a way that he would fall from the lift on the ride down? Could arsenic be administered with that sort of accuracy? Or had that just been a lucky coincidence? Maybe Cox had been poisoned earlier in the day and . . . Ray made a mental note to check on the time factor: How long did it take for pentavalent trioxide to kill a man? For that matter, had the amount in Cox's bloodstream been enough to end his life if he hadn't fallen? Time and potency. He would ask Glen's friend at the ME's office.

A few paces ahead, Ehrlich reached an embankment of slick boulders. Swearing, he began scrambling over them with the grace and speed of a drunken turtle. As Ray waited, he considered the other scenarios that were crowding his mind. What if they were making things too difficult? What if Cox really had taken his own life? What if, for some inexplicable reason, he came to the end of his rope, self-administered the poison, then either fell or maybe even jumped to his death? A lot of "what ifs." And several extraneous factors made that scenario unlikely: the airline reservations, the success of the deal with Fukutomi, the link with the State Department, and now an affair with Mrs. Mancini.

No, Ray decided, starting into the boulders. Suicide

was a stretch. The note, the plane tickets, the rental car with the keys locked inside . . . Cox had been bugging out. Why? Because Ron Mancini had found out about the affair? Maybe. Or because he had something valuable? Eddie Fukutomi's computer chip? Or . . . What about blackmail? Could he have been blackmailing Louise, threatening to tell her husband? Not a good idea. If she called his bluff, his only play would be to tell a mobster that he was committing adultery with his wife. Not smart. Scratch blackmail.

They were approaching the parking area when Ray remembered that there had been two reservations to Tokyo. Whom was Cox planning on taking? Louise Mancini? Were they planning to run away together? Had Ron figured it out and taken steps to ensure that it didn't happen?

A Dodge splashed up and double parked a few yards from the trail head. Ray recognized who it was before the doors even popped open. Feds. Predictably, the passengers who got out were dressed in trench coats, hats, and sunglasses.

"Dark enough for you?" he asked. The light was bad even without Ray-Bans.

"Officer Attla," Agent Pool grunted, stone-faced. "Sheriff Redfern." He glanced at Ehrlich but apparently found him unworthy of a greeting.

"What are you doing here?" Bailey wanted to know.

"We're big race fans," Ray said.

The wind came wailing over the ridge and both agents had to grip their hats to keep from losing them.

"I'll bet," Pool muttered. "Don't suppose you have any information that might assist us in our investigation?"

"Don't suppose," Ray replied.

"Do you happen to know if Sheri Groves is racing tonight?"

"Try the registration tent next to the Porta-Pottys," Ray said. "They might be able to help you." Before Ray could come up with another smart-alecky comment, a gust snuck up and lifted the hats from both agents, whisking them to treetop level before depositing them halfway across the parking lot.

As they sprinted to fetch them, Glen said, "You could at least be nice to them."

"Why?" Ray asked as they piled into the Wagoneer.

"Because you're a professional law enforcement officer."

"So?"

"So they're professionals too," Glen pointed out. He released the parking brake and gave the ignition a try. The Jeep quaked and belched a puff of smoke before falling silent. "We're all working toward the same end. Just because they're Federal and we're local shouldn't hamper our relationship or our efforts."

"It shouldn't. But it does."

"It's never a good idea to burn bridges." Glen paused and turned the key again. The engine made a noise like a wounded moose before dying. "Blast!" Clenching his teeth together, he glared in the direction of the engine and twisted the key. When this didn't produce the desired results, he pounded on the dash, "Blasted thing!"

Ray pulled his hood back up and opened the door. "Got a flashlight?"

Glen rooted under the seat. "Here."

From the backseat, Ehrlich whined, "I'm freezing. Shut the door."

"Pop the hood," Ray instructed. "And keep trying to start it."

"Shut the door!" Ehrlich demanded.

Ray complied and sloshed to the front of the Jeep. The latch clunked and he raised the hood, suspending it with a metal rod. Using the beam of the flashlight like a doctor's probe, he examined the "patient": rotting hoses, frayed belts, grayish-green corrosion that obscured not only the terminals, but the battery itself . . . His diagnosis? Terminal.

In the cab, Glen continued to attempt to spur the truck to action: ignition click, the rhythmic bark as it tried to catch, the high-pitched shriek as it lost the battle.

To get a good look at what was happening, or more importantly, what wasn't, Ray realized he would have to get under the Jeep. He glanced at his legs. His slacks were soaking wet, muddy to the calves, the soles of his shoes ferrying a full inch of soil. The damage had already been done. Grabbing hold of the grill, he lowered himself into the mud and slid between the front tires. If he were a mechanic, this bit of alligator repair work would cost Glen big bucks.

With the help of the flashlight, Ray noted that the garage had fixed the brakes, but nothing else. The strut mounts were still bad. So were the struts. Glen needed new shocks as well. He followed various cables with the beam, looking for a short, a loose wire . . . anything.

Overhead, somewhere beyond the air filter, Glen was begging the "blasted thing" to run.

Ray covered his mouth against the smell of gas and burnt oil. Moving the flashlight to the right, he was reaching to wiggle a cluster of cables when he saw the box: black plastic with wires protruding from one end. His hand froze.

The engine complained again as Glen continued his relentless attempt to resuscitate it. Following the wires with the light, Ray managed to trace them up to the distributor.

"Stop!"

THIRTY-FOUR

"STOP!" RAY SCRAMBLED out from under the Jeep in a panic. "Stop!" He pulled himself up by the door handle and pounded on the driver's side window. "Stop!"

Glen looked at him like he was insane. "What's the matter?"

"Don't touch the ignition! Take the key out!"

"Why?"

"Just do it!"

Glen did. He rolled the window down and held up the key. "Okay. Now what?"

"Out! Get out!" Ray opened the door and yanked him out by the arm. He motioned to Ehrlich. "Come on!"

"I'm cold."

"You're fixing to be warm. Real warm. Get out!"

"What's going on?" Glen wondered.

"Get clear," he said as he forcibly removed Ehrlich from the backseat.

"Clear of what?"

Ehrlich sneezed as he emerged into the drizzle. "I think I'm coming down with something. Probably pneumonia."

"Move away from the car!" Ray urged. Out of the corner of his eye, he saw the FBI agents returning from their hat-retrieval mission. They were headed for the trail. "Pool!" he shouted, backing away from the Wagoneer. "Get over here!"

Pool and Bailey met them a row over from the Jeep. "Yeah?"

"We've got a problem."

"Call a cop," Pool shot back. He started for the trail.

"I'm serious."

"You guys need a jump?" Bailey asked.

"No."

Pool stopped a dozen paces away and turned back toward them. "You suddenly remember something that will slam dunk the case? Who killed Cox, for instance?"

"Actually," Ray told them, "I was hoping you could call in the bomb squad."

The smirk on Pool's face evaporated. Ehrlich swore.

"There's a bomb?" Glen asked, dumbfounded. "In my Jeep?"

Ray nodded. "There's a black box down there, hooked to the distributor."

"You sure it wasn't a catalytic converter?" Bailey asked.

"Pretty sure," Ray answered. While he wasn't Mr. Goodwrench, he could at least tell the difference between an anti-smog part and an explosive device.

Ehrlich cursed again, his breathing rapid. "We could've been killed."

Pool ignored this. "Take a look," he told Bailey.

"Okay," Bailey grunted. He trotted to the car as if Pool had asked him to get his sunglasses from the glove compartment.

Ray watched him peer into the open hood. "It's underneath!" he called without taking a single step toward the Wagoneer. "On the right!"

Bailey bent and crawled under the truck. "Be careful!" Pool yelled in a fatherly tone. "Don't touch anything!"

Thirty long seconds passed. The wind rose in waves, tearing at their jackets. Droplets assaulted their cheeks.

"Bailey?!" Pool shouted.

Obediently, the junior agent scooted out from beneath the front end. Walking back, he wiped his hands on his saturated trench coat. He looked like he had taken part in a mud wrestling competition for secret agents.

"There's a bomb all right," he said. "Not very big. But big enough to do the job."

Glen offered thanks to God. Ehrlich took the Almighty's name in vain.

"First the brakes," Ray said, "now a bomb."

"The brakes?" Pool asked.

The wind roared over the ridge and the five men formed a hunched half-circle, backs to the stinging rain.

"The lines were cut this morning," Ray answered when the gust had passed.

Bailey extracted a pad and tried to record this, but the storm made the task nearly impossible.

"Call the squad in from Anchorage," Pool told him. The underling nodded and pulled a phone from his coat. "You guys need a lift?" Pool grinned victoriously.

"What's the catch?" Ray asked.

"You have to tell us what you know, quit treating us like the enemy."

"You're not the enemy?" Ray asked.

Pool removed his Ray-Bans and blinked at him sleepily. "Help us out with this investigation, fellas."

Ray glanced at Glen. A ride was a ride. "Okay."

"What about my Jeep?" Glen asked.

"It'll be disarmed and impounded. But you'll get it back . . . eventually." He turned to Bailey. "Stay here and wait for the squad to show. Don't let anyone near the car."

Bailey's face dropped. "How will I get back?"

"I'll pick you up in a couple of hours." Pool led them to the Dodge and when they were all inside, said, "Now tell me about this bomb."

"We already did," Ray said. He waved as they passed Bailey's bent, waterlogged figure. Bailey didn't wave back.

"Who wants you guys to back off?" Pool asked as they reached the highway.

Ray considered his choices. They could stonewall Pool. But that didn't seem prudent given the situation. The guy might just deposit them at the side of the road. They could give him a few tidbits to chew on, satisfy him until they were safely back in Girdwood. Or they could actually cooperate, share information, try to solve the case. The last seemed the most practical, but it depended on Pool's willingness to form a partnership.

"Any ideas?" Pool prodded. The wind swept them sideways, threatening to push them onto the shoulder. In the backseat, Ehrlich swore at the expanse of Turnagain Arm. Pool gripped the wheel and corrected for each gust. "Any guesses?"

"Ron Mancini?" Ray offered.

Pool forgot the road. He looked over at Ray, blinking. "Ron the Don??"

"He's staying up at Alyeska."

"I know. But . . ." Pool stared at the highway vacantly. "Why would Mancini want to kill you guys? Did you do something to perturb him?

"We didn't do anything," Glen said. "We didn't even question him in Cox's murder."

"Cox's death," Pool corrected carefully. "It's not a homicide case, per se."

"Says who?" Ray asked.

"We haven't ruled out accidental death or suicide," Pool told them.

"We have," Glen said.

"Would you like to elaborate?"

Not really, Ray thought. "Well, you know about the note."

"Right." Pool nodded.

"And the plane tickets?"

"What plane tickets?"

"And the affair with Louise Mancini?"

"The what??" Pool lost his concentration and the

Dodge lost the road. They skidded onto the gravel shoulder. He and Ehrlich traded curses. Glen prayed energetically. When Pool regained control, he said, "Start at the beginning. Take it slow. Tell me everything."

Ray grudgingly complied, filling him in on the main points of the case: from finding the body to finding the bomb in the parking lot, everything except the envelope.

When he finished, Pool blew air at the windshield. "What a mess."

They traveled the next two miles without speaking. When the turnoff to Alyeska was in sight, Pool asked, "So you think Mancini killed Cox?"

"Possibly," Ray answered. "He had motive."

"You said you talked to the girl who worked the upper lift that evening. What did she have to say?"

Ray shrugged. "Not much. She saw Cox come up. Saw him go down."

"Tell him about the woman," Glen urged.

"What woman?" Pool asked.

"She saw Cox come out of the lodge with a woman. Or, at the same time as a woman. Apparently they talked, but Sheri wasn't paying that much attention and didn't know if they were actually together."

"Did they ride down together?"

"No. She doesn't know how the woman got up or down. But she's pretty sure she didn't ride the lift."

"What about a description?" Pool asked.

"Vague. Sheri was a hundred yards away. But it could fit Mrs. Mancini."

Pool grimaced and shook his head as though it ached.

"Now it's my turn," Ray said. "Why did Cox have a fake ID?"

"That's classified."

"Don't give me that garbage," Ray complained.

"I'm serious," Pool said. "I'm the special agent in charge, and I don't even know the full story on this guy."

"You have to give us something."

Pool sniffed, eyes darting from the windshield, to Ray, back to the windshield. "He worked for the State Department," he finally confessed.

"We know that. What did he do for the State Department?"

"That's classified."

Before Ray could argue, Ehrlich said, "He stole things." Both heads swiveled radically.

"He what??" Ray asked.

"Watch yourself, Mr. Ehrlich," Pool warned gravely. "Don't say anything you'll regret. Do you know what the sentence is for breaching matters of national security?"

"What sort of things did he steal?" Ray pressed.

"Secrets," Ehrlich said.

"Mr. Ehrlich . . . !"

"Industrial secrets."

Pool whipped the car onto a pullout and it skidded to a halt. "This is a Federal investigation. That information is classified. I swear to you that if it leaves this car, you'll be prosecuted to the full extent of the law. Do you understand me?"

"Yes, sir," the three men chimed.

After glaring at them through bulging eyes, Pool hit the gas and the Dodge fishtailed back onto the road, the rear tires spewing gravel.

"Cox was an industrial spy . . . for the government?" Ray wondered aloud.

Pool put his Ray-Bans back on and adopted a stern expression.

"How do you know?" Ray asked Ehrlich.

"I just do," he answered. "We were friends. He told me things."

Ray closed his eyes and visualized the envelope again. Could it have held that computer chip? Had Cox stolen one . . . for the Pentagon?! Did the U.S. Government really engage in that sort of thing? Would they stoop to thievery to keep in step with foreign technology?

"We'll need to talk to Mancini," Pool said out of the blue.

"I hope by *we* you mean the Bureau," Ray said.

"Oh, no. You guys are the ones with the theory and the trail of evidence. You have to come too." Pool smiled. "He's leaving in the morning. After breakfast with Fukutomi. We'll catch him early."

Ray reflected on Pool's choice of words. *Catch him?* Catching Mancini at breakfast was about as comforting a thought as catching a polar bear in the middle of devouring a fresh kill.

"I'll pick you up at seven."

"I have services tomorrow," Glen tried. "The first one's at eight."

"I'll pick you up at seven," Pool said, as if he hadn't heard. "Our meeting with Ron won't take long."

"I'm not going," Ehrlich said. "I'm a private citizen. You can't make me."

"Fine," Pool said.

Ray pointed at the condos. "That's me."

The Dodge swooped into the lot and jerked to a stop next to the curb.

"See you in the morning, partner," Glen said glumly as Ray got out.

"Right." He waved a finger at Glen, frowned at Pool, ignored Ehrlich.

The headlights of the Dodge veered away and Ray found himself standing alone in a blowing mist, barely able to make out the closest condo, much less the surrounding mountains. It was a fitting allegory, he thought, for the case he was marooned in: cold, foggy, disorienting, but probably within walking distance of the answer. Was that answer Ron the Don Mancini? At the moment, he didn't really care. He was simply glad that the vacation day from hell was finally over.

Trudging toward the condo, he was debating whether

to take a shower or just slip off his filthy, wet clothes and fall into bed, when he heard a thumping sound. Before he could classify it or even turn around to look for the source, the sky erupted in fireworks.

➤➤ THIRTY-FIVE ◄◄

IN THE FIRST instant, there was no pain, just a shower of yellow sparks and the dull sense that something had collided with the back of his head. The concussion wave ran down his spine like a bolt of lightning and exited his body at the knees, causing them to buckle. For a millisecond he was totally disoriented. As he sagged forward, his mind worked in slow motion. What was happening?

Before he could come up with a satisfactory answer, a second round of mortar impacted the small of his back. Through the veil of stars, he saw the sidewalk coming at him, then he heard a sickening thud. Something tore into his side, just below his rib cage.

Suddenly the pain caught up with him: crisscrossing fingers of searing electricity. He blinked at the hairline cracks in the wet sidewalk, fighting to remain conscious.

There was a brief lull. The world seemed to be holding its breath. Ray could hear his heart and lungs responding to the attack. His mouth was salty with the taste of blood.

He was about to make an effort to rise, or at least roll over, when something stoked the fire in his side. By the third or fourth jab, he realized that he was being kicked.

Ray felt a heavy weight crash onto his back. Air left his body in a short, gasping hiss. Stars danced over the sidewalk until his entire field of vision was bright and glittery.

Someone whispered gruffly, "Had enough?"

Ray had the feeling that he was about to die and thought that perhaps he had just heard the voice of God.

"Leave Cox alone!"

He tried to make sense of this. Leave *who* alone?

"Drop the case. Or you're dead." This was punctuated by another kick to his side.

Through the pulsing buzz that filled his ears, Ray recognized footsteps. Whoever had just knocked the stuffing out of him was leaving. Finally. Thankfully. An engine started in the distance. It revved. Wheels spun. A car screeched away.

Lying facedown on the sidewalk, Ray could feel the cold rain on his neck, soaking his hair. But he was sweating, overheated and nauseated. Eyes closed, he felt the universe circling above him. He was sinking, twirling, falling.

His last semicoherent thought was of being thirsty. Thirsty and anxious for a chance to get back at whoever had sucker punched him from behind.

When he awoke, he was stiff and cold. Shivering, he winced at the thick web of pain that seemed to encompass every nerve, every fiber, every cell of his body. For a long moment, he couldn't remember where he was, why he was wet, why his head felt as though it had been bashed repeatedly with a two-by-four, why he couldn't swallow, why his side felt like a postoperative wound. As his eyes focused on the sidewalk, it slowly came back: Alyeska, the Bird Creek race, ambushed . . .

Holding his breath, he brought his watch up to face

level and squinted at the digits: 11:10. Even squinting hurt. Without moving his head, he glanced at the sky. The light was diffused by clouds, making it impossible to decide whether it was 11 A.M. or 11 P.M. He examined his watch again and, after several seconds, was able to make out the tiny P just above the time. P.M. Night. He had been prostrate in front of the condos for . . . an hour? Less? According to the chill in his bones, it had been days. Weeks. An eternity.

He considered getting up, but various parts of his body argued with this, unanimously rejecting the idea. It would require too much effort and produce too much pain. Yes, he needed to attend to his injuries. Yes, staying out here on the concrete, in the rain, put him at risk for hypothermia. But no, remaining still for another five minutes would not kill him. In fact, there was a chance that it might even help. Maybe if he rested long enough, his energy would return. Then again . . .

Ray rolled gently onto his good side. A hot fist squeezed the cavity beneath his rib cage. The parking lot blinked in time with his heart and the stars returned.

Closing his eyes, Ray concentrated on remaining conscious. He tried running down the events of the day. He visualized Cox's body lying beneath the lift. At least the guy hadn't been kicked to pieces, he thought. Glen appeared, bearing the stretcher: wild red hair, blue eyes, classic Native facial structure. The mental video fast-forwarded to Amy Yasaka. He lingered on a frozen image of Yasaka bending over him in the hallway: dark eyes, flawless skin, perfect lips . . . A deep breath caused her to disintegrate and she was replaced by yellow streaks. Ray swore against the heat that pulsed up and down his side.

He forced himself to move on: Cox's hotel room, the note, the tickets . . . A full-color movie of the ride up the lift began to roll. Ray watched the trees pass under his feet. The face of the midway kid flashed into view. He was gulping down dope. Suddenly Ray was coming back down. Glen was beside him. Down below, the two suits came into view. They were too large, almost as tall as the lift house itself.

The images slowly dissolved and Ray opened his eyes. Thinking through the case was more taxing than relaxing. It was such a complex, chaotic mix of people and happenings. He hadn't even gotten to the brake lines, Mancini, the affair his wife was having with Cox. And then there were Fukutomi and Eddie, and that chip, and the infamous disappearing envelope, and the bomb, and the beating . . .

Now there was a puzzling trio of questions: Who had taken the envelope? Who had rigged Glen's car? Who had used Ray for kickball practice? Better yet, why? He had no idea where the envelope could be. Presumably the Wagoneer had been sabotaged, twice, to convince them to give up on the case. A logical assumption. But if it was true, then why would they bother to jump Ray, pummel him, and issue a threat? Wasn't that a little redundant? Wasn't the bomb sufficient to get the message across?

Unless . . . Maybe whoever was responsible for the bomb knew that it hadn't detonated. Maybe they followed them back from Bird Creek and . . . No. If the intention was to kill Ray and Glen in a fiery blast, why not jump them both and, instead of getting in a few kicks, finish them off for good? It didn't make sense. Then again, neither did lying on the sidewalk in the middle of the night, on vacation, in the rain, trying to sort things out.

As if prompted by Ray's silent complaint, the wind rose dramatically. He could hear it coming, advancing across the lot, droplets attacking cars, splattering against the asphalt, hitting the walls of the northernmost condos in staccato sheets. When it reached him, Ray's already damp pants began to soak through. Time to come in out of the rain.

His first attempt to get up was rewarded with a surge

of electric stabs that brought tears to his eyes. He moaned, cheek pressing into the concrete, as if it might offer some vague relief. Still lightheaded a minute later, he made a second attempt. This time he succeeded in reaching a sitting position. The drizzle merged with an array of Fourth of July sparklers. Water ran down his brow, into his eyes, along his chin.

Struggling to get his feet under him, he considered the warning again: "Drop the case." Gladly, if this was the alternative. He balanced in a crouch, using his hands to keep from doing another faceplant into the sidewalk. "Leave Cox alone." Okay. No problem. Will do. After gathering his resolve, he willed himself up. Surprisingly, his legs responded and he found himself standing. Listing to one side like an ailing ship, but standing.

He eyed the condos. Warmth, water, dry clothes, a comfortable bed, Margaret . . . They were all waiting just fifty feet away. Ray wasn't sure he had fifty feet in him.

He began the journey with a stagger, almost tripping off the curb. He stood firm, knees locked, waiting for the pain to subside. When it did, he shuffled forward.

There was a crooked man, he thought, pulling himself along, who walked a crooked mile. He was definitely crooked, and the distance seemed like a mile.

Blinking away the rain and the pounding in the back of his skull, he wondered if he would be permanently crooked. Was that dull, nagging sense of dementia here to stay? Did he have a head injury? A concussion? Was he bleeding internally? He reached a hand up and dabbed at his cheek. Crusted blood.

The admonition echoed through his mind, "Leave Cox alone."

Still thirty feet from the condo door and closing at the speed of glacial ice, he tried to classify the voice, but couldn't. It was nothing more than a hoarse whisper.

He ran the tape recording again: "Leave Cox alone . . . Drop the case. Or you're dead." Almost no inflection. Very mechanical. Neither high nor low, male nor female. Could it have been Hat Trick Benny? Yes. Except that Hat Trick probably wouldn't have had the self-restraint necessary to leave Ray alive. What about one of the security guards from the hotel? They had seemed more than willing to beat him into a puddle on the sidewalk.

Twenty-some feet.

Ray analyzed his two options: Hat Trick Benny or the Asian brute squad. Benny was certainly up to the task. And if the attack had taken place *after* he'd confronted Ron the Don about his wife's affair with Cox, it certainly would have been motivated. But it hadn't.

For the first time, Ray wondered about Glen. Had he been thrashed and threatened? He decided to check on the chaplain if and when he made it into the condo.

Fifteen feet and closing.

The Amazon and her sidekick from the hotel . . . Ray could think of no reason for them to use him as a human punching bag. Besides, there were two of them. Only one person had ambushed him. Or at least it seemed that way. Could there have been two of them? He didn't have a chance to see anything except an extreme close-up of the concrete.

Ten feet.

He was within spitting distance now, under the protective covering of the extended roofline. The wind gusted through the breezeway like an invisible river.

Six feet.

His legs were shaking, his limbs not so much in pain as weak.

Three feet.

Ray leaned the final yard, fishing into a pants pocket for a key. He found it and blindly tried to fit it into the lock. Looking down made his head do timpani rolls.

After two failed attempts, he hit the lock and forced the door open. It creaked loudly. He slid inside and shut the door, exhausted to the point of collapse. Feeling his way down the darkened hall, he flipped on the bathroom light and stared into the mirror at the ghoulish reflection. His face was cut and bruised, already swelling, and most of his hair had escaped from the confines of the ponytail band. Ghastly.

The cardinal rule from now on, he told himself as he labored to rise, was to spend his vacations far, far away from any and all police work. No more busman's holidays.

He slipped off his jacket and let it fall into a wet heap on the floor. The shirt followed. He grimaced at his side. It looked as bad as it felt. It took several minutes to successfully rid himself of the heavy, sopping slacks.

Bracing himself against the cabinet, Ray stood there in his underwear, wondering what to do next. Call a doctor? Call Glen? He cupped his hand and gulped cold water from the faucet. When his thirst was satisfied and he could swallow without a composed effort, he flipped off the light and went back into the hall. Keera was asleep in the extra bedroom, a nest of stuffed animals hedging her in. He mentally blew a kiss at her.

As he approached the main bedroom, he could hear the deep, rhythmic, breaths of a sound sleeper. He navigated past an open suitcase and pulled back the comforter on his side of the bed. The sheets were hot, the electric blanket glowing on high. Ray sank into it, groaning softly.

He was still trying to find a comfortable position when Margaret rolled over and muttered drowsily, "Hi, honey." An arm swung in his direction, coming to rest directly on the grapefruit. Ray grit his teeth together, determined not to scream in agony. Exhaling, she puffed, "How'd it go?"

"Fine," he lied.

"Good." She gave his side a playful squeeze.

He flinched, biting his lip.

"I was kind of thinking that when you got back we could . . . *you know.*"

You know?! Ray glanced at her in horror.

"But then I got tired waiting. And now I'm too sleepy."

"Aw . . . shucks."

"Maybe tomorrow." She smacked her lips and turned away from him.

"Yeah . . ." Ray sighed in relief. "Maybe."

➤➤ THIRTY-SIX ◄◄

A COLORLESS VOID. Space stretching forever. Silence.

The featureless canopy abruptly collapsed, draping itself over him like a velvet cloak. It was pleasant at first. Comforting. But the wrap quickly tightened its grip, binding his limbs, robbing him of breath and sight. He could feel it dragging him away. And then, without warning, he was falling. Into a deep pit. A bottomless grave.

The free fall stretched . . . slowed . . . stopped inexplicably . . . He found himself hanging in a limbo without light or life. He floated through the emptiness . . . drifted . . . began to pick up speed . . . began to soar.

The gauzy, electric mist shifted, parting to reveal an alpine Eden: rolling carpet of emerald lichen, ranks of willows, bushy alders lining a placid stream that snaked across the valley. On the far side of the meadow, mountains rose up dramatically.

He stood in bright morning sunlight and breathed in

the sweet scent of fireweed. Maybe he was dead. Maybe this was paradise.

There was a stirring in the brush nearby and a bushy white fox trotted into the meadow. With a strange sense of clarity, he realized that it was Kajortoq, a character from Inupiat mythology. And for an instant, he knew that he was dreaming.

He watched as Kajortoq sniffed the air for game. The beauty of this summer day was lost on her. She was weak with hunger, weary from hunting. After a long moment, she snorted in frustration. Her head drooped and she was about to slink back into the trees when something out on the tundra caught her eye: a young bull caribou! She moved toward it and, upon reaching the animal, greeted, "Good day, young nomad."

The bull kept his head to the tundra, never acknowledging her presence.

"I know a place where there is an entire field of tasty moss," she told the caribou.

The bulging eyes glared at her. "And where might that be?"

"It's a secret, hidden place that I discovered only this morning," the white fox said. "There is so much moss that it would take days for you to eat it."

"Will you show me?"

Kajortoq smiled. "Certainly. Follow me to the trail that runs along the cliff, the one over the sea. I will show you." And she started off.

The caribou followed, head held high. When they reached the trail, the caribou hesitated. It was narrow, the cliffside treacherous.

"The road is difficult," the fox said, "but the moss and lichen are worth it." The caribou grunted and began clomping his way behind the fox.

"Careful," the fox warned periodically as the path grew more and more precarious. The caribou labored along, hooves slipping on loose rocks, until they came to a section where the trail had been washed away in a mud slide.

"Where is the moss?" the caribou asked, losing patience.

"Just around the next bend," the fox told him. "We only have to jump this small gap and then we will find it."

"I cannot," the caribou confessed, clearly frightened.

"Of course you can," the white fox assured him. "I jumped it only this morning. And you are much more agile than I."

The flattery worked. After stamping his hooves, the bull galloped forward, leapt, and landed on the other side.

Before he could catch his breath, something dove at him out of the sky. The caribou grunted and flinched, its hooves slipping on pebbles still glossy from the morning dew. The assailant, a bird, swooped in, cawing angrily until the bull lost his grip on the cliffside and fell in a blur of clawing limbs.

Kajortoq cursed the tragedy before setting out on a slow, studied descent to the beach. As she went, she searched for the carcass. When she reached the rocky shore without finding the bull, she wondered aloud, "Where is my caribou?"

"Your caribou?" a voice called. It was Raven. He was circling in the sky, a piece of fresh meat clamped in his mouth.

"What have you done with my caribou?" Kajortoq demanded.

Raven landed on a nearby stone and cackled at her. "It was indeed your trickery that led him here. But it was my cleverly timed assault that sent him to his death. It was my eye that found him, my beak that picked him clean."

Kajortoq lunged at Raven, snapping her sharp teeth. The arrogant black bird flapped its wings casually and lifted into the air, easily dodging the attack. "Anyone can deceive a fool," Raven mocked. "But the prize goes to the shrewd."

"Is that right?" Kajortoq was holding a gun, aiming it at Raven. Except she wasn't a fox anymore. She was a woman with dark, penetrating eyes. The rest of her face was obscured by a revolver that was almost as large as her head.

And Raven . . . was now a man, a man cowering behind his hands, begging for mercy. "Please . . . ! Please . . . I won't do it again!"

"I'll just bet," the woman scoffed. "Now you're *my* prize."

The man bolted. There was a blinding flash. An explosion. Smoke. A bird squawked pitifully. A woman sighed wearily. Far away, a dog barked.

Morning light was spilling in from the window, cutting the ceiling into two neat halves. He realized that he had been dreaming, but couldn't recall what it had been about. The details were gone, whisked away by his conscious mind.

Twisting beneath the soft sheets, he put his arms around Margaret.

She stirred. "Ray . . ."

He kissed her ear, her neck . . . As he worked his way down her naked back, he was struck by the fact that Margaret was sleeping without a nightshirt. Apparently she really had been waiting to surprise him last night. And that perfume . . . Intoxicating.

He massaged her shoulders, traced her spine with a fingertip. Her waist was pencil thin, the curve of her hip firm. Had she lost weight?

She stretched and turned to face him. "You've been thinking about this since you first saw me, haven't you?"

Ray was about to assure her that yes, from the day they had met, he had, when he opened his eyes . . . and saw . . . Amy Yasaka grinning at him.

Shrieking, he backed away as though she were wielding a hot iron.

"What's the matter?!" She reached for him, lips first. He lost his balance and fell out of bed.

Ray twitched awake, gasping as though someone had been trying to smother him with a pillow. The sheets were twisted around his legs, stuck to his clammy skin like fly paper. He glanced over at Margaret. She was sleeping peacefully.

Sitting up, Ray closed his eyes as a killer headache made its presence known. When the brunt of it had passed, he checked his watch: 6:42. He gently probed his side. Ow! It was swollen and very tender.

Leaning back against the pillow, he shook his head at the bizarre dream. Amy Yasaka? Sure, he found her attractive. But fantasizing about her was rather disturbing. On the heels of this thought, the other elements of his active dream life came wandering back: the white fox, the caribou falling from the cliff, Raven . . . What was it? Zoo night? And he hadn't even eaten pizza for dinner. Maybe the mystery assailant had knocked something loose inside Ray's head.

The white fox, Kajortoq, was simple enough to explain. She was a character in one of Grandfather's tales. Fueled by hunger, she had tricked the caribou and led him to his death. Except, in the old story, Kajortoq had been responsible for caribou's fall, not Raven. And Kajortoq had eaten her bounty. Only later was she deceived by Raven.

Ray could still see Kajortoq pulling a gun, transmogrifying into a woman, Raven shape-shifting into a man. Trying to make sense of that made his temples pound. It was utterly illogical and without explanation. Of course, that was often the way with dreams.

Suddenly, Keera's words echoed in his mind: "*He fell down, Daddy.*" It was indeed strange how her admonition and Cox's death seemed to parallel the Kajortoq myth. Grandfather would see something significant in that. He would say that the tuungak were trying to tell

Ray something, to warn him, to "lead him through danger ways."

Dismissing the dream, Ray padded into the bathroom. Walking didn't feel great, he noted en route. His side pulsed with pain and his head was clanging like an overplayed cymbal. Both cheeks burned. There was a sore spot between his shoulder blades. Not in prime shape, he decided, but he would live.

The mirror had a different opinion. He looked like a boxer who had just fought a particularly nasty bout, and lost.

Ray spent the next ten minutes dabbing away crusted blood, swallowing Advil, brushing his teeth. He had just pulled on a pair of jeans and a sweatshirt and was trying to put on his socks without doubling over when there was a knock at the front door.

He groaned at his watch. The Fibbies were right on time. Picking up his Nikes, he tiptoed to the door and squinted through the peephole. Glen, Agent Pool, and Agent Bailey were huddled outside. Ray opened the door and managed a half-smile.

"Ready?" Pool grunted. When he saw Ray his mouth fell open. "What the—?"

"What happened?!" Glen gasped. "Are you all right?!"

Bailey fumbled with his jacket, hurriedly unharnessing his sidearm. Pointing it at the sky, he cut his eyes back and forth, as if Ray's attacker might still be on the premises.

"Somebody jumped me last night," Ray told them.

Bailey put his revolver away in favor of a notepad. "What did he look like?"

Ray shook his head. "No idea. They got me from behind."

Glen shook his head at the atrocity. "Have you seen a doctor?"

"I'm okay . . . I think."

Pool frowned at him. "You still want to come with us to see Mancini?"

Ray didn't. He was tired, ailing, in desperate need of rest. The mugging was the perfect excuse to avoid visiting Mancini. In fact, if he milked it enough, it might even get him free of the case altogether. He could relax, recuperate, try to salvage his vacation.

But instead of scaring him off, the attack had produced the opposite effect. Now he was mad. For the first time since discovering Cox's body, he was determined to figure out who had killed him. And, in the process, figure out who it was that had greeted him in the parking lot. Revenge, Ray realized, was a potent fuel.

"Wild dogs couldn't keep me away."

▶➤ THIRTY-SEVEN ◀◀

"LET ME WRITE Margaret a note." Ray left the three men at the door and stepped into the kitchen. He wrote Margaret's name on the back of a flyer for the alpine slide, then jotted a short message:

Had to run an "official" errand. (Ugh!) Be back in time for church.

Love,
Ray

The bit about church was a little over the top, he decided as he set the note next to the coffeemaker. But running off at the crack of dawn to do police work while they were supposed to be on vacation was not going to earn him any brownie points. Going to church, on the other hand, would. Especially if he did so without grumbling, with at least the pretense of a positive attitude. Margaret wasn't stupid. She would see through this. But she would appreciate the thought behind it.

When he returned to the door, the men were gone. A horn tooted and he saw the dirty white Dodge parked next to the curb.

He grabbed a jacket and went out in his bare feet, closing the door as quietly as possible. Carrying his socks and shoes, he was hit by a sense of déjà vu. Just about twenty-four hours earlier, he had been sneaking out of the condo with his mountain bike. It seemed like weeks ago.

Approaching the Dodge, he silently regretted biking the ski runs. If only he had stuck to the valley trails. If only he had avoided the lift. None of this would be happening. Or at least it wouldn't be happening to him.

He climbed into the back next to Glen and started pulling on his socks. This proved to be painful. Bending at the waist sent rivulets of fire up and down his side. After donning one sock, he raised up and waited for the burning to subside. "What did you find out about the bomb?" he asked, breathing hard.

"It's at the lab in Anchorage now," Pool said, accelerating out of the lot.

"Looks professional, though," Bailey said.

Ray wondered if Bailey would know a professional bomb if he saw one. He folded in half to attend to the second sock. As he did the car filled with stars.

"The good news is that they saved the Wagoneer," Glen told him.

"Oh, that is good news," Ray muttered.

"The squad disarmed it," Bailey said. "No prints. Definitely professional."

"Yeah." Ray leaned back. Maybe Glen could put his shoes on for him. His stomach was in the act now, threatening to convulse. Thankfully, it was empty.

"Donut?" Bailey asked. He thrust a cardboard box of pastries into the backseat.

Sweating now, Ray rolled down the window and stuck his head out. "No thanks."

"They're Jean's," Glen told him as he snatched up a sticky bun. "Homemade."

"No thanks." Swallowing hard, Ray sucked fresh air into his lungs.

"I'll take another," Pool said.

The box was retracted. Ray rolled up the window and peered down at his feet. They looked like they were a hundred yards away.

"Want some help?" Glen asked, munching.

"No. I got it." He made no move to put the shoes on.

"Here. Let me do it." Glen crammed the remainder of the bun into his mouth and took one of the Nikes. As he worked it onto Ray's foot, he said, "You know, Ray, you've gotta learn to let people help you. I'm all for being independent but there's something to the concept of receiving. If you can't receive, you're going to miss out on a lot in life."

Ray could feel a sermon coming. "Thanks for the tip. Did anybody call Mancini to tell him we were coming?"

Pool nodded. "Yep. He sounded happy as punch."

"You see, Ray," Glen continued, tying the first shoe, "if you can't receive from people, how can you receive from—"

"You guys know anything about an envelope?" Ray asked.

Pool's head jerked. "What sort of envelope?"

"One that Cox had with him when he died?"

Bailey and Pool put their heads together and began conferring in whispers.

"There was no envelope on the body," Glen said. "I was standing there in the parking lot when the troopers recorded his possessions. There was a watch, a wallet, cash, pictures, credit cards, a passport, a business card . . . No envelope."

"Did you see an envelope?" Pool asked.

"Maybe."

"What do you mean, maybe?" Pool twisted to face him. "Did you see it or not?"

"Maybe. What was in it?" Ray asked.

Bailey leaned over for another conference. They were pulling into the hotel lot before Pool said, "That's classified."

"So you know about the manila envelope?" Ray asked.

"I didn't say that," Pool argued.

"What manila envelope?" Glen wondered.

"If Cox was carrying it on him," Ray speculated, "it was obviously important."

"I said it was classified," Pool grumbled.

"My guess is that it contained some sort of industrial secrets. He was employed by the State Department. Maybe the boys back there had him doing spook work. Maybe they had him snatch the NVSC chip."

The Dodge lurched into a spot and Pool jammed it into park. Wheeling around in his seat, he snarled, "Where did you put it?"

"Put what?" Ray couldn't help grinning. Both cheeks punished him for this. "You mean the super chip? Is that what was in the envelope?"

"Say there *was* an envelope." Pool sighed. "Say it did contain something important. Not the NVSC. But something involving—"

"National security," Bailey interjected with a serious expression.

"If the envelope was on Cox when he died," Pool continued, "on him when he was found, but disappeared before the body reached the bottom of the mountain . . ."

"That means you have it," Bailey said, eyes boring into Ray. "No one else was alone with the body."

Ray thought this through. He had discovered Cox and seen the envelope. Then Glen and Hans had shown up, carted the body down the mountain, and handed it over to the troopers. "Maybe I was the only one to be alone with the body," Ray agreed, "but I don't have the envelope."

Pool stared at him, obviously unconvinced. "We're talking about more than simple obstruction of justice here. If you are in possession of or have suppressed or destroyed a critical piece of evidence in this case, you could be looking at felony charges."

"Not to mention murder," Bailey said.

"Murder?!"

"How do we know that you didn't kill Cox and take that envelope?" Pool asked.

Ray squinted at the logic, or lack thereof. "Right. I pushed Cox off the lift. Then I found his body, reported it, started investigating the incident, nearly got blown up by a bomb, and got beaten to a pulp. All of that was an elaborate ruse to throw you off the trail. Good job, agents. You've got your man." Ray presented his wrists for cuffing.

"You could have discovered the envelope accidentally," Pool tried, "and pocketed it. The rest . . . All of that could have been the result of various parties knowing that you have something they want."

"Namely?"

"Classified information."

"Uh-huh . . ." Ray muttered. "Next you'll accuse me of having an affair with Mrs. Mancini. Sorry to disappoint you guys, but the only sin I committed was spotting Cox under the lift."

"And rifling his pockets," Pool added.

"Who said I rifled his pockets?"

"You're the one who brought up the envelope."

"I was checking for ID." Ray sighed.

"Why didn't you tell us about the envelope earlier?" Bailey asked.

Ray paused, picking his way through the menagerie of answers: because you're Feds . . . because you hijacked the case . . . because you didn't give us all the related facts, and still haven't . . . because I don't trust you as far as I can throw you . . . The only reason he was breaching the subject now was that the heat had been turned up several notches. He and Glen had nearly been blown to bits, and he had been jumped, thrashed, and threatened, all in the same evening. Someone, perhaps several someones, had taken an active interest in Cox and whatever it was he had been up to before his untimely death. The case had grown too big, ugly, and dangerous for a Barrow cop and a Girdwood chaplain to handle.

"I'm telling you now," Ray said. "And I'm asking for your help."

"There you go," Glen gushed. "That's a good first step in learning to receive."

Ray wanted to tell Glen what to do with his "learning to receive" spiel. Instead he said, "You be straight with us. We'll be straight with you."

Pool popped open the door and adjusted his Ray-Bans. "Fair enough."

They started for the entrance, walking four wide, like members of *The A-Team*.

"Tell us about the envelope," Pool said without looking at Ray. "How big was it?"

"Nine by six manila, folded in half."

"Was it heavy?"

"No." After a half dozen paces, Ray said, "Tell me about Cox. Was he a spook?"

"That's classified," Bailey answered.

So much for teamwork, Ray thought.

Pausing in the covered drive-through, Pool cautioned, "You two are here to observe and assist. We'll direct the questioning."

"Yes, sir, Mr. Special-Agent-in-Charge, sir," Ray replied glibly.

Ignoring the remark, Pool led the way past the valets, through the revolving door, swaggering like John Wayne en route to a WWII battlefield.

Despite the hour; the lobby was bustling with the frenetic energy of a holiday airport: a cluster of guests at the desk, an impatient group huddled around the concierge station, a line of patrons waiting at the coffee stand, formations of businesspeople crisscrossing the atrium . . . There was baggage everywhere, stacked in neat ramparts, strung along the walls, piled in leaning heaps.

"You believe this place?" Pool wondered as he fought his way into the corridor. "They don't get this much traffic at the Olympic in Seattle."

"Must need a machete during ski season," Bailey said.

"Actually, this is peak," Glen told them. "It's busier now than during skiing."

A school of Japanese executives in crisp, dark suits flowed past. Ray scanned the faces for Eddie Fukutomi. Still craning, he had just decided that the men represented a different corporation when someone gasped, "What happened to you?!"

Ray turned and found himself standing toe to toe with Amy Yasaka. Grimacing in sympathy, she reached a hand up and gently brushed the back of her fingers against his cheek. "What happened?" she asked again.

"I tripped." When the look of concern intensified, he added, "I'm okay."

She didn't seem to believe him. "What are you doing here?"

He gestured at the three men snaking away down the hall. "I'm with them."

"Still on the job?"

Ray missed the question. He was busy trying to figure out the mechanics of this woman's eyes. Light actually seemed to emanate from them. Her smile, he noted, caused her entire countenance to glow.

"Ray? Hello?"

"Huh? Oh . . . the case . . . yeah . . . We're still at it."

"Any big breaks?"

He shook his head. "Not yet. But . . . We're here to talk to Ron Mancini."

Her eyes widened, sparkling. "What's he got to do with it?"

"That's the question of the hour," he answered. "Apparently his wife was having an affair with Michael Cox."

"You're kidding!? And you think . . . ?"

"If it pans out, it could be motive," Ray shrugged, wondering why he was volunteering confidential information. The answer was obvious. Standing this close to Yasaka, even here in a bustling hallway, had a weakening effect on him. Flashes of the erotic dream filtered through his mind.

"Are you sure you're okay?" she asked. "You look a little pale."

"I'm . . . fine." He tried to blink away the images: tangled limbs, Yasaka without a stitch of clothing . . . "Just tired. I didn't sleep that well last night."

"I'm surprised you could sleep at all after yesterday. And with this." The hand brushed his eye. "Mr. Mancini is with the Fukutomi group in Banquet Room C. You know where that is?"

Ray shook his head.

"Come on." She took him by the hand and began pulling him through the flux of people. Ray made a subtle, polite attempt to loose himself, but Yasaka only tightened her grip, yanking him forward like a parent towing an errant child. When they reached the inner atrium, she stopped, released Ray's hand, and produced a credit card. She slipped it through a device mounted at doorknob level and a panel in the wall magically opened.

"Secret passage?" Ray asked.

"Shortcut." She winked at him and started down a

flight of concrete stairs. As he followed, the door sprung shut, nearly catching his foot. The resulting thud echoed gloomily, as if they had just entered the catacombs beneath Rome. Actually, Ray decided as they made their way beneath a thick bundle of pipes and wires, the "shortcut" was probably every bit as dank as the catacombs: cold, damp, mildewy ... The only upgrades were a paved walkway and a series of bare light bulbs hanging at twenty-yard intervals.

"Is this the private entrance to the executive suites?" he joked, hurrying to keep up.

"Beats fighting the crowds," Yasaka shot back. She made a sharp left turn and another set of stairs presented themselves. Trotting up them, she used the same card to satisfy this door, and stood waiting for Ray to catch up.

He mounted the steps puffing and emerged into a large kitchen. Cooks were laboring at oversized stainless steel stoves while workers in hair nets and rubber gloves prepared salads and filled gleaming tubs with scrambled eggs.

There was a sudden hush and all heads turned toward Ray. "Hey, Ralph," Yasaka called to one of the cooks. She grabbed Ray's hand again and led him through a side door, into a carpeted hallway. Two short corridors later they reached a door marked SERVICE ENTRANCE—BANQUET ROOM C. A waiter was rolling out a long food gurney.

Yasaka nodded at the door. "There you go. Good luck."

"You're not coming?" It sounded more desperate than Ray intended it to.

She smiled at him. "To tell Ron the Don that his wife was having an affair and accuse him of murder? Sounds like great fun. But I'll pass. Let me know how it goes."

Ray watched her leave. She was right, he decided. This was a doomed mission. What did they expect Mancini to do? Confess? More than likely he would have them thrown out and then sue for harassment. Grounds for suspicion or not, it would take a grand jury to get any answers out of him. And even then it would be like pulling teeth.

Leaning forward, he snuck a peek into the room. Round tables with white linen covers had been set up on a semicircle, facing a long, elaborate breakfast bar. There were several dozen people in attendance. Mostly Japanese. He spotted Eddie Fukutomi sitting at the center table. Mrs. Mancini was seated next to him. Then came Ron. Across the table was the elderly Asian gentleman Ray had seen in Mancini's company earlier. Grandfather Fukutomi, he assumed. They were raising glasses, toasting something.

Ray leaned in further, sweeping the room with his eyes. Where was Hat Trick Benny? He had to be somewhere close by. Glen and the Fibbies weren't there either.

For a brief instant, he considered entering the fray alone. The idea was laughable. Facing Mancini with the full power and authority of the Federal Bureau of Investigation would be bad enough.

He took a small step backward and felt something bore into his back. It was small, round, about the size of a dime. The barrel of a 9mm, he guessed.

"Move and you're dead."

Ray chose not to move.

THIRTY-EIGHT

"WHAT DO YOU think you're doing out here?"

Ray mentally compared the voice to the one from the night before. It was different. Lower. Raspier. "I was looking for the bathroom."

The remark caused the gun to dig into the flesh between his shoulder blades.

"You think you're funny?"

Before Ray could answer, his arm was wrenched behind him and he was thrust at the wall. He impacted cheek first and sagged as pain clouded his vision.

"How's that for funny?" A hand patted Ray down roughly, the gun still pressed into his back. His keys and wallet were confiscated.

"You're a pig." The statement was laden with disdain.

"I prefer the term swine."

A fist found his sore side, driving him to his knees. "I don't like pigs," the man explained, as if this justified the blow. " 'Specially pigs with attitudes."

Jaw clenched, Ray was inhaling and exhaling through his teeth. "I'm here to speak with Mr. Mancini," he managed between breaths.

"Is that right?" The wallet and keys hit the floor. "Then get up. Let's go see him."

Using the wall for support, Ray scrambled to his feet. When he bent to retrieve his things, a shoe impacted his rear end.

"I'm gonna put my piece away, seeing as how this is a business breakfast and all. But you give me an excuse to hurt you and I will. I'll twist you like a pretzel."

Rising, Ray realized that he was caught in the vicious gaze of Hat Trick Benny. The scrappy thug yanked him up by the arm. Brushing Ray's jacket as though he cared about his appearance, Benny grinned maniacally. "And I'd love every minute of it."

Ray believed him. There was something odd about Benny's eyes. It was like looking into the eyes of a rabid dog. Add a two-day scruff of beard and a crooked nose, and you had one mean-looking guy.

"Go." He pushed Ray through the door.

As they made their way to the head table, the room grew quiet. Snippets of Japanese were exchanged, a flash bulb went off. Ray felt like a circus performer being ushered into the center ring.

When they reached the table, Eddie Fukutomi nodded warily. "Officer Attla." He looked surprised, even a little rattled by Ray's arrival. His expression shifted to one of concern when he noted the condition of Ray's face. "What happened?"

Ray shrugged. "I slipped in the rain."

After gawking at him for a moment, Eddie asked, "Have you had breakfast?" He gestured to an empty chair.

"Actually, I'm here to speak with Mr. Mancini."

The elder Fukutomi glared up and said something in Japanese that didn't sound complimentary. Sighing, Eddie launched into a reply in his native tongue.

On the other side of the table, Benny was whispering to Mancini. Ron nodded, frowned, swore. He waved his hand in irritation and Benny backed up a step.

"What is it you want, Mr. Allan?" Mancini asked.

"Attla," Ray corrected. He jerked his head from side to side, hoping to see Glen, Pool, and Bailey inbound.

Apparently they had stopped off for coffee.

"What do you want?" he repeated impatiently. Next to him, Mrs. Mancini batted her long eyelashes at him. She was wearing a fire-engine-red blouse that succeeded in covering only the bottom third of her chest. Sitting at the table, her lower body hidden, she looked like an advertisement for the Miracle Bra.

"Uh . . . We just wanted . . ." Ray stuttered, trying to think of a way to stall.

"*We?*" Mancini turned to his wife and they both laughed obnoxiously. "*We* who?"

"I'm with the police department in Barrow."

"Barrow??" More laughter. "What's that got to do with me?"

"I'm participating in a Federal investigation. Agent Pool contacted you."

If this rang a bell with Ron, he did an excellent job of concealing it.

"We're looking into the death of Michael Cox."

"Oh, yeah . . . That was a shame. A real shame," Mancini lamented gruffly.

Ray snuck another look at the entrance. No Fibbies.

The mock grief evaporated. "So what do you want?"

To get out of here alive, Ray thought. He glanced at Mrs. Mancini. "Perhaps we could talk in private."

Mancini cursed at the suggestion. "Just tell me what you want."

"It has come to our attention that Mr. Cox was . . . acquainted with your wife."

Mancini sat up taller, eyes narrowing. "What??"

He looked to Mrs. Mancini for help. She was killing him with her eyes. "We've been informed that Mr. Cox and . . ." As he paused, she warned him with a minuscule shake of her head. Apparently Mr. Mancini was not privy to this information. Shifting on the fly, he asked, "Were either of you at the top of Mount Alyeska on Friday night?"

Swearing, Mancini squinted at him. "What kind of question is that?"

"We're just wondering if you saw something that might help put this thing to rest."

"Neither of us were up there Friday night," Mrs. Mancini said. She punctuated this with a stern glare. Weaving an arm around her husband's neck, she added, "We were together, the whole evening, here at the hotel."

Ron held a finger to her lips. "Don't say anything else to this guy. He's not looking for witnesses. If Mr. Cox died by accident, he wouldn't need witnesses." He summoned Benny with a nod. "You just want to know if I have an alibi. You're looking to dump a murder in my lap."

"No," Ray assured him. "We're just trying to piece things together."

"Talk to my lawyer." Mancini reached for his fork and began downing eggs Benedict like a prisoner of war. "A guy tries to go straight . . ." he mumbled through a mouthful, "and this is what he gets?" Aiming his fork at Ray, he growled, "You'll be hearing from my lawyers, Officer Attla."

"That's not necessary," Ray said.

"Harassment, defamation of character . . ." Mancini muttered, flailing his fork. "I'll have your badge."

Across the table, Mr. Fukutomi was chattering like a frightened squirrel.

Scooping up another load of eggs, Ron grunted. "Get rid of him."

Ray didn't like the sound of that, but Benny did. Smiling as if he had just been ordered to take a day off with pay, he took hold of Ray's wrist and twisted. There was a sickening crunch and Ray was suddenly dancing on his toes, wishing he could fly. After tiptoeing him past the serving line, Benny deposited Ray unceremoniously in the hallway, finishing the job with a flourish that sent him skidding along the carpet.

He heard Benny laugh and braced himself for a kick,

covering his head with his arms. When it didn't come, he peered up and saw Pool, Bailey, and Glen standing over him. From the door, Benny said, "See you later." He blew Ray a kiss. "Promise."

Pool pulled Ray to his feet. "You and Hat Trick got a date?"

"Very funny." Ray wiggled his wrist. Amazingly, it didn't seem to be broken.

"What happened?" Bailey asked. "Did you talk to Mancini?"

"Sort of."

"I thought I told you to let us handle it," Pool scolded in a fatherly tone.

"I was going to. But you guys apparently took the scenic route, via Juneau."

"We stopped for a quick espresso," Glen explained. "We lost you and we saw this coffee bar, so . . ." He grinned apologetically.

"What did he say?" Pool wondered, sipping his latte.

Bailey pulled out his pad to record Ray's findings.

"Before or after he threatened to sic his lawyers on me?"

"Did he know about his wife's affair?"

Ray shrugged. "Hard to say. Mrs. Mancini got pretty nervous when I mentioned Cox. And Ron got all hot and bothered at the mere suggestion that there might have been something going on between the two of them."

"He did it." Pool described Mancini in less than flattering terms. "He found out that his wife was cheating on him and he killed Cox."

"Or had him killed," Bailey threw in.

"Maybe," Ray conceded. "Maybe not."

"We'll get him," Pool vowed. "We'll nail his ugly hide to the wall."

"Did Mancini have an alibi for Friday evening?" Bailey asked.

"According to his wife, they spent the evening together, here at the hotel."

"What about the envelope?" Glen wondered. "Did Mancini know about that?"

"We didn't get that far," Ray said.

There was a thumping sound and they turned around to see the brute squad inbound: broad shoulders and thick limbs encased in maroon blazers and slacks.

"Problem?" the woman grunted. The question was addressed to Ray.

"No problem here," he replied.

"We got a call about a disturbance," the man said. Pointing, he informed, "That's a private affair going on in there."

"We know," Pool said. He displayed his badge. "This is a Federal investigation going on out here."

The woman sniffed at this. "Got a warrant?" she asked.

Pool shook his head. "Do we need one?"

"You do if you plan on harassing our guests," the male guard said.

"We're finished anyway," Ray told them, palms raised in a show of good faith.

"Then maybe you should be on your way." The man took a step forward and his partner took up position in front of the door to Banquet Room C. Arms on hips, they looked like linemen preparing to go down into three-point stances.

The woman glared at Ray. "Hit the road."

Ray stared back, dazed. "Say that again."

"Hit the road!" Her hands balled into fists.

He glanced at her feet. They were large, her ugly shoes probably a men's ten. The voice sounded viable. Could she have beaten him to a pulp on the sidewalk last night? Ray felt sure that she could have. But why? Why would a hotel guard care if he was investigating the death of a guest?

"We're going," Ray promised.

When they had entered the main mall area, Pool grumbled, "I could get a warrant and shut this whole place down." He swore at the raised roof, as if to prove this claim.

Ray shook his head, uncertain that Pool had the pull to close a five-star hotel. "It wouldn't do any good. Besides, I'm not convinced Mancini's involved."

"Oh, he's involved all right," Pool muttered. "He did it."

They passed several shops before Bailey asked, "If Mancini didn't do it, who did?"

Ray sighed. "I don't know."

"What do we do now?" Glen wondered. He sounded lost.

"We get a warrant and take Mancini into custody," Pool said.

"It's your case, so you can do whatever you want," Ray said, "but if I were you, I'd keep poking around."

When they reached the fountain, Bailey asked Ray, "What are you going to do?"

"Head back to the condo, get cleaned up for church," he told them. "This afternoon I plan to take my daughter on a nice long bike ride."

"And a picnic," Glen added cheerfully.

"Exactly. Then this evening I'm going to drive my wife and daughter back to Anchorage, hop a plane and go home."

"And leave us to deal with Mancini," Pool complained.

"It's a Federal investigation," Ray reminded. "I'm just an observer, remember?"

Pool cursed under his breath.

"Did you ever turn up anything on those bogus Fibbies?" Ray asked casually. When neither agent responded, he groaned, "Don't tell me . . . it's—"

Bailey nodded. "Classified."

"Give me a break . . ." Dealing with Ron the Don Mancini was just what these guys deserved, Ray decided as they weaved down the corridor, into the lobby.

The atmosphere had changed radically. All but one tour group had departed, the desk was quiet, and the stacks of luggage had been reduced to a collection of stray suitcases. There was no line at the coffee stand, no mob at the concierge desk.

They went single-file through the revolving door, walked across the lot, and were getting into the Dodge before Pool confessed, "Got a report on some Nikai activity."

"Nikai?" Ray asked. He slid into the backseat beside Glen.

"Japanese mob family," Pool explained.

"What's that got to do with anything?" Ray asked.

"They own this hotel," Bailey said. "And they own a company that's in direct competition with Fukutomi."

Ray stared out at the mountains, trying to make sense of this. The sun had burned away the leftover fog and was radiating through the trees. "Why would Fukutomi have a meeting in a place owned by a competitor?"

Pool glanced at Bailey, sighed, then groaned, "Tell him." When the underling balked, Pool insisted. "Tell him!"

"The hotel is formally owned by a corporation called Nakasawa Enterprises," Bailey explained without enthusiasm. "It's actually part of the same conglomerate Fukutomi belongs to. But about three years ago, Nakasawa was penetrated by the Nikai. Now it's virtually run by the mob. The connections, however, are subterranean. There are a dozen front companies, all sorts of foreign bank accounts . . . It's a real mess."

Ray nodded, in full agreement with at least the last assessment.

"We've been trying to build a case against Nakasawa for six months. They're buying up real estate and hotels here in the States and using them to traffic drugs, trade arms, launder money . . ."

"Eddie and Mr. Fukutomi don't know about this?"

"I seriously doubt it," Pool said. "Like we said, this is classified. We're talking deep. The Fukutomi people think that by staying at the Prince, they're supporting their own conglomerate, lining their own pockets rather than stimulating the U.S. economy."

Glen was nodding as if this was old hat.

"Are you saying the Japanese mob killed Cox?" Ray was genuinely confused.

"No," Pool answered. "But we do think that they may have posed as the FBI agents who questioned you."

Ray closed his eyes, visualizing the faces of the man and the woman who had met them at the bottom of the lift. "They weren't Japanese. They were both blond," Ray argued. "I never heard of a blond Japanese."

"Ever hear of a red-headed Yupik?" Glen submitted.

Pool snorted, "Ever hear of a wig?"

➤➤ THIRTY-NINE ◀◀

"WIG OR NO wig," Ray argued, "they weren't Japanese."

"You sure about that?" Pool asked, frowning. "They were wearing shades, right?"

"Yeah, but . . ."

"So you didn't see their eyes. How tall were they? As tall as you?"

"Well, no, but . . ."

"What about their skin? Were they Caucasian?"

"I assume so . . ."

"They were pretty dark," Glen volunteered. "Like they'd spent some time in the sun. And the lady was wearing makeup. Kind of a thick layer."

"So it's possible that they were Nikai," Pool pushed.

"It's possible that they were alien visitors from another galaxy," Ray said. "Just not very probable." He shook his head at the idea. "Japanese mobsters masquerading as Fibbies? Dressing up in wigs and makeup? I'd be more inclined to believe it was someone from our own government. The CIA likes to play those kind of games. Don't they?"

"It was not the Agency," Bailey quipped.

The shocks on the Dodge creaked as they bounced over a pothole. Ray gazed out the window, unwilling to concede the issue. Cox had been on the State Department's payroll, having an affair with Ron the Don's wife, responsible for sealing a lucrative international trade agreement . . . And as if that wasn't enough, the Japanese Mafia had been after him? Next Pool would be telling him that Cox had played a role in the assassination of JFK.

Ray massaged his temples. His head was pounding, bolts of pain shooting along the back of his skull, down his neck. "Why would they be interested in Cox?"

"That's what we're trying to figure out," Pool said. He turned in at the condos. "We think it may have something to do with that envelope."

"The one that you're not willing to admit exists?"

"That's the one." Pool cut straight across the lot and pulled up to the curb.

Ray reached to open the door, then stopped. "I'm no Federal agent, but it seems to me that Cox must have stolen something. Something important, like that computer chip." When Pool and Bailey didn't respond, or even blink, he continued, "What if the plan was to hand it over to the State Department, then run off with Mrs. Mancini? But somebody got wind of it. Say these Nikai people." He shrugged. "And they poisoned him."

"Huh-uh." Pool shook his head. "First of all, why would the Nikai go to the trouble of impersonating the FBI to find out about Cox, if they had already killed him?"

"Because . . . They killed him, but didn't get the chip?" Ray guessed.

"Mancini did it."

Ray sighed at this. "I don't know . . . Poisoning doesn't seem like his style. If he was jealous and angry, wouldn't he have sent Hat Trick Benny on a house call?"

"Not if he's trying to go straight," Pool rebutted. "Maybe he's toning down his strong-arm tactics. He is, after all, a semilegit businessman now."

Ray leaned back in the seat. "What about the State Department?" Pool and Bailey seemed to stiffen slightly. "Say they wanted the chip for military purposes, for the good of the American economy in general, to keep step with the Japanese . . . who knows why. And say that Cox managed to obtain it, but wouldn't hand it over. Maybe he got greedy. Maybe he upped the price at the last minute or something. He might even have threatened to sell it to another buyer. The Nikai for instance."

The Dodge idled quietly. When fifteen seconds had passed, Ray prodded, "Well?"

The agents shared a conspiratorial glance. "They *are* law enforcement officers," Pool pointed out to his partner. "And they *are* assisting in a Federal investigation."

"But this is classified," Bailey whispered back urgently. "We could get canned."

"What?" Ray wondered. Then it dawned on him. Leaning forward, he said, "Let me guess. The State Department already has the Fukutomi chip."

Pool huffed at the dashboard.

"Am I right? Did Cox get it for them?"

Sighing, Pool twisted in his seat. He glared at Ray, then at Glen, warning them with his eyes. "Let's get something straight. This entire conversation never happened. You repeat any of this and we'll deny it. Furthermore, the Bureau will then prosecute you to the fullest extent of the law. You'll do thirty years. Do you understand?"

"Threat received," Ray said.

Pool grimaced at them with the intensity of a man passing a kidney stone. "Off the record, under your hats . . . It is possible that the State Department may be in possession of certain items which involve the national security of the United States."

Wading past the language, Ray said, "How'd they get the chip?"

"I am not at liberty to comment on that at this time," Pool said mechanically.

"It must have been Cox," Ray said. "He really was a spook!"

"I am not at liberty to confirm or deny that statement at this time."

"And he stole the chip for the State Department."

"I am not at liberty to—"

"We get your drift," Ray told him. "You're saying that the U.S. Government is guilty of theft, but had no motive in the murder of Michael Cox. They already had what they wanted, so they had no reason to kill him."

Pool repeated his mantra.

"Interesting. So if that envelope didn't contain the chip, what did it contain?"

"If we knew that," Pool admitted, "we could pack up and head for home."

"Sounds like a grand idea." Ray eyed his watch: 7:49. "You're gonna be late for your service," he told Glen.

"They won't start without me."

Ray got out and leaned into Bailey's open window. "What a soap opera. Makes me glad to be a lowly borough cop." He smiled at them. "Good luck."

"You'll be around the rest of the day, right?" Pool asked. "In case we need you?"

"Till four. Then I'm gone." He patted the roof. "Have fun trying to lasso Ron."

"See you in church!" Glen called.

Not if I see you first, Ray thought. As he started for the condo, he heard the Dodge's transmission adjust to a new gear, then the sound of the tires slinging gravel as they raced away. If only Margaret's conference were over and they could leave now.

Unlocking the condo door, he stepped in and found Margaret and Keera at the breakfast table eating cold cereal and toast. They were wearing bright, flowery dresses, their hair up in matching styles that involved colorful ribbons.

"Wow! Don't you ladies look beautiful? Where're you off to?"

"Better hurry," Margaret said with an edge of irritation. "We're gonna be . . ." Her voice trailed off as she looked up from her bowl and saw his face. "Raymond!" Her tone conveyed both concern and anger. She shot out of her chair. "Does it hurt?"

"Not really," he lied.

"What on earth did you do to yourself?!"

"Actually, someone did it for me." Ray tested the bulge with a finger.

"Have you seen a doctor?"

"No. I'm fine. It's nothing."

"Right . . . What happened? Did you get into a fight?"

"Not exactly." He went over and gave Keera a gentle hug. "How's my girl?"

"Fine, Daddy." She stuffed an overburdened spoonful of granola into her mouth, then mumbled, "Are we gonna have a picnic today, Daddy?"

"You bet."

After another shovel of cereal, she asked, "You found the lady, huh, Daddy?"

"What lady?"

"The one who was there when the man fell."

Ray didn't understand the question, but pretended to. "No, honey. I sure didn't."

"But Daddy . . ." she whined. "You did too!"

"Okay, honey. Whatever you say. I better get ready." He went into the bathroom and shut the door. Leaning into the mirror, he admired his swollen face for a moment. "I haven't got a tie," he called as he started to brush his teeth. After washing his face and downing another trio of Advil, he emerged from the bathroom and announced with as much cheer as he could muster, "I'm ready." On the way to the door, he snatched a piece of leftover toast. "Do we have to do this?"

"Don't start." Margaret ushered Keera, then her husband outside. "You promised."

"I know but . . . Can't we just relax? Maybe go for a nice bike ride."

"How are you going to ride a bike with that coconut on your side?"

Ray hadn't considered that. "I don't know. Carefully."

"Besides, I can't go biking," she said, closing the door.

"Oh, yeah. Then how about a nice walk?"

"We're going to church." Taking her daughter's hand, she set off for the rental car.

Ray rolled his eyes at Keera, eliciting a giggle.

"Don't egg him on, honey," Margaret said.

They got into the car and Ray was about to turn the key when images of Glen's Wagoneer flashed through his mind. "Just a second." He got out, popped the hood, and examined the engine, checking the brake lines, the ignition wires . . . No bomb.

"What are you doing?" Margaret asked as he got back in. "You got grease on your new shirt."

He tried to brush it away, but the spot only got bigger. "It'll wash." Starting the car, he breathed a sigh of relief. He was tired, sore, in no mood to go to church. And yet, as they drove down the road, past the main lodge area, he reveled in a liberating, almost giddy sense of release. He was off the case. Cox and his various activities—be they legal or illegal, moral or immoral—were no longer his headache. It now belonged to the FBI. All he had to do now was survive church and he would be free and clear of Glen. In a matter of a few short hours, they would be leaving Alyeska. Ray was ready. Enough vacation. It was time to go home.

When they reached the rustic church building, the unpaved parking area was half full. Ray pulled in next to a black BMW sports car. It was new, clean, by far the nicest vehicle in attendance. "Tourists," he grunted. He started to get out, then noticed that Margaret was bent forward slightly, eyes closed, frowning sadly. "What's the matter?"

She held a hand up. Breathing through her mouth, she managed, "I'm . . . okay . . ."

"What is it? Raymond Junior giving you a hard time?"

"Who??" Keera wondered.

"Your baby brother," Ray said.

"We don't know what it is," Margaret countered. She sighed heavily, opened the door, and got out. "Your Daddy's just hoping for a boy."

"He's right, Mommy. It's gonna be a boy," Keera said confidently.

"And just how do you know that?" Margaret asked.

"'Cause I wanna brother."

Ray nodded. "Fair enough."

Music met them as they cut across a path in the lawn: guitar, bass, drums . . . It reminded Ray of a garage band warming up.

"Come on," Margaret urged. "They're starting."

As they approached the front door, Ray reflected on the situation. Yes, they were headed straight for a church building, but with his wife on one side, his daughter clinging to his finger on the other, his second child present, though hidden, and sunshine transforming the hillsides into a glorious, effervescent mural that bested the work of any human artist . . . things could have been worse.

⋙ FORTY ⋘

"GOOD MORNING! WELCOME to Girdwood Chapel!"

The greeting was so cheery, the smile behind it so effervescent, that Ray had to fight the urge to turn tail and run. It came from a frail, Native woman of about seventy with silver-blue hair tied up in a bun. She shoved her bony hand at Margaret, then at Ray. After patting Keera on the head, she gushed, "We're so happy you could join us today!"

A man appeared at her side. He was about the same age as the woman, a couple of inches shorter, and a good seventy-five pounds heavier. "Wonderful to have you!" He shook their hands with the same unbridled enthusiasm before passing them each a yellow paper that had been folded in half. "Would you like me to help you find a seat?"

"No," Ray answered a little too quickly. "We're fine."

The man nodded, still smiling. Next to him the woman was all teeth. They stood watching, as though Ray were about to perform a trick.

He led the way across the small entryway and pulled open one side of a double wooden door. Music blared out of the sanctuary in a sudden rush, as if it had been welling up, waiting to escape: a blend of thumps, cymbal crashes, and beaten guitar strings.

Keera wrinkled her nose. "What's that noise, Daddy?"

Ray shushed her with a finger and ushered her inside. The room was surprisingly small and dark. Overhead, two short banks of fluorescent lights flickered unevenly, causing rust-red indoor/outdoor carpet to glow like a radioactive substance. Metal folding chairs had been set up in rows that faced a low, bare plywood stage. They were nearly full, most of the attendants standing and singing. The stage itself was a thick forest of music stands, amplifiers, microphones, and instruments. Four young musicians were swaying to the beat, "jamming."

Ray followed Margaret into the last row of chairs and started to sit down. She tapped him on the shoulder, shaking her head.

"Stand up, Daddy," Keera implored.

Bracing himself against the seat in front of him, Ray surveyed the room. He recognized a few faces from the meeting the night before at Glen's place. Two of the three grungers were present. The two young blonds were three rows ahead. The woman in the wheelchair was over on the side. He made out the back of Jean's head. No John.

An overhead transparency was being projected onto a white sheet tacked up above the stage. Ray eyed the lyrics to the song in progress and was about to sit down, proper etiquette or not, when something whacked him on the back.

"You made it!" John enveloped him in a bear hug, as if he had just reached the top of Everest. Leaning back, he noticed Ray's face. "What happened?"

"I got hugged."

John laughed boisterously. "Mind if I squeeze in here?"

Ray swore under his breath and motioned for Keera to scoot down. Glancing up, he saw a hand waving across the aisle. Ray peered behind John and saw Amy Yasaka smiling at him. She mouthed, "Hi, Ray."

"Who's that?" Margaret wondered in a whisper.

"Manager of the Prince," Ray whispered back.

"She's beautiful," Margaret acknowledged. "Isn't she?"

Ray declined to comment. He wasn't stupid. Redirecting his attention toward the stage, as though suddenly very interested in the music, he watched the guitarist bring the song to a close. Glen appeared and mounted the stage, taking up position next to a podium that appeared to be made out of a section of totem pole.

Most of the congregation remained standing as Glen launched into a prayer that covered everything from the weather to the finances of the church to the spiritual state of all three branches of the Federal government. After a solemn "Amen," the band led them through several more songs. Ray sank to his seat and watched the seconds tick off on his watch. Glen finally returned and rambled off several announcements. Then he told the kids it was time for Sunday school. The adults were encouraged to "greet" each other.

"I don't wanna go!" Keera was telling Margaret.

"But there'll be other kids your age, honey."

"I'm not going!" She was wearing that look, the one that meant that she wasn't going to give in without a knock-down-drag-out fight.

"Yes, you are!" Margaret insisted. She took hold of Keera's hand, but Keera jerked free.

"No!" The volume was increasing.

Before Ray could intervene, a hand patted his shoulder. He turned, expecting another of John's bear hugs. But it was Glen.

"I need to talk to you for a minute."

"What about?" Ray asked suspiciously.

Glen motioned toward the back door.

As Ray rose to follow him out, Margaret bit off in exasperation, "Take her!" He scooped her up by the waist and was rewarded by a shrill, piercing shriek that brought an abrupt hush to the room. Keera began flailing her arms and legs madly.

Ray grunted at Glen, "Go!"

They trotted through the entryway and out onto the sidewalk. Ray sat down on the curb and held Keera like a human straightjacket. A minute and a great deal of shouting later, the fit came to a sputtering end and Keera relaxed in his arms.

Glen stroked her head. "Ruby does that too." To Keera he said, "Sometimes you just have to blow off steam."

"I don't want to go to Sunday school," she whined.

"That's okay," he assured her with a smile. "Ruby's going to be in there."

This drew a glimmer of interest.

"I think they're making musical instruments today. Might be kind of fun."

There was a brief moment when it seemed that Keera might capitulate. Then she snorted, "I don't wanna go." Gasping, she began to cry.

"You don't have to go," Glen said. He shrugged at Ray.

"What did you want to talk about?"

"Oh . . . When I got home a while ago, there was a message on my answering machine. This guy I know, he runs a coffee bar in Whittier. He's into mountain biking. Rides all the time. Anyway, he was up doing the backside of Alyeska on Friday evening."

Ray caught the significance. "Did he see Cox?"

Glen shrugged. "I don't know. He just left a message that said he was up at the top on Friday night, and that he had something to tell me. It might be nothing. But if he did see Cox, he may have seen the woman too."

Ray nodded at this. "Call him back and find out."

"He didn't want to talk over the phone. He said he wanted me to meet him this morning in Whittier."

"So meet him."

"I can't. I have services. Then I've got a potluck. Then a softball outing thing with the youth. I won't be free until maybe four. Three-thirty at the earliest."

"Guess he'll just have to wait."

Glen produced a pair of tickets and handed them to Ray. He asked Keera, "Have you ever ridden on a train?"

She brightened at this. "No."

"Would you like to?"

"Yeah! Daddy! Can we? Please?!"

Ray glared at Glen before examining the tickets. They were open date VIP passes to the Portage/Whittier Railroad. He handed them back to Glen. "You go."

"I can't. At least not today. The last train is at three."

"Daddy!" Keera pleaded. "Please can we go on the train?!"

"You don't have to pay for them or anything, and the only other way to get there is by boat," Glen explained. "I've got others. The vice president of the railroad comes to church here about once every six weeks or so. He gives me a fistful of passes every time." He stuffed them into the pocket of Ray's shirt. "You two go. It'll be fun."

"Yea!" Keera hopped out of Ray's lap. "Let's go tell Mommy!"

"Mommy . . ." Ray sighed. "Yeah, what about Margaret?" he wondered aloud.

"She's got a conference, right?"

"Right, but . . ."

"Jean can run her over there between services." He glanced at his watch and gasped. "I gotta get back in there."

"A train! A train! We get to ride on a train, Daddy!" Keera did a celebratory dance.

"You'd better get going if you plan to make the nine-thirty." He extracted his flip phone from the pocket of his pants. "Here. Just in case you need to get ahold of me."

"Glen," he protested. "This guy in Whittier doesn't know me from Adam."

"I'll call him after church and let him know you're on your way. It may turn out to be a wild goose chase. Or it may turn out to be enough to get Mancini indicted.

Either way the scenery's great." He looked at Keera. "And there're two really long tunnels."

"Tunnels?! Daddy, tunnels!"

"His name is Pete. He runs Pete's Coffee." He shot them a parting grin. "Have fun." With that he hurried back inside.

"Daddy, tunnels! And a train!"

"After that scene," Ray said grumpily, "you think you deserve to ride on a train?"

She nodded emphatically.

Groaning, Ray led her back into the entryway. "Wait here a second." He tiptoed into the sanctuary and whispered into Margaret's ear. "Glen gave us train tickets. Keera absolutely refuses to go to Sunday school anyway, so . . ."

"So you're going to spoil her by rewarding that behavior," Margaret whispered.

"If you don't think we should go . . ." Ray said, hope fading. He had already decided that taking Keera on a train *would* be fun. And, best of all, it would give him an excuse to skip out on church! The idea of traipsing to Whittier to talk with some joker that he didn't know and wasn't interested in getting to know didn't particularly appeal to him. But then neither did sitting through one of Glen's sermons.

"No. Go ahead."

"Okay. Jean'll run you back to the conference." He kissed her lightly on the cheek as a peace offering. "See you this afternoon."

She sighed, then mouthed over her shoulder, "I love you."

"I love you too." *Even when you're pregnant,* he thought. Hormones were no fun. Mood swings were dangerous, emotional firestorms potentially lethal. But all the crabby, irritated feelings in the world could not keep him from adoring this woman.

As he turned to leave, he noticed Amy Yasaka. She was sitting, straight-backed, listening intently as Glen read from the Bible. In every way—hair, cheekbones, complexion, clothing—she was like a fashion model. But as he started for the entryway, Ray decided that Yasaka had nothing on Margaret Attla. Now *there* was a classic beauty.

➤ FORTY-ONE ◄

"DADDY, CAN I sit in front?"

Ray shook his head. "You know Mommy's rule. No kids in the front seat."

"But I wanna sit in front!" Keera's tone foretold the approach of another fit.

"You can't, honey," Ray explained calmly. "There's an airbag."

"I wanna sit in front!" This time it was a demand. "I'm *gonna* sit in front!!"

Unlocking the door, Ray vacillated, uncertain which course to take. If he gave in, Keera would probably quit screeching, but he would be feeding into the "brat syndrome." If he stood his ground, she would dedicate herself to making his life miserable for the next hour or so. Parenting was such a fulfilling experience.

"You can't sit in front, Keera." He opened the back door and was about to help her inside when she charged him like a rhino. Banging into his leg, she kicked and punched wildly. He took her by the wrists and "encouraged" her to get in, then held her wriggling form in place with one arm while buckling the safety strap with the other.

Hurriedly climbing into the driver's seat, he started the engine. As he put the car in gear, he noticed a woman standing at the edge of the lot, waiting as her dog sniffed the grass. She was squinting in their direction, hand on her brow. He waved and smiled nervously as they rolled past, half expecting the woman to rush home and call child protection to report a suspected incident of abuse.

Five minutes later, as they were approaching the highway, the fit still in progress, Ray braked onto the shoulder. "Do you want to ride on a train or not?"

Keera glared back. Thrusting out her lower lip, she whimpered, "Yes, Daddy."

"Then stop this."

Sniffing, she nodded, conceding defeat. "I will."

Ray pulled back onto the road and turned toward Portage. Taking a deep breath, he marveled at Keera's will. It was strong, growing more inflexible by the day. The terrible twos hadn't been so bad. But four was turning into a real battle.

A mile down the highway, Ray noticed a silver Taurus looming in the rearview mirror. It was too far back to make out the occupants. FBI? Nikai? Or innocent tourists headed for Portage Glacier? He decided to keep an eye on it.

"Daddy? Can we get a donut?" Keera's voice was weak and mournful, as though not getting to sit in the front seat was a trauma that would someday require therapy.

Still emotionally drained, Ray said, "I don't know."

"Daddy!"

"If you start again, I'm turning around. I don't like it when you act that way and I don't want to spend the day with you if you're going to behave like a brat. Understand?"

"Yes . . ."

The remainder of the trip was quiet. Keera looked out

the window with a forlorn expression, sighing heavily at regular intervals. Ray watched the Taurus in the mirror, doing his best to ignore her sulking. As they rounded the bend and the rail yard came into view, she magically snapped out of it. "Daddy! There's the train! There's the train!"

"Sure is." He eyed the clock on the dash. They would have to hurry to make the 9:30. Turning into the parking area, he was relieved to see the Taurus continue on. Tourists. Nothing like a weird murder case to give you the heebie-jeebies. He found a spot along the north end of the lot. "Come on. We don't want it to leave without us."

The idea of rushing to make the train thrilled Keera. Suddenly she was animated, ready to run for it. "Hurry, Daddy!" she kept saying.

They reached the ticket office platform just as a voice on the loudspeaker announced: "All aboard the nine-thirty to Whittier."

Ray handed the VIP passes to a woman at one of the windows. She glanced at them and slid them back at him. "You're all set. Enjoy your trip."

The locomotive belched smoke, causing Keera to squeal, "Hurry, Daddy!" She pulled him forward as though this was the last train out of a city under siege. When Ray slowed to flash the passes at an attendant, she urged, "Come on!" Dragging him up the stairs, and into the car she dropped into the only empty booth in evidence and beamed at him. "This is gonna be the most fun ever! When are we gonna start going?"

"Soon," Ray assured her. Despite her occasionally infuriating behavior and marked moments of willful disobedience, Keera was a doll. Ray's doll. Irreplaceable. Without equal. Ray wondered how he could ever love their next child as much as he loved this one. It didn't seem possible.

"Daddy? When are we gonna—?"

The train whistle blasted, rattling the windows, and

they lurched forward. Keera grinned as though it were Christmas morning and pressed her face against the window. "We're going, Daddy!" She pointed at the parking area. "There's our car, Daddy!"

Ray nodded. Settling back, he angled himself at the window. The tide was out on Turnagain Arm, the silty gray waters replaced by an expanse of mudflats that gleamed under the summer sun like melted chocolate. Off to the left, the emerald-green bluffs of the Kenai Peninsula rose gently from the inlet. The track curved across a marsh until they were afforded a view of the Chugach Range, 4,000 vertical feet of rock and ice.

Five minutes into the trip, with the train hugging the hillside, puffing east on a collision coarse with a mountain, Keera sighed. "When are we gonna get there, Daddy?"

"In another forty minutes or so."

Keera deflated, as though this represented an eternity. Sprawled across the seat, legs dangling in the aisle, she frowned up at the ceiling. "I'm bored."

He realized for the first time that he had neglected to bring a book, a toy, a snack. He was unarmed aboard a train with a four-year-old. Not an enviable position.

"Do you have any crayons?"

Ray shook his head. "What if we play I Spy?"

She sat up as rigid as a stick. "Okay! I getta go first! I spy something . . . green."

Ray began guessing, rattling off anything and everything visible through the window, green or not: grass, clouds, sky, trees, stream . . .

Keera giggled at his attempts, rolled her eyes, saying, "Daddy, that's not green!"

They had each had three turns and Ray was in the process of trying to think up some other distraction to keep his daughter occupied when the train whistle sounded. Someone in the next booth said, "Here comes the first tunnel."

Keera forgot about I Spy. "How long is the tunnel, Daddy?"

"I don't know. We'll have to wait and see."

Thirty seconds later, they reached the tunnel. The running lights of the car had apparently shorted out, leaving them in total darkness.

"Daddy!"

"I'm right here." He fumbled and pulled her into his lap. "It's okay, honey."

They exited the tunnel with a whoosh. The sunshine was blinding. Before Ray's eyes could fully adjust, the train entered the next tunnel.

"You could develop film in here," Ray heard someone say. When they emerged into the light, again they were on the outskirts of Whittier. It was a dirty-looking town: rail yard, freighters anchored in the bay, a factory building, dull brown docks ... A small tourist trade had sprung up along the water, a sparse collection of trinket shops and food stands.

As the train creaked to a halt, passengers began clamoring for the door, as though the thirty-minute stopover would hardly be enough to appreciate the metropolis of Whittier.

Following Keera down the steps, Ray was about to ask one of the railroad attendants about Pete's Coffee, when he spotted it: a shack not much bigger than an outhouse stationed just fifty feet from the rails. Painted lime-green, it was tough to miss.

Ray led Keera to it and they stood in line behind an elderly couple who had been sitting near them on the train. The man running the stand was asking them where they were from, how their trip was going. He was about sixty, with a kind face partially hidden beneath a silver, out-of-control beard. A short gray ponytail bobbed as he turned to face his equipment. His denim shirt had "Pete" stitched on the pocket and his baseball cap declared that Pete's Coffee was the "best joe in Whittier." Not much of a claim, Ray decided.

"Do we get a donut now?" Keera wondered.

"I'm not sure they have donuts. But we'll see."

When the couple had paid for their lattes and were toddling off to do the town, the man in the shack said warmly, "Welcome to Pete's Coffee. What can I do you for?"

"Are you Pete?" Ray asked.

He glanced down at his shirt and smirked. "Must be."

"I'm Ray Attla."

Pete wiped his palm on a rag before shaking Ray's hand. "Nice to meet you, Ray Attla. Now, what can I get for you?"

"Did Glen call?"

"Glen?" His face twisted as though he had never even heard the name.

"Glen Redfern."

"Oh! *Glen.* Sure." He reappraised Ray. "You the cop from Barrow?"

"That's me."

Pete smiled down at Keera. "And what's your name, little lady?"

"Keera," she peeped. Without being asked, she held up her fingers. "I'm four."

"Well, Miss Keera-who's-four," Pete said, "are you hungry?"

"I wanna donut."

"Don't have any donuts, but I've got muffins and scones." He lifted the clear plastic lid from a platter and presented it to her. "Pick your poison."

With wide eyes, Keera studiously selected a chocolate chip muffin.

"What about you, Ray?" Pete asked.

"I'm fine, thanks."

"How about if I whip you up a latte?"

"Okay."

Pete set to work, loading the sieve holder with grounds from a canister.

"About Friday night . . ." Ray prodded. "At Alyeska . . . ?"

"Oh, yeah." Pete poured milk into a chrome pitcher. "I was about to ride the backside," he explained, feeding a thin, hinged pipe into the pitcher. "And I went into the lodge to use the facilities." He paused, twisting a knob on the espresso machine, and it howled like a stricken banshee. After sticking a thermometer into the pitcher, Pete crossed his arms. "The place was empty except for a girl mopping the floor, and these two people sitting in a booth: a man and a woman." He eyed the thermometer before continuing. "I didn't think anything about it, of course. Until I read the paper yesterday afternoon."

"It was in the paper?" Ray found this strange. Why had the Fibbies allowed that?

"Just a blurb about some unidentified tourist who fell off the lift. It said they thought it might have been suicide." Pete twisted the knob again, putting an end to the shrieking steam. "Hang on a sec."

Ray watched as Pete set the pitcher aside and positioned two shot glasses on a metal grid. He pushed a button and the banshee renewed its shrill, angry song. With the quick, practiced movements of a bartender, Pete silenced the machine, slung the espresso into a tall paper cup, spooned milk into it, and slapped a lid on top.

"What do I owe you?" Ray asked, wallet in hand.

"It's on the house." Pete smiled at them. "Anything for a friend of Glen's."

"Thanks." He wondered if Pete would be as generous to someone who was merely an *acquaintance* of Glen's.

"Anyway, I put two and two together and thought maybe that was the man I saw up top."

Ray dug out the creased sketch. "Is this him?"

Pete squinted at it. "Yep."

"And he was with a woman?" Ray confirmed.

"Yeah."

"What were they doing?"

Pete shrugged. "Talking."

"Did they seem happy? Angry? Friendly?"

"To tell you the truth, they seemed like they was having a business meeting."

"Why do you say that?"

"I don't know. The clothes he was wearing were casual, but nice. Yuppie style. And they looked kind of serious, like they were talking real estate or something. Oh, and there was an envelope on the table."

"What kind of envelope?" Ray asked, pretty sure that he already knew the answer.

"Manila. But not one of the big ones." Pete paused and shook his head. "Hard to believe the guy went and killed himself. Bizarre."

Ray nodded his agreement.

Another couple, this one in their early twenties, arrived at the shack and ordered coffee. Pete served them with the enthusiasm of a carnival barker.

When they had started for the docks, Ray asked, "Can you describe the woman?"

Pete sighed. "I didn't get a real good look at her. She had her back to me. But . . ."

Ray mentally anticipated Pete's description: dark hair, flirty outfit, buxom . . .

"She had dark hair," Pete started.

"Yeah . . ." He made a chopping motion at his shoulder. "About this long?"

"Uh-huh. Real shiny. And she was dressed nice. You know, expensive-looking."

Gesturing to his own chest, Ray said, "What about . . . you know." He glanced down at Keera. She was working on the final third of the muffin, her mouth ringed with chocolate, her fingers and shirt stained brown. It was as though the muffin had attacked her. "Was she . . . uh . . . well endowed?"

Laughing at this, Pete said, "Not that I recall." He closed his eyes in concentration. "No. She was kind of flat-chested."

"Flat-chested??"

"One other thing," Pete said. "I'm not certain, 'cause I didn't get a full-on look. But as I was comin' out of the bathroom, I saw her profile for just a second. I may be wrong but . . ."

"But what?"

"I *think* she might have been Asian."

➤➤ FOURTY-TWO ◄◄

"*ASIAN?!*" RAY BLINKED at this. So much for Mrs. Mancini. She had probably never in her life been described as flat-chested. And even if Pete had somehow missed her cosmetically enhanced breasts, he could never have mistaken her for an Asian. Jewish maybe. Otherwise, Louise was a stereotypical New York Italian.

"Korean . . . Japanese . . . Vietnamese . . ." Pete shrugged again. "I may be off the mark, but I remember thinking as I was leaving the lodge that she was pretty. You know, trim and all, like a fashion model. Reminded me of one of them high-class B girls from 'Nam."

"What's a B girl?" Keera wanted to know.

"Could you identify her if you saw her again?"

One side of Pete's mouth twisted up. "I don't know. I doubt it. Like I said, I didn't get that good of a look."

"Is there anything else you could tell me about the woman?"

Pete scratched his beard. "Don't think so." He gave

the counter another swipe with his cloth, then glanced beneath the bar. "Dang!" Stepping out of the shack, he swung down a hinged door and fastened it shut. "Hang on. I gotta make a milk run."

"Listen, thanks for your help, Pete. I don't have any more questions," Ray said. "Except, why couldn't you tell all of this to Glen on the phone?"

Pete grinned at him. "I was incountry—'69, '70, '71. Special ops." He sniffed, as if this explained everything. "Covert stuff." The grin disappeared. "Nasty stuff. Things you can't tell anybody." His face seemed older now. "I learned something."

"What's that?"

"That you can't trust the government. It's an immoral monster that feeds on money and power." He looked at Ray through sad eyes. "Call me paranoid, but since then I haven't written a letter or made a phone call that I haven't made sure was about things I didn't mind Big Brother knowing about. Maybe they aren't listening in. But then again, maybe they are."

He shook Pete's hand. "Thanks for the latte."

"Anytime."

Ray nudged Keera and she peeped politely, "Thank you for the cupcake."

"You're welcome, little lady."

Watching him trot off, Ray realized why Pete was so enthusiastic about Glen. Despite the overbearing sermonettes, Glen seemed sincere in his desire to help people. And Pete needed help. He was a friendly, likable guy on the outside, a wounded soul on the inside.

"Daddy, can we get back on the train now?"

"Don't you want to walk around Whittier?"

Keera glanced at the town. "Do they have a toy store?"

"I doubt it."

"I wanna get back on the train."

He followed her back to the same car. "Why don't we sit on the other side?"

"I like these," Keera whined, plopping into the same seats.

As she fidgeted, flopping one way, then another, twisting, dangling limbs onto the floor, kicking the wall, Ray tried to analyze what he had just learned. Cox had been on top of Alyeska on Friday evening with a woman. But that woman had not been Mrs. Mancini. At least, according to Pete of Pete's Coffee. The first question was, how reliable was Pete? The guy's idea of a good time was riding the backside of Alyeska. He suspected the government of reading his mail and bugging his phones. Was he suffering from delayed-stress syndrome? Maybe he had hallucinated on Friday night, mentally placing an Asian face on that woman, a face from his tour of 'Nam.

"Stop kicking the wall, honey."

Keera frowned at him, shoulders sagging.

On the other hand, Ray thought, if Pete was right and someone other than Mrs. Mancini had been meeting with Cox, discussing a manila envelope . . . Who could it have been? And why?

The train tooted its whistle, summoning the travelers from their sojourns in Whittier. "Here we go!" Keera shouted. She started kicking the wall again.

"Please stop that," Ray said in a calm tone.

Keera complied, bouncing up and down on her bottom, then beating the window with a fist. "Did you bring any snacks, Daddy?"

"No."

She was stricken. "I'm hungry."

"You just had a muffin."

"And I'm thirsty. I want a drink of water."

"We'll get you one when we get off the train."

"I want one now."

"I don't have any water, honey."

Keera stared at the harbor as though concocting a plan to siphon its contents.

When Pool heard Pete's account, Ray thought, he would say that the Nikai had been up there making some sort of deal with Cox. The deal soured and the lady slipped him some arsenic . . . No. Pool was sold on Ron the Don having committed the crime. So the Nikai had been dealing. And Cox was about to make a bundle of money and leave the country, when Ron came looking for his wife's gigolo and . . . Ray shook his head at the scenario. Surely Cox's death was more logical than all of that.

The whistle sounded again and people began clambering aboard, seeking out seats with the urgency of immigrants fleeing a war-torn city. Keera maintained a steady cadence on the window, giving the influx an added sense of desperation.

An *Asian* woman . . . Who? Ray drew a blank, then tried to fill it. A member of the Nikai? Why not a Communist dissident from North Korea? "Stop hitting the window."

Keera gave it a parting blow. After a brief pause, she began swinging her legs, flapping her shoes against the floor to produce an amazingly irritating thunka-thunka.

Ray set the Asian woman aside, focusing on what Cox might have been dealing. Secrets. Industrial secrets. That seemed obvious. But what, precisely? The manila envelope rematerialized. What was in that envelope?

The man in the next set of seats turned around and glared at Keera, then at Ray.

"Please stop, honey. You're too loud."

"When are we gonna go?!"

"Soon," he told her. But not soon enough.

If Cox had stolen or, in the spook vernacular, *procured,* the super chip for the State Department, as Pool had implied in vague, noncommittal terms, then. . . . Maybe Cox had taken another chip and was selling it to the Nakasawa. They were basically in competition with Fukutomi and would, no doubt, pay top dollar. Except . . . ripping off one chip would be difficult enough. Two? That seemed highly unlikely. How could Cox have maintained his cover as an executive, forging an agreement between Suntron and Fukutomi, while pocketing super chips at every turn?

After a long toot, the train hissed and began jerking its way forward.

Pressing her nose against the window, Keera announced, "We're going, Daddy!"

"Uh-huh." Pool's Ron-the-Don-did-it theory certainly was simpler than anything Ray could come up with. It didn't hold water. But it was simple. Motive: jealousy. The perpetrator: a known mobster with a history of violent crime. And if Pool could build a case, it just might take Ron down. That would be something in itself.

As they approached the first tunnel, Ray sorted through the tangle of facts. If Ron wasn't involved. . . . If Pool was right about the Japanese mob . . . If that had been a member of the Nikai meeting with Cox just before his death . . . Maybe Cox had been playing both sides. All three sides: taking a salary as a negotiator for Suntron, selling secrets to the State Department, selling secrets to the Japanese.

The train shuddered around a curve and suddenly they were engulfed by darkness. Keera squealed in a mixture of delight and terror. "It's okay. I'm right here." Ray groped across the car for her hand. He found her foot. The tunnel, he decided as he tickled her ankle, was an apt allegory for the Cox case. He was working blind, grasping for one thing, getting something altogether different.

According to Pool, the Nikai owned the Prince Hotel. That was rather disconcerting. Whether or not they were involved in the murder, having a foreign crime group invest in property in the United States qualified as a threat. What else did they own? He wondered how many people knew that when they came to the five-star hotel at Alyeska they were lining the pockets of the Japanese Mafia? For that matter, did the employees know? Did Amy Yasaka realize that her boss was . . . ?

The train clattered out of the tunnel, and the car was

flooded with sunlight. Keera sneezed. "How long until the next tunnel?"

"Not long."

She stood, twirled a clumsy pirouette, and aimed for her seat. Missing, she stumbled, careened off of another passenger, and fell straight-legged to the floor. Though unhurt, she let out a wounded howl.

"You're okay." Ray reached to help her up, but the light retreated with a whoosh as the train chugged into the second tunnel.

Keera shrieked again, this time without even a hint of amusement.

"I'm right here." Waving his arms in the darkness, Ray tried to find her. "Keera?"

There was a muffled cry . . . the scuffling of shoes.

"Keera?" He rose, stumbling as the train bounced and shifted its weight on the track. "Keera?" Bracing himself against the wall, he knelt and ran a hand over the floor. It was empty. "Keera??"

When she didn't respond, he felt a twinge of panic. "Keera . . . ??" He swung his arm again. She wasn't on the floor. Her seat was empty. He blundered forward, hand outstretched, and found the beefy shoulder of another passenger.

"Sorry." He turned his head in the direction of the front of the car. The darkness was all-consuming, the tunnel seemingly endless. "Keera?!" He patted his pockets for a flashlight. There was a penlight in the bullet pack on his bike. A lot of good that did right now. "Keera!"

Taking a deep breath, Ray tried to calm himself. She couldn't have gone far. Not on a moving train. She was probably playing hide-and-seek like they did before bedtime at home. When he found her, he would have a little talk with her about sticking close in public places, especially in the dark. "Keera??"

There was a flash and the train raced back into the daylight. Squinting, Ray surveyed the floor, the seats, the rest of the car. "Keera?!" He tapped the grumpy man on the shoulder. "Did you see my little girl go by?"

He shook his head, unconcerned.

"Did anyone see my little girl?"

More heads shook. A few passengers regarded him with suspicion.

His heart raced. "Keera??!" He hurried to the front of the car, checking under seats, peering over backpacks and bags, glancing down the stairs. She had to be there somewhere. "Keera? This isn't funny. I give up. Where are you?"

No answer. Just the rhythmic clicking of the rails. He ran to the back of the car and was greeted by rows of vacant stares. "Have you seen my daughter?" When the response was negative, he tried to smile. "She likes to play hide-and-seek." Heart booming in his ears, he rushed down the steps, into the lower berth.

"I was upstairs with my daughter," Ray explained, out of breath. "She's four. Dark hair. About this tall." He put a hand out. "She likes to play hide-and-seek. In the tunnel she . . ." His voice trailed off. She what? Wandered off? Ran away?

"Did she come down here?"

Frowns, puzzled expressions, a chorus of "nos." Passengers muttered in hushed tones. Nothing like a frantic, possibly drunken Eskimo to make the trip memorable.

Ray bolted back up the steps, clinging to a hope that Keera would be in her place, banging the wall, giggling at having fooled her father. He arrived at their booth and stood, paralyzed, staring at her empty seat. "Keera!"

Out the window, the metallic roof of the depot was aflame in sunlight. It was a half mile away, the train meandering toward it.

"Keera!!"

The locomotive groaned, creaked, began braking far in advance of the station. Ray could have covered the distance more quickly on foot. Instinctively, he tried the window. It slid down four inches. Not enough for a four-year-old to fit through. He checked the other windows with a twist of his head. They were all the same. And there was no exit in the upper berth. Taking the steps by threes, he jumped to the lower level and examined the exit. The two sides butted together with strips of black rubber, like the door of a bus. It was shut tightly. He tested it with a shoulder. Keera couldn't have opened it.

"Keera!!"

He waited as the train rolled for what seemed like a lifetime, slowing, slowing, but never stopping. When it finally ground to a halt, the door spit air and grudgingly opened. Ray leapt out and ran for the engine, fifty yards down track. Forty . . . Thirty . . . He was straining to cover the distance, yet seemed to be moving in slow motion.

One of the engineers, a thick man in a baseball cap, was stepping out as Ray sprinted up the gravel siding. Startled by the sudden, seemingly hostile approach of a six-foot Native, the man turned and scampered back onto the train like an overweight squirrel.

"Call security!" Ray demanded. He bounded up the steps and found two men waiting for him, backs to the wall, both holding revolvers.

"Already did," the one with the baseball cap said. "Now just take it easy, chief."

"My daughter's missing," Ray explained, taking a step forward.

The guns reached toward him. "Don't come any closer."

Ray lifted his hands in a show of good faith. "My daughter . . . she's missing!"

"Is that right?" The capped man gave his partner a quick glance, eyes rolling to imply that this guy was a nut. "And you think she's up here in the engine with us?"

"We were riding the train from Whittier," Ray tried. "She disappeared in the tunnel." He reached for his ID.

"Don't you move, chief."

There were voices outside. Shouts. A frantic cadence of dress shoes fighting gravel. After a series of deep thunks, Ray was yanked backward. He fell, spun, and sprawled on hands and knees. A heavy, unfriendly weight drove him to the ground and a hand began patting him down. More shoes arrived. The shouting crescendoed.

Ray felt his wallet being removed from his pants pocket. An instant later someone said, "He's a cop. Name's Raymond Attla." After a pause, the same voice wondered, "Should we let him up?"

There was no verbal answer. But the weight lifted and Ray rolled over, sitting up. "My daughter's missing," he told them.

A dozen eyes blinked at him stupidly.

"We were on the train. She disappeared in the tunnel."

"In the tunnel?" one of them asked. He was distinguished-looking and had a radio.

"Yeah. One minute she was sitting there. The next minute she was gone."

"How old?" Before Ray could answer, the man mumbled something into the radio.

"Four. Dark hair. Wearing a purple windbreaker and flowered dress."

After repeating the information into the radio, the man asked, "Which car?"

"The one without lights."

"Car Three." He gestured in the direction of the train and the other men ran down the track. "Lost child, Car Three," he told the radio.

"I don't think she jumped out," Ray said, cringing at the image this produced. He swallowed hard and realized that he had begun to cry.

"Don't worry," the man said in a fatherly tone. "She couldn't have. Just hang tight. We'll find her." He marched off with a confident stride.

Still seated in the gravel, Ray considered following

him. But what was the point? He had searched the car. Keera wasn't there. She simply wasn't there.

Head in his hands, he swore softly, repeatedly . . . tried to breathe, tried to pretend that everything was okay. Surely this would turn out to be a fluke. A mistake. A game of hide-and-seek gone bad. Surely she would pop out of a hidden compartment, whining for a donut, demanding to sit in the front seat on the ride back to Alyeska.

He closed his eyes and willed himself to determine what had happened and why. He could see Keera twirling, falling, sitting there on the floor. He could feel himself reaching for her and . . . Nothing. Darkness. She was gone. Vanished. Ray's palms were wet with tears when the man returned.

Looking down at Ray, he announced, "Mr. Attla, we've got a problem."

▶➤ FORTY-THREE ◀◀

PROBLEM . . . THE WORD echoed in Ray's head. "What kind of problem?"

"We checked the car, but there was no sign of your daughter." The man shrugged apologetically, as though they had been unable to locate a lost wallet.

"How could she just disappear?" Ray asked the sky.

Grimacing, the man told him, "We checked the emergency door and it turns out that it had been deactivated."

He shrugged. "They're all secured electronically, controlled by an automated system. You can't manually open or close an exit without setting off an alarm. It's a safety precaution. But in this case . . ."

"The door was broken?" Ray could feel the despair subsiding, bald panic giving way to a smoldering rage. "My daughter fell out a faulty door?!"

The man shook his head. "No. The sensors were purposely circumvented."

Ray squinted at this. "What are you saying?"

"Someone tampered with the emergency door on the car you were on."

"Tampered with?" Ray's overwrought brain couldn't process this.

The man's radio squawked. He lifted it to his ear, listened, then mumbled, "Code Adam." When he realized that Ray had overheard, he said, "Code Adam is—"

"I know what it is." Ray staggered to his feet, drunk with terror. Code Adam was the double-talk most law enforcement agencies used when a child was abducted.

"We searched the train," the man said with a frown. He shook his head slowly.

"Maybe she fell out," Ray said, more willing to accept a horrible accident than a calculated act of violence.

"I have people checking the tracks right now," the man assured him. "We're running cars from both ends. They'll meet in the middle in about five minutes. If she's out there, we'll find her." The radio stole the man's attention. He stuck it to the side of his head. "I'll be right back," he promised before wandering down the track.

Ray's hands were trembling. The anger had been short-lived. Now he felt weak, impotent, numb. If Keera had been abducted . . . *Abducted?!* His legs threatened to give way. If someone had taken her . . . His stomach twisted and he bent to retch. As he did, something bobbed in his jacket pocket. The phone. Wiping his mouth on a sleeve, he dug it out and glared at it. Who could he call? Who could make all of this go away?

He punched in Glen's number. After four rings, the machine picked up. Jean's voice cheerfully told him that he had reached the office of the Girdwood Chapel. She and Glen weren't available, but they would return any messages in a timely fashion.

Ray snapped the phone shut, cursing the machine, cursing Glen, the train, the mountains, the universe. How could someone take his daughter? Beyond the moral issue, how, in practical terms, could they snatch her from a train? A moving train? How??

The Taurus from the highway! The sedan came jarring into his consciousness. Had it been following them? What about the woman in the church parking lot? Had they been under surveillance? Had someone been shadowing them all morning? Tailing them from Girdwood to the train? To Whittier? Had someone been listening in on their meeting with Pete? Suddenly Pete's paranoid, untrusting attitude seemed justified.

Ray's mind raced, accusing any and all suspects, no matter how outlandish: the FBI, the Nikai, the State Department, Ron the Don, Hat Trick Benny, the hotel security guards. Or was it just a lone sexual predator with a thing for little girls? Another bout of nausea seized him, squeezing his internal organs into a tight ball. Before it had passed, the phone beeped. He stared at it, dazed, disoriented.

It rang three more times before he unfolded it. "Glen?"

There was a click, as though the line had been disconnected.

"Hello? Glen?" He was about to hit the power button when he heard a faint wind on the other end. "Hello?"

The wind rose and took on a regular pattern: breath.

"Who is this?"

Several seconds later, a voice whispered, "We have her."

Ray couldn't breathe.

"Understand?"

"No," he answered truthfully. "Is she . . . ? Is she . . . ? Did you . . . ?"

There was a rustling noise.

"Daddy!?"

"Keera!!" He cradled the phone to his face, wishing he could transform himself into a sound wave, bounce off the satellite uplink and beam to wherever it was they had her. "It's okay, honey. I'm going to come get you as soon as . . . Keera? Keera?!"

"Go to the laundromat at the cutoff to Girdwood. Bring the envelope. Wait there until we call. Notify the authorities and she's dead."

"I don't have any envelope," Ray pleaded.

"You've got forty-five minutes . . . starting now."

"I don't have the envelope! Hello?!" Ray denounced the situation with a thunderous swear. Kicking the gravel, he slipped the phone back into his pocket and leaned against the engine, exhausted.

His overwrought mind began a frenzied assault on the problem. Whoever had taken Keera knew Glen's cellular number and knew that Glen had given him the phone that morning. So they *had* been watching. Otherwise . . . No. That was crazy. Glen? No. It was too absurd. But the mere suggestion triggered a landslide of wild thoughts.

Ray had seen an envelope on the body. It had contained some sort of information. Information that was extremely valuable. The envelope had been on the body when Ray turned it over to Glen. Yet it hadn't made it to the troopers at the bottom of the mountain. Or at least it hadn't been reported. Glen? Why would the chaplain/sheriff steal an envelope off a dead man? Ray could think of no good reason, yet he could come up with no other person who had the opportunity to take it.

And then Glen had tagged along to help Ray investigate. Or to ensure that he didn't turn up any crucial evidence or leads. To keep an eye on him? Had Glen arranged for someone to meet Ray outside the condo last night and beat him silly?

What about the trip to Whittier? Was the whole thing a setup? Was Pete a fake? Had he really been up there when Cox was? Had he really seen Cox with an Asian woman? Or was that just a story to help clear Mrs. Mancini?

Conjecture gave way to illogical speculations. Maybe Glen was working for Mrs. Mancini, helping to keep her husband from finding out about the affair. Or maybe Glen was working for Ron the Don himself. Maybe Pool was right after all. Maybe Ron had killed Cox in a fit of jealousy. Or had Glen killed Cox?

Except . . . If Glen was involved . . . what about the brake lines and the bomb in the Wagoneer? Were they part of an elaborate ruse to make Glen look like an innocent victim?

And . . . If Glen did have the envelope . . . he certainly wouldn't have taken Keera. Whoever had stolen his daughter knew about the envelope, assumed that Ray had it, and desperately wanted the information it contained. So that meant . . . *What* did that mean?

Ray rubbed his eyes, stemming the tangential flow of thoughts. *Focus!* Determining who was behind it all didn't matter nearly as much as getting Keera back. To do that, he had to figure out where the envelope was and get his hands on it. Maybe Glen had it. But if he didn't, if he really was what he seemed to be . . . who else could . . . ?

He glanced at his watch and cursed again. He had wasted several minutes floundering on a sea of improbables. He now had thirty-nine minutes to figure out how to get ahold of an envelope that he had only seen once and wasn't even sure existed anymore.

Before he could decide, cognitively, what course of action to take, he was running, feet beating the gravel, arms pumping. He went straight toward the rental car, not certain where he was going, just that he needed to get there fast.

Fitting the keys into the door lock with a quivering hand, he yanked it open and slid inside. He barely gave the engine a chance before jamming the gearshift into drive and slamming his foot down on the pedal. The Toyota skittered out of the lot, showering the other cars with pea gravel and sending a cloud of dust drifting toward the depot. The front tires squealed as Ray sped onto the highway without regard for traffic. Horns sounded at the maneuver. Ray ignored them. Accelerating, he passed one car, another, another . . .

If Glen didn't have the envelope, he thought, whizzing past a camper, who did? Pool? If he did, he wouldn't admit it. Cox had been trying to sell whatever was inside, Ray presumed. But to whom? And why had he been killed? Had the deal been completed first? Or had the sale stalled, the goods withheld? Either way, the envelope had been on Cox's person. If Glen hadn't lifted it, who had?

This was pointless, Ray realized, doing ninety-five on a straightaway. He was getting nowhere fast. He was rocketing down the highway, putting countless families and individuals in harm's way in a vain attempt to recover his daughter. Where was he going?

At the turnoff to Girdwood, he yanked the wheel to the right, cutting off a Winnebago. As he shot up the hill, he glanced in his rearview mirror. The gas station and storefronts on the corner were quickly shrinking. Still, he made out the sign for the laundromat. According to his watch, he had thirty-one minutes to get back to the washeteria with the envelope. Impossible.

In another minute the road to Glen's house appeared. Ray slowed, trying to imagine Glen as a villainous industrial spy, then gunned the engine. Glen wasn't his favorite person, but unless he was an actor worthy of an Oscar, he hadn't taken that envelope. Yes, Ray thought in a moment of clarity, the opportunity had presented itself. But Glen wasn't a criminal. A nuisance. A bother. But not a thief or a murderer.

Seconds later, the church flashed by on the right. The lot was still half full with late-service attendees. Ray passed a line of slow traffic. At the lodge, he abandoned the road momentarily, streaking across a field rather than following the curve of the pavement. Bouncing back onto the asphalt, he shifted, forcing the car to maintain its speed.

As the Toyota roared north, past the condos and the conference center, an image of Margaret materialized: eyes vacant, face twisted by grief. The death of a child, someone had once said, was the most debilitating of life's losses. Worse than divorce or even the death of a spouse. The pressure on Ray's chest increased. *Keera . . .*

The right tires drifted onto the shoulder, then jumped the curb, tracking down the sidewalk as the road emptied into the hotel parking area. Ray hit the brakes and the Toyota skidded sideways, plowing to an unceremonious stop on the lawn next to the entrance.

Two doormen rushed to greet him, eyes wide. "Hey! You can't park there!"

Ray ignored them, darting for the door. He still wasn't sure why he was there or what he was going to do. The car had arrived at the Prince of its own accord, as if guided there by some unseen force.

He bumped through the revolving door and found that the lobby had returned to a state of controlled bedlam: guests besieging the front desk, surrounding the concierge station, assembled in a curling line at the coffee stand. A new collection of luggage had been piled along one wall and another band of tourists stood nearby, awaiting their bus.

Ray took it all in, the noise, the busyness, the movement, and wondered why he was there. He could feel time silently slipping away—Keera slipping away. The sense of helplessness was rising, panic causing the room to collapse in on him. How could anyone take a child? How could they steal a little girl and use her to get some stupid envelope?

He was debating whether to turn and start back to the laundromat without the envelope or call in Pool, despite the warning, when he saw her. She was standing in an open door to the right of the main desk, speaking to someone in a hotel uniform. He watched her gesture, watched the way her hair danced, grazing her shoulders as she talked. He studied her figure: the dark skirt that accentuated her trim hips, her stocking-clad legs, the silk blouse, the curve of her neck, the perfect skin. She was elegant and alluring. *Like a fashion model.*

Ray stared, mentally placing her at the top of Mount Alyeska, at a table with Michael Cox. Before he could fully evaluate this, his mind fit her with a blond wig and dark glasses. As it did, he realized that she was conversing with one of the security people—the man who had nearly broken Glen's arm and had later tried to pick a fight with Agent Bailey. Switching his attention, he went through the same process with the security guard: blond hair, glasses, mustache . . . Though Ray hated to admit it, Pool had been right. The two fake FBI agents that had shown up at the bottom of the lift had been Japanese. Amy Yasaka and the male guard were Agents Moore and Randolph.

It made sense, Ray decided, in a backward sort of way. The hotel was supposedly owned by Nakasawa. And Yasaka managed it. Apparently her duties went beyond making sure everyone had enough towels.

Was she a member of the Nikai, as Pool suggested? Had she met with Cox on top of Alyeska? Had she killed him? More importantly, did she have the envelope? It was time to find out.

As if alerted by an acute intuition, Yasaka turned abruptly and strode into the corridor. Ray jogged across the lobby, through the obstacle course of stray baggage, wandering children, and artificially important business people.

When he reached the corridor, Yasaka was unlocking the secret door she had led him through earlier.

"Amy!"

She either didn't hear him or wasn't going to acknowledge his presence. With the bustle and din, the former seemed likely. Until now, she had been extremely cooperative. But why not? Especially if she had been lying through her teeth, doing her best to muddy the case in an effort to avoid being arrested for murder. Ray shifted all the suspicion, anger, and ill-will he had briefly held toward Glen and foisted it onto Yasaka. "Amy!"

Without so much as turning her head, she slipped through the door. Ray ran to catch it, arriving just as it clicked shut. He kicked the panel in frustration.

His watch reminded him that he now had only twenty-four minutes left. He gazed vacantly at the fountain. Call Pool? Go back to the laundromat?

As he started forward like a sleepwalker, his eyes slowly focused and he became aware of a figure coming at him down the corridor. It was a man: average height, wiry, with a sharp, insolent face. And he was grinning with all the warmth of a barracuda.

Ray froze. Had he been seen?

In the next instant he got his answer. Hat Trick Benny's smile grew and he mouthed a greeting: "Time to dance."

➤➤ FORTY-FOUR ➤➤

THOUGH NOT SCHOOLED in lip reading, Ray got the message. Hat Trick was either planning to make good on his promise to twist Ray into a pretzel, or had been dispatched by Mancini to punctuate the need for Ray to back off. Ray wasn't going to hang around to find out which it was. He turned and bolted, barging through clusters of guests like a runaway halfback. Even without looking back he could tell that Benny was in pursuit, probably closing.

He turned the corner and burst between two bellboys guiding overburdened luggage carts. Leaping a small boy like O.J. in his glory days, Ray made a sharp left. He had no idea where he was going, but that was nothing new. When he finally snuck a glance over his shoulder, he paid the price by colliding with a stocky man in a three-piece suit. Rolling, Ray sprang to his feet, calling, "Sorry!"

Urgent footsteps told him that Benny was behind him, coming hard. Another turn led Ray into a narrow service hallway. It was short, with only one door. He put his shoulder down and rammed through it, spilling into a pantry closet. For a moment he thought he was trapped. Then he saw the other door. *Thank God!*

He snatched two industrial-sized food cans from the shelves before banging into the kitchen. The cooks, their tasks momentarily forgotten, glared at Ray.

"Call security!" he told them.

Ray slid behind one of the stainless steel tables and ducked his head. Before the workers could say anything, the pantry door flew open.

Benny paused to survey the room. Without rising, Ray flung a can of tomato sauce in the general direction of Benny's head. It missed, hitting a pot, but was enough to make him flinch. Before he could recover, Ray launched the second salvo: forty-two ounces of halved pears in syrup. The can impacted Benny squarely on the forehead, knocking him backward. He staggered, swearing, and fell through the pantry door.

Reaching a hand up on the table, Ray found a chrome spatula. He wanted to look for a knife, but could hear Benny getting up. He judged the distance to the opening that led into the refrigerators and walk-in freezer. Was there an exit in there?

Then he remembered the door to the underground passage. Crouching, he scurried toward it. He waved the spatula at the chef in a threatening manner. "Open it!"

Flustered, the man started to object, glanced at the spatula, then changed his mind. Pulling a card from the pocket of his white smock, he zipped it through the scanner. The door hissed and opened of its own accord.

As Ray dashed through, a spark flashed on the metal door frame. Paint chips lifted into the air and another bullet ricocheted into the passage. Ray flattened himself against the floor and used his arms to drag himself clear. Two more rounds followed him into the passage before the door shut.

He jumped down the stairs and hit the ground running. With his body laboring to escape, his mind was fixated on Keera. Where was the envelope?

He tore along the passage until he found the secret door that Yasaka liked to use. It was knobless. No handle. No bar. Nothing. Just a slot for a card. In the distance a door creaked open, clanked shut. Benny was inside.

Ray put his shoulder into it, winced with pain, kicked it, slammed it with his fists. The thing wasn't moving.

Cackling laughter wafted down the passage. Apparently Benny was enjoying himself. And after all, this was his kind of place: a mock-sewer ripe for vermin.

Retreating from the door, Ray stumbled along in the opposite direction, away from Benny, away from the kitchen, away from the one cut-through he was familiar with.

"I'm ready to dance!" Benny called energetically, voice echoing.

Ray came to another door. No knob. He didn't even bother to swear at it. Instead he hurried on. Time was running out. He had to get out. He had to get the envelope. He had to get back to the laundromat.

"Just you and me, hotshot," Benny said happily from somewhere in the recesses of the passage. "No guns. No knives. Man to man."

Somehow, the idea that Benny was going to show mercy by killing Ray with his bare hands didn't offer much comfort. He reached another door but didn't slow down. The reality of the situation was sinking in. He was trapped.

The thin trail of light finally came to an end. There wasn't even a door. Just a concrete wall. Ray turned around, shaking his head at the futility of trying to hide.

He heard Benny's shoes scuffing along the floor, then saw him round the corner, teeth gleaming. The guy was having a blast.

"I been looking forward to this," Benny said. He wasn't even out of breath. Holstering his gun, he made a show of popping knuckles. "You want it slow or fast?"

Ray wasn't thrilled with the choices. "So your boss killed Cox?" he asked. It was more an attempt to prolong the inevitable than to glean information.

"Mr. Mancini doesn't do nobody." Benny rolled his shoulders. "You ready?"

"No." Ray raised the spatula at him.

Benny laughed. "I'm gonna find a new home for that thing."

Ray believed him. Tossing it behind an air duct, he asked, "So *you* killed Cox."

"I would have loved to."

"But you didn't?"

Benny rushed him with the agility of a cat, performing a roundhouse kick before Ray could decide what was happening. From the ground, the passageway spinning over him, Ray said, "Ron must have been ticked when he found out about his wife's sleeping companion."

This seemed to interest Benny. "You mean her sleeping around?"

Ray tried to nod, but a shoe to the groin knocked the desire from him.

"Mr. Mancini isn't stupid. He knows Louise has . . . needs." When Ray didn't respond, Benny added, "What do you think he hired me for?" He collected Ray and leaned him against the wall. "I'm more than a bodyguard. I'm her chaperone and keeper."

Ray saw the punch coming and pooled his strength to move his head out of its path. Benny's knuckles bounced off his cheek, into the concrete. Hat Trick did a dance, accompanying himself with a storm of profanity. "Now I'm fixing to hurt you."

Fixing to? Ray thought. He braced himself, wondering how long he would remain conscious. Benny flexed his fist. The smile was gone.

The tapping filtered in like something out of a dream: a faint, echoing patter. It reminded Ray of Betty, the dispatcher in Barrow. Betty always arrived on the dot of eight, poured a cup of coffee, then walked down the hall to the radio room in those dress shoes, tip-tapping out a pleasantly predictable rhythm.

Benny hesitated. He heard it too.

Ray saw her outline before he saw her face. But there was no mistaking the silhouette. Amy Yasaka marched around the corner with an air of authority.

"You're not supposed to be down here," she informed Benny, as if he were some junior high punk who was playing hooky from class.

He sneered at her. "Is that right?"

There was another noise, heavier steps approaching.

"And just how are you planning to—" Benny started to challenge. His voice trailed off as the female security guard appeared.

Benny sized her up, sniffed, swore, reached for his gun. The woman mirrored his movements, producing a cannon of her own. The standoff stretched. Rather than force the issue, Benny just stood there. Ray could almost see the wheels turning in that demented head of his: Take on this beast and possibly get himself killed, or talk his way out and make a clean exit? Benny was ruthless, maybe even psychotic, but he wasn't stupid.

"Firearms are not allowed on the hotel grounds," Yasaka informed him.

"I've got a permit," Benny returned, his eyes never flinching from the guard.

"I'm afraid I'll have to ask you to hand over the weapon."

Yasaka said this in such a nonchalant manner that for a moment, Ray thought Benny might comply. Instead he cleared his throat and expectorated, hitting Yasaka on the shoe. With an ugly grin, he then began describing her in less than respectful terms.

Interrupting, Yasaka said, "You spit on my shoe!"

Benny laughed. "I'm gonna do more than that to you, baby, if you don't—"

The ultimatum was cut short when Yasaka emitted something akin to a shriek. She whirled, was inexplicably airborne, and had kicked Benny twice in the head before he could blink. He stumbled backward, dropping the gun, and Yasaka pounced on him like a wild animal:

a chop to the neck that made Benny gasp, a blow to the ribs accompanied by a sickening crunch, a hard knee to the groin. Benny collapsed to the concrete with a thud, blood trickling from his nose. Yasaka gave him a couple of kicks for good measure.

Ray stared in disbelief, unable to marry this woman's elegance with her fierce, almost supernatural ability to reduce a hit man to dust. As he watched her adjust her skirt and swipe a stray lock of hair out of her face, Ray asked, "Learn that in Nikai school?"

"My folks enrolled me in karate when I was four," she said with a wink. Retrieving Benny's gun, she emptied the chamber with the smooth movements of a card-carrying NRA member.

"Don't suppose you happened to be milling around outside my condo last night about ten?" he asked her. If she was a member of a Japanese mob family, had posed as an FBI agent, and was skilled in martial arts, why not a mugger too?

She shook her head, then nodded at the guard. "That was Suzi." The woman grinned, as though thrashing a police officer had been a real treat. "Sorry about that," Yasaka apologized. "But it was for your own good."

Ray tried to figure out how getting the stuffing knocked out of him was for his own good. "How's that?"

"This thing is dangerous and you're out of your element," she explained. "That was just a warning, to keep you out of harm's way."

Fingering his side, Ray decided that it hadn't worked. Harm had found him. He checked his watch and cursed. "I need the manila envelope."

Her eyebrows rose. "What manila envelope?"

"You know what I mean. I need it. They've got Keera."

"Who's Keera?"

"My daughter. They took her."

Yasaka was genuinely puzzled. "Who took her?"

"I don't know." Ray sighed. "Whoever's after the envelope. Do you have it?"

"No."

"I'm not playing around here. Neither are they. I need the envelope."

"I don't have it."

"Who does?" When she didn't answer, he clenched his jaw. "Who does?!"

The guard took a step forward, gun still at the ready, now aimed in Ray's direction. "It's okay," Yasaka told her in a soothing voice, as if she were calming a guard dog. "Come on." She turned and trotted along the passage.

"I don't have much time. I need that envelope!"

Yasaka waved him along, mounting the first set of steps they came to. After unlocking the door, she ushered him through. "I'm not sure who has your daughter, but I've got an idea. And I think I know who killed Cox."

"Where's the envelope?"

"I don't have it." She set off down a sterile, tiled hallway, heels clacking. "But I may have figured out who does. The only problem is getting him to tell us where it is."

"Him? Him who?"

Yasaka stopped at an unmarked door and entered a code into the keypad lock. She opened the door and gestured for him to enter. The room was small and stark: white walls, a single metal table, four folding chairs. Three were empty. The fourth was occupied by Jack Ehrlich.

He looked up as they came in, face flashing with hope, then falling in despair. He hadn't shaved and his hair was twisted into a lopsided spire, as though he had just climbed out of bed. Returning his attention to the tabletop, he swore.

"He killed Cox?" Ray asked. Ehrlich didn't seem capable of murder.

"I didn't kill anyone!" Ehrlich blurted in a panicked tone. "I'm innocent!" His head drooped toward the table. "I demand to see my lawyer. I didn't do anything."

"Ray's daughter has been kidnapped," Yasaka told him.

"I didn't do it!"

"But you'll be charged as an accomplice if you don't hand over the envelope."

Ehrlich's eyes darted about the room nervously. "You're not a cop."

"I am," Ray said. "And if anything, I mean *anything*, happens to Keera, and you could have prevented it . . ." Ray completed the threat with a glare.

"We already know you rode the lift up on Saturday morning," Yasaka said. "Right after it opened. We know you hiked down."

This information clicked a switch in Ray's brain, completing an especially troublesome piece of the puzzle. "You stole the envelope off the body?"

Sweat popped out on Ehrlich's brow.

"You must have gotten to the body after I did, but before I came back with Hans."

"We know that you opened a Swiss bank account yesterday," Yasaka continued, applying pressure like a seasoned law enforcement officer. "That you had a deposit of two million dollars wired to that account at five-thirty-two this morning."

Ehrlich slammed a fist into the table. "You can't hold me! You're not the FBI!"

"But we can give them a call," Yasaka said. "If you'd like us to."

Ehrlich's shoulders slumped in defeat. After a long hesitation, he sighed, "Mike had a sweet game going. I just wanted a piece of it. That's all."

"Where's the envelope?" Ray asked.

"I knew what he was doing," Ehrlich confessed. "Playing both sides like that. No wonder he got killed."

"The envelope!" Ray demanded in a growl.

"I figured I could finish what he started, make a quick bundle, and get out before anyone caught on."

"The envelope!"

"I can't give it to you," Ehrlich said, shaking his head. "They already paid me for it. If I don't show up with it, I'm dead meat."

Taking Ehrlich's neck in both hands, Ray lifted him from the chair. "Hand it over or I'll pinch your head off of your shoulders." He had never in his life seriously considered committing murder, until that very moment.

Ehrlich tried to swallow, but Ray's grip prevented it. Instead he choked, "What'll happen to me?"

"You think I care?"

"Relax, fellas." Yasaka gently removed Ray's hands. "Give us the envelope and we'll see that you're protected."

"*Protected?*" Ehrlich asked skeptically. "What's that mean?"

"We'll get you out of the country."

"What about the money?"

"Beggars can't be choosers," she replied. "You don't really have a choice. You're looking at prison if we notify the Feds. A hit squad if your buyers don't get the goods. And I'm not sure you'll make it out of this room alive if anything happens to Ray's daughter."

Ehrlich's chin quivered at the prospects. "I was just trying to—"

"Give us the envelope!" Ray took him by the neck again and began to shake.

Head bobbing, eyes bulging, Ehrlich finally caved. "Okay! Okay!" he coughed. After a deep breath, he disclosed, "It's under tower two."

"Where??" Ray wondered.

"Up on the mountain. Under the chair. I wrapped it in plastic and stuffed it into the cushion that's wrapped around the pole of tower two."

Ray took a fistful of Ehrlich's shirt and yanked him toward the door. "Show us."

➤➤ FORTY-FIVE ◆◆

YASAKA LED THEM out of the room, down the hall, and through a heavy metal door marked EMERGENCY EXIT. They emerged from the rear of the hotel onto the platform of a deserted loading dock. The midday sun was partially obscured by a band of low, gauzy clouds and a meager drizzle was falling, giving the asphalt a glossy sheen.

"Over there," Yasaka said, pointing to a cherry-red Forerunner.

Ray nudged Ehrlich toward the truck. The man was moving with the speed of oil after a hard freeze. "Come on! We're running out of time."

Before they could fasten their seat belts Yasaka had the Toyota in gear and was screeching out of the service lot. She banked hard as they reached the front of the hotel, purposefully abandoning the pavement in favor of an overgrown, double-track. Tall stocks of rabbit grass disappeared under the hood like waves beneath a speed boat. Yasaka rammed the stick into a new gear, accelerating. The Forerunner bounced wildly, shocks compressing and expanding, tires fighting for traction.

Ehrlich swore as the cab tilted up and they nearly rolled.

"Shortcut," Yasaka explained, shifting. The Forerunner rumbled over an outcropping of rock, then raced down an embankment, directly toward a creek. When it hit the water, it sent up a rooster tail twice as high as the cab. The stream wasn't wide, but it was deeper than it looked. The water level rose, engulfing the wheels, covering the fenders. The floorboard began to fill up.

"Don't worry. We won't stall," Yasaka said, busy navigating the Toyota.

Stalling wasn't Ray's main worry.

"We've got a snorkel," she explained, nodding at a thick, black rubber pipe sticking up in front of the grill. The water was only six inches from the top of the pipe.

Ray eyed his watch, wondering how they could possibly get to the laundromat on time, and simultaneously wondering what would happen to Keera if he drowned. The engine hesitated, then the truck dragged itself onto the opposite shore. They four-wheeled through a line of willows and dwarf pines before shooting into a steep, grassy clearing. Yasaka pointed the Forerunner straight up the hill.

It wasn't until he saw the chairs hanging in the air that Ray realized they were on the ski run. Tower one whizzed by. Yasaka shifted, aiming for the second tower. Skidding to a halt, she grunted at Ehrlich, "Get it!"

He sighed, but made no effort to get out. Ray popped open the door and leapt out, scrambling into the over-sized hole surrounding the steel pole. There were several empty beer cans, part of a newspaper, a half-dozen crumpled trail maps . . . No manila envelope.

"It's not here!" he shouted.

"Yeah it is," Ehrlich replied without enthusiasm. "Look behind the pad."

There was a short ladder affixed to the tower. Just above it, a vinyl-covered cushion had been strapped around the pole, presumably to keep skiers from bashing their brains out. Ray quickly mounted the rungs and stuck his hand behind the pad. Nothing.

"Ehrlich, it's not—!" he started to repeat. But jabbing

his hand further in, he felt something. He used his thumb and forefinger to work it free. A plastic Ziploc dislodged and fell into the hole. Ray turned loose of the ladder and jumped in to retrieve it. The bag was clear, the only thing inside a small, creased manila envelope. Without checking the contents, he stuffed it into his jacket and clambered back up and into the Toyota.

"You got it?" Yasaka asked.

"Yeah. Let's go."

Yasaka performed a 180 that lifted the left side tires off the ground. Suddenly they were hurtling toward the lodge.

"I'm supposed to go . . . to the laundromat . . . out by the . . . highway," Ray told her through clattering teeth. It felt like the gray matter was rattling inside his head.

In the backseat, Ehrlich was whimpering, alternately groaning and swearing.

The oil pan scraped the ground as the slope bottomed out and they caromed back onto the pavement. Yasaka took the direct route: over a curb, through a concrete island, across a lawn. When they reached the main road and managed to merge into the traffic without causing an accident, she asked, "How much time?"

Ray shook his head. "Two minutes. We'll never make it."

"We can try."

We can die trying, Ray thought as Yasaka took up a position in the left lane and stayed there, passing cars as though they were frozen in time.

They had just flown by the church when the phone rang. Ray flipped it open. "We're not there yet, but we're only a few minutes away. And I've got it."

"Got what?"

"Who is this?"

"Glen. Is this Ray?"

Ray swore under his breath. "Get off the line!"

"What's going on?"

"They've got Keera. And we're supposed to be at the

laundromat right now," he blurted. "Now get off the line
and don't call back!" He hung up.

They rounded the bend and the highway came into
view. Yasaka was doing 102, dodging traffic going both
ways. Ray watched the gas station and storefronts grow
in size, glanced at the phone, checked to make sure it
was on.

He checked his watch again. "Time." The laundromat
was still a quarter mile away. The phone was silent. He
tried not to think of what they might be doing to Keera.

The Forerunner skid to a flamboyant stop directly in
front of the laundromat seconds later. Ray got out and
ran inside. There were only two people there: an elderly
woman folding clothes and a long-haired teenager lying
across three seats, reading a magazine. Washers and dryers were humming. No thugs. No kidnappers. No Keera.

Ray looked at his watch, checked the phone for a dial
tone, turned it off again . . .

"Well?" Yasaka asked when she came in.

Ray's chest was rising and falling, but he couldn't get
enough air. "We're late."

"Not very late."

"The degree doesn't matter," he snapped. "Late is late.
And Keera—"

"They won't hurt her," she assured him.

"You don't know that." Ray could feel the tears coming again.

"I know that they want that envelope. And without
your daughter, they won't get it. They need her. At least
for now."

Ray sank to a seat next to the teen and wiped his eyes.
"Who's they?" Ray asked. "The State Department? Ron
the Don? The Japanese mob? The FBI?" This drew a
glance from the teen. Ray pulled out the plastic bag and
held it up. "Why is this so important?"

Yasaka looked around the laundromat, as though the
FBI might be lurking behind one of the dryers.

"You're with the Nikai, right?" Ray said.

"Who told you that?"

"I made the connection myself."

"Impressive," she said. "But wrong. I'm a special investigator, with the JIA, Japanese Investigations Agency."

Ray tried to suppress a curse, but failed. Next Glen would admit to being a CIA operative. Ehrlich was probably Elvis in disguise. "You were up there with Cox."

Yasaka answered with a single nod.

"And you killed him."

The teenager's head turned slightly.

"That wasn't us."

"Who was it?"

Leaning against a dryer, she shook her head at the question, then pointed at the Ziploc. "That's what got him killed."

"Why? What's in it?"

She opened the plastic bag, unfolded the envelope, and tipped it on end. A mini-CD in a hard plastic shell slid out. "The chemical formula for a new type of metal, a metal that will revolutionize the microchip industry. Cox stole it and was auctioning it off."

"Who was bidding?"

"Oh . . . Let's see . . . Nakasawa . . . the State Department . . . my people . . ."

"Who won?"

"We did."

"Then why didn't he give it to you Friday night? That was what the meeting on top was for, right?"

"Yeah. But he got greedy. Suddenly our bid wasn't enough. He claimed that he was leaving the country with his girlfriend and needed more."

"His girlfriend being Mrs. Mancini," Ray said.

"When I said I'd have to clear it with my superiors," Yasaka explained, "he threatened to turn around and hand the formula over to the State Department."

"So who poisoned him?"

The teen craned his neck, nearly falling from his perch.

Yasaka put the disk back into the envelope and handed it to Ray. Before she could reply, Glen burst in.

"Ray! I got here as quick as I could. You okay? What's this about Keera?"

"Someone kidnapped her," he disclosed wearily. "They took her while we were on the train. And they want this." He held up the envelope for Glen's inspection.

"What is it?"

"A disk with some sort of formula on it."

"The formula for a new metal," Yasaka emphasized.

"I thought everyone was after a computer chip," Glen said.

"The chip is a breakthrough," Yasaka admitted. "But this," she said, tapping the envelope with a fingernail, "this is the revolution. It will alter manufacturing and information exchange worldwide."

Glen blinked at the envelope. "What's that have to do with Keera?"

"Someone apparently thought I had it," Ray explained. "So they took Keera to force me to hand it over."

The teenager sat up, stretched, and pretended to check his wash.

"Is that what you're doing here?"

Ray's shoulders drooped. "Yeah. Except we're late. And they haven't called."

"They will," Yasaka promised.

Without warning, Glen launched into a prayer, fervently invoking heavenly assistance. He was still at it when Ray asked Yasaka, "Did you cut the brakes?"

"No," she answered.

"Did you plant the bomb?"

"No."

"Then who—?" Ray's question was cut short by the phone. The pulse sent shivers along his spine and down

his legs. The room seemed to waver. He flipped it open
and hit the button. "Hello?" he managed, voice cracking
like a schoolboy's.

"You're late."

"So are you," he answered, immediately regretting it.
This was no time to be a smart aleck. The last thing he
needed to do was give these people any added incentive
to hurt his daughter. "I'm sorry. It took longer to get the
envelope than I thought it would."

"You've got it?" The caller sounded surprised, relieved.

"Yeah, right here. What do you want me to do?"

Yasaka leaned in to eavesdrop. Glen's prayer dribbled
to an end and his mouth hung open. The kid was watching them, wide-eyed, magazine drooping in one hand.

"Take the highway to the pull-off at milepost fifty-
three."

"Then what?"

"You'll see. You have seven minutes to get there. And
this time, don't be late."

"What about Keera? I want to talk to her."

"You can. If you make it to the drop-off in seven
minutes—starting now. Bring the envelope, and leave
your pals behind."

"Pals?" Ray wondered.

"Miss Yasaka and Sheriff Redfern."

Ray swung his head around and glared out the window, half expecting to find a surveillance van parked
outside. Instead, he saw a bicycle, a decrepit old Honda,
Glen's Camry, and the Forerunner with Ehrlich still in
the backseat.

"You better get going. You now have six minutes and
forty-seven seconds . . . forty-six seconds . . . forty-five
seconds . . ." There was a click and the line went dead.

Ray stuffed the phone into his jacket. "I need a car."

"I'll drive you," Glen offered.

"No. You have to stay here. I'm supposed to go alone."

"I'll set up a support team," Yasaka said, reaching for a phone of her own.

"I'll call the FBI," Glen said.

"No!" Ray ordered. "They said alone. Just me. No support teams or Feds."

"They won't know we're there," Yasaka assured him, dialing.

"You're willing to bet my daughter's life on that?"

She paused. "You can't go alone."

"I can and I'm going to," Ray said. "I need a car!"

She frowned and dangled her keys at him. When he tried to take them, she pulled them away. "You have to make me a couple of promises."

"What?" Ray asked impatiently.

"First, if things go bad"—she stuffed a business card into his jacket pocket—"call."

"Okay." He snatched away the keys and started for the door.

"And, after all of this is over, you have to come to Japan."

Shouldering through the door, Ray ran to the Forerunner. "Why?" He yanked Ehrlich out by the arm. Ehrlich stumbled and hit the ground swearing. Ray started the truck and ground the gearshift into reverse. He backed out and was fighting to find first when a hand reached through the open window and gripped his shoulder.

"Promise me you'll come to Japan and testify," she demanded.

He gunned the engine, but the Toyota lurched and died. Ray cursed and started it again. "Testify?!" he asked angrily. "What are you talking about?"

"At the trial against Fukutomi. We're putting the last touches on the case right now: racketeering, industrial espionage, a dozen violations of international contract law . . ."

Ray gave up on first and jammed it into second, heaving away with the grace of a stricken rhinoceros.

"Not to mention murder," she called after him. "And kidnapping!"

➤➤ FORTY-SIX ◀◀

RAY SCREECHED ACROSS the parking lot and accelerated through an obstacle course of gas pump islands. He was already looking beyond the station, analyzing the heavy flow of traffic on the highway, when a woman stepped out from between two parked cars carrying a cardboard tray filled with paper Coke cups. She gasped and retreated, abandoning the tray. Ray slammed on the brakes and watched as the soft drinks impacted the hood and exploded. The truck skidded sideways, the back end colliding with a trash barrel. Before Ray could stop the slide, he was careening into a drainage ditch. Shifting, he regained control and raced along the bottom of the narrow ditch, tires spinning in the deep, boggy muck. He hit the wipers and in one swipe was rendered blind. Groping for the washer switch, he felt the front end jerk upward, heard the suspension scream.

Suddenly he was weightless, his body straining against the safety harness. The Forerunner soared in a clumsy, abbreviated arc. When the front tires hit, the

Toyota seemed poised to flip. Instead it bounced, the rear end leaving the ground twice.

Horns blared. Ray heard wheels locking, the sick crunch of metal meeting metal, glass shattering. Out the side window, he noted that he was moving perpendicular to the highway, straight for the inlet. Yanking the wheel hard left, he held his breath as the Forerunner tilted, threatening to roll.

When the tires were committed to pavement again, Ray found the switches and cleaned the front and back windows. He winced as he glanced in the rearview mirror. The highway was blocked in both directions: cars stopped at odd angles, hoods crumpled in half, radiators steaming. An RV lay on its side like an injured elephant.

Ray hoped no one was hurt and had to fight the impulse to turn around and find out. He checked his watch. Four minutes. Shifting, he pressed the pedal to the floor.

The highway was clear for a mile, giving him the opportunity to do 84, 91, 103 . . .

Yasaka's voice echoed in his mind and, for the first time, Ray became cognizant of what she had just said. Kidnapping? Fukutomi had something to do with Keera's abduction? And what was that about murder and industrial espionage?

Passing a pickup, then a Volvo, Ray tried to make sense of it. The Japanese police were putting a case together against Fukutomi? Okay, maybe they had violated a few treaties or something. But murder and kidnapping? If the formula for the metal belonged to them in the first place, why would they . . . ?

Ray veered and swept past a bus, a van, a beer truck . . .

Unless Cox had stolen it and they were trying to get it back. When the attempt failed, they tracked it to Ray. In order to "encourage" him to turn it over, they took Keera. Still, killing a man and holding a child hostage?

According to Pool, Cox had taken one of the new super chips for the State Department. Why commit murder and kidnapping for a formula, but not for a ground-breaking chip? Wouldn't a computer company be more worried about that than the chemical breakdown of some metal? Unless, as Yasaka had explained, the formula was really that critical, a true revolution in metallurgy.

Whatever their motivation, Ray decided, watching for mileposts, the people involved in this tangle of deception, thievery, and greed were clearly desperate. It dawned on him that Ron Mancini was now on the board of Fukutomi. Maybe Pool was right after all. Ron the Don *had* killed Cox. Only for a wholly other reason. Instead of doing it out of jealousy, he had done it for money, to preserve Fukutomi's worldwide dominance of the high-tech industry. The kidnapping, the bomb, the brakes . . . Those were all part of Mancini's business plan: success by fear, intimidation, and elimination.

It fit in Ray's mind. Mancini had killed Cox for the disk, without realizing he was erasing his wife's lover. Or maybe he had known about the affair. Two birds with one stone. Either way, Cox was dead and Mancini was the odds-on favorite for guilty party.

A green steel stake bearing a white 51, flashed by. Ray slowed to ninety. Thirty seconds later a chipped, bullet-ridden sign announced SCENIC OVERLOOK. The pull-off materialized an eighth of a mile ahead and Ray braked hard.

He performed a 180, slinging gravel, before bringing the Forerunner to a halt. Jumping out, he hurried to the side of the overlook and found . . . nothing. The sun had won a momentary victory over the stratus clouds and was bathing the Kenai Mountains in a hundred shades of green. Turnagain Arm was quiet, the tide out, the mud flats glistening.

Ray scanned the inlet, peered over the edge at the cliffside, shook his head at the empty parking area. Nothing. No one. No sign of Keera.

According to his watch, he was exactly on time. Fifteen seconds passed. Cars rushed by in a whoosh of air, tires, and wet pavement. Thirty seconds. Sea gulls cawed overhead. Forty-five seconds. Ray glanced around, helpless, making a conscious effort not to give up hope. After two excruciating minutes, the phone finally rang.

"You're quick."

"Where's my daughter?"

"Where's the envelope?"

Ray patted his jacket. "Right here."

"Toss it."

"Toss it?" Ray surveyed the mudflats again. There were no footprints, no tire tracks, just lonely brown puddles and low mounds of wet clay.

"Over the side."

"But what about—"

"Do it now or you won't see her again."

Ray hesitated. The disk was his bargaining chip. Without it, he would be in no position to negotiate Keera's release. Were these folks as hot and bothered about the disk as Yasaka made them out to be? Would they agree to a one-for-one exchange if Ray pushed the issue? Was it worth putting Keera at risk to find out? Did he have a choice?

"Toss it!"

"I have to see her first." Had he just signed his daughter's death warrant?

"Toss it!!"

"I'll give it to you when you give me Keera."

"Toss it or you won't—!"

"I'll give it to you when you give me Keera," he repeated with artificial bravado. "We do a straight exchange or . . . I walk."

There was a pause. To Ray, it was terrifyingly long. Sweat mingled with droplets of drizzle and ran down his forehead, into his eyes. Finally, there was a heavy sigh on the other end of the line. "Come down the trail."

"What trail?" Ray asked. But the line was dead. He leaned over the edge of the escarpment. There was no trail, only forty feet of slick granite face. He trotted to the west end of the pull-off. The rock was sheer, the drop almost fifty feet. Sprinting east, he noticed a bent, rusted sign at the far extreme of the parking area: DANGER—STAY OFF MUD FLATS. Beneath this, smaller print provided a detailed description of the perils of straying onto the flats.

Directly behind the sign, a fresh set of bootprints left the pull-off and disappeared over the side. Apparently someone had been unconvinced by the grim warning from the Department of Natural Resources and had decided to see for himself just how hazardous the area really was. Ray followed them, using his hands to scramble down a tight V in the granite. The rock along here was slippery, damp from the light rain, and encrusted with clumps of moss and lichen.

After backing down a short section that qualified as a technical free-climb, Ray found what he assumed was the trail: a polished ledge of humid granite not quite as wide as a man's shoe. It went down the bluff in a ragged zigzag of sharp cutbacks, disappearing before it reached the flats. Ray started down with the concentration of a tightrope walker.

Halfway down, he looked up and realized that the Forerunner, the highway, the traffic, the pull-off itself had disappeared. Twisting, he followed the narrow path down another steep switchback, fingers clinging to rifts in the cliffside. He was in the process of finding a foothold to lower himself to a stone platform that jutted out like a diving board some fifteen feet above the mud, when someone grunted, "Stop there!"

Ray tried to, but lost his grip and slid the final two yards to the platform, skinning his knuckles before landing hard on his hip. He bit his lip as pain radiated down his leg.

"The envelope," the voice demanded.

Rising stiffly, Ray turned to face his adversary: a man crouching at the mouth of a misshapen opening in the rock face. At least he assumed it was a man. The figure was dressed in a long black rain parka, jeans, and hiking boots, the face was obscured by a ski mask, the hair hidden by the hood of the parka. Two dark eyes stared out from the neoprene.

"Where's my daughter?"

"Where's the envelope?"

Ray removed it from the pocket of his jacket. "Where's Keera?"

The man nodded at the malformed cave.

"I can't see her."

"She's there."

For the first time, Ray noticed that the man was holding a gun. It was small and blended with the black gloves. He tried mentally to put Ron Mancini into the hood and mask. No. Mancini was more rotund. And the voice was wrong.

"Keera?" Ray called. There was no response.

"Throw me the envelope."

"Keera?!"

The gun reoriented itself, barrel aimed at Ray's chest. "Throw it to me."

Ray eyed the opening: a ragged oval of deep shadow. Was he about to pay a ransom for his daughter and get an empty cave in return?

The man stepped forward slowly, revolver held high. After glaring at Ray for a moment, he snatched the envelope away with the acuity of a rattlesnake.

"Give me my daughter!" Ray demanded.

Ignoring this, the man tore into the manila envelope and fumbled with a single gloved hand until he had the disk.

"Keera!" Ray called.

The man pulled a notepad computer from his parka and shoved the disk into the mini-drive. He watched the screen as the device whirred.

"I want my daughter!"

"Shut up!" the man said, gesturing with the gun. He tapped the keypad, waited, tapped it again. Nodding, as though satisfied, he deactivated it with a perfunctory finger and stuffed it and the disk into a pocket. "Did you copy it?"

"I'm not even sure what it is," Ray confessed. "Why would I copy it?"

"Did you?" The gun added emphasis to the question. "No."

"Good. Because I'll run a diagnostic later. And if you did, I'll be back to visit your daughter." Before Ray could respond, the man turned and ran, leaping from the rock ledge. He fell gracefully, impacting the soft clay in a standing position, and sunk to mid-calf. It reminded Ray of a maneuver he had seen Spiderman do in a cartoon. Except that now the man resembled a fly trapped in a web: legs half swallowed by the gummy muck.

As the man thrashed and cursed, fighting to free himself, Ray bent into the cave. "Keera?!" His voice echoed back at him.

Squeezing inside, he crawled along on all fours. The cave was bigger than it looked. Despite the darkness, Ray could tell that the inner cavern was wide, the roof high and rising. Water trickled in the distance and a moldy smell assaulted Ray's nose.

"Keera?!" Her name bounced from wall to wall before he heard a tiny, dampened response. "Keera?" Another soft return. He clambered blindly toward the sound.

A few yards later, he bumped into something. It was softer than rock, dryer, more solid than mud. A duffel bag, he realized. His fingers trembled as they worked to unfasten the top clip. Reaching in, he felt hair. "Keera!!"

There was a muffled whine. Ray cradled the entire bag and scooted his way back to the opening of the cave. In the faint light, he gingerly removed a piece of duct tape from her mouth and examined her face: tired eyes, dirt-smudged cheeks, chapped, bleeding lip. "It's okay now," he soothed. "It's okay."

"Daddy!!" She hugged him with what seemed like superhuman strength.

"Are you all right? Did they hurt you?"

"No."

Ray was crying freely now. "I'm so sorry, honey."

"It's not your fault," she said in a remarkably mature tone.

"But I should have been watching you more closely." He held on to her desperately. "I should have—"

"Daddy, I was scared."

"I know, honey. So was I." Ray was suddenly bone-weary, uncertain whether he could summon the strength to exit the cave, wondering how they would ever make it back up that rock face.

"Daddy, can we get a donut on the way home?"

"Sure, honey," he said, amazed at her resilience. But a pastry wouldn't be enough to bring closure to this experience, he knew. Keera needed to see a doctor first, then a psychologist. Though she seemed healthy enough, getting kidnapped and stuffed into a wet, black hole in the ground had to be traumatic. He silently prayed that she wouldn't be scarred for life.

Ray glanced over the ledge and saw a pair of holes where the man had landed. They were full of water. Beyond them, a deep set of footprints weaved across the flat, marching straight into the inlet before disappearing into the glare of the sun. The perp had escaped.

➤➤ FORTY-SEVEN ◄◄

"LOOK DADDY!" KEERA pulled away from his embrace and pointed, face animated.

Ray squinted at the horizon. The sun had seared a hole in a band of whirling, gossamer clouds, transforming the mudflats into a shimmering vat of bronze. Covering his brow with a hand, he blinked at the blaze. "What is it, honey?" Before she could answer he heard it: the rhythmic thump of steel beating air. The volume rose, then changed pitch as a helicopter roared over.

"Look Daddy!"

"It's a helicopter," Ray said, nodding. "I saw it."

"No. Lo-ok!" She drew the second word out until it became an elongated whine.

A mile out, the helicopter banked, slowed, and began to circle.

"Daddy! Look at the man!"

In the next moment, the ridge of clouds reasserted their control of the sky, eclipsing the sun. The mudflat was suddenly restored to its bland, featureless state. And for the first time, Ray saw the boat: a flat-bottomed skiff parked at the water's edge. There was someone in it, sitting at the rear, manning an outboard engine.

Closer to shore, Ray spotted another person: muddy

pants, muddy boots, mud reaching halfway up a black, hooded parka. The kidnapper. He was moving away from them, toward the boat, trudging laboriously through the glutinous soil.

The helicopter hovered directly over the boat and began losing altitude.

Ray stifled a curse. This guy was no dummy. He had planned his escape for low tide, arranged for a boat to meet him, arranged for a copter to whisk him out of there. It was slick. Foolproof. Or so it seemed, until the man stopped. He began waving at the boat. One of his hands reached toward the helicopter. A trio of muted pops reached them seconds later. The helicopter dove and jinked away toward the opposite shore. It was then that Ray noticed the mark on the front of the cabin. It was a search and rescue helicopter, not a getaway vehicle. Maybe it was looking for him and Keera.

The man continued his trek toward the boat, each step more arduous than the last. He was pulling at his thighs, sloshing through the increasingly wet mud. Ray saw him fall, then flop around like a fish, unable to right himself.

The sun made a cameo appearance, reflecting off a squat, silver wall that was hurrying inland: a bore tide. A big one, probably three feet high. Maybe the plan wasn't so foolproof, Ray decided. The copter had been an unexpected nuisance rather than a tool. And now the tide was returning. Not just rising, rushing in to fulfill its reputation as one of the highest, most severe in the world. If the mud didn't swallow the man, the silt in the water would take him down. He had about two minutes, Ray guessed, to find a way out.

The helicopter inched back toward its former position, only to be fired on again. It dodged and circled out of range. The man stood there for a few seconds, gun at his side. His head swung from the boat to the shore and back again. Then he must have noticed the bore tide coming. Leaping forward, he tripped and had to swim to the surface of the mud. When he was upright again, he turned and started for shore. It was a pitiful sight: a man struggling for his life, battling sea, land, the very earth itself in a frantic attempt to survive. If he was smart, Ray thought, he would toss the gun and wave the helicopter in.

"Daddy, he's gonna get hurt," Keera said. "Just like the man he made fall."

The man dragged himself along, his progress negligible, the tide gaining. His timing probably would have been perfect, Ray noted. The tide would have reached the boat just as he did and he could have floated away into oblivion. Except for the bore.

The man had plodded and slipped his way to within an eighth of a mile of shore when he looked back and saw the wave rushing at him. It was fifty yards away . . . forty . . . thirty . . . He fell to his knees and began crawling. The mud, as if sensing the approach of the sea, lost what little solidarity it had and began absorbing his limbs.

"Give up," Ray implored. Despite the fact that this man deserved to die a horrible death for his crime against Keera, Ray found himself unable to root for the demise of another human being. He turned Keera's back to the event. "Call in that copter!"

The man was up to his elbows in mud, his legs hidden from the calves down, when the bore overtook him. It splashed up his back, sending a spray into the air.

The helicopter shot forward, zooming to attempt a rescue. But the man wouldn't allow it. Floundering in the tide, brown water licking at his hips, lapping at his chest . . . he somehow managed to lift the gun and get off a shot. The helicopter wobbled and retreated.

The section of inlet where the man was trapped couldn't have been more than three feet deep. But the level was rising dramatically. With water washing up over his shoulders, he tried to turn onto his back. Probably hoping to float, Ray thought. But floating wasn't an option in Turnagain Arm. The attempt failed and the man's head disappeared. When he bobbed back up, he was clawing at the mask, ripping away the hood.

Just before he disappeared from view, Ray caught a glimpse of the man's face. Even from a distance, even with clay-matted hair, even with the wild-eyed expression of someone who knew beyond a doubt that he was about to die, Ray recognized him. As the inlet hungrily claimed yet another victim, dragging the man down into its silty, unforgiving womb, Ray closed his eyes and told himself that it made sense. It was horrible. Enough to turn his stomach. But it made sense.

➤ FORTY-EIGHT ◄

WHEN THE TIDE had engulfed another quarter mile of mud and the body was visible only as a slight abnormality in the surface flow, the helicopter moved in to perform a recovery. It was hovering just a few feet above the sea when a side door slid open and a man clad in bright orange coveralls and an orange helmet appeared. Attached to the helicopter by a harness and safety line, the rescuer hopped into the water astride a tiny, yellow raft. Using it like a kneeboard, he paddled into position and began probing the water with a grappling hook.

"The water got him," Keera said. "It got the man, didn't it, Daddy?"

"Yes, honey." Ray watched as the hook snagged something. The man worked it, secured another line, then gave an exaggerated thumbs up to the helicopter.

The entire ensemble jerked, then started up like a tangled fishing lure.

As the helicopter rose, it reeled in its catch. When the helmeted man reached the cabin, a pair of hands yanked him through the door. The soggy bundle dangling below was trailing streams of water. Ray wondered if the search and rescue team would even bother attempting resuscitation. After the body had swung its way up and was drawn into the hatch, the helicopter accelerated in the general direction of Girdwood.

When it was gone, Ray eyed the cliffside. "How did you get down here?"

"He carried me, in a backpack thing." She pointed at the cave. "It's in there."

Ray glanced at the opening, then back at the bluff. "Think you can climb up? If I help you?" He wasn't even sure he could climb up.

"I don't think so, Daddy," she told him. "It's too hard. You have to carry me."

Sighing, he bent to enter the cave. "Stay here. I'll see if I can find that backpack." He groped forward, waving a hand in front of him.

"Daddy!" Keera called.

"What?"

"Hurry!"

Swearing softly, Ray backed his way out. "What's the matter?"

"Daddy!!" She sounded like she was calling to him through a gale.

He emerged from the cave into a violent storm of wind and noise.

"Look Daddy!" Keera shouted. She was hopping up and down, pointing. Guarding his eyes with a hand, Ray looked and saw the source of the squall: the helicopter. It was levitating at their level, just yards from the cliffside.

The door slid open and the man in the orange outfit motioned to them. Lifting a long, steel basket, he clipped a rope to the harness on his chest and, assisted by another man in orange, sidestepped down, onto one of the feet of the helicopter. Before Ray could decide what he was up to, the man had abandoned the pontoon and was swinging at them with the skill and agility of Tarzan. He made a smooth two-foot landing on the ledge.

When the basket was seated on the rock platform, he knelt and snapped on an umbrellalike set of lines, linking them to the main rope. Turning, he pulled two more harnesses from his bulging vest. "Put these on." He assisted them into the devices, yanking on cords and making adjustments. "You'll be sitting in the basket," he explained. He helped Keera into her place, then showed Ray where to sit. "Hang on."

He took up position on the rim of the sled and waved at the helicopter. "Go!"

The pilot waved and a fraction of a second later, the basket jumped sideways and up, and they were airborne, pitching wildly from side to side, spinning in dizzying circles.

"Daddy!"

"It's okay, honey." Ray found Keera's hand and squeezed it. The only good thing about the swinging motion, he decided, wondering if he would vomit, was that it made you forget about the inherent danger involved in the maneuver.

The pendulum slowly lost momentum, but the spinning continued. Ray was able to make out bits and pieces of the cliff on half of each rotation, flashes of water and mountains on the other. They seemed to be traveling forward, gaining altitude. A few seconds later, they floated to a stop and the basket wavered beneath the hovering copter. There was a mechanical grinding sound, and they lurched upward, the bay ingesting rope at a slow but steady pace. When they reached the pontoons, the man in orange sprung onto one of the feet and directed the basket toward the open door with an arm.

The sled was whisked inside and deposited onto the floor with a clank.

Before Ray could even unhook, the helicopter was moving. One of the men in orange was wrapping Keera in a blanket, checking her pulse, looking at her pupils, sticking a thermometer into her ear . . . "Do you hurt anywhere?" he asked.

"No." She looked even smaller than usual.

Another man began the same routine with Ray. When he finished attending to his abrasions, he folded a blanket around Ray's shoulders. "You hurt anywhere?"

"Lots of places," Ray answered honestly. "But not from this particular outing."

The man consulted with Keera's attendant, then muttered something into his headset. To Ray he said, "We'll be down at Alyeska search and rescue in five."

Ray glanced around the cabin. "What happened to the man in the mud?"

He frowned at an elongated black plastic sack laid out on another sled. "We did mouth-to-mouth, but . . . He never stood a chance. If he hadn't started shooting at us . . ."

Keera crawled into Ray's lap. "Are we almost there, Daddy?"

"Almost." He pulled her against his chest. "What about the guy in the boat?"

"We contacted the Coast Guard. They'll pick him up."

Ray leaned back and watched as the three men methodically repacked ropes and secured the basket to the wall. "How'd you know we were out there?"

"Got a call from Glen Redfern," one of them replied without looking up from his work. "He and John are buddies." The man gestured at the cockpit.

Craning his neck, Ray managed to see the pilot. Despite the helmet and dark visor, he could tell that it was John the hugger.

"He's kind of a nut," the man explained. "But he's an incredible pilot."

"The best," one of his partners agreed. "They don't come any better than John."

Ray nodded, truly thankful, yet amazed that he owed his life, and that of his daughter, to the chaplain of Alyeska and an overly friendly, far too happy member of Girdwood Chapel. Keera twisted in his lap and Ray realized that she was asleep.

Moments later, they were falling. The drop slowed and the pontoons touched down with the delicate grace of a ballet dancer. Keera didn't even stir.

The whine of the engine relaxed, the lights blinked, and one of the men popped the hatch. The other two helped Ray to his feet. Cradling Keera, he leaned on the men for support and gingerly climbed onto the asphalt tarmac. A few feet away, the pilot's door flew open and John bounded out.

"Was that cool or what?!" he shouted.

Before Ray could respond with "or what," an entourage raced to greet them: Glen, Amy Yasaka, Agents Pool and Bailey, all hunching in respect for the decelerating rotor.

"Are you all right?" Glen gushed, obviously worried.

"Yeah. We're okay."

"Thank God," he gasped breathlessly.

Pool and Bailey were less ecstatic: blank faces, matching sunglasses, arms crossed. The consummate Fibbies.

"Have you two met Ms. Yasaka, of the JIA?" Ray asked.

"JIA, huh?" Pool grunted.

"So this is your daughter." Yasaka smiled at Keera. "Was she hurt?"

"Not physically. And to tell you the truth, she seems to have taken it all in stride. I think she'll be fine. I *hope* she'll be fine."

"I hope so too." Yasaka peered into the copter bay.

"Eddie didn't make it," Ray told her.

"What happened?"

Ray waited as the men unloaded the body bag. "The

tide got him." Sighing at the tragedy, he said, "It serves him right really, for what he did to Keera, but . . ."

Ray started for the small building at the edge of the tarmac, Yasaka on one side, Glen on the other, the Feds following like guard dogs. "I think I understand most of it—why Eddie killed Cox. That's who killed him, isn't it?"

Yasaka nodded. "We think so. Either he or one of his people poisoned Cox at the meeting on Friday evening."

"And he did that because Cox stole the formula?"

Another nod.

"Mancini was simply a victim of circumstance. He didn't do anything, he was just in the wrong place with a bad reputation."

"We're looking into that," Pool informed from a couple of paces back. "We're sure he's dirty. It's only a matter of time."

Ray rolled his eyes. "Eddie cut the brakes on the Jeep and planted the bomb?"

"He had someone do it," Yasaka said.

"To keep us from mucking things up?"

"Right."

"My question is why? Why was Eddie obsessed with a metal that his company held the patent on? If Cox stole it, why couldn't Eddie just inform the authorities and have him arrested on charges of industrial espionage? And why wouldn't Eddie allow himself to be rescued? He would have done time for kidnapping, but that's better than dying."

Yasaka shook her head. "Not in our culture, it's not. Eddie lost face with his grandfather. It was an honor thing. He was supposed to take his grandfather's place at the helm of Fukutomi. But as the reins were being turned over, a couple of disastrous things happened. First, one of the super chips was ripped off."

"The United States Government was not involved in any fashion," Pool claimed.

Yasaka ignored him. "That was a real blow to Eddie.

It brought him down several notches in his grandfather's eyes. The second thing was the metal. It was a real feather in his cap until old man Fukutomi found out how Eddie obtained it."

"Namely?"

"He ripped it off from another company."

"You're kidding?"

"No. He stole the formula from Nakasawa when it was in the development stage, had his engineers generate a prototype, and got to the patent office first. We were about to nail him for that. Strike number three was when Cox ripped off the formula. Mr. Fukutomi knew that if that metal was purchased by a competitor and/or Eddie's indiscretion came to light, it would mean death to the company. So he gave his grandson an ultimatum: Get the formula back or else."

"Or else what?" Ray wondered.

"Or else he would disown Eddie. No more executive status, no more obscene salary, no more perks, no more family fortune. Not to mention the social shame that the old man would heap on him. Eddie couldn't have gotten a job at McDonald's after that."

"Sounds to me like Mr. Fukutomi is just about as culpable in all this as Eddie was."

"He'll be charged with conspiracy to commit murder," Yasaka assured him, "along with conspiracy to commit kidnapping, conspiracy to commit fraud . . ."

Ray slumped to a bench built into the outer wall of the building, bone-weary. "What a mess." He reached into a pocket and discovered a set of keys. "Your car's parked at the pull-off at mile marker fifty-three."

Accepting the keys, Yasaka said, "So you'll come to Japan? To testify?"

"I guess."

"That's saying you can extradite Mr. Fukutomi," Pool inserted. "The Justice Department will push to keep him here since the murder took place on American soil. In that event, we'll need Ray to testify here in the States."

"We may also need you to testify against Mancini, if we can put the case together," Bailey added helpfully.

"It's wonderful to be needed." Ray muttered.

Keera yawned and her eyes fluttered open. She glanced around, unsure of her surroundings, puzzled by the six faces looming over her. "Are we going on a bike ride now, Daddy?"

"No, honey."

"I'll get the car," Bailey said, trotting off.

"Is Mommy done with her con-ferns?"

Ray examined his watch. "Just about."

"I can't wait to tell her."

"To tell her what?" Ray asked. That you were kidnapped? That Daddy lost you on the train? That you saw a man eaten by Turnagain Arm?

"About the helicopter, Daddy," she chided, as if the answer was obvious. "I never got to ride in a helicopter before. Did you?"

"Once."

"It was sooo fun. I'm never ever gonna forget it."

"Me either, honey." Ray sighed. "Me either."

➤➤ FORTY-NINE ◄◄

HOLY, HOLY, HOLY . . . Lord God Almighty . . . Early in the morning our song shall rise to thee . . .

Ray stared at the hymnal without seeing the words. He made no effort to sing or even follow along. Fatigue prevented it. He was so tired, he felt sick. And yet here he was enduring an especially potent form of torture. If the Nazis had threatened prisoners of war with church attendance, he decided, all manner of secrets would have been disclosed and they might have won the war.

At the end of the first verse, the organist launched in a labored musical interlude, hands striking the keys with obvious frustration, feet pumping the pedals as though the instrument was a reluctant mare that required forceful goading.

Closing his eyes, Ray reminded himself that his presence at the service was a form of concession, his way of doing penance for a grievous sin: allowing his daughter to be abducted.

God in three Persons . . . blessed Trinity.

Glancing sideways, he realized that Margaret wasn't singing either. She was admonishing him with an expression that wordlessly assigned blame, as though Ray had betrayed her, had purposely put *her* daughter at risk, purposely tried to extinguish the light of *her* life. Keera was snuggled safely in her lap, smothered in a fierce embrace.

He checked his watch and found that they were only twelve minutes into the hour-long service. He began following the second hand with his eyes, wishing he could somehow shift time into overdrive.

Holy . . . holy . . . holy . . . Lord God Almighty . . . All Thy works shall praise Thy name in earth, and sky, and sea . . .

The funny thing, Ray decided, was that Keera seemed the least affected. Unlike her mother, she was calm, relaxed. As she reclined in Margaret's lap, feet kicking the pew in front of them, it was difficult to tell that anything out of the ordinary had happened.

Maybe Grandfather was right, he thought. Maybe Keera was special. Of course she was special in the way that all children were special in the eyes of their parents. But, according to Grandfather, Keera was different. The old man liked to say that she had been marked by the tuungak before her birth, predestined to an unusual future. The experience at Alyeska had certainly fit the bill in terms of being unusual.

He reached over and patted her hand. This drew a glare from Margaret. The plane ride to Barrow after church was looking to be long and quiet. The four months remaining in the pregnancy might be pretty *interesting,* as well. Hormones and weight gain were a volatile combination by themselves. Toss in a husband who couldn't keep up with his daughter and you had the ingredients for an incendiary device.

God in three Persons . . . blessed Trinity.

The music finally ended after a loud, frivolous organ finale, and the sanctuary fell silent. The rector popped out of his chair and marched across the stage, black robe fluttering behind like a cape. When he reached the podium, he gripped it with both hands, and gazed out at the congregation with a dour expression.

"Let's pray."

Heads rocked forward. Ray shifted in his seat, stealthily catching a glimpse of his watch.

The rector began mumbling through a list of things for which he and, presumably, those in attendance were thankful. Without conscious effort, Ray found himself reflecting on his own list. He was thankful for many things, the two most important sitting right next to him in the pew. Unfortunately, one of the two was as mad as a hornet at the moment. But Margaret, no matter her emotional state, despite any and all mood swings, was the love of his life. Always. Forever. After seven years of marriage, she could still make his heart skip a beat. And Keera . . . she was a treasure, a jewel. He cut his eyes at Margaret's stomach. The next child, boy or girl, would be too. Kids were just like that. As much work and trouble as they were, they made you laugh, smile, count your blessings.

"For these gifts, we give thanks," the rector was saying. He then shifted gears, offering up a "wish list" of items and actions that included everything from solving the drug problem in America to making sure street people had enough to eat.

Ray was about to check his watch again when a tone sounded. The rector paused. Heads twisted in his direction. The tone sounded again. A phone. *His* phone. As he dug into the pocket of his jacket, he could feel Margaret shooting fire at him with her eyes. The phone rang again before he flipped it open and silenced it with his thumb.

The rector sniffed before continuing his marathon petition.

"Hello?" Ray whispered. At the other end of the line, a tiny voice said something that Ray couldn't quite make out. "Hello?" he said a little louder.

Margaret shook her head and muttered under her breath.

Rising, Ray hurried out of the sanctuary, into the foyer. He hit the volume button and the voice became audible. ". . . And let you know what was going on."

"Glen?"

"Yeah. Can you hear me? I've got lots of static on this end."

"I can hear you," Ray groaned. "What is it?"

"Things were a little frantic right before you left and I didn't really get a chance to say . . . you know . . . thanks."

"For what?"

"For helping me with this case. You took me by the hand and led me through it."

"No problem." He hadn't led Glen so much as towed him. And calling it a case was a little generous. It was more of a happenstance. Ray had found a body and, over the course of a couple of days, been inexplicably caught up in the process of determining what had occurred and who had committed various crimes. It was investigation by blind luck.

"I couldn't have done it without you, Ray."

"Likewise."

"I also wanted to wish you, and Margaret and Keera, our best. Hope to see you all again soon."

"Me too," Ray lied.

"Actually, there's a chance that . . ." Glen's voice trailed off.

"That what?" Ray asked. He peered through the crack between the two doors and saw men passing collection baskets.

Glen chuckled. "I shouldn't say anything else."

"About what?"

"I don't want to spoil the surprise."

"Fine."

"Just remember that God—"

"I know." Ray sighed. "Works in mysterious ways."

"No. I was going to say, has a sense of humor."

"What's that supposed to mean?"

"You'll find out. Take care, Ray."

"You too." He hung up. Glen was a strange guy, he thought for the hundredth time that weekend. His hand was on the door handle when the phone pulsed again. He caught it on the first ring. "What is it, Glen?" he answered in irritation.

"Glen? This here's Billy Bob. Is this Ray?"

Another of his favorite people. "Yeah. What's up?"

"The captain asked me to call and find out what was goin' on down there."

For the past several hours, Ray had forgotten all about the captain, Billy Bob, and life above the Arctic Circle. "The case is closed. I'm heading home in about an hour."

"Didya figure out what happened to that fellar?"

"Yeah."

There was a pause. Billy Bob clearly expected him to elaborate.

"He was murdered."

"By who?"

Ray sighed. "It's . . . complicated. Just tell the captain that the case is closed. The FBI and the JIA are handling the details."

"That JIA?" he asked in a twang.

"I'll explain later."

"Fair enough, partner. Guess I'll see you in the mornin.' Huh?"

"Yeah."

"Oh, I almost forgot. We got us a call in here earlier from somebody down in Gird-wood. A chaplain, said he knew you."

"Glen."

"Right. Glen Red-furn."

"What did he want?"

"He was in-quirin' 'bout a permit fer a church meetin'. Said he and his wife was thinkin' 'bout comin' up this summer."

"You're kidding."

"No, sir." Billy Bob laughed.

"What's so funny?"

"Better watch out, Ray," Billy Bob warned. "Sounds to me like you got a preacher on yer tail. You're gonna get ree-ligion whether ya like it or not."

"Wanna bet?"

"See you in the mornin'."

"Right." Ray snapped the phone shut, turned it off, and slipped back into the sanctuary. Was there no getting away from Glen?

The choir was performing another hymn, complete with dreary organ accompaniment. As he sat down, Keera climbed into his lap. The hymn droned on. Without warning, Margaret reached over and took his hand. There was forgiveness in her touch, love in her eyes. Ray didn't understand the radical shift in mood, but wasn't about to question it. As she leaned on his shoulder, placing his hand on her swollen stomach, he marveled that suddenly all was right with the world. Sure, he was sitting in church, and yes, Glen was threatening to visit Barrow, but there were worse things than that. He could bear almost anything, as long as he had these two wonders at his side.

Between fat, annoying organ chords, the choir tried with little success to reach a harmonic blend.

Keera looked up, grinning. "Daddy, we're getting a baby boy!" She whispered this as if they were going to pick up her sibling at Wal-Mart after the service. Patting Margaret's stomach affectionately, she added, "Uncle Glen can bab-tights him."

"*Uncle* Glen?" Ray whispered. Since when was it *Uncle* Glen?

"You mean 'baptize,'" Margaret corrected.

"Yeah." Keera beamed. "And he can bab-tight me too."

The subject of *bab-tighting* was a matter open to debate, something he and Margaret had yet to hash out. But thankfully, the idea of Glen performing such a ceremony was rendered moot by distance. "How could Glen do that from Girdwood, honey?"

"They're gonna come visit."

"Is that right?"

She nodded confidently.

Rolling his eyes at Margaret, Ray whispered, "She has some imagination."

Margaret shrugged and took his hand in hers, implying forgiveness. "Maybe. Maybe not."

Ray blinked at her, terrified by the alternative.

AN ARCHEOLOGIST DIGS UP MURDER IN THE ALAN GRAHAM MYSTERIES BY

MALCOLM SHUMAN

THE MERIWETHER MURDER
79424-1/$5.99 US/$7.99 Can

BURIAL GROUND
79423-3/$5.50 US/$7.50 Can

ASSASSIN'S BLOOD
80485-9/$5.99 US/$7.99 Can